A STUDY IN SURVIVAL

ENDYMION COLLEGE
BOOK TWO

W. H. LOCKWOOD

CASTLEFIELD PRESS

For a list of potentially sensitive content and for more information about the series, please visit the website at www.whlockwood.com.

Please note, this book is written in Australian English and abides by Australian grammar and punctuation conventions.

Behind every exquisite thing that existed, there was something tragic.

— OSCAR WILDE

AUTHOR'S NOTE

Dear Reader,

Sorry about this.

A STUDY IN SURVIVAL

W. H. Lockwood

CONTENTS

CHAPTER 1

RETURN TO ENDYMION

E velyn shaded his eyes from the bright lights of the lecture theatre as he quickly scanned the audience to find Anna. He flashed his boyish smile as they exchanged a secret acknowledgement of one another, and he commenced his lecture.

"My name is Evelyn Worthing." He wrote it in quick and elegant letters on the blackboard. "That's Evelyn, as in Adam and Eve."

Anna's sigh was just as audible as any other student in the lecture theatre that day.

Candide, by her side, laughed quietly. "He's shameless."

"Welcome to Gothic Literature," Eve began. "I'm going to be asking a lot of you this term. We'll be hitting all the greatest works of the genre. Jane Eyre, A Sicilian Romance, The Private Memoirs and Confessions of a Justified Sinner, The Woman in Black, The Turn of the Screw, Dr Jekyll and Mr Hyde, and of course… The Monk." Eve raised a knowing eye towards an almost wholly ignorant audience, only Candide clapping as quietly as possible in scandalised delight. "It's going to be dark, it's going to be dramatic, and it's going to be *very* romantic."

Anna, who had arrived at Endymion College three months prior with nothing more than some classic books and a very nice fountain pen, was probably the happiest person in the lecture theatre that day. Studying literature at Endymion College, the dream of a lifetime, was as fulfilling as she had ever dared to hope it might be. She lived in her own gorgeous apartment with the smartest, sweetest, most brilliant woman she had ever met, and above all, she was thoroughly, deeply, all consumingly in love with the person she wholeheartedly believed to be the most wonderful man to have ever walked the Earth.

"If you want to experience passion—deep, true, incessant passion…" Anna's suggestive eyes locked briefly with Evelyn's. He smiled and blushed lightly, then turned away to maintain his composure and continued, "Then you must read Gothic literature. Every essential ingredient of human nature is here in these novels and I apologise in advance for the trauma we are all about to experience together. Characters you love are going to suffer. Characters you hate will triumph. You will grasp hold of one last shred of hope, only to have it pulled away from you at the last. It is Gothic literature, and it is the very essence of life."

Anna watched Eve's energetic, elegant movements with the same rapture she felt the first day she saw him, back when it felt impossible he would fall as hard for her as she had for him. Yet today, there were only two people out of the hundred or so attending who knew that only an hour earlier Anna had been lying in the lecturer's bed, the crisp winter sunshine streaming in through the open window, illuminating Evelyn's ethereal beauty as he traced his fingers over the palm of her open hand, kissed the underside of her arms as he pushed them gently over her head, kissed her lips, her neck, her breasts, trailing one hand down over her hips, over her belly, down, down, then tracing up the inside of her thigh, slowly, slowly, deliciously, pausing, until just when she thought she might scream in anticipation—

"Excuse me."

Anna pulled her legs in close to make space for the woman to pass. She did so politely, of course, but remained quietly resentful of the unnecessary interruption to her stream of delightful memories. Then, as the woman took a seat right beside Candide, Anna was doubly annoyed to recognise her as one of the many admirers who were always turning up at Eve's door unannounced. This one she had sent away twice before, and that day, for the third time, Anna was unpleasantly struck with how beautiful the woman was, even sitting next to and compared with Candide.

Her skin was dark and smooth, there was an adorable sprinkling of even darker freckles across her nose, and her hair, piled high in a black tower on her head, must have been long and luxurious. When she put on her glasses, her big brown eyes became even bigger and more beautiful, and her already painfully cute nose became even cuter.

Anna scowled at her.

Why did this woman need to climb over her and Candide to sit right there? Why this particular spot in the whole theatre?

With a worrying twist of guilt, she wondered, was she onto them?

Eve's voice drew her attention back to the front of the theatre.

"We begin our course with one of the greatest gothic novels of all time, The Picture of Dorian Gray by Oscar Wilde. A tale of corrupted innocence? Or a tale of innate darkness? We look into the very soul of humankind and we ask, can we face what we find there? What is it that makes a person good or bad? How far can a person be pushed before they break? And when they do break, whose fault is that? Does the same darkness exist inside all of us? Or does it take one specific wrong person, in the wrong place, at the wrong time, to cause a catastrophe?"

Anna flipped open her leather-bound journal and applied her golden fountain pen to the expensive paper which she could ill-afford, taking notes in her most practised cursive, because only that could do justice to words spoken with such enthusiasm for what she believed to be the greatest art of all.

"We will ask," Eve continued, "what is art? Is it moral? Is it corrupting? Is it anything at all, in and of itself? Or is it merely reflecting back to us the hideousness of this world we created for ourselves? And what does that say about you, the passive viewer who stands back to behold such horrors playing out in front of your eyes? The characters in these stories—their strug-gles, their vices, their virtues—what does the reader put them through with their craving for 'art'? Be it a book, a piece of music, or a portrait, is the horror in the work itself? Or in the depraved eye of the beholder? It's my hope that by the end of this book, we will have answered some of your burning ques-tions, but I can't guarantee you won't uncover more hideous mysteries along the way."

By the conclusion of the lecture, there wasn't a student in the room who didn't go directly to an atmospheric corner of Endymion College and open *The Picture of Dorian Gray*. Anna was no exception. She alternately sniffed and feasted her eyes on her new book as she drank her coffee in a quiet corner of her favourite cafe between classes. She then brought forth her dog-eared copy of *Brideshead Revisited* and made her way first to the lecture, then to the tutorial, for Great Romance Novels of the Twentieth Century. Following that, Anna made her way to Evelyn's apartment alone.

Anna had lost her beautiful skeleton key. She didn't dare go back to the office to tell the intense and immensely handsome man who'd given it to her that she'd been so careless, so while she waited and hoped it would turn up, she was reliant on Candide for entrance to their apartment.

To save an enormous amount of trouble and, Eve said, to avail himself of every possible opportunity of seeing her, Eve had given Anna a key to his apartment. She had told him that sort of commitment should not be proposed for at least two years, but he reasoned, logically, he had already trusted her with far more than that. She acquiesced on the condition the key go back to him as soon as hers should appear. But after almost two months of this secret arrangement and still no sign of her missing key, Eve and Anna had settled into what they both considered a perfectly blissful existence, all but living together.

That afternoon, when she got home, Anna turned the heating up high, made one of Eve's nice teas, and sat down on his couch to get some reading done. She remained that way, feeling an uncomfortable camaraderie with Mr Gray for a good few hours, until the failing daylight alerted her to Eve's imminent arrival.

He had told her he had a mountain of work to get through that evening, so he would be very busy and quite unavailable.

She had said she understood.

Accordingly, she got up from the couch and moved the coffee table off the plush, shaggy rug, over to the edge of the room.

She took off all her clothes and stretched herself out long on the floor of Evelyn's living room, completely naked. She opened up his thoroughly annotated copy of *Confessions of an English Opium Eater* and read and waited.

Upon his arrival, Anna needed only to throw him a half smile, and Eve didn't stand a chance.

She slept very soundly right there on the rug for the rest of the night, blissfully unaware of how late Evelyn sat up beside her to get his work done.

When she finally woke in the morning, well-rested, fresh and happy, she rolled over and kissed Eve's sleeping face. He opened his lovely eyes, brushed her messy hair behind her ear and said, "Anna, we need to talk."

CHAPTER 2

A HANDSOME ALLOWANCE

Back in her own apartment, Anna threw herself down dramatically on the couch. "Eve's kicked me out until he finishes his essay. Talk about frustrated. Let's get drunk."

"Okay, Anna, two things," said Candide, emerging from the kitchen. "One, there are things I don't want to know about you and Eve. And two, a friend of yours is here."

"What friend? I don't have any friends." She looked towards the hanging door and there, following languidly behind Candide, with a handsome smile on his handsome face, was that handsome man whom she'd first met three months ago in the office.

He flicked his dark hair back, offered a lightly sardonic smile, and drawled, "Well, I don't know about you, but this 'Eve' sounds like a bore to me."

Both women bristled immediately, two sets of eyes flaring, two sets of lips pushing into irritated pouts.

"Read the room, Percy," he mumbled to himself, then with a casual airiness, "Don't take any offence. I don't even know the man. Or woman? It was supposed to be a compliment. In that, you don't sound half as boring as he does."

"What the fuck is this?" Anna blustered.

"We're off on the wrong foot." The sexy office man walked calmly across the room and eased himself into the armchair by Anna, crossing one long leg over the other, and settling his blue eyes on her. "I'm Percy Ashdown, and I've come to take back something you have which is mine." He raised an eyebrow and nodded his head, somewhat comically to Anna's eye, though possibly meant to be debonair.

Then she remembered: the key was lost.

He wanted it and it was a special secret and it was lost.

She had to stall.

"Oh, I remember now…" she said unconvincingly. "Percy Ashdown."

His face broke into a smile that said he knew she had no real idea what was going on, but he was happy she was playing the game. The slight challenge she saw there made Anna more keen to play whatever the game was, but quite beyond that—perhaps it was his smile or his eyes or his expression—she suddenly felt an unexpected connection to him. She sensed an odd familiarity she couldn't place. It wasn't only that he'd made a strong impression on her when she met him three months earlier, as he certainly had. There was something more. Something she couldn't put her finger on.

Anna's intrigue of both Percy's person and his purpose only deepened when, just for a few seconds, she noted his eyes lift, gazing past her. She followed the line of his sight to the demon warding symbols still plastered all over the wall. She waited for him, expecting the question which she and Candide had a fake answer already prepared for, for any guest who might ask, but he said nothing at all. When their eyes met again, it was almost as though it hadn't happened. Almost, but not quite. There was intelligence in his eyes. Understanding.

Or had she imagined that?

Whatever the mystery was, Anna was determined to get to the bottom of it. "Would you like a drink?"

He held her gaze steadily. "I would."

"Is there wine, Candide?"

Candide's head tilted in a curious manner at the sudden change in Anna. "In the kitchen."

"I'll get some."

"I'll come." Percy stood, forcing Anna to brush close past him on her way to the kitchen.

Unfortunately for Anna, even all-consumingly in love with Eve, she did have an eye for beautiful men, and she could hardly help taking to Percy on account of his good looks. And nice perfume. Add to that his taste in dress and his elegant manner and she would have been smitten if not for her firm attachment elsewhere. Which is all to say, she didn't mind brushing past him one bit.

Percy took a seat on the kitchen worktop by the window, one leg up on the bench, in what must have been a studied pose. Even so, it had the desired effect of making him look very elegant and sophisticated indeed. Anna poured a glass of wine for herself and handed one to him, neither of them saying anything, both quietly enjoying a conspiracy of sorts. They already had an unspoken kinship, the way some people do instantly upon meeting, but while Anna attempted to keep her enjoyment secret, Percy's mischievous eyes on Anna revealed all.

Candide, casting a suspicious gaze over the two of them, interrupted the thick silence: "He says he's living down the hall now."

"That's odd. I thought it was all being refurbished," Anna replied.

"Not Room 238," he said.

"But that's right opposite..."

Percy raised a vaguely knowing eyebrow at Anna and she decided she had best stop talking lest she reveal too much about her secret relationship.

Candide ran interference. "Anna, I have a friend coming over."

"Friend? What friend?" Percy disappeared from Anna's radar instantly, replaced with a fast flash of jealousy.

Candide, who knew Anna inside out by that time, gave her a kind smile. "Don't worry, she's really nice. You've probably seen her around. I didn't think you'd be here, because, well, you never really are these days, otherwise I would have mentioned it. Jesus, do you mind?"

Percy had lit a cigarette and was following along with the conversation, apparently enraptured. "Oh, sorry," he said, and kicked open the latch of the kitchen window. "It's only when I drink wine. Tell me about this 'friend' of yours."

There was a knock at the door, which brought an anxious frown over Candide's face, directed squarely at Percy. "Anna, please take care of this whole *situation*, okay?"

Anna shrugged innocently. "I swear I hardly even know him."

"Why are people always saying that?" he waffled out on a puff of smoke.

Candide gave the two a wary look on her way out, and Anna peeked around the kitchen doorway to see who this friend was.

It was her!

It was that beautiful girl who kept hanging around Eve's door —who interrupted her daydreams in Gothic Literature.

"I don't believe it," Anna said under her breath.

"Neither do I." Anna jumped, not realising Percy had snuck up and was watching over her shoulder. "She's beautiful. Just look at her. She's like some kind of goddess."

Anna scowled up at him.

"Not that you're not," he said, grinning back down at her. "Just in a different… less ethereal way…" Her mouth dropped open, but he was back to studying the guest the same second. "But oh my god, look at them together."

It was true. There was kissing of cheeks and Candide's pale hair swished delightfully into whomever's thousand gorgeous dark ringlets. Their long arms wrapped briefly around graceful necks as the gift of wine was transferred from one to the other, and Anna felt sick with jealousy at the same time she felt angry at this woman for worming her way into their lives.

"She's bad news," Anna muttered, half to Percy, half to herself.

"Don't worry," came his fast and firm reply. "I'm not going anywhere." Anna looked at him disdainfully, which only seemed to increase his enjoyment. "Moral support. And entertainment. Act natural."

Percy hurriedly took up his position and his pose again, and Anna, following his lead, took up her wine and whispered, "Give me one of those."

Percy, accordingly, lit a cigarette and passed it to her.

Candide looked so happy when she came into the kitchen that Anna felt hideously guilty about having to tell her what this woman was really after.

"Anna, this is Aubrey," Candide said.

Anna, having made sure to have both hands occupied with her wine and cigarette so she was unable to provide any physical welcome, gave Aubrey a neutral face with a cold eye as best she could. "We've met."

"Oh," said Candide, not a little taken aback by her frosty response.

"Not formally, I don't think," said Aubrey, smiling sweetly. "Anna, is it?"

"It is." Still Anna made no move to welcome their guest. She wanted to add that she was Professor Evelyn Worthing's permanent, full-time lover and partner, but she knew she absolutely could not, so instead she stayed mute and distant.

"I'm Percy. It's so nice to meet you, Aubrey." He slid down from the bench and kissed her on both cheeks. "Don't worry about Anna. She's been drinking."

Aubrey laughed uncomfortably, Percy laughed a little too loudly, Anna glared at Aubrey and Candide grabbed two wine glasses and the bottle and led Aubrey away to the living room as quickly as possible.

"She's clearly the worst," whispered Percy. "What should we do? Out the window? Shallow grave?"

"She's after my boyfriend," Anna confided, then wished she'd never said anything.

Percy didn't miss a beat, though he threw it off casually enough. "So Eve's a man, after all, is he?"

"What?" She blushed. "That's none of your business."

"Oh, Anna, I couldn't care less. I can help you, though." He, eyes staring down into his wine, ran his finger around and around the rim, yet he had her full attention.

"How?"

The glass began to sing. "Want me to seduce her?"

"No!" she gasped.

"Nothing untoward about it." He shrugged, taking a sip. "She's gorgeous. Wouldn't you prefer she was with me rather than throwing herself at your lover?"

"Percy, no, not under these circumstances."

"What circumstances?"

"I don't know." She coloured twice as red. "*These* ones."

"It would be entirely her choice. I doubt she could resist me, though."

"No."

Percy topped up both their glasses and hopped back onto the bench. "No, you're right. Best she hangs around here with you and Candide. Maybe you'll become best friends. Eventually. Maybe she'll get over her infatuation with your boyfriend the more time she spends with him." Anna blanched a little, knowing that was entirely impossible. "And after all, I'm sure you and he are completely solid. Come to think of it, though, he did send you away for the night…"

"Percy!" she snapped.

He raised a quieting finger. "I'm just thinking out loud. I mean, I'm a man, and I just—well, you have to wonder about a relationship when a man goes off sex."

"He hasn't gone off sex!"

"Hasn't he?" He looked at her with exactly the sort of patronising sympathy that made her want to slap his face, whoever the hell he was.

"Who asked you anyway?"

"No one. As usual. But you're right. Only you know how solid you two are, and there's nothing a beautiful woman like Aubrey can do to interfere if you're really completely sure that's the case."

Anna said nothing and smoked her cigarette broodingly, looking Percy up and down. He really was gorgeous. His cheekbones were high and prominent, his eyes a dashing, stormy blue under dark brows. His hair was straight, dark and thick, except at the tips where it curled just a little, and he threw it with an air of carelessness that can only have been painstakingly studied, and which fooled all who did not study those sorts of things themselves. His swarthy complexion and wide shoulders gave him a more rugged aspect compared to Evelyn's statuesque beauty and, Anna considered, his presentation was also the opposite of Evelyn's relaxed, natural elegance.

Percy's brown brogues were shiny and expensive. His heavily starched, pale-blue shirt was pressed firm and crisp in every corner. His brown belt was new and flawless, and the expensive watch on his wrist flashed brilliantly as he sipped his wine. Overall, he gave the impression of a man of wealth and taste, blessed with show-stopping good looks, which were only accentuated by an air of impulsivity and adventure. Then there was that beautiful, confident smile, and a warmth in his tone and deportment that set Anna at ease in that curious way.

She had to admit, it would take him about five minutes to seduce her under normal circumstances.

If that…

As though having deliberately waited for her to complete her silent appraisal of him, Percy finally spoke again. "I have these linen sheets on my bed, and they're just that perfect amount of worn where it feels like sliding into a cloud."

Anna stifled a laugh, and instead went for an unconvinced sounding, "Mmhmm…"

"And we're having this impromptu party…"

"Mmhmm…"

With a sly glance at her from beneath his long lashes, "And I'm a very generous lover."

She almost fell off the bench. "Fine. Fine! Go seduce her." Anywhere else, surely, was better than him being in her kitchen practically seducing her. "But only if she wants to. And don't be mean to her."

He turned his handsome head to look back at her as she shoved him towards the door. "I'm insulted."

"No, you're not."

"I'm not. I'm very likely to fall for her, anyway. You'd be amazed how quickly I fall in love. So don't worry. One hour from now, she'll be in good hands." He smiled so lasciviously with the final comment that Anna immediately felt guilty about their plan, but Percy was out the door before she could stop him.

CHAPTER 3

A FIERY INTERACTION

To Anna's great surprise, Percy became a different man the moment he passed through the doorway. His movements became calm, deliberate, elegant. The posing, jovial Percy of the kitchen disappeared in an instant, and Anna suddenly had the disconcerting feeling she was in his home rather than the other way around.

Candide and Aubrey sat together on the couch, deep in conversation. Percy deftly filled both their glasses, Anna's and his own, and sat back in the armchair, quietly and unobtrusively tuning into their conversation. To all appearances, he was genuinely interested, appropriately disinterested, and he started making incisive comments and dropping surprising jokes with a warmth that made everyone feel at ease. Everyone except Anna. She flopped back into her armchair and crossed her legs defensively, nursing her wine like it was a newborn kitten.

She studied this new woman, finishing her conversation with Candide, her sparkling eyes instantly including Percy and Anna in her story as though she weren't evil personified. They were very nice eyes, big and brown with thick, black lashes. She was, annoyingly, probably the prettiest woman Anna knew besides Candide. Anna flung her legs the opposite way in irritation. They all laughed at whatever Aubrey had said, Anna having been too busy examining her to notice what she was saying. She looked across the room in disgust.

There were Aubrey's really very nice brown boots, unlaced and left next to the door. She wondered how much they cost. Rolling her eyes, Anna turned her head back and took in Aubrey's thick, charcoal grey tights, her brown pencil skirt, and her white silk blouse tucked in at her neat waist. Burgundy nails held the wine glass and took it to her dark red lips as she hid her beautiful smile for a brief moment to take a sip.

Anna willed her to spill the wine on her shirt.

She did not.

Her make-up was done very nicely. Too nicely. Had she been hoping to run into Eve here?

"Anna, you're being awful," Percy whispered when the other two were talking. "Do you want Aubrey to leave?"

Anna glared at him. "No." She refocused her gaze on Aubrey, forced a smile and said loudly, "I'm sorry, Aubrey. I didn't realise I was being *awful*. I will stop immediately."

Aubrey blushed and glanced over at Candide, who smiled at her apologetically, then sent a confused look to Anna.

"Aubrey, what are you studying?" asked Anna, the simple question laced with bile.

"Medicine," Aubrey replied softly.

"You're a medical student?"

"I am."

"Then what on earth are you doing in our Gothic Literature class?" Anna kept her eyes steady on Aubrey as she awaited the response.

Aubrey, clearly disconcerted, pressed forward, keeping her own voice calm, if a little less confident than it had been before. "I have a spare class this term, so I thought I might branch out a bit."

Anna tilted her head to the side, her fake smile and dull eyes practised from the myriad men and women she'd dispersed from Eve's door before they simply decided to start locking it and ignoring the knocks. "So why not one of the other literature classes? Why this one in particular?"

"I—"

"You don't have time for this class," Anna pursued. "Some of these novels are huge. On top of your already heavy workload, one imagines. Seems like a pretty big sacrifice. What is it that makes *this* class so attractive to you?"

Aubrey gave a curious, confiding little nod, as though Anna had exposed her already. She glanced over at Candide, the corners of her sensuous mouth lifting a little, turned back to Anna, leaned forward and lowered her voice. "I'll tell you a secret. I found out someone I like was taking the class, so I enrolled." Aubrey's eyes were on Candide again, who stared back at her with her big green eyes, smiling sweetly, a light flush on her cheeks. Anna narrowed her eyes at Candide in disbelief at the betrayal. "And I'm cheating a little too," Aubrey continued in a too-cute, off-hand sort of way. "I actually love the genre and I've read almost all of these books before. It should be one of my easier classes." She laughed gently, as did Candide and Percy.

Anna, however, was furious now. Aubrey could easily work her way into Eve's heart with that kind of taste and knowledge outstripping her own. She had already managed to charm Candide somehow. What a snake.

She glared at Aubrey, wondering if she should have one more drink before making a scene and kicking her out. Almost definitely. It was good wine. She drained her glass and held it out for Percy to refill.

He did so, she thought, somewhat reluctantly, leaning closer than necessary, speaking more quietly than necessary. "Anna, come for a cigarette."

"I don't want a cigarette. Anyway, didn't you have lots of things you wanted to say? You know, to Aubrey?"

"No," he replied swiftly. "I want to go to the kitchen. For a cigarette. With you. Won't you come?"

"Aubrey," she continued loudly, paying no attention to the way Percy then hid his face in his beautiful hand, "I don't think that's a very good reason to take a class. You know, just because you like someone, because for all you know, they might already be involved with someone else, and it's kind of a stalkerish thing to do."

"Anna!" Candide looked more shocked than angry, but still really quite angry.

"She needs to know," Anna went on, doubling her ire at Aubrey. "Some people don't appreciate being stalked is all. But there's plenty of time to change classes, which would be the right thing to do. You know, to save yourself the embarrassment."

Aubrey sat very straight, head held very high, and fixed Anna with flaming eyes. She spoke low and calm, but the sort of calm before a tornado. "Okay, that's enough. What is your problem?"

Anna leaned in further still, perfectly confident in her ability to deal with this pampered princess. "You really want to know?"

Candide placed her hand on Aubrey's knee and squeezed, effectively stalling the poisonous response that was no doubt on Aubrey's red lips. "Aubrey, please give me five minutes. I'm sorry. I just need…" Candide's eyes snapped across to Anna, hard and cold. "Anna, come to the kitchen with me. Right now."

Anna glanced over at Percy, who had averted his own eyes, staring down at the floor, foot tapping slowly, but with an alarmingly amused suggestion of a grin on his face.

She glared one more time at Aubrey for good measure, huffed, and followed Candide, who turned on her angrily, in loud whisper, as soon as they rounded the corner. "Why do you hate Aubrey so much?"

Anna reacted with equal indignation and a louder whisper than Candide's. "How could you bring her here?"

"Because I like her!"

"Of course you like her!" Anna scoffed. "She's throwing herself at you."

With a bewildered shake of her head, "And what's wrong with that?"

"Because why would she do that?" Anna coughed a little, so harsh had her stage-whisper become. "Come on, don't you think it's a bit weird?"

"Weird? Why would you find that weird?"

"Candide…" Anna took a deep breath and controlled herself, feeling the full weight of her responsibility to disabuse Candide of the belief she seemed to have that Aubrey was genuinely her friend. "I don't think you can know this, but she's been hanging around here for months. Pretty much since we met. I have had to get rid of her so many times."

Candide's angry face turned blank. "Wait, what? How many times have you gotten rid of Aubrey?"

"Maybe two or three." Anna shrugged. "But it feels like a lot. And she keeps coming back, even though I've been quite firm with her. She's clearly a stalker, and she needs to go."

"Oh, Anna." Candide sighed, in the way only a long-suffering friend can, raising her long fingers to her temple. "I can't believe you did that. I told her I live here."

"Obviously!" How else would this stalker have found her way over tonight? Anna would have to spell it out very plainly. "She keeps turning up at Eve's door. She just told you she only enrolled in the class because she likes him. And you're still being nice to her! Why are you doing this to me?"

Candide stared aghast at Anna for a good five seconds, before furiously spitting out, "To *you*! Are you seriously telling me *that's* what all this is about? Eve! Everything is always all about Eve!"

Anna looked back at her like she was mad. "Well, of course it is. I didn't want to have to tell you all this, because I didn't want to hurt your feelings, but we've all had several drinks now, so I should just come straight out with it—"

"Anna, stop."

"No, you're not listening to me—"

"Anna!" Her loud voice finally snapped Anna out of her selfish train of thought, enough to at least try to tune in to whatever Candide was trying to tell her. "She's been by Eve's place because the door is always hanging open there. Or at least it used to be, before you came along. She has no interest in Eve. She's been there looking for me. Because I asked her to come here."

"But why would you tell her to do that when…" Her confidence slipped slightly. "But that was months ago, and…" She felt her stomach tighten. "What? Oh…"

Candide nodded slowly, like Anna was an idiot, which Anna may have started to suspect was a fair assessment. "Hard to believe, isn't it? Someone likes me better than Eve. Yet somehow his very existence is still managing to ruin things for me."

"She came to see you? All those times? And. Oh. And sit with you in class…" Anna turned a sickly shade of pale, arms closing over her stomach. "Oh no. Oh no. I'm so sorry."

Candide calmed a little with the realisation, and her tone shifted from angry to let down, with a strong side of frustrated. "Anna, you are so obsessed with Eve, it's like you can't see anything else. Honestly, it worries me sometimes."

"I'm not obsessed. I'm not, it's just…" She was obsessed. There was little use denying it. If they weren't together, which was rare, she was thinking about him, watching every other student's eyes in every lecture, jealous of them all adoring him, trying to pass him their numbers, still turning up at his door unannounced, having to wait silently inside until she heard them drift away with a sigh. Anna felt, to an extent, it was only to be expected she would lump Aubrey in with all the rest. Though now she remembered, Aubrey didn't actually ask for

Eve when she came by. She only looked annoyed that Anna was alone in Eve's apartment, claiming it was a study group, which it very obviously was not. And she left as soon as Anna told her to... "I'm so sorry. Please, let me go and tell her I'm sorry."

Candide shook her head resolutely. "No. No, I don't want you to go in there right now."

"But will you please tell her I'm sorry? I didn't know. Candide, I'm the worst."

"Anna, you are lately."

"I'm sorry—"

"No. Listen to me." Candide kept her voice quiet, low enough that what sounded like Percy making an endearing attempt to keep Aubrey entertained all this time almost drew Anna's attention away, but she snapped back with the following words: "This isn't even about Aubrey. I haven't said a word to her about you and Eve, but she's going to figure it out after that performance. So is Percy, whoever the hell he is. Anna, this isn't okay. You must know how much Eve has on the line dating you. You need to reel in your jealousy now. I told you it would be like this."

"I know, I know. I didn't think—"

"No, you didn't. A lot of people around here want Eve to fail, and I don't know if you realise this, but you are key to that happening. He's going to get fired if one wrong person finds out about you."

Anna averted her eyes guiltily as she mumbled, "Eve never gets annoyed with me—"

"That's because he's obsessed with you too!" Candide snapped. "And he probably thinks you would know better than to behave like this. You're being really immature, and weirdly insecure, and—"

"Candide—"

"No! I'm really upset with you about this whole mess. And you know what else?" As Candide's voice became louder and faster and hotter, as she launched into a seemingly unstoppable rant, Anna suddenly became aware of a strange glow in Candide's eyes. A strange sort of hyper-colour greenish hue to them. "You always buy the cheap milk. Don't use the nice one if you're going to buy the cheap one."

She was right. Candide's milk was so nice but so expensive, and Anna knew she should definitely stop using it. But what was that odd glow... A trick of the light? Or something more? "I'm sorry—"

She was talking about dishes and clothes and heating, but then she spat out, "And you're boring, Anna."

Anna gasped, a hand on her lips in shock.

"You've become a total bore. Just so you know. And... and..." Before Anna could properly react to the insult, Candide's voice cracked as she forced out the words, "And I miss who you used to be. When we were close and... before you and Eve became so... so... intolerable!"

A groaning weight of guilt fell hard on Anna's chest as she realised how long Candide must have been stewing over everything. How lonely she must have been in this strange apartment, Anna never home, Anna always, always with Candide's best friend. And now here she was, ruining whatever was happening with Aubrey. She reached out a hand, but Candide pulled hers away. "Candide—"

"No. I'm going to go out there now. Can you, I don't know, be in here or something? Just not be there."

"Yes," Anna replied softly. "Yes. I'll stay out of the way. Sorry."

Candide turned to leave, but Anna reached again for her hand and this time she caught it, pulling Candide back to face her. "Please don't hate me. You know I love you, and I couldn't handle that. I'll make it up to you."

Candide, who had attempted a hasty exit in order to hide her tears, threw her arms around Anna's neck.

Anna pressed her hands against Candide's back and pulled her close. "I know I'm awful," she whispered. "I'll fix it."

Candide kissed Anna's cheek as she stood tall again. She left the kitchen with only a conciliatory half smile and not another word, but with time for Anna to see her eyes were back to normal, except for the sadness. Definitely a strange trick of the light, Anna concluded, wiping the cuff of her sleeve beneath her own eyes.

Anna followed Candide enough to peer around the corner after her. The way Aubrey looked at Candide as she came back made it all so obvious. She clearly adored her. And Anna, clearly, was a shit.

"Aubrey," Anna called. "I'm sorry. Please pretend I never said any of that."

She retreated into the kitchen before Candide or Aubrey could see her, intent on quietly hating herself for a while.

Naturally, Percy arrived seconds later, not even trying to hide the smirk on his face.

CHAPTER 4
WORTH GETTING STABBED FOR

"I tried to tell you," Percy drawled, pushing himself back up onto Anna's kitchen bench.

"You didn't try hard enough," she snapped, before hiding her face in her hands, groaning, "God, was it that obvious the whole time?"

"It really was," he laughed.

"Ugh. I hate myself."

"You should."

"I do!"

Anna made herself busy finding and opening another bottle of wine.

Percy fell silent and watched her.

She felt his presence—his eyes on her. She knew her taut movements were a giveaway that she was aware of him, but she gave him no more confirmation than that. She hopped up on the bench by the window. He continued to study her, and she felt the strain of needing to look up at him, to break his stare, but she couldn't bring herself to do it, the spark and the intimacy of his contemplation too much to acknowledge openly. Instead, she watched out the window into darkness, the treetops of the forest lit by the moonlight. Eventually, he spoke, only this time it was serious and reflective. A touch sympathetic. "Anna?"

"What is it?"

"Is Eve really that awful?"

Now she did look up, and she fixed him with a warning in her eyes.

He didn't flinch from her harsh gaze in the least. "Do you really think he would have his head turned so easily?"

"No. I don't," she said quietly, her fingers fiddling with the bottom of her wine glass. "Not ever. I don't know what's wrong with me. And could you please just forget I said anything about him? It's very complicated."

"Is it?"

"It is."

But Percy, apparently, wasn't about to let it go. "It's not okay for him to make you feel that way—"

"Will you stop!" she snapped. "He doesn't make me feel that way. *I* make me feel that way. I wish it wasn't true, but it just is." Percy didn't seem the least bit judgemental of her terrible behaviour that night, which somehow set her on edge even more. She felt a strong need to defend Eve, assuming, as Percy must, that any of this was somehow his fault. "Maybe you've never been in love—"

"I have been in love. And he never made me feel like that." He delivered those words in such a sad, wistful, resigned sort of way that Anna was stopped in her tracks.

"Are you in love?"

"Not now."

"I'm sorry."

"It's easier."

"Is it?"

"It is."

Percy flipped open a golden cigarette case, offered her a cigarette, and placed another between his beautiful lips. He slid off the bench, approached, and bent his head close to hers to light both cigarettes with the one flame.

His glorious eyes suddenly flicked up to hers up for a brief, intimate, stomach-flipping moment, then illuminated by the fire, millimetres from touch, she noticed for the first time that one of his handsome brows ran above the line of an old scar, just above his right eye, slicing straight his eyebrow through at the edge.

Anna's hot blood turned thick in her veins.

Even as Percy's lips pulled into a wicked smile, as scandalous blue eyes held her exactly where she was, all she saw in her mind's eyes was that night, three months prior, when she had revealed the secret of her skeleton key to Eve. When he had asked her, with such vehemence, who had given her the key. When he had told her how vital it was to tell him if the man who gave it to her had a scar—a scar just the same as Percy's.

She remembered the darkness that clouded Eve's face that night. She would never have known him capable of the emotion of hatred had she not seen it then. Whoever this man was, Evelyn clearly knew him and held a passionate dislike for him.

But if Eve knew who he was... Percy must have known Eve, too.

And Percy knew she was in love with Eve.

And Percy was pretending he didn't know Eve at all.

But no...

Surely there were other men with scars under their handsome eyebrows all the world over. This man was only Percy from the office of Endymion College, so Eve must already know him. He was funny, if a little odd, and she felt perfectly safe with him. He was, surely, just a student doing part-time administration in the office.

But what if he wasn't?

Percy, by this time seated opposite her again, had caught the pale change in her aspect. "What is it?"

"Where did you get that scar?"

He neither coloured nor stalled, not even for a second. "A Belgian monk stabbed me."

Anna almost spat out her wine. "A Belgian monk!"

"No, seriously," he replied, utterly unperturbed. "He had something I wanted, and I had a very hard time taking it from him. That's not all he gave me."

Percy began to unbutton his shirt with long, sensual fingers. One button, then two, then three. Anna felt herself getting slightly hot all around her neck and chest, and she hated herself for the flush Percy would no doubt see on her.

He was still busy with his buttons, though.

Four. Five. He pulled his shirt to the side, slowly, expertly, revealing first his luscious collar bone, tilting his neck in the opposite direction to accentuate the entire area as he slipped the shirt down over his lovely shoulder. He rested his finger on a scar at the top of his large, beautifully sculpted biceps, though she could hardly force her eyes to his arm, given how much of his well-built chest he had unnecessarily revealed.

He took in her frozen breathlessness in one glance, smiling rakishly. His words alluded to none of that, of course. "This scar is also from his dagger. But clearly I bested him, because here I am to tell the tale."

"I wonder what could be..." She licked her lips. "Worth getting st-stabbed for..."

"That's a conversation for another time." He took up his wine, and he left his shirt hanging open, so Anna forced her eyes back out into the wilderness.

One's lover's enemy must be one's enemy too, she told herself, unconvincingly.

"Please, could you do your shirt back up?" Her weak voice wavered only a little this time, encouraging some pride in her progress.

The corners of Percy's handsome mouth tilted further at her supplication, and she sneakily turned her gaze back on him as he undertook the requested task, which they both knew he knew she would do. She didn't care. She ran her eyes over the gorgeous body and handsome face for pure enjoyment, before focusing more seriously on that scar above his eye.

It did nothing to lessen his overall pleasing aspect.

If anything, it made him more mysterious and intriguing.

Possibly more handsome.

That wasn't the point, of course.

"The one on your arm looks far fresher than the one above your eye," she said. It was a direct challenge.

Languidly, "It's amazing what they can do with a laser these days."

"Is it?"

"It is." Then, after a brief silence, and a long, inquisitive drag on his cigarette, "You know, Anna, in the nicest way possible, you don't seem like you belong here."

"Then will you explain to me exactly how I got here?" Her eyes were piercing and cold and worked to disconcert him exactly as she had intended. He knew something. It was just the slightest twitch at the corner of his mouth, only the vaguest dimming of the confidence in his eyes. It was only for a second that he finally lost that minuscule touch of his composure, but it was enough for her watchful eye to catch.

"Sounds like there's some sort of mystery here," he said.

"Seems so." She took a breath of her own smoke. "What will you tell me?"

Then in quick-fire, "I can't tell you anything."

"Can't or won't?"

"Can't. I don't know what you're talking about and you're being weird."

"What are you even doing in my kitchen, Percy?"

"Do you want me to go?"

"No."

Percy and Anna watched each other, both making their own calculations. He hadn't asked once for his key, not since he arrived. He drank with her and sat with her and talked with her. Could it be that he was simply enjoying her company as much as she enjoyed his?

No.

He knew or wanted something, and she knew he wasn't going to give it up yet.

She also knew, unfortunately, she couldn't hide out with him in the kitchen forever, because Candide hadn't been back and she was almost definitely going to need the apartment to herself if things were going well. "How long do you think we can hide in here?"

He took her meaning, his gaze on the kitchen door. "They're very quiet."

With a slight blush, she muttered, "I think I need to go. Somewhere. Will you come sit on the stairs with me?"

"Okay. But bring the bottle."

As they passed through the living room, they found it deserted. Anna's eyes involuntarily went towards the bedroom, where she knew she probably shouldn't let them go, and in the quick glance she found Candide and Aubrey, sitting on Candide's bed, knees drawn together. Candide's fingers gently gripped the top of Aubrey's blouse, the other hand was lost in her hair, and Aubrey ran a hand over Candide's shapely hip, the other on her thigh, at the hem of her skirt, kissing her.

Was it their first kiss?

Anna couldn't help but think of Eve—of how hard it had all been in those early days.

She felt slightly envious of Candide, this woman so open and honest in her interest, making clear and undeniable advances. Nothing in their way except Anna's stupidity. Not like the mess of lies Eve and Anna were still burdened by daily.

Percy's voice, close and quiet by her ear, shot a little tingle down her back. "I don't think you're supposed to watch."

"I'm not," Anna blustered, fumbling with the door as an unsavoury scarlet washed over her complexion.

She followed him out into the frigid hallway, where they sat at the top of the frozen stairs, neither particularly minding the chill, as they had all the warmth of alcohol on the inside, and all the warmth of their new, strange friendship on the outside.

"I'm surprised you would want to come out here," Percy said, leaning back against the stone bannister, "seeing as it's haunted and all."

Anna laughed.

Percy gave an odd smile. "Why are you laughing?"

"I didn't think you were the sort to believe in ghosts, is all." She lit two cigarettes and passed him one.

"I believe in ghosts. And so should you. Hasn't anyone ever told you this building is haunted?"

"Candide did, once, I think…" She frowned. Anna had a clear memory of standing in the courtyard with Candide that first day, looking up at the apartment, talking about the rumour of a haunting… but she couldn't remember why Candide had brought it up in the first place, or how the ghost story had ended. She blinked away the vision that went nowhere. "I've been here three months now, and I've never seen a thing. In fact…" Then she caught herself. She was about to tell him they had played with a ouija board once, planning to leave out all the details of the demon that came through and the nightmarish events that followed, but then she wondered, a little absently, not for the first time, why they had decided to do the séance in the first place. It was rather an odd thing she and Eve had puzzled over together on occasion. That the two of them should have been brought together in such strange circumstances, doing a séance for no apparent reason… It must have been someone's stupid idea. But she couldn't remember whose… How had she even ended up in his apartment that first night?

"In fact, what?" Percy was watching her very carefully. Almost studying her. He seemed to be hanging on her every word, and she felt a small flush of self-consciousness.

"Nothing. I don't really know what I was going to say. I wish I could believe in ghosts, but I've never seen one…" His incisive eyes remained steadfast, unsettling her, like he had since that first day. She tried to sound casual. "I love ghost stories, though. Have you ever seen a ghost?"

Finally, his gaze fell away, down into the darkness below, and the words slipped slowly, heavily, from his beautiful lips. "I have."

"Really?" She leaned a little closer. "Was it scary?"

"It was terrifying." Even in the black of the hall, she believed she saw a slight shudder, his eyes stoney, a touch of panic all about him.

Her curiosity very quickly got the better of her. "Do you know a good ghost story?"

Now he looked back at her, but not as one preparing to enter into all the intimacy and excitement of a creepy tale told in a dark, haunted building. He looked genuinely scared, as though he could see the apparition even now in his mind's eye. He looked unsure, wary, as though he thought he'd perhaps best not tell her. But he said, his tone serious, nothing light or fun or joking about him, "I know the best and most horrifying ghost story of all. The most harrowing and terrifying of all, because it's true, every word of it. And if I tell you, your life won't ever be the same again."

Utterly beyond help, Anna scooched a little closer still, and whispered, "So… will you tell me then?"

At that, his face broke into a lovely smile. Far too lovely, far too fond, with his blue eyes dancing in the dark. He leaned back on his elbows, stretched his legs out long on the stairs, and dipped his head back to contemplate the ceiling. "Anna James…" He sighed her name in a way she didn't know he could, before tilting his head towards her, intimately, lips much too close to hers. "Did you ever get the feeling you've made a terrible mistake?"

With the warning boom of her heart in her chest, Anna straightened her posture, and redirected her concentration to her wine glass, and not at all on Percy's handsome form stretched out there, long and lean, right in front of her. "What have you done?"

"I don't know." He turned his eyes away from her again, as he oh-so-casually let fall the words, "If only you could remember."

Her relative ease turned to horror in an instant.

Remember? She remembered everything. Didn't she?

She rubbed her always-aching shoulder and shuddered. She could see the demon, remember kissing him, remember herself stabbing a priest with a salty scalpel, remember the death and the screams and the blood.

But how did Percy know? What could any of it have to do with him?

There was no way. He must have been talking about something else.

But what couldn't she remember?

There was something there. There was always something there, but it was forever just out of her reach. The more she tried to focus on it—on the séance and the ouija board and her reasons for being there with Eve that night—the more she could feel it slip away. Every single time.

None of the intimacy between Percy and Anna had dissipated. If anything, it had intensified as he waited for her to pick up whatever crumb he had just dropped. His barriers, she was sure, had gone down several seconds earlier, and it was the best chance she would get. "Who are you?"

"I'm just Percy."

"And what do you know about me?"

"Anna." He sat up, close, his whole body turned towards her, fixing her with burning eyes so intent it scared her a little. "I'm going to need you to find that key."

She broke into a nervous, slightly hysterical sounding laugh. "Oh. I thought you were going to say something awful to me. The key. Don't worry, it will turn up. I know it's in the apartment somewhere."

He didn't relent, his tone, if anything, becoming more urgent. "Anna, you can't know how important it is."

"Okay, got it." She took a deliberately distracting draw on her cigarette. "Is it antique or something?"

"Or something." His index and middle fingers raised, cigarette wafting between them, to point instructively at her. "Tomorrow, I don't care how hungover you are, turn that place inside out until you find it. It's vitally important. Please, will you do it for me?"

"I will." She made herself smile to ease the tension. "Are you going to lose your job over this?"

"My job?" He looked briefly confused, then also smiled. "Oh yes… Yes, I might. If I'm not in the office, that's probably why. Please do try to find it."

"All right. I promise."

A silence fell between them as he relaxed back into his provocative pose, and as her heart rate slowly returned to somewhere close to normal. He dropped his head to the side and took a long inhalation of smoke. "I'll do you a deal."

She raised a curious eyebrow. "And what deal is that?"

When he grinned across at her, it was far more dashing and cheeky than she would have liked, especially when he leaned in again and lowered his voice to an intimate whisper. "If you find that key, I'll tell you my ghost story."

A not too dissimilar grin swept across Anna's face. "If it's as scary as you say, then you have a deal."

"It's scarier."

"I'll find it."

"Good." He let his entrancing eyes wander slowly to her lips, then, hotly, brought them back to meet hers. "Because I would very much like to see you again. And soon."

That was flirting.

That was definitely flirting.

It was flirting, and it was the step over the line Anna needed to snap her back to reality and realise she was sitting on a dark staircase in the middle of the night, drunk, with a handsome, entertaining, very sexy man who was not her partner.

This was the time to end the conversation. "My boyfriend," she said. "I should probably—"

An impatient finger tapped his ash into the empty black. "I didn't mean anything by it."

"No, I know." Didn't he? "But I should—"

And just like that, he launched into a series of totally unrelated and thoroughly beguiling stories about his time studying in Italy. He told very good stories, and a great many of them, and she could never have said exactly where the time went, because for the next few hours, or however long it may have been, Percy and Anna lost themselves completely in amiable conversation.

Art was Percy's main area of interest, but he was easily as well-read as Anna and shared some of her favourite novels. She was surprised to discover he had never studied at Endymion College until now, leaving the expensive private school he, for some reason, avoided naming, before moving to Padua for several years to become fluent both in Italian language and Renaissance art. Latin, it transpired, was a special interest, but this he passed off as too similar to Italian to warrant her particular appreciation of his skill.

He spoke beautifully and there was an unusual, clipped edge to his accent, which she attributed to travel and money. All night, he listened carefully to every word she said, and he held her completely transfixed with every thoughtful reply of his own, always funny, always fascinating, seeming almost to wind a spell about her that made time and reality drift away.

"And that," he concluded, "is how I almost destroyed a Caravaggio."

Anna laughed at the conclusion of his meandering, long-winded story, unsure whether she believed a word of it, but she had decided some time earlier that if it were at all possible for the things he said to be true, he was exactly the man to pull them off.

They were both comfortably quiet for a time, smoking, drinking, then he broke it all to pieces when he said softly, "You're too good for him, you know."

Anna sighed and leaned her head against the railing. "You don't know anything about him."

"Of course I do," he muttered. "Everyone does."

Her eyes snapped over to him. "Then you do know who he is. And you lied to me all night."

He gave a careless shrug in response. "I thought you would rather I pretend I didn't know."

"And why would I want you to do that?"

Percy was perfectly relaxed as he replied to her growing perturbation, "You let slip the minute you walked in the door. Would you have preferred to spend the evening trying to backtrack? I know you need to keep your relationship secret. It was ever so with students and professors. It would have only made you uncomfortable had I said anything."

It was, to her wine-addled brain, a reasonable explanation, but that did little to quell the small panic that she had been so stupid, and had let her secret relationship be uncovered so easily. "Percy, please don't tell anyone."

"I won't." He gave her a reassuring smile. "Of course I won't. Your secret is safe with me." But then, with a mischievous glance, he added, "So long as…"

Why was it she couldn't quite suppress her smile at his suggestive tone? "So long as what?"

"Let's keep this between us. This conversation, the key, everything that happened tonight. Let's not talk about it until I see you again."

"And why not?"

"Because… Well, I'm mostly thinking of you, and, I don't know him personally or anything, but if I was Eve…" A sparkle through the long, black lashes. "I might not take too kindly to you being here, alone, with me, all night long…"

Her lips parted in protest, but just as quickly he went on, "Obviously it was all totally innocent, but why put the idea into his head? It just feels right to do it this way. And I'll keep your secret for as long as you need me to, because we're friends now, aren't we?"

"I guess we are," she replied, though she neither agreed nor disagreed openly with his suggestion to keep their friendship secret. Of course she would tell Eve. He wasn't the jealous type, and she didn't see anything untoward about what had happened with Percy that night. Two friends chatting over wine. For hours.

And hours. One very, very handsome... A little flirtatious perhaps... But what of it? She genuinely liked Percy. She did, very much, want to be Percy's friend. She told him as much. "You know, it's strange, but there's something oddly familiar about you. Like something I can trust. Even if I probably shouldn't."

He glanced across at her with a sweet, heartfelt warmth which seemed to cement the odd bond they'd formed that night. "You'll figure it out soon enough." He took a drag on his cigarette, blowing rings of smoke into the black of the hallway, before following Anna's eyes as she looked wistfully towards Eve's room. "Go on," he said. "You have to go to bed some-time. And it would hardly do for you to come back to my apartment. Much as I'd like to invite you."

She addressed this latest none-too-subtle flirtation with a mock-scowl, before sighing out, "He told me not to come tonight."

Percy chuckled, warm and deep. "Anna, if a girl like you turns up at a man's door at three a.m., looking like you do, and he turns you away, it's already over."

She bit her thumb, eyes on the door. "I don't want to bother him."

Percy watched her bite her thumb and consequently doubled down on his supposition. "Trust me, you'll be very welcome. Now go. I'll clean up here."

Anna's eyes lit. "Really?"

Percy's eyes dimmed, just a little. "Really. Goodnight, Anna."

"Goodnight, Percy." She smiled at him, then tripped lightly down the hallway into darkness. He heard a faint knock, then saw her happy face illuminated in the warm glow of Evelyn's apartment. An arm reached around her waist, then she was gone, her laughter filling the hallway briefly before the door closed behind her.

Percy drank his wine, stubbed his cigarette out on the stairs, then left the glasses outside her door, carrying the bottle downstairs with him, and back out into the icy courtyard.

CHAPTER 5

THE KEY TO EVERYTHING

Anna awoke, groggy, with a light headache, to see Evelyn standing in front of his mirror, his fresh white shirt tucked into his brown woollen trousers. He pulled the shoulder strap of a pair of suspenders up over his shoulder, then down again, seemingly undecided whether to wear them.

"Oh my god, you look amazing," Anna moaned, ready to make a crumpled mess of his nicely pressed clothing.

He threw an anxious glance her way, then back to the mirror. "I don't know… I can't find my belt. They'll have to do."

"Oh… Sorry…" Anna slipped an arm down the side of the bed and pulled out the belt she'd hidden sometime the night before. "I just thought if you weren't too busy this morning…" She held the buckle on the end of her long index finger, and with an expert shift of her hips, let the sheets slip down to expose her breasts.

A small, delectable slit opened between Eve's gorgeous lips, and within seconds, he was on top of her. His mouth crashed against hers, he threw off what was left of the sheet between them, and she lay back as he worked his way down her body, her perfectly naked flesh pressed luxuriously against his pristine, crisp clothing, pulling at his hair gently. His hands wrapped around her ribs, and he took her nipple between his teeth. He kissed and kissed down her belly, sliding down between her thighs, when he dropped his face against her pubic hair and groaned. "No, no…" He lifted his head to survey her, laid out before him, and groaned again. "Ugh, why do you have to be so lovely all the time?"

She shifted her thigh up against his cheek. "Really? Not even a little while?"

He wrapped his fingers around her leg, kissed her thigh, closer, closer, placed one incensing kiss far too near to her clit, and, "No." He escaped from the bed before she could catch him with her ankle, and shoved some books from his bedside table into his satchel, mumbling all the while, "I can't even look at you or I'll never get out of here. I'm going to be late. Again. And now I'm in suspenders."

"But they look so good," she breathed desperately.

"Goodbye!" And he, really very abruptly, left the apartment.

Anna, once she recovered from the crushing blow of having slept through the opportunity for morning sex, lay for some time between Evelyn's soft sheets. She consoled herself with the idea that as she had chosen to study literature, she was actually working hard at obtaining her degree by reaching one arm out into the cold to grasp a copy of *Jane Eyre*, and pulling it back into the bed with her.

She lay there at least another two hours before she remembered that Candide had told her she would be leaving the apartment at midday, and that if Anna wanted access to it, she must be home by then. That gave her only minutes.

Anna dragged herself out of the cosy bed, into yesterday's clothes, stole Eve's nice milk from his fridge, and made her way barefoot down the hall to Room 235.

As she lifted her hand to knock on the door, she was almost flattened by Candide leaving for the afternoon. "Perfect timing." Candide sped past her, then spun around. "Oh!" She thrust a pointing finger past Anna. "Look what I found."

Anna entered the apartment and there, on the brand-new coffee table, sat her beautiful skeleton key, sparkling in the late morning sunshine.

"The key!"

"Actually, Aubrey found it," Candide said proudly.

"Where was it?"

"Uh. Don't ask."

"Okay… But this is great!"

Anna put the milk down on the coffee table and grabbed the key. The key, which she almost instantly dropped. As she turned back, Candide was greeted by a face of unmistakable horror. Anna's temple broke wet with sweat. Her hands began to shake. "Candide, I remember… I remember everything…"

Candide walked slowly back into the apartment. "What's wrong?"

"Don't you remember?" Anna searched the room frantically. "The ghost. Don't you remember him?"

Candide tried to follow Anna's eyes, darting back and forth— the demon warding symbols, the ghost warding symbols, the hanging door. "Please stop whatever you're doing."

"We need to find him!" Anna ran to the bedroom window, the one where the ghost had last been seen.

Nothing.

Candide chased after her. "Find who?"

"The ghost!" Anna cried, then, eyes wide and wild, it clicked. "No. It's Percy. I need Percy!"

She ran down the hall and banged on the door of Room 238. Silence met her waiting ears. "Percy! Percy, come out here right now!"

She banged on the door again, and still nothing.

She ran back into the apartment and froze in the centre of the room, turning on Candide with unsettling intensity. "You… You… Candide, you have to hold this key. Hold it with me."

Candide studied both Anna and her key with a doubtful eye. "Anna…"

Anna thrust out her hand, shoving the tip of the key towards Candide's face.

As much to get the thing away from her as anything else, Candide took the other half tentatively, and in less than a second, her face mirrored Anna's, her eyes enormous with awe, surprise, horror. "Oh. Oh, Anna… How did we forget that?"

Anna shook her head, still gripping the key tight. "I don't know. I don't understand any of this."

Candide blinked her intelligent eyes three times, and announced, "It's a spell. It has to be."

Why did Candide always know all the things? "A spell? Spells are a thing now?"

"Yeah," Candide nodded authoritatively. "I think spells may have always been a thing."

Slowly, disbelievingly, "Really? Because this feels like a new development... in our lives..."

"It does. But it's not if you really think about it." Anna, not for the first time, pushed herself to keep up with Candide's brain, and failed. Happily, Candide continued, "I think we should go over everything we both know so far, and put all the pieces together. It's probably really important that we pause, right here, and make sure we're clear about everything that's happened so far and how we got here."

"Yes. Good idea, Candide. We don't want anyone getting lost at this point. It's been months since all that ghost stuff happened."

"And it's possibly a little complicated."

"Then let's lay it all out."

Candide, still holding the key, led Anna around to the couch where they both sat, leaning close, gripping tight. "Anna, do you remember that day in the cafe, I told you J—uh—'*he*' put the demon warding on our walls, but it was the wrong warding?"

"Yes. That was the day the ghost came into my lecture."

"Yes. Remember I told you he locked the ghost out? When he was possessed, he specifically locked the ghost out, but not demons. He tricked us into thinking we were safe, so he could come back at any time. That's what those first sigils are on the wall for."

"Yes, but why don't we remember all of this?"

"Because the ghost sigils block our ghost. In fact, they block anything to do with our ghost. Do you remember, that day when you came in, I'd just been reading about the ghost sigils in the Necronomicon. You walked in and told me about the ghost, and I'd already forgotten all of it—the ghost, what I'd just read, all of it, until I touched you. You had the key with you, didn't you?"

"I must have," muttered a bewildered Anna.

"So you see, it's all our conversations about the ghost, the séance, the memories, anything we read about it, all of that gone. Or scrambled. That's the reason we forgot all about him. But you remember all of it now, don't you?"

Anna nodded vigorously. "I do remember. But I only remember this exact minute. Before you found this key, I could remember the demon, I could remember how we met, and everything we did, except not a thing to do with the ghost. It's all come back just now. Everything."

Candide smiled at the success of the explanation. "Anna, that's a classic uncloaking spell."

"Classic?"

"Classic!"

Narrowing her eyes in an attempt to continue to follow, "To be clear, what you're saying is, there's a spell on this key and it uncloaks what that warding has cloaked?"

"Yes. Or any warding at all. It will uncloak any cloaking spell." Right there, Candide seemed to catch herself. She straightened, averted her eyes, gave a little shrug. "At least, I believe that's how this sort of thing works."

Anna felt a small chill creep down her spine. "Um... I know you like ghost stories, too, but... Seriously, why do you know this?"

"Just..." With a distracted flick of her hair over the shoulder, "Just the book." The way she kept her face forcefully blank, her voice casual, like it was barely worth mentioning at all, did nothing to relieve Anna's growing concern.

"The Necronomicon? That book?"

"Yes."

"The Book of the Dead?"

"Yep."

"So, you've memorised all this information from the Necronomicon?"

Anna thought she saw a small blush and a flutter of the eyes as Candide studied the ceiling. "I mean, it's just random knowledge I picked up here and there. I'm not an expert or anything."

She was lying. Anna knew she was lying, and Candide knew Anna knew, so Candide swiftly moved the conversation along. "If you drop that key, the warding will take over again, and you'll forget the ghost and every word we ever said about it. Everything to do with its existence."

Anna nodded her understanding. "What happens if you just touch me and not the key?"

Candide first put a hand on Anna's arm, then let go of the key. "That works. Just like in the cafe. I still remember everything. But, listen, why do you have this key? This isn't basic magic. Whoever cast this spell, whoever gave this to you, they know what they're doing. It's a very powerful spell, and it's not easy to pull off."

Anna's eyes flared at the thought. "It's Percy. He's done something, and he's the missing link in all of this. We need to find Percy."

Anna was up off the couch and out the door by the time Candide mumbled, "Percy? Percy, the sexy office man?"

"Yes! It was Percy who gave me this key! We need to go to the office." Anna was halfway down the stairs already, yelling over her shoulder, so Candide reluctantly slammed the door and ran after her. They made their way across the freezing courtyard, Anna still barefoot, and into the building opposite, down the long corridor, arriving breathless at the office desk in what felt like seconds.

"Hello? Hello!" Anna smacked her hand down repeatedly on a small bell.

"Anna, why are we…" Candide, hands on hips, doubled over, took a moment to catch her breath from the run. "Anna, why did we need Percy again?" Anna linked her arm through Candide's. "Oh!"

"Can I help you?" A neat, older, bespectacled woman made her way slowly out of the back room to greet them.

"Percy!" Anna virtually shouted at the poor woman. "Is Percy working today? I need to see Percy straight away!"

The woman, taken back by Anna's over-excited, particularly messy presentation, was slow to answer. "There's no Percy working here."

"What?" she cried. "You didn't fire him already, did you?"

The woman squinted. "I'm sorry?"

"I have the key!" Anna slammed it down on the bench with a shaky hand. "Please, everything is fine now. Percy doesn't need to be fired. I have the key."

The woman looked long and hard into Anna's face, then turned her eyes to Candide's far more serene, competent, washed and well-presented face.

"Does a man called Percy work in the office?" Candide asked sweetly. "We had reason to believe we could find him here."

"I'm sorry, dear, no. There's no Percy working here at all. I don't even know anyone called Percy—" She paused, tilting her head to the side, as a vague recollection popped into her mind. "Hold on. You don't mean *little Percy*, do you?"

"Little Percy?" Anna repeated. She thought over the powerful stature of that beautiful, tall man, his broad shoulders, his whole physique altogether comforting to the point of being an almost overwhelmingly luscious presence—the disdainful curl of that sensuous lip, the way his muscular arms—

"Yes, little Percy. Well, I suppose he's not little anymore," she laughed. "Oh, but he hasn't been around here for years. Last I heard, he was in Morocco. But you'll have to come back when Harriet is on and ask her. She's his mum, you know."

"Percy's mum works here!" Anna yelled.

"Well, of course," the woman smiled, politely enough, but keeping a sensible distance from Anna. "If that's the Percy you mean."

Anna nodded furiously. "When will she be back? We need to see her at once."

"She should be in Monday week. I'll leave a note for her if you like?" She began moving things around the desk, searching for a notepad.

"No, no. I really need to see Percy immediately. How can I get in touch with her?"

"You can't, dear." Her shrug was as unhelpful as her tone was resolute.

"Can't you send her a message or something?"

"No, not while she's away." She spoke a little slower now, a little firmer. Probably preparing for an argument, Anna thought. Or maybe hiding something. Maybe hiding Percy… "But I don't think it can be Harriet's Percy, anyway. He wouldn't come by Endymion without stopping to say hello to me. He's an absolute doll, that boy."

No. She *must* be hiding something. This was the exact spot Anna had met Percy three months before. He was hardly forgettable. She must know. Anna leaned a little closer. "Can't you give me her details?"

The woman took a step back and crossed her arms. "Absolutely not. Whatever it is will have to wait."

Anna looked over the woman's shoulder and around the office for some sign of Percy, then, failing to find anything, she narrowed her eyes at the woman, ready to make all manner of possibly absurd accusations, until Candide's shout snapped her out of it.

"Anna! I've figured it all out!" Anna turned to Candide expectantly. "Thank you so much, and sorry for the inconvenience," Candide called to the woman as she dragged Anna back down the hallway.

"What? What is it?" whispered Anna, as soon as they were back in the atrium and Candide only held her arm, rather than pulling it half-off in their flight.

Candide looked straight into her eyes and spoke very sternly. "Anna, don't be rude to the office ladies. They have a very hard job for much less money than you would think."

"I wasn't being rude." Anna blushed, then redirected, "Also, you'd think Endymion College could afford to pay her better."

"Yes, you would. And yes, you were about to be rude." Anna looked down at her feet guiltily. "She doesn't know anything. We'll come back and see Harriet next week, but before then, we'll just ask around a bit. We'll find Percy. There's no rush. We'll deal with the ghost situation without him, and then when we do find him, I'm going to punch him in the face."

"Me first," Anna spat.

Candide reached awkwardly around Anna's arm to check her watch. "Listen, I have a lecture in a minute, so I'm going to have to let go of you, and then I'll forget about our ghost again. Can you go back to Eve's apartment until we sort this out? I don't want to leave you in a haunted room again."

"It's fine," Anna sighed. "I'll just put the key down and forget all about it, apparently."

"If you're sure. We'll meet up later and talk this through with Eve, and we'll make a plan. Can you maybe make a note before you put your key down or something so we don't get lost again?"

"Okay, yes, we do need to do that, and I will, but... Will you have dinner with me tonight? Just us? I want to make you something."

"Oh, that's so sweet." It warmed Anna's heart to see how quickly Candide's face lit, then made her a little sad again to see the avoidant eyes and the light blush. "I don't want to make you not see Eve. I was just… being jealous, I guess."

"No, I want to. I miss you. We should do something. Just the two of us. If you're free?"

Candide raised her shoulders, far more shy than usual. "I was supposed to be seeing Aubrey. I guess I can shift that to this afternoon…"

"Are you sure?"

"Of course."

Utter relief washed over Anna. She could easily see the many ways she'd been a terrible friend, but never for a second had she stopped adoring Candide, regardless of the delightful distraction that Eve was. "Did you tell Aubrey I'm sorry?"

"Yes. She's so lovely. She's all right with it."

Anna scanned Candide's eyes. "I am really sorry."

"I know you are." Candide, who still held Anna's arm, leaned in for a long hug. "Tonight?"

"Yes. I'll see you then. If not before."

"And when will you see Eve?"

When indeed. Anna hadn't yet mentioned having met the man with the scar to Evelyn, although she spent the better part of the night with him. It had been late when she got in after all, and she had been distracted… But now it had become vital to tell him. As she worried over how deeply Percy must have been involved all along, she wondered how Eve would react when he found out what she'd done, given his clear dislike of the man.

She had to talk to Eve. Immediately. "I'll try find him before dinner. If you see him, will you tell him I'm looking for him?"

"If I find him, I'll bring him home so we can all talk, okay?"

"Perfect."

They parted ways.

Anna's trip back across the courtyard grass was far slower, more gingerly, one thousand times colder. Her feet were painfully numb as she put her hand on the handrail and made her way up the frozen stone staircase. She had come to be very comfortable in the building, but now, with the key in her pocket and the memories of the ghost fresh in her mind, everything was unsettling. She remembered the feeling of the ghost's hand on her skin, when it came to her in the lecture theatre, when it woke her in her bed. She moved quickly to the warded safety of her own apartment and looked through the windows. No one there.

She told herself she was safe in the building, as she had been for months.

Her feet ached.

A warm shower would probably help.

Anna gathered her belongings, and once again made her way down the dark, dark hall.

As she passed Percy's door, exactly opposite Evelyn's, she stopped and held her ear against it.

Not a sound.

CHAPTER 6

A SURPRISE ENCOUNTER

Winter at Endymion College was always freezing cold, and a good number of students, including Anna, delighted in the opportunity to wear their softest jumpers and scarves, and most dramatic coats and boots. Even so, that day, as Anna stepped into the perpetually frigid bathroom, there was an edge to the cold that felt unnatural. *Super*natural. Instantly she saw her breath turn to fog before her eyes. But then anyone who attends a gothic university on a cold continent in winter will tell you that is quite normal.

She assessed the row of showers, all three of them just as cold and empty-looking as usual. Then she studied the four toilet stalls that ran along the back wall. One, two, three doors open, and the last, just open a crack. Almost closed. Was that normal? Anna had no idea. She had never seen another person other than Eve or Candide in this bathroom, and that was generally by appointment, so never had she had the smallest fright.

This time, however, the hairs on her neck stood up, and had she been the sort to listen to her intuition, she would have returned immediately to her room or left the building altogether. Alas, it was rarely in Anna's nature to listen to her intuition until the threat was clear and present. Still, she was no idiot. She did not approach the door at once, but stood back some distance and lowered herself to the floor to look for feet. She saw none. Of course this information was insufficient to satisfy her, so carrying her hairdryer, the heaviest weapon she had to hand, she quietly approached the door. Standing as far away as she could manage, she kicked that door hard, and it made a thunderous bang, which caused her to jump, but also convinced her that indeed, there was no human lurking in the toilet stall.

Calming herself, but unable to shake off the feeling that she wasn't alone, she again inspected all the stalls, then turned on the hot water and showered, dressed, dried her hair.

She had almost finished her make-up when that toilet door, the last one, creaked. A swish of red appeared beneath the door. A bathrobe? It stood to reason that some other students at some point must use this bathroom. There were students living downstairs. Weren't there?

The robe slid around the base of the toilet and she felt a slight revulsion at whomever was inside the stall, allowing their clothing to sweep the toilet floor. It continued to move around as the… person?… turned towards the door. Anna gathered her belongings, alarm-bells going off in her mind, though the logical part of her brain still told her nothing had ever happened here, not once, in this creepy, weird, freezing bathroom.

A red hand, gloved perhaps—perhaps not—reached fingers around the side of the bathroom door. It began to open, slowly,

slowly, the sound of the robe shuffling and sweeping the floor all the while as the door creaked.

Anna fled.

Before she could see who was behind that door, before she even considered saying a word, she ran down the hall and slammed her own apartment door closed behind her.

And there, before her very eyes, was Percy's beauteous form spread out on her couch.

"You!" she yelled furiously, clutching her key tight in her hand.

"You found it!" he exclaimed happily, a stupidly handsome grin on his stupidly handsome face.

"This is all your fault!" she yelled. "Everything is all your fault!"

"In a manner of speaking."

His calm voice only made Anna angrier, though it should hardly have been possible for her to be any angrier. "How dare you! Who even are you? How did you get in here? Does your mum work at the office? How the hell!"

"Calm down," he drawled. "You don't want the neighbour to hear."

"Yes, I really do."

"No, Anna." His tone became quiet and quite serious, even if he didn't shift in the slightest. "You do not want Evelyn to know about me."

Anna's already overtaxed mind reeled. Even now, even after whatever it was he had done, was he still going to ask Anna to keep his secret? "Why on earth not?"

Stupid, handsome, suggestive, raised eyebrow. "He wouldn't like us spending time together."

"But what can you mean?" Anna threw her lustrous hair back proudly and looked down her nose at Percy. "Evelyn loves me. He trusts me implicitly."

"He shouldn't, though, should he?"

That same proud face now showed a touch of horror. "What do you mean by that?"

He held her gaze steadily. "Exactly what I said."

"That's not a bit true."

"Isn't it?"

She thrust an angry finger in his general direction. "Don't think I don't know what you're doing. We're not here to talk about me. You're trying to trick me and throw me off the scent."

Still relaxed, still smiling, as though she had invited him over for tea and biscuits, "Anna, I'm your friend. I hadn't intended to be, but as it goes, I rather like you. Now, I have done a few things I perhaps shouldn't have and I want to make amends for that. That's why I came here yesterday."

"You just came for your key!" she shouted. "Your weird, haunted key! Why did you give me a haunted key?"

"No." He shook his head gently, confidently, infuriatingly. "I didn't come for that. Not really. I came to see you. And here I am again, and I have a lot to tell you. Really, quite a lot to explain. So come sit with me and we'll talk." He swung his feet down to the floor, so she begrudgingly dropped her belongings, slipped her key into her pocket so she wouldn't forget any important details, and threw herself down beside him. "Good.

Now the first thing I want to say is that I am actually really sorry for all the trouble I caused you."

"Trouble!" she spat.

"Yes." He waved his fingers as though her repeated brushes with death were nothing. "All of that."

She turned her body to face him, jabbing one knee into his slate woollen trousers. "Percy, do you have any idea—"

"Anna." His voice was low and strong, and now, as he turned his body to her and leaned in close, his blue, blue eyes met hers with such an intense, burning sincerity that it disarmed her immediately. "I know *everything*."

The way he said it... "Everything?" She faltered. "No, Percy, you can't possibly know what I—what we've all been through."

"I do know, Anna. I know all of it."

"All?"

"Yes."

"Everything?" Her voice broke at the word. She knew the key was magical somehow. What else could Percy have done? How much could he really know? Without her even realising her tears had started to fall, she lost all her remaining strength. She was in the room again—in the room with Joe Bruno—and she was kissing him and she was loosening his belt and she was undoing his buttons and he had no control over his own body as she did those despicable things to him, and all her feelings of self-loathing and guilt boiled up inside her. She saw flashes—a shard of green glass, blood and more blood, a decapitated head, another, another, and Joe's smashed face lying on the floor, gasping for air. Percy reached for her hands and squeezed them tight. Then he put one hand under her chin and turned her face up to his.

"I knew you would be strong enough to handle whatever happened. But I never thought that would happen to you. If I'd had any idea, I never would have let you become involved in any of this."

"How can you know?" She looked into his eyes pleadingly, as though his words, his explanation, were enough to erase all the trauma she was holding on to if he would just say the right thing—as though this man was the key to everything—the one who could answer all her questions, take away all her guilt, and make everything like it was before.

She broke his gaze, staring down at his strong, manly hand holding both of hers, his other hand still under her chin, stroking her cheek gently with his thumb, her tears falling on him one by one. "Percy, I need you—"

He cut her short. "It's all right, Anna. I'm here now. And I'm going to fix everything. I'm going to take care of you."

"Oh, Percy—"

"Anna…" he whispered, as his face moved closer to hers, his gentle hand guiding her by the chin, slowly, almost imperceptibly closer. She looked back up to his handsome face only to see his eyes closing.

The very second she realised his intention, even before she could lift a hand to slap his face every bit as hard as she intended, she was almost frightened out of her seat by the apartment door slamming shut with a deafening bang.

Evelyn stood before them, his face a mask of fury, his lovely hands formed into two tight fists and his chest heaving with rage.

"Anna, get away from him!"

"Eve! It's not what it looks like!"

"Anna, he's dangerous!"

As Anna attempted to stand, Percy grabbed her wrist and wrenched her back down sharply. She turned to face him, horrified at the change from only seconds earlier. It was as though he were an entirely different person. She saw nothing but darkness and anger and a malignant air which she shrank from even as he held her tight.

Percy's eyes were fixed on Eve, a burning hatred emanating from his every pore, a malicious smile marring his handsome face as he snarled, "Welcome home, little brother."

CHAPTER 7
A TENSE CONVERSATION

"**G**et your hand off me immediately!" Anna snapped.

Percy, as though startled out of a trance by her words, let go his grasp in a second, and she sprung towards Evelyn, who reached out for her.

She jumped back from him. "Wait. Before you touch me, there's something you need to know." Eve's eyes went sharply to Percy and back to Anna, marking the first time he had ever doubted her, be it only for a split second. "I have a key. The key has a spell on it. And when you touch me, you're going to remember some terrible things."

"What terrible things?"

"About a ghost."

"What ghost?"

"Are you ready?"

"Yes!"

She reached for his hand and watched his eyes as his expression changed. It was not as she had expected. First, the recognition, the horror, then within seconds it deteriorated back into anger, fury.

"Percy! Percy, you did this! You absolute bastard! I should have known it was you!"

"Well, you didn't," he shrugged. "Because you're an idiot."

"Because you put a spell on a key! And gave it to my girlfriend! God, I hate you so much!"

"Good, because I hate you too so much."

"Shut up, Percy!"

"You shut up, Evelyn!"

"Brother!" Anna gasped.

"Only half!" Evelyn spat.

"The worst half by far," Percy retorted.

They heard laughter in the hall. Anna and Eve exchanged panicked glances, and seconds later, Aubrey and Candide were in the room. Candide's face fell immediately, and she looked to Anna for an explanation. "Anna… what's… You've got people over?"

"Yes. There are people here." Candide gave up on her instantly after her stupid response and looked instead at Eve to fix the situation.

"Aubrey!" he said, with an undeniably fake, overtly anxious smile plastered on. "Hi!"

"Professor Worthing. What are you doing here?" Aubrey was also smiling, but they all noted an edge to her voice.

"Uh." Eve folded and unfolded his arms, hid his hands in his pockets, felt his glasses there, pulled them out. and started fiddling with them. "Essay," he mumbled, pushing his glasses over his nose and into place. "I had to come and get an essay."

"You did?"

"Yes," Anna breathed, enraptured. Eve was now wearing suspenders *and* his thick-rimmed black glasses, and therefore Anna found herself at a severe disadvantage. Had he rolled his sleeves at that moment, which he considered doing, the jig would have been entirely up. As it was, Anna managed to hold herself together enough to agree, rather robotically, with Eve. "I did not give him my essay last term, and he has come to get it."

"Ah ha," said Aubrey.

They all stood still.

"Anna, go get your essay," Candide hissed.

"Yep. I'm going to get it." She lingered a second longer, then disappeared reluctantly into the bedroom to search for something she could pass off as an essay.

Aubrey looked Eve over from head to toe. "Do you always do house calls, Professor Worthing?"

"No. Never. It's just..." He reached an arm up, playing distractedly with the hair at the nape of his neck that way he did. "Her scholarship. She's probably going to lose it... Because of the essays. So I came to get it. How are you enjoying Gothic Lit?"

"It's good." And she pressed her lips tight together.

"Good," Eve nodded. "That's good to hear."

Silence. Long and painful silence in which Evelyn almost visibly wilted under Aubrey's unrelenting gaze.

Anna returned. "This is my essay. Thank you, sir, and I'm sorry I didn't get it to you sooner. It won't happen again."

"That's okay, Anna. You don't have to call me sir, by the way." She blushed and hid a smirk. "I'll take this essay and go now. Percy?"

Percy, quietly watching all with an amused eye, said, "Oh, I'm not going anywhere with you, Professor Worthing."

Eve's beautiful lips drew tightly to the side. "Yes, you are, Percy."

"No."

"You're leaving right now."

"No. I'm fine here."

"Get out, Percy!" Anna shouted.

He tilted his nose up at Eve. "Not until he goes."

Eve looked at his brother furiously, but spun around and walked out without another word.

"And close the door behind you!" Percy called.

They heard Eve's apartment door slam shut and Percy ran out the open door, his footsteps sounding loud on the stone stairs as he fled. A second later, they heard Eve's door slam shut again and a second set of footsteps quickly descending the stairs.

Candide slammed their own door. "Okay, who wants coffee?"

Aubrey wasn't about to be distracted. "Anna, is that man bothering you?"

"Man?" Anna blinked stupidly. "Which man?"

"Professor Worthing. Is he bothering you?"

"No. No, not at all. He's very nice. A very nice man."

"I'll bet he is," Aubrey said.

"I'll vouch for him," said Candide. "I've had a few of his subjects. He's very nice."

"Anna, I'll level with you," said Aubrey, her eyes all at once worried, sympathetic, and angry. "I've noticed him hanging around you. The way he looks at you. I know you've been to his apartment."

Anna's mind flashed back to one of the times she had sent Aubrey away from Eve's open door, and her stomach pressed into a knot. "Study group…"

"Yeah, I remember. Study group for one, wasn't it?"

Shit. She swallowed hard. "No… no…"

"You told me no one else is allowed in the study group. Doesn't that seem unusual to you?"

Aubrey was so nice, so genuine, and Anna really shouldn't have been so rash that day. She squirmed, trying to think of a way out. "No… That was different…"

"You're not interested, are you?"

"In Professor Worthing? What? No." Anna forced a laugh. "What do I want with a fusty old professor guy? Ew."

"Ew." Candide nodded emphatically.

"He's only a few years older than you," said Aubrey.

"Yeah, but just the whole vibe. That whole... academic thing..." She thought of his suspenders over his crisp white shirt, unbuttoning his shirt, running her hand over the scar she herself had given him as he grasped her naked flesh tight, the hairs on his chest, his lovely belly, the way he could so easily pick her up and thrust her against the wall... A blush rose to her cheek. "Fusty," she sighed.

Aubrey shook her head sadly at the hopeless state Anna appeared to be in. "Candide, don't let him in here again. I'm telling you now, I don't trust him. And Anna, you can talk to me, okay? If you ever want to report him, I'll tell them everything I've seen. Or listen, if you're not comfortable doing that, I can go ahead and report him for you?"

"No!" Anna cried. "Aubrey, please no. There's really nothing going on. Really. He barely even talks to me. And thank you. Thank you for looking out for me. I don't deserve it after the way I treated you last time you were here. I wanted to apologise for that."

"Anna, that's okay." Aubrey shot a knowing sort of smile at Candide. "Candide explained everything."

Anna looked over at Candide's averted eyes. "She did?"

"She did. And your secret is safe with me."

"Oh. Okay..."

"Coffee?" said Candide, wandering innocently away from the conversation.

"Yes," said Anna, relieved at the distraction, whatever it was based on. "And I'm going to go get it while you two stay here and sit and talk. To each other. For a while. I need to sort that coffee out."

Instead, Anna ran to the bedroom window and looked down at the courtyard. Unable to see Percy or Evelyn from her vantage point, she returned to the living room where Aubrey sat suspicious, and Candide sat irritated.

"Candide, actually," Anna waffled, "will you come help me make coffee?"

"No, Anna," came the cold response. "I will not come help you make coffee."

"But I might need some help—"

Through gritted teeth, "Anna, go make the coffee."

They heard Eve's door close again, and it was clear from the look on Anna's face she intended to run straight down the hallway to him.

"No!" Candide snapped at her, as if she was she was a puppy, about to eat a poisonous mushroom off the ground. "Coffee. Just like normal."

Without another word, but with a brain like a hornet's nest with a brick thrown in it, Anna went straight to the kitchen to make coffee to make small talk until she could unburden herself of the thousand questions burning inside about Eve, Candide, and especially Percy.

CHAPTER 8
A FORGETTABLE DINNER PARTY

The calm with which Candide presided over the conversation made Anna wonder if she too should perhaps take up yoga. Candide must still think Eve needed to know about the key. Perhaps she assumed Anna had already told him, which she had, more or less. But she couldn't possibly know Percy was Evelyn's secret brother! Or could she? Did she already know that? Had she decided to keep the explosive secret from Anna even as a man named Percy with a scar above his right eye sat in the kitchen drinking wine with her best friend and Evelyn's beloved half the night? She couldn't know! Or could she?

Then Anna remembered.

Everything to do with the key was forgotten by Candide. All she knew was that Eve and Percy had been here, and that they had left around the same time.

Anna was itching to reveal the truth, but she was painfully careful, even as she passed Candide her coffee, to not so much as brush her hand while the key remained in her pocket, lest she accidentally transfer the shocking information.

So, Anna sat and sipped the first of several cups of coffee, and slowly, slowly, she became distracted by Aubrey's conversation.

Aubrey, it transpired, had been raised by a doctor and an architect, both wealthy humanitarians. Her mother took her family around the world with her as she offered her medical skills in impoverished and war-torn countries, where Aubrey and her four brothers and sisters either lived in compounds and were homeschooled, or were sent to boarding schools overseas if the country was just too dangerous. They made five, the brothers and sisters, so they were never lonely, and Aubrey considered her upbringing exemplary, having enrolled in medicine to follow in her mother's footsteps.

Aubrey's father, the artist of the family, made sure his children were particularly well-schooled in the arts, and when they were at home, either in London or New York, Aubrey had access to the family library, proclaimed to be her favourite room in the house—either house.

Anna chose not to say anything about what it must be like to have an entire library in your house, trying to avoid making a fool of herself by showing her appalling lack of knowledge about such a standard household requirement. She found something slightly hurtful about the way Candide understood it to be a basic truth in life. Of course the library is the best room in any house, she laughed. Anna knew in her soul Candide would never intend to hurt her, but as she sat in the armchair, watching Candide curl her legs up close against Aubrey, who leaned in close to her and rested a hand on her thigh, as though the two had already known one another for years, and as she watched their closeness grow right in front of her eyes, Anna saw something she had never fully realised before. There was an understanding between the two, in addition to all the other interests and the physical attraction they shared, that came from their wealth.

They simply saw the world that little bit differently than how Anna saw it.

She wondered what Eve's reaction to the conversation would have been, as having always had to keep their relationship secret, she had never witnessed any close interaction between Eve and one of his own kind, other than Candide. She hated the thought of being on the outside of anything involving Evelyn, yet she already felt a vague distance grow as she listened to Candide and Aubrey. Neither Eve nor Candide had ever mentioned having a library in their home. Something which she now attributed to delicacy. And their awareness of the need for that delicacy around Anna roused only shame inside her.

No, not only shame.

Shame with a bitter twist of resentment.

But although she felt that sudden and slight distance from Eve, although she felt Candide slipping away from her, although she felt herself somewhat locked out of their basic understanding of reality, which is a gap that people from vastly different classes never truly can bridge—although she was quietly aware of all those things, her feelings were only more complicated by the fact that she couldn't find it in herself to dislike Aubrey for awaking all these unpleasant ideas. It would have been so much easier to have a single point of anger to pour out all the discomfort.

Alas, Aubrey was very funny, very clever, and had that relaxed air about her that people who never stay in the same place for too long always seem to have. Her voice was soft and warm and her accent fascinating, a mixture of all those places she grew up, all those nannies and teachers and boarding school children all mixed into one. In addition, from what Anna could tell, Aubrey was also very kind. She was kind to Anna even though Anna had been revolting to her, and with Candide she had a comfortable yet respectful way about her. Confident in her movements, but not expectant. Candide, of course, was putty around Aubrey, and even Anna couldn't help but feel somewhat swept up in her hopeless romanticism.

"Aubrey, would you like to stay for dinner?" Anna asked. "I'm going to go make it now."

Candide's lovely green eyes showed Anna that all was forgiven from the previous day. It clearly meant a lot that Anna could put her own desperation to see Eve aside for her, although Candide could not possibly know quite how desperate Anna was.

"I can't." Aubrey gave a very sweet and apologetic smile. "But thank you. I switched some things around to come over now, so I'm busy later."

"Oh. Well, I'm glad you did."

"Me too," said Aubrey.

Anna went to the kitchen to prepare their meal, wondering when she would finally talk with Eve. She was so happy to have won Candide back that she daren't try to run out now and risk causing a scene if Aubrey caught her sneaking into Eve's apartment. If he was even still there. So she waited, and she chopped vegetables, and she waited.

Eventually, Aubrey took her leave, and seconds later Candide was in the kitchen.

"Isn't she lovely?"

"She's so lovely."

"She's awesome."

"She is."

"Do you like her?"

"I very much like her." Anna smiled across at her love-stricken friend patiently. "She's very sweet and funny and lovely. You've done really well."

"Isn't she great?" Candide pushed herself up onto the bench and stared out the window, eyes glazed with ardour, while Anna stirred the pots, biting her tongue all the while, waiting, until finally Candide asked, "So, what happened back there?"

Anna dropped her spoon and turned excitedly to Candide. "Okay, so first, I don't know if our bathroom is haunted. Oh wait, can you link arms with me or something?"

Candide scrunched her nose up. "What?"

"Just…" Anna huffed a frustrated breath, and pulled Candide off the bench, gripping her wrist tight.

At the touch, Candide was hit with the initial shock of a flood of memories, but she quickly continued, "A ghost in the bath-room? No, please, no. Same ghost or something else?"

"I don't know. Maybe even a person? Some unhygienic, shuf-fling person? So anyway, that's first. Then I came home and Percy was here, and he apologised for giving me the key." Anna let go of Candide, whose brow drew into a confused frown, until Anna directed her, "Can you get the wine? I'll take this through."

They made their way into the living room where Anna lit some candles, Candide poured the wine, and they took their seats at the table.

"Rest your foot on mine so you don't forget anything," Anna said.

"Huh?" Another distrustful nose scrunch.

With a firm nod and authoritatively raised eyebrows, "Please?"

Candide pushed her lower lip out a little, but stretched her foot across onto Anna's, and a second later, "Oh, well, that's something. At least Percy knows how awful he's been if he's apologised."

Anna quietly dropped the bomb. "And then he tried to kiss me."

"What!" Candide yelled.

"Aha," Anna nodded.

"But he knows you're seeing someone?"

"Yes, he knows! And he knows it's Eve too."

"No!" Candide gasped.

"Yes!" Anna affirmed.

"Shit." Candide took up her wine, while wondering aloud, "How does he know you're with Eve? And did you slap him?"

"No." Anna waited until the glass was at Candide's lips, then added, "Because Eve walked in on the whole thing, caught him in the act, and yelled at him."

She spat the wine back into her glass. "Oh my god!"

"Aha," Anna nodded.

"So dramatic," Candide sighed over another sip. "And is that when we came in?"

"Just about. But…" Anna sat a little taller and rearranged her cutlery and wine glass as a small twist of anxiety started up inside. "Um… There was something else…"

Candide leaned in close. "What?"

"Oh…" She glanced at Candide, then away again. "Oh, I think Eve should be the one to talk to you about this. It's…" She wrinkled her lips in apology. "I don't know if he has a secret."

Candide looked as insulted as Anna had expected her to. "I know everything about Eve."

Of course she did. She must. They were best friends. They'd lived together for years. But then why didn't Candide say a thing about Percy? Anna asked, with some trepidation, "So you knew about Percy?"

"What?" Candide's voice quieted, and she leaned in closer still, in readiness for a secret. "What about Percy?"

The natural gossip in Anna fought hard for escape, but she managed to hold a lid on it. "So you *don't* know about Percy?"

Candide's fingers began to tap on the table. "What about Percy?"

Anna shook her head resolutely. "Candide, this will just have to wait until we see Eve. We need to talk to him. You need to talk to him."

"But—"

"I'm probably way off anyway," Anna deflected. "Suffice to say, he was pissed to see Percy, and not just because of the kissing thing."

Candide jabbed at her steaming rice in irritation, but soon settled her desperate curiosity enough to reflect, "Is it bad we're having this nice dinner and Eve probably really needs to talk to us about whatever happened today?"

A knock at the door.

"Eve!" they shouted.

Candide was up first. She flung the door wide open and yelled in his face, "Eve!"

"Candide!" He just about yelled back, dropping a fast kiss on her cheek, then pulling back with an excited, "You and Aubrey?"

"Yes!" Candide squealed with delight.

"Good for you." He relaxed against the doorframe as another dreamy haze descended over Candide's face.

"She's so pretty," she marvelled.

"She's beautiful," he concurred.

"Isn't she? And she's so smart."

"I know she is." He nodded in sincere and empathetic agreement.

"And she hates you."

Eve's happy face dropped. "Oh no. Sorry. What did I do?"

"She's onto you and Anna. Thinks you're a sleaze."

"Oh." He bit that sexy lip of his right there in perfect ignorance of the effect it might have on Anna, quietly watching in
the background. "When are you going to tell her?"

"About us? I don't know. I mean, we only just…" She gave a
bashful shrug. "You know…"

And he was straight back to the fond smile of a doting big
brother. "Made it official?"

"Yes!" She gave a fluttering of her hands for emphasis. "Yes,
it's official!"

"I love that!"

"Me too!"

Eve was yet to notice Anna, sitting in darkness, lit only by
candlelight, and she slightly wished she could become invisible
and continue to watch him talk with Candide, so sweet and
unconsciously charming as he was. Of course, she was equally
happy when he did spot her and a warm flush rose to his cheek
at the sight of the woman he loved best in all the world quietly
adoring him.

"Hey, gorgeous," he said.

"Hey, beautiful," she replied.

Candide moved aside for him. "You two are actually quite
sweet now I have a girlfriend."

Eve spun around to Candide with another one of those
flooring grins of his. "We both have girlfriends!"

"How nice is this?" she laughed.

Though he still appeared to be perfectly happy, his tone softened a little as he made his way over to Anna. "I wanted to talk
to you two because something really odd happened today

and… I don't know… I'm confused and…" He leaned over to kiss Anna. As soon as their lips met, he pulled back in horror, then his face went blank. He looked at Candide. He looked at Anna. "Did… I feel like something weird happened just then… Did it?"

Anna said nothing and waited.

He leaned over and kissed her again.

The same thing. The complete horror when their lips touched, then blank confusion, only with that stressed hand at the nape of his neck.

"I take it back," said Candide, watching him. "You two are weird."

"That…" Another compellingly handsome yet questioning scan of both of them. "Did something just happen?"

Anna found herself perfectly bemused by the bizarre situation, having the key in her pocket, allowing her to be the only person in the room who knew what was happening. With a sly grin, "Eve, aren't you going to give me a kiss?"

He smiled his beautiful smile. "I can't believe I haven't done that yet." He leaned in.

"No, don't!" Anna laughed, pulling her face away. "Don't. It's too cruel." Eve's look of confusion, mingled with a little hurt, reduced her levity somewhat. "No, no, I love you so much. Just wait one minute. I want to figure something out. You were saying something weird happened today?"

"I was…" Damn, he looked good with those glasses on, especially as he pushed the black frame up his nose following the thwarted kiss. "I remember coming here, and I remember meeting Aubrey and… And then everything's kind of…"

Anna waited. He would not, or could not, say it. His eyes scanned over the apartment, as though trying to fit his memories of the afternoon back together.

Fascinating.

Anna prodded, "Do you remember who else was here?"

"You, me, Candide and Aubrey... and then I... I must have left, only I don't remember leaving... But then I was at home again... But you weren't there... And I don't remember—"

"You don't remember anyone else?" Anna watched him keenly.

He frowned. "Was there someone else?"

Really fascinating. Anna turned her investigation to Candide. "Candide, do you remember who was here?"

"Yes!" she cried, far too excitedly. "It was—"

"Shhht!" Anna hissed, chopping her off before she could ruin the game. "Eve, what do you remember about when you were here?"

He leaned back against the couch, fingers tightening on the ornate mahogany, thinking hard as he stared at the floor. "It's like... something's missing. Or like a weird dream, because I can't put it all together. I remember being so angry when I was here, but I can't put my finger on why."

Candide piped up helpfully, "Probably because Percy tried to kiss Anna."

"What!" Eve shouted.

"Candide! One thing at a time!" Anna attempted to shush her.

"You said he knew!" Candide threw back.

"Clearly, he forgot!"

"How could he forget?"

Eve watched the arguing, but it wasn't until he spoke that the pair realised the effect the news had on him. His tone became low, with a metallic edge to it, and a familiar darkness clouded his face. "I never heard you mention anyone called Percy."

"No, I never did," Anna replied softly. Then she hastened to add, "But listen, enough, because you're all acting very strangely. With good reason. Come sit and I'll explain everything."

But Eve kept his distance. "Anna, if someone called Percy has been anywhere near you, that's something I really want to know about."

"Sit!" she snapped, and he did as told. Candide followed, excited, and Eve remained quietly apprehensive as Anna explained, "We're all going to need to hold hands for me to tell you something, and you're both about to get a really big shock. So prepare yourselves."

A chuckle sounded in the back of Candide's throat at the seemingly ridiculous preparations, while a slight tic across Eve's cheek was the only sign he showed of his much deeper concern about whatever Anna was readying them for.

"You two hold hands first." Anna tried to keep a serious look on her face as she directed them, because it really was terrible for everyone else to be unable to remember, but it was also an incredible magic trick to her. Eve and Candide held hands, then looked at Anna expectantly. "Let's see if this trick stretches as far as three people…" And she reached for Eve's hand.

"That absolute bastard!" he shouted the second their fingers touched.

Candide jumped at the response Anna had been expecting, then doubled her grip on him. "Percy?" she asked. "Because he kissed her?"

"Not kissed!" Anna spat. "Tried to!"

"Yes. Yes, I remember everything now," Eve muttered. Anna and Candide waited for him to speak again, but he said nothing at all, staring hard at the table, his lips drawn tight as his mind worked overtime. Anna felt his hand pull back, as though he had thought to try forgetting again, but then changed his mind, and he held her fingers slightly tighter.

After a time, Candide decided to forcefully pull him out of the tense reverie, asking casually, "So, are you going to tell us what's going on with Percy?"

A flush, an embarrassed smile, a knee shaking anxiously under the table. "I actually really don't want to talk about that." He looked over at Anna. Behind his sweet, uncomfortable, unsure smile, she could see real sadness, real pain. "I wasn't..." He swallowed. "I wasn't expecting this tonight."

"Eve," she said gently, "did you forget about him when you weren't touching me?"

"I don't know—"

Anna wrenched her hand away.

Eve's face cleared in an instant. He blinked twice, and the same light befuddlement settled over him. "What were we talking about?"

"Candide, do you remember what we were talking about?"

"We were talking about Percy."

"Percy?" Eve said, darkening again in exactly the same manner as he had a few minutes earlier. "I've never heard you mention anyone called Percy."

Anna leaned so close in her study that she was almost touching him again. "You don't remember talking about Percy just now?"

"No, I don't." He flung himself back against the chair frame in his miserable confusion. "Should I remember? What's going on?"

"It's because of my magic key." Anna clasped his hand again.

A look of alarm crossed Eve's face, then he fell silent for at least a full minute, ruminating.

Candide jiggled in her chair, itching to ask him about it all, so Anna kicked her shin to prevent her. The two scowled meaningfully back and forth for a time, until Eve broke the tension apart with the unexpected statement, "He's put a spell on me."

"What?" asked Anna, as though she hadn't heard the clearly spoken comment.

"Told you," said Candide.

Eve made no response to either comment, continuing his stream of thought aloud. "And the key. He's put a spell on me, and a spell on the key. He can do that, the complete shit that he is. And I don't know how to undo it. And I don't know how to handle this." Rather than let go, he dragged each of their hands to his forehead, hiding his face and groaning. "Why would he do this? Why now?" He was quiet again for a time, his eyes hidden, until he let out a long breath, and placed all their hands back down softly, calming his tone. "I want to help you with this ghost thing. And this key thing. And…" He straightened with an unconvincing smile. "It's fine. I'll be fine.

I'll be totally fine. Soon." His foot that had recommenced its tap-tapping on the floor suggested otherwise.

He still hadn't mentioned to Candide that Percy was his brother. He still hadn't given them an ounce of detail, and he was still, very obviously, trying to hide the fact that he was probably as upset about the situation as Anna had ever seen him feel over anything.

The fun and games came to an abrupt end in Anna's mind as she witnessed Eve's struggle with whatever was going on. Something of a locket clicked shut then and there, with Evelyn safely inside, and like the soft flick of a securing key, Anna announced, "I'm not going to let you remember him."

Eve's face turned a greyer shade of ashen as he understood very quickly that he was powerless to control the situation, because Anna, once set on something, was a very sexy but completely imperturbable immovable object. "No, you can't do that." Though he knew the protest would only make Anna more determined, which it did.

She wrapped her fingers a little firmer around the palm of his hand and pulled it close to her chest. "We know Percy did this. And I know who he is now. If you're not touching me when I'm holding the key, you're going to forget you've seen him anyway, so it's a waste of our time and our energy for you to be upset like this. And I'm not going to let it happen."

"Anna, no. I can't just walk out and leave you to deal with this." Worried, he may have been. Turning himself inside out with anxiety—it was his natural state. But having someone who loves you as much as Anna loved Eve will always warm the coolest heart, and the slightest something of a smile bloomed in his cheeks and eyes

"You won't," she said, offering her own adoring smile. "When we need you—when you need to know something—I'll make sure you know it."

"It's not right—"

Her tone changed to clipped. "Don't you trust us?"

"Of course I trust you, that's—"

"Good then. We'll take care of it. Right, Candide?"

Candide nodded her bewildered but enthusiastic assurance.

"Anna… I can't…" But even as he said it, she could see the thought of forgetting Percy, for a time, was clearly very tempting for Eve. Yet, he avoided the specific topic with a quiet, "I don't want to miss out on all the ghost stuff."

"I promise you'll be in on all ghost shenanigans."

He smiled slightly, searching Anna's eyes to confirm her confidence in letting him forget. He must have found what he was looking for, as he offered no more resistance than a fetching pink tint about his cheeks.

Candide looked back and forth between the two of them as they came to their silent agreement. "I feel like maybe I've missed something really important here."

Anna searched Eve's worried countenance. "Can I tell Candide what happened with Percy earlier today?"

Eve took the lead. "Candide, remember when we were kids, and I told you that guy was my brother, and then he disappeared, and I told you he wasn't my brother at all, and I said I lied about the whole thing?"

"Vaguely."

"He was my brother. Percy is my brother, and I'm sorry I lied to you. Don't be mad." Anna could see the hazy sheen dulling his eyes, the look of hopelessness at having to explain right here, right now, and she knew, whatever the history was, it must be extraordinarily painful.

She pulled her hand away without another word about it.

The teary haze remained in his beautiful eyes, yet he was perfectly happy again in an instant. He and Candide laughed awkwardly to find themselves holding hands, which they soon dropped, and Anna placed her foot on Candide's with a finger over her lips to encourage her silence.

Meanwhile, Eve's brow creased, his smile dropped, and, "Oh no, I've just realised," he said in his usual sweet, gentle tones.

"What?" Candide and Anna watched him apprehensively. "What is it?"

"You're doing a thing. You've got candles and wine and everything. Why didn't I even notice that?" The same confusion that had marred his beautiful face for most of the night returned, then, "I think I need to go. Let's talk later."

"Candide, will you hold my key, please?" She passed it across. "Eve, how about that kiss?"

That lovely, loving smile. "I can't believe I haven't kissed you yet."

In that instant, in the way he looked at her, the way he spoke, Anna knew she would have destroyed worlds for Eve. The peace and happiness he felt there and then was something she could so easily deliver. And she resolved to do exactly that for as long as she could.

She lifted her foot from Candide's, and just as the confusion descended, Eve kissed her, and everything was utterly perfect in both their worlds.

That is, until Eve leaned back in his chair, and Candide jabbed Anna hard with her foot, bringing the memories flooding back.

"Okay," he said, standing up. "I guess I'll see you tomorrow."

"No, Eve," Anna replied. "You have to stay, because I have a lot to tell you. Go get a glass. You're going to need a drink."

CHAPTER 9

SECRETS AND CIGARETTES

Half an hour later and a glass or two in, Evelyn said, "So, there's a ghost haunting this apartment, but no one knows unless they're touching the special key, which has some kind of spell on it, but I can't touch it or it will upset me for reasons you're forbidden to explain to me?"

"Yes!" Candide clapped. "You've got it!"

Eve's face darkened. Again. "Anna, the man who gave you that key—"

Anna remained stern and confident, even if she flinched inside at his fast return to Percy. "Eve, do you remember how annoyed I was last time you brought that up?"

"Yes, but—"

"But nothing. Don't bring it up to me again. I mean it."

Candide deliberately interrupted any possible reply. "So we need to figure out what to do about this ghost. Does he need to get back into the apartment? Presumably, we have to find out what's keeping him here."

"All right," said Eve. "Let's go to the library."

"What? Why?"

"Study." He cast a dramatic eye over Anna and Candide, before continuing, "We do the séance tonight."

"No!" Anna and Candide yelled in unison.

"No, Eve. That would be a very bad idea," said Candide.

"Really, let's never do that again," Anna agreed.

"Again?" asked Eve.

"Ugh, this is so painful," Candide moaned. "Eve, don't you remember the séance?"

"Candide!" he harsh-whispered. "I thought we agreed…" He trailed off with a none-too-subtle glare.

"Oh." She blanched. "Oh." She stumbled. "Uh. Not that séance. Oh…"

Anna looked at her suspiciously. Even now they were keeping their secrets, which was only fair, because she had explicitly told Eve long ago that she didn't want to dredge up their past if it made him miserable. And then, with the spell on the key, they had forgotten so much anyway… But while it hadn't once bothered her before, the information suddenly seemed pertinent. Any information to do with séances or picking locks or stealing cars or why on earth literature professor Evelyn Worthing apparently wasn't shocked or shaken by the revelation that she had a ghost in her apartment and a magic key.

Eve, unaware of Anna's musings, continued to attempt to run distraction, much like Candide had. "So, have either of you noticed anything at all weird in this apartment? Like an ancient object that a spirit might attach to, some kind of container with weird residue, bones hidden in the walls?"

"Eve?"

"Yes?"

"You're curiously relaxed about this news."

"No. No, I'm not." He sipped his wine. He felt her eyes. "Not at all. I'm not relaxed. It's terrible news. I hate ghosts."

Candide bit her lip and avoided Anna's hard gaze, looking instead at Eve, who locked eyes with her for a few seconds longer than usual, then looked back at Anna, a worried, melancholy expression on his face. Eve said, "Candide, would it be all right with you if I had a talk with Anna?"

She scoffed. "I think that would be a very good idea."

"Cigarette?" he asked.

"Yes," Anna replied.

Candide handed the key back to Anna, and Anna said, "Candide, when I take my foot away, I honestly don't know how much of tonight you're going to remember."

"That's okay. Can you just remind me to go look for some kind of uncloaking spell? Or something that will circumvent a cloaking spell?"

Anna removed her foot from Candide's, waited for the usual befuddlement, then, "Candide, you were just saying you need to research cloaking spells. Can you go check in the Necronomicon? We're going for a cigarette."

She remained seated. "Was I?"

"You were, but there are some complicated things happening that I can't go into right now. Super complicated. But we really need to know about cloaking spells. Could you do that for me?"

"Um. This is all very odd…"

"Please?"

"Okay…" Candide reluctantly walked into the bedroom and pulled the *Necronomicon* from under her sheets.

Eve watched Candide in dismay. "Is that where you're keeping it now?"

"Just for now."

"Do you…" He paused with a waver of his lower lip that was somewhere between shocked and furious. "Do you sleep with it?"

Candide was immediately on the defensive. "What's wrong with that? Anna sleeps with books all the time."

Assuming his parental tone, "Do you remember when we were told to not even touch that book?"

With the same old childish smirk, "I don't think you should take advice from demons, Eve."

"No, I suppose not," he admitted, mildly checked. Then added, "I think it's probably a very bad idea to spend that much time with it, though."

Candide's final response was an apathetic shrug, and a redirection of her concentration to the ancient tome.

Anna turned her full attention on Eve. "Cigarette, then?"

He gave a final reprimanding glare to Candide, then nodded at Anna.

She opened the hanging door, and they each settled down with their wine in what had become their usual places. Eve had never made a second mention of how strangely the door was set back from the edge, and both had fallen in love with the intimate space over the last three months. Occasionally they even closed the little blue hanging door behind them and spent hours talking and reading in the sunshine on their tiny private balcony. Not tonight, though. Tonight there was a distinct wintery chill in the air, and Anna was glad she had thought to grab her coat on the way out.

She took a sip of wine to warm herself.

Eve lit two cigarettes, passed one to Anna, then said, "Anna, I have to tell you something."

With a nervous smile, "I figured that. But please remember you can't touch me at all right now, or you're going to have to deal with key stuff, and that's bad."

"All right."

"Okay."

He took a deep breath. "Okay... so... when Candide and I were kids, our parents had a paranormal club. You already know that. But what I haven't told you is that the club had consequences they were either unaware of, or in denial about, and sometimes..." He paused, and gave the sort of slight nod that is meant only to convince oneself to go on. "Paranormal things would come for us. And we learned to—to try to deal with that, a long time ago, and, well, for most of our lives." He looked across anxiously. "And I wish I told you sooner. About that."

"Oh." Anna let the enormity of the confession wash over her. A series of gates seemed to burst open, one after another, slowly at first, then more and more until she was hit with a wave of appalling understanding. She tried to make it okay. "I wasn't expecting that. Not entirely. So…" But she, the more her imagination delved into the confession, became less and less okay. "You've always known about those things?"

His eyes were still keen on her, watching every sign of with-drawal—of the realisation of betrayal. "I'm really sorry I didn't tell you."

"And that…" Her stomach twisted in on itself. "Everything we went through wasn't new to you at all?" She began to feel sick. "Were you just pretending?"

Eve reached out a hand, by instinct, then withdrew it sharply, gripping the edge of the stone wall beneath them. "No. Anna, no. It was all new. What happened to us. Just not, you know, that supernatural things exist. And dealing with sometimes… *unusual* situations. But except for not telling you that we had been in circumstances not totally unlike that before," he shrugged apologetically, "really quite a few times, the rest was all very true and very real. The way I felt about everything that happened between us, and about you, that was all true and real. Please don't doubt that."

She blinked at him in shock. "How many times?"

Eve shook his head and said softly, "I don't know. Many. But not for a few years, until that happened. And never a demon possessing a priest trying to kill us. And I never exorcised anyone before. That was totally new." She withdrew her gaze from him and tapped the ash off her cigarette before drawing deep on it as an excuse to not talk. Eve, meanwhile, fell into a brief silence of his own, until he explained, "We had hoped dealing with paranormal things was over. Me and Candide. And I'd hoped I would never have to dredge it up and that you..." He watched her profile in the dark, but didn't try to take her hand, desperately as he wanted to. "I hoped that you would never need to know. And that you wouldn't have to be involved in any of it. Not ever. I'm sorry."

"Is that the thing you wouldn't tell me? In the church."

"Yes."

"Is that why you can hot-wire a car?"

"Yes."

"I wondered about that." She took another sip of wine and puffed some more on the cigarette held in a shaky hand.

Three months he had kept the secret. And so had Candide. Her partner and her best friend kept this enormous secret that coloured every single interaction they had ever had.

Three months of... She sifted through the many memories, sweet, fun, loving—the best three months she could remember having in her whole life, and attempted to weigh the impact of this lie. But those memories supplied a great deal of confused conversation, bashful and slightly unnerving references to something they'd never been able to fully remember, because until that very day—until Anna had her hands on her key—she could barely remember half of what had happened. Certainly no more than Eve could, which made his lie... far less upsetting.

In fact, something about the idea tickled her somehow.

Eve, who, it seemed now, must have known ghosts inside out, orchestrated a séance with Candide, during which both pretended to be entirely ignorant of the supernatural. And that back when they were stupidly trying to hide their relationship from her, too. One ridiculous thing after another and all in a misguided attempt to keep her safe. And that, she couldn't help but feel, summed up so much of what she loved about Eve. Those ludicrous, confused, occasionally infuriating, but always sweet and genuine things he did.

And it had been all over, hadn't it? The ghost and the demon and supernatural things.

Until Percy had shown up…

She looked across at Eve. So worried. So sad. So anxious. He was doing everything he could to not reach out for her, though he didn't entirely understand why he wasn't supposed to. He simply trusted her enough to do what she asked him to do.

And she had her secrets, too.

There were so many things she had never told Eve…

"Anna, that's why I didn't want us to be together. I love you and I…" He glanced across sheepishly. "I don't want you to die, basically. And I didn't want to fall in love with you, and I didn't want you to fall in love with me, because I thought that would put you in danger. But then I fell in love with you, anyway. And I feel terrible about that."

"Eve, you can't say things like that." Even so, her words came out on a laugh at his usual messy delivery of rather a lovely message.

"Sorry. I don't mean it like that. I just…" He took a deep breath, stared down at his knees, and launched into one of his quickly spoken, long and rambling explanations. "I don't know if this is ever going to stop, and I don't want you to live like that. And I think I've probably been incredibly selfish and weak by letting this happen—between us—but when you said you would stay with me… I really wanted that. I wanted to be with you. And I wanted to pretend things could be normal, and maybe I really believed they could be. For a while. And I guess I hoped if I never mentioned it, it would stay in the past and we could move on together. Now I think that was unrealistic. But maybe not. Maybe we'll just figure out this situation with the ghost and that will be it, and all the supernatural things will be finished. I don't know. I should have told you months ago. It wasn't fair of me to let this relationship carry on without you knowing what you might be getting into." Finally, his eyes met hers again. "I could understand if you felt betrayed."

She was, by this time, mostly oddly bemused, but what little flint was left inside softened completely at his words. "No, Eve. Never by you."

"And…" He sighed, not for the first time, but in a way that put her on edge about what was coming next, as he ploughed forward regardless of his evident misgivings. "My father is missing. Presumed dead. Maybe because of supernatural things. More likely shacked up secretly with a woman half his age. We really don't know what happened to him."

Now it was Anna who wanted to reach out for Eve, who delivered the message so quickly and calmly, just the same way he reminded her some mornings she had forgotten to pack a book she needed. "That's a different kind of awful. Are you okay?"

A flicker of tension ticked across his cheek, but his too-relaxed voice said, "Yeah, I'm fine. It's been a really long time since he disappeared. It's just not something I could talk about. Or that I wanted to talk about. But it might come up sometimes with Candide, and you should know, because I don't want you to think I'm keeping that from you, too."

A touch of guilt squirmed inside, as though her immediate reaction to the first secret had forced him into something he didn't want. She left it for Eve to either build upon or put to bed. "All right. Is there anything else you want to tell me?"

He thought for a moment and she saw his face harden a little. Lips flinching to the side, his eyes staring at nothing, as though he hated it. "No. No, there's nothing else."

Not even a word about Percy.

How bad could it all be?

Her curiosity disappeared with his apologetic frown and, "Nothing except that I love you and I'm sorry. Are you very angry with me?"

As though she could ever stay angry with Eve for more than five seconds. "No, I'm not angry with you. I'm appalled at your parents, though."

He smiled softly. "Me too. For the most part."

She knew, from what he'd told her in the past, he'd been regularly left alone to fend for himself and Candide from the time they were seven and four. The creeping gravity of that began to overtake her now, as the thought of a child dealing with anything approaching the horror of her paranormal experiences hit her. She moved a little closer, her hand mere millimetres from Eve's. "You were so little. You must have been terrified."

"It's over." He raised his shoulders, as though shrugging off the ghosts of the past with the small, easy movement. "That's all over. I only wish I'd told you sooner. It was just nice, all that not being real for a while." He laughed, defeatedly, then went on, "But it's who I am, and it's Candide too, and you have a right to know. Especially because I know I…" His little finger lifted slightly, with the restrained urge to brush hers, and his beautiful eyes flicked across to measure the effect of his comments. "I know I made things hard for you... And this is why. And you need to know it's not unrealistic that things like that could happen again in the future. To me. Paranormal things."

How she wanted to throw her arms around him. "Doesn't it never stop?"

"Maybe?" He shook his head. "I don't know. But you were here when we decided to keep the Necronomicon, so I guess you already know it's probably just a matter of time until something comes for the book."

It worked as well as any closing argument might have. There wasn't a thing about the horrible secret she could hold him responsible for. She'd asked him to keep up a happy pretence when he tried to tell her the truth that first night. Neither of them remembered everything after that. But most of all, he was right on this last point. She had decided, with Candide, to guard that book until they could discover the original owner and shove it down his throat. So she turned her body towards him, planted two palms on the cold stone, leaned close and said, "Evelyn, I don't care about any of it. I love you. And that's all that matters."

His relief was visible in every inch of him, from the delighted, disbelieving smile, to the curve of his shoulders, to the hand that came close to taking hers, until he settled on saying only, "I love you, too."

And just like that, Anna heard herself say, "Eve?"

Perfectly attentive, perfectly serious, "Yes?"

Then, as casually as Eve had delivered his own horrifying story, Anna told him something she had never once intended to tell him or anybody else. "I don't have parents."

"You don't?"

"My mother is also missing, also presumed dead. But my dad is actually dead. He died when I was nine."

Eve swung his legs up and turned to face her, a distracting sympathy and sadness written in his expression. "I'm so sorry. That's awful."

Anna reached for a fresh cigarette and lit it with quick hands. She had said it now. There was no going back. And she wasn't sure she wanted to go back, even if she probably should. She shot a sharp stream of smoke into the night, and eyeing the moon over the forest, asked, "Have you ever seen a real dead body?"

His answer was immediate. "I have."

She studied him for a moment, wondering if she should risk telling him, but he was calm and quiet and he made her feel safe, just like he always had. "Then you know it's not like movies, and they don't stay nice and firm for long once the blood stops flowing. Especially if they're on their side or something. Everything kind of... melts." She fell silent as the memory came back, fresh and clear, as though it had only happened the day before. But then some memories are always fresh and clear, no matter how much time has passed.

She watched the ash from her cigarette float down and down into darkness, and pressed forward. "So, this one time, I was stuck alone with my dad, dead, in the house, for three days, waiting for my mother to come home. She is, or was, a drug addict—not a fancy one like your mum, but like, a scary drug addict. And she was out doing that. And whatever else she was doing. So…" A hollow laugh worked its way up her dry throat. "That was a bad week."

She didn't need to look at Eve to know how appalled he was. She could hear it in his voice. "Three days alone?"

Having been quite calm and forthright until now, Anna's voice began to shake a little. "Mmhmm. It was a bad area, and the house was all locked up and the keys were in his pocket. Under him… and I just couldn't." She wiped away a tear at the recollection. "The phone was cut off, so… I just sat. I read books so it didn't seem real, and I waited. And I hoped she would come home. Eventually." The frightened child that was still inside Anna, shoved deep down and smothered in a thousand layers of anger and cynicism, made herself known in a flush of disgust and fear. Anna countered by throwing her hair back and drawing even deeper on her smoke. "That's the weekend I stopped believing in ghosts. That's the weekend I stopped believing in God. And the smell. I can't describe the smell. An overdose isn't pretty. And I couldn't even open a window."

This last comment she accompanied with an awkward, almost apologetic laugh, which did nothing to lessen Eve's silent horror. Therefore, she found herself compelled to continue. "After that, it was me being passed back and forth between my mother and my dad's sister for years. My dad's sister blamed my mother for what happened to her brother, and she hated me because she hated my mother, so… Both places were bad. My aunt's place was definitely cleaner and safer, at least." The unclean and unsafe place, despite her unprecedented openness, was ground she refused to walk back over. She drew the story to its quickest close. "When my mother eventually went missing, permanently, I ended up with that aunt. For a few years. Until I finally got accepted into Endymion College."

"I'm so sorry all of that happened to you." He was so close now. She could virtually feel the tension in the arms he needed to put around her.

"No, don't be." She stubbed out her cigarette in a crack in the stone. "It's just life, isn't it?"

"No. It isn't."

"It is." She smiled sadly in response. "For a lot of people, it is. People I think you rarely come into contact with. And it could have been worse. It was winter. I couldn't imagine the smell in summer."

He didn't laugh at her morbid joke, which prompted her tone to turn a little less nonchalant. "Most people like me, we're born into that life, and we die in that life. We don't get to come to a place like this. For so many people, it's…" She paused, trying to get a grasp on something so elusive. "It's strange, and it's cruel that a place like this even exists. It's like this secret palace at the bottom of a lake. You know it's there, but it's so untouchable it may as well not be. I knew about it. And I wanted it. And I would have done anything to be here."

Eve's deep understanding of her showed itself in his softly spoken reply. "Your Endymion College brochure."

That feeling he always gave her—that being punched in the guts, in a nice way—swept over her. "You remember."

"Of course I do. You said how important it was to you. Ever since you were a kid. Is that why?"

She nodded, and she let a few perfectly unguarded tears fall. "Those few days, in the house, I just, kind of, stared at the brochure, in between books. I picked it up somewhere because it… I don't know, it looked… so beautiful. It's not the sort of thing that should ever have been in my house, or in my life at all. Everything looked so clean and elegant and the people looked so happy and... It was all I wanted. It was all I ever wanted. This safe, beautiful place. I lost myself imagining being here and what it would be like and... It is like that, Eve. It never feels quite right, but somehow it does. I'm just lucky that books, study, all of that was my escape from reality. That's why I did so well at school, I think. I wouldn't be here if not for that need to disappear. To escape into another world. But so often, still, I think, how can I be here? How can that really have happened to me?" A memory of their first night together in that very spot, behind the hanging door, came back, and she said, "It scared me so much when you told me I wasn't supposed to be here."

He shifted with his guilt at himself. "No, of course you belong here. I wish I hadn't said that. That was just—"

"But I am here." She smiled and brushed away her tears along with his attempted apology, sitting a little taller to look into the loyal and adoring eyes that never left her face. "And we're together. And all the things you told me tonight, believe me, I would rather deal with ghosts and demons and anything like that the world can throw at us, rather than what I've already dealt with, if it means I can stay here. I'm an adult now, and I have autonomy, and I can choose to fight or to run. Having that choice is everything. Being here, with you, is everything to me."

She felt the whisper of his frustrated sigh on her cheek. "Okay, seriously, get rid of that key. I can't just sit here like this."

She let out a little laugh. "Okay. I guess I could..." She took the key from her pocket and slid it across the floor back and into the apartment.

Evelyn's arms were tight and warm around her the very same second. She leaned her head on his shoulder and stayed there, safe and loved, just as he was, neither of them wanting to let go ever again. He kissed her hair, played gently with the strands, and she knew only the rise and fall of his breath, and the strong beat of his heart, until she said, "Please don't let any of this change the way you feel about me."

"Anna, no." His voice was as firm as he pulled back with a gentle hand on her cheek. "No, it never would. Nothing ever could."

"And, please, can we never talk about it ever again? I never told anyone before. I don't know why I even told you. I…" She looked up into his beautiful grey eyes, keen and clear and sparkling. "You're my person."

"I am. Forever. It's you and me forever, Anna. I love you so much." He turned her face up to his and kissed her, and she had never felt so completely accepted as she did in that moment.

"I never thought it was possible to love someone so much," she whispered, then kissed him again. "Thank you for telling me about you and Candide. Things make a lot more sense now."

"I felt really awful keeping that from you. And Candide wanted to tell you months ago. At least she won't be bothering me now." He laughed softly.

Anna laughed too, imagining the heated conversations they'd probably had when she was out of earshot. "She's too good to you."

"I know she is. She puts up with a lot."

Anna looked across the long room at her best friend, cross-legged on her bed, long blonde hair spilling over the Necronomicon. "What's she even doing over there?"

"We need a spell, apparently. You'll need that key to understand. When I'm done with you. Which won't be for a while." Accordingly, he wound his arms around her as much as he could without crushing her.

She accepted another kiss on her cheek, then said, "Don't be different, okay?"

"I promise I won't." And this he sealed with yet another kiss.

Satisfied, Anna called to Candide, "Why aren't you smoking and drinking with us?"

Candide frowned, as though she'd forgotten them entirely, then she flipped the giant book closed and wandered over to sit with them. "I don't know if I mentioned it, but I have a hot, sexy girlfriend, and she's going to be a medical doctor, and I want to smell nice when she kisses me, so then she'll want to kiss me again. So I'm done smoking until she falls for me." Candide reached over and picked up the key. She sat quite still for a few seconds, then said, "Are you two finished talking?"

"Yes," said Eve. "Anna knows everything."

"Well, that's a relief." She looked to Anna. "You're okay?"

"Totally fine. I probably should have figured it out, but it's so far-fetched."

"Right? I told him to tell you ages ago, just so you know."

Eve laughed. "And when are you going to tell Aubrey about us?"

With a look of complete disgust, "Oh, no, I'll never tell her."

"Never!" repeated Anna, ten times louder.

"No, never." Candide, apparently mildly shocked by Anna's implication that this secret was unreasonable, asked, "Why on earth would I do that?"

"Hypocrite," Eve chuckled, on a breath of smoke.

Candide gave one of her carefree shrugs. "Things got weird for you two."

"Yeah, that's true," Eve said.

"Aubrey isn't Anna," she went on. "She doesn't even know about those sorts of things."

Eve nodded. "You've got to keep it that way."

"I'm determined to. We're going to fix this whole situation, then no more paranormal stuff ever again."

"That's such a luxury, not having to worry about that," Eve reflected.

Anna shook her head, watching the pair of them. "You two have this all figured out, don't you?"

Candide leaned across, as though the great secret hadn't already been revealed. "We had a rule about this. A *firm* rule, before you came along. But you're different."

"Only because of circumstances." Anna wondered if she would ever have found out if not for the day's events.

"It doesn't matter how we got here," Eve interjected. "I'm just happy we don't have any more secrets."

Anna wasn't sure she agreed with Eve's perspective, especially given she knew he was keeping at least one more huge secret up his sleeve. But she knew Eve loved her. Whatever was between Percy and Eve, he was happier not thinking about it, and she was determined to protect him from every awful thing in the world she possibly could, so her only response was a reassuring smile.

"Okay." Candide clapped as an end to the conversation. "Now we have all the emotional stuff out of the way, we can get back to the action."

"Ugh!" Eve pulled sharply away from the wall he had been leaning against.

Anna ran a hand over his shoulder. "What is it?"

"It's…" He inspected the wall, his elegant fingers running over the rough stone and smooth mortar. "Look, there's a hole here. The coldest air just shot out of there."

"Where can it lead to?" Anna climbed to her knees, peering over his shoulder. "It doesn't go outside. It's some kind of cavity."

Candide's keenly incisive eyes examined the curious black gap, and, "Oh shit!" she exclaimed. The three exchanged glances, awaiting an explanation for her shocked words, but unfortunately, the explanation was easily twice as shocking. "You don't think there's a kid's body walled-up in there, do you?"

"What?" Anna stared at Candide in surprise, mingled with a touch of revulsion. "Why would you say something like that?"

Candide's hard green eyes stared back at her like she was an idiot, then she sighed out, "Come here and lean against me or something."

"Oh." Anna's brow drooped. "Is this a key thing?"

"Yes."

"Okay." Anna shuffled over, linked an arm through Candide's, then a few seconds later, her eyes were wary on the offending wall. "No. No, that's too hideous to be true."

Candide evidently disagreed. "Well, shit. Looks like we have to go to the library again."

Eve leaned in, raising one handsome eyebrow in excitement. "Are we going to do a séance?"

"No, Eve," Candide sighed out patiently. "We need to get this cloaking spell figured out so we can all be on the same page already. *And* we're going to need the blueprints for this building. If there's a dead child in that wall, we need to find him, pull his body out and give him a proper burial."

CHAPTER 10
BACK TO THE ACTION

Anna, Eve and Candide had agreed to meet at midday in the library, citing busy mornings of tutorials, lectures, and breakfasts with beautiful students. Upon her arrival, Anna went straight up the winding staircase and followed the glorious balcony around to the occult section, where she found Candide and Evelyn already hard at work.

Evelyn sat in the corner of one gigantic old leather couch, his legs crossed and a huge, leather-bound book balanced on one knee. That knee was clad in heavy cotton navy-blue trousers. His head was tilted towards a soft banker's lamp, which lit his thoughtful face and the tips of the tendrils of his luscious hair, which he played with absentmindedly as he studied, his black-framed glasses sitting just so on his beautiful face.

Anna could still hardly believe she was the person that spectacular man was waiting for, but when he sensed her approach, when his adoring gaze met hers, they slipped straight back into their perfectly imperfect romance, and all her worries ceased to exist.

"Anything yet?" She lightly passed her enchanted skeleton key to Candide, then dropped into the seat beside Evelyn. He slid one beautiful, tender arm around her waist and pulled her in close to him, dropping the first of several light pecks on her lips, each of which lingered a little longer until they quite forgot Candide on the opposite couch, coming to grips with the magic of Anna's key.

She waited patiently enough as the two went through their lightly nauseating ritual after having spent maybe an hour apart, then interrupted loudly, "Only bad news so far."

Eve pulled back, failed to resist one more kiss, then revealed, "Candide says someone put a spell on me."

"A spell on Eve and a spell on the key," Candide said urgently, as though the pair might slip back into their galling distraction. "Two separate spells. It's the only thing that makes sense. Without the key, Eve can't remember that thing we don't want him to remember, but you and I still remember that thing, whether we're touching it or not. So, it seems to me, something else must be blocking that memory for him specifically."

Eve switched one disgruntled leg over the other. "Why is the second spell only on me, though?"

"I think it may be too complicated to explain just now," said Candide, with a particular sort of glance at Anna.

Anna, taking the hint, added, "We'll leave it for later, then. The question is, what can we do about it?"

Candide snapped shut her heavy volume, threw it down on the desk with a bang, then pushed forward another book she had left open for Anna to see. "Only the person who cast the spell can undo it, but we can do our own spell, on top of that spell, to uncloak everything that's being cloaked. Just the same as the spell on the key, that's uncloaking the ghost for us."

Anna's eyes grew wide with fear. "The ghost? There's a real ghost involved?"

"Anna, there's a…" Candide's bored tone changed quickly to irritation. "Oh, God, just come sit over here."

With some trepidation, Anna moved across to the other lounge, Candide shuffled up so their legs were flush, and Anna said, "Oh! Right. If there's a spell to let us see and talk about the ghost, can we just do that right now? Because this whole memory misunderstanding thing is getting old."

Candide nodded her vehement agreement. "I'll do it as soon as we get back to the apartment. We need to charm an object, so we'll do all our keys then, I guess. That way we'll always have them with us."

"Sounds good. You have a spell?"

"I have one right here."

Anna looked over the dusty book Candide indicated with a head tilt. "This is the weirdest library."

"And the best," Candide agreed. A little too contentedly, to Anna's eye.

"I thought…" Anna meandered over the idea, wondering if perhaps she shouldn't say what she was thinking. No. She was definitely going to say it. "Didn't you say the spell on the key is a very powerful spell? Don't you need advanced magic skills or something to do it?"

"Uh…" More blushing and looking away—something that was rarely in Candide's nature. "I'll just give it a shot. I've been practising a little. Here and there."

Eve, until that time resigned to his position of ignorance, looked up from his book. "This is new." Anna could see the effort he was putting into trying to sound light. "What magic?"

"Just with…" Candide's fingers drew a distracted trail over her page, and a barely audible muttering slipped out. "Just the Necronomicon."

Eve's book fell straight to the wooden floor, sending a harsh echo throughout the cavernous library. "Black magic!"

"Shhh!" Candide cast her eyes around to assure their privacy, picking Eve's book off the floor and placing it gently back down on the table, with a pointless, "It's not that bad."

He, of course, wasn't about to be mollified by such a spurious claim. "First you sleep with the book and now you practise its magic?"

Candide hissed back, "Would you keep your voice down? I think you're overreacting slightly."

Eve did not keep his voice down. "Overreacting? Anna, am I overreacting?"

Not wanting to be involved in this latest squabble, Anna mumbled, "Uh. Maybe? I mean, she's an adult so she can make her own decisions."

"That's right!" said Candide.

"But the book is said to drive people insane," Anna continued.

"Insane!" Eve blustered.

"Anna, don't tell him that," Candide snap-whispered.

"But," Anna went on, "that's probably nonsense. Claiming someone's insane often just means they're a bit unusual. And powerful. At the same time. And powerful, unusual people scare people. Especially when it's a powerful and unusual woman."

"Especially when it's a woman," Candide reiterated pointedly at Eve.

"And you know, they burned a lot of women for being too powerful and not toeing the line," Anna said.

"That's right," said Eve, as though it proved anything at all.

"But we've moved beyond that," Candide replied. "And now I can do whatever I want."

His voice fell a little quieter, but just as urgent as ever, as he turned to Candide. "Please don't choose to do that. Please."

"Eve, it's fine—"

"Please, Candide." His middle finger pushed his glasses back up his nose, and he rattled out, "I've been very supportive about you changing from art history to ancient history. I think you need to eat more vegetables, and I haven't mentioned that once. Until now." Candide's face drew into a deep scowl, which didn't pause his series of remonstrances. "I also think you go out far too often and I let that go, too. But this—the Necro-nomicon—this is where we need to draw a line."

"We?"

"Yes. *We*. Together."

She looked at him long and hard, just as he held her gaze and awaited her response.

Finally, she relented. Somewhat. "We can talk about it. After all this ghost stuff is taken care of. And after we talk, if you want me to stop, I will. But I don't think you'll mind when you understand. It's really not that big of a thing."

Eve smiled like a kid who just scored an extra hour of video games. "Okay. We'll talk. Thank you."

And they were straight back to best friends, virtual brother and sister. The heartfelt love in the way Evelyn and Candide interacted with each other pained Anna, unwillingly, somewhere deep in her gut. To see how close a familial bond could be. It fascinated and drew her in, having never had the same experience before. She wondered what it must have felt like for the two of them to have each other all their lives. She wondered how different she might have turned out had she not been an only child.

Eve, satisfied with his progress, ignorant of Anna's thoughts, moved the conversation along, as usual, as though the intense interaction with Candide had never happened. "Did you say we need the plans for your apartment because of the crack in the wall?"

Equally serene, Candide confirmed, "Yeah. We need to find out what's behind it."

"And downstairs," said Anna. "I wonder if it all used to be connected."

Eve's handsome head turned sharply. "Downstairs?"

"Yeah, downstairs. The apartment beneath ours."

"What do you mean?" He leaned forward in curious perplexity. "A basement of some sort?"

"No." Anna pursed her lips with a touch of confusion. "I mean the ground level apartment."

He looked at her, blank.

"Downstairs, Eve."

He shook his head.

Strange.

She attempted to explain again. "Eve, you know how we walk up a flight of stairs to get into our apartment?"

"Yes!" he said proudly.

"So, if you didn't go upstairs, what would be under it?"

Blank.

"The ground floor, right?" she tried.

He shook his head, frowning. "I don't understand. There is no ground floor. Yours is the ground floor."

"But it's upstairs."

Deeply troubled at the two strands of conflicting information trying to twist themselves together in his mind, he looked to Candide for help.

"It's not the ground floor, because there's a drop from the hanging door. And..." In equal perplexity, Candide licked her lips and thought hard over the facts she remembered. "Our view. It's up so high, but..." She raised her eyes to Anna. "There is nothing beneath. How's that possible?"

"This is incredible," said Anna, shuffling forward a little on the couch. "Part of the building is actually missing in your minds, isn't it?"

As Candide and Eve exchanged another worried look, Anna wrapped her fingers around Candide's wrist, provoking the announcement, "It *is* the first floor!" She dropped back to Anna's side. "I think we really need those plans."

"I'm on it." Eve left to locate the records.

Candide watched him descend the stairs with a worried eye. "Do you think he'll be able to find them? I have to wonder how far the cloaking goes. Would it cover the blueprints, too?"

"It should be fascinating to find out." Not for the first time, Anna felt a guilty amusement at the way things were unfolding. It was bizarre, to be sure, yet how comparatively dull things might be had she not been assigned Candide as a roommate— had she started seeing, or fallen in love with, anyone but Eve.

Candide's hesitant voice broke into her thoughts with words and a tone that dispersed the amusement. "Did he tell you anything about Percy?"

"No. Even when he was telling me about your past with para-normal things, and about his dad—"

Candide cut her off, shocked. "He told you about his dad?"

"He did." It must have been an even bigger admission than Anna had realised.

"Huh." Candide's gaze fell over Anna in an odd sort of way. Was she annoyed? She looked annoyed when she swished her hair over her shoulder and doubled her attention on her book, seemingly putting an end to the brief, private conversation with cold silence.

Anna had the distinct feeling she'd overstepped some sort of line, so she attempted to wind the conversation back a little, to before Eve's dad was mentioned. "He wouldn't allude to Percy at all. Nothing. How bad do you think it is?"

Candide raised one shoulder a little, her eyes fast on the book. "I honestly had no idea he existed. I don't know how this is even possible. I lived with Eve since I was fifteen. Before that, I was there pretty much all the time. I've spent half my life there…" She sent a quick glance back to Anna, guarded, but confiding. "I have a vague recollection of a boy hanging around there when we were kids, but I would never have known it was Percy. My aunt never mentioned him, neither did my parents. I don't understand how they could all keep him such a secret if he's really Eve's brother. And why would they do that? What can possibly be bad enough to just…" Anna bent her head a little closer to hear Candide's whispered words. "What could make a whole family and their friends delete a little boy like that?"

"More secrets?"

Anna peeped over her shoulder at her beautiful partner, maintaining a respectful, if curious, distance to their huddle. "We're talking about the thing you're not allowed to know about. Did you hear?"

"No."

"Good. Plans?"

"No."

"Why?"

"They've been removed from the library. On permanent loan for several years now. Care to take a guess who's borrowed them?"

So he knew. Just like that. How stupid of them both to let Eve be the one to look at the records. Because Percy clearly knew something about the ghost. And Percy had told Anna to never, ever open the hanging door. And there wasn't a thing wrong with the door, or the space behind it, except that it led to the spot in the wall that may have encased the ghost-boy's corpse. And how on earth would Percy know that unless…

A sharp chill swept down Anna's back. No wonder they had all disowned Percy. No wonder the very thought of him upset Eve the way it did.

She spoke to Eve with a good deal of sympathy, hiding the growing terror. "I'm sorry you had to see his name there."

Eve's ever-present worry resurfaced with that tiny hint. "See whose name there? Is there someone you were expecting?"

"Um…" was the brilliant reply Anna came up with in response to the probing question.

"Nobody's name," Candide cut in hurriedly. "Who is he?"

Eve, against his better judgement, pressed his lips together in a patient grimace, took a long breath, and continued to play the game. "It's not a 'he'."

Candide let out a small laugh. "Well, I can't think of a woman… who…" And there she drifted off with eyes as big as petrified saucers.

"So, who has it, then?" Anna pushed.

Breaking the troubled stare he shared with Candide, Eve revealed softly, "My mother."

CHAPTER II
LIBRARY RESERVATIONS

Anna was on her feet as quickly as Eve's words registered. "Let's go visit your mum."

And she was halted just as fast when Eve moved forward, uttering a panicked, "Oh no. No. You can't meet my mother. Not ever."

This time his comment was like one of those not-nice gut-punches, which dropped Anna back into her seat, with a weak, bewildered, "Oh. Okay, Eve."

Eve, realising immediately that he had once again fucked up, rushed out, "Anna, she's really a terrible person." He crouched down beside her. "Key."

She slapped her key down on the coffee table.

Taking her hands, watching her expression, he said, "Really. I don't want to put you through meeting her. That's all."

She was both embarrassed and surprised by the brittle, pathetic sound of her voice when she asked, "You think she wouldn't like me?"

His thumb ran a circle across the back of her hand, and he rested his chin on her knee. "She wouldn't like anyone. It's not about you. I don't like her, and I don't trust her, and I don't want you anywhere near her."

Anna's fingertips pulled at the strands of his blonde hair, wanting to believe him, but with that ever-pounding reminder in her head and her heart that she was not the sort of girl Evelyn Worthing brought home to mother. She wasn't the sort of girl anyone brought home to mother, ever.

"We told you it's complicated." Candide's quiet, apologetic words seemed to back up Eve's explanation, settling Anna just a little. She sent Eve a small, reassuring nod.

He sent his soft smile back, then his perfect chin on her knee was replaced by the donk of his forehead as he moaned to Candide, "What are we going to do?"

She gave her usual helpful shrug. "You'll just have to go over there and get the plans."

"I can't." On his feet again, he commenced a pace of the thick maroon library carpet. "There's no way I can get them out of there without her noticing. I haven't visited in six months. She'll know something's up. She'll be watching me like a hawk."

Candide started piling her library books up in preparation to depart. "Sounds like you need someone to run distraction."

With a relieved smile, he asked, "So you'll come?"

Without even looking up, she replied, "No."

He paused in his pacing. "Just like that?"

"Yes."

"Okay, another day then." He made a move for his satchel.

In one fast lunge, Candide snatched the satchel off the arm of the lounge before he could grasp it. "We need them today. Take Anna."

White as an infuriated sheet, he snatched at the strap. "No."

She wrenched it out of his reach and shifted it behind her back, waggling her eyebrows at him. "Yes."

He attempted a side-step. "Candide, No."

She fronted up to him. "Eve, Yes."

"I'm right here," Anna mumbled. "In case anyone forgot…"

"No!" he snapped.

"Yes!" she shouted.

"There's no way that's going to happen." With all the guile of an agile big brother, he slipped a foot around behind her leg, brought it down on the back of her knee, and she dropped to the couch.

She took his bag with her, deliberately landing on it, so he had to wrestle her to try to get her off it, while she kicked at him, insisting all the while, "Eve, Anna can do it. She's smart. Smarter than you. She'll figure it out."

"Candide, let it go," Anna sighed, elbows on knees, chin on palms, watching the skirmish with a bored, dejected face. "Eve doesn't want her to meet me."

"Anna, please, it's not like that," he huffed, shoving his fingers in Candide's armpit to tickle her into submission. It worked like a charm, and even though he received a smack to his jaw for the affront, he successfully plucked the bag out from beneath her, then was promptly kicked in the hip, landing on the floor in front of Anna with a bump. He threw his bag over his shoulder, criss-crossed his legs and fingers, and leaned forward, a near-mirror to Anna. "When I tell you she's awful… I've never seen a person who could deal with her. More than one gir-ah-*friend* has left the house in tears." She frowned. He frowned. He carried on, "And never talked to me again. She won't tolerate anyone. Except Candide."

"Aunt Addie loves me," Candide added with a self-satisfied smile. "She's an ogre to everyone else, though."

"Even me." Eve grimaced.

"She's trying to look out for you," Candide replied.

"She doesn't have a maternal bone in her body," said Eve, "except where you're concerned. You know, I'm not even surprised to find out she's mixed up in this."

"I can't say I'm too shocked either," said Candide.

They fell quiet, Eve still scowling and shaking his head at Candide's suggestive head tilts.

"Eve," Anna said, after watching the two increasingly irritate each other for a time, "it seems to me you can either do this alone, or take me. If it's true what you say, then don't introduce me as your '*gir-ah-friend*'." She enjoyed the embarrassed blush, and proceeded, "Just tell her we're working on a project or something. I'll find a way to distract her for as long as you need. Do you know where she would have the plans?"

He leaned his face down into his hands and rubbed his eyes, but by the time he propped his chin up on his palms, Anna could see he'd had a tentative change of heart. "In a safe, I suppose."

"Great. How long can that take? I'll keep her busy, you sneak out to the safe and come back. Done."

One of his lovely hands raised to his temple, as he tilted his head, lightly embarrassed. "There's more than one safe…"

"Two?"

"Six."

"Are you kidding me right now?"

"I wish I was."

"Rich people stuff?"

"Yeah. It is. It might take a while."

"Mmm." She smiled. "Is your house super big too, and it will take you forever to walk around it?"

Eve bit his lip in that painfully sexy way that Anna could barely resist, and she dug her fingernails into the leather couch lest she jump on him right there in the library. "Eve?"

"Mmm?" Why did his sweater move across his chest like that when he shifted his head to look up?

"Can you steal the key to the library? In case we ever needed to come here at night when it was all closed up?"

"Yeah, I could do that. Why?"

She shifted in her seat. "No reason."

Anna coloured. Eve coloured. Two pairs of eyes began to sparkle.

"It is a big place," Candide said with a flat tone that brought Anna straight back to reality from the delicious fantasy forming fast in her mind. "But you can do it. You took out a demon. I don't think Aunt Addie's going to give you too much trouble. And I think, regardless of what he says, she should get used to you being around."

Eve's wide smile and alluring blush indicated that he agreed, Anna, a force to be reckoned with, was going nowhere far from either of them any time soon. He slipped his hand into Anna's. "Do you really think you could put up with her?"

Anna's eyes flared excitedly at the thought of taking the great Lady Adeline Worthing down a peg or two. "I can't wait," she said. And she meant it.

CHAPTER 12
WORTHING HOUSE

Evelyn telephoned his mother to advise her of their visit, then suggested they take Anna's car. She wondered what Eve's car was like, but didn't put up a fight. She loved to drive and was more than happy to show off her skills and driving soundtrack. The journey would be an hour each way, so they set out immediately, Anna deliberately refusing to so much as brush her hair because deep down she felt the need to anger and oppose Lady Worthing, as though this small act of disrespect and rebellion would go some tiny way towards avenging herself for all Evelyn's difficulties growing up.

Anna was possibly not ready to admit it to herself yet, but in the back of her mind she wondered whether if she forced Lady Worthing to dislike her from the start, then she would never have to feel as though she had failed in any attempt to impress her.

The further they drove, the greener the surroundings became. Mile by mile the houses got larger and further apart, until eventually they all remained large, and began to grow older and older. Bit by bit, Anna lost her pluck slightly, coming closer to something so familiar to Evelyn that was so very alien to her. "It's really nice around here."

She tried to sound casual, but she knew she had failed to hide the note of bitterness in her voice when Evelyn reached across, gently tucked a strand of hair behind her ear to see her face better, and replied, "Don't let this change anything between us. I hadn't planned to do this so soon."

She glanced across at him quickly and pasted a reassuring smile on her face. "It's all right. It's not an 'us' thing. We're here to get a job done. That kid needs his bones buried and we're going to get it done for him. Now where's your house?"

"Next right."

The 'next right' was a private road that led to a private drive-way. Two large, red-brick pillars either side of the drive held in place a twisting, black, wrought-iron gate. She pulled the car up and Evelyn climbed out to unlock the padlock, then he kicked the gates aside with a comfortable, familiar motion that disconcerted her even more. She drove through, crunched to a stop on the gravel, and took in the sight as she awaited him.

The evergreens of the suburbs were left behind and except for the occasional burst of colour from one or two, they entered a virtual ossuary of trees, their long, naked limbs and branches every shade of ochre, brown, and grey, through to black. Even without their leaves, the great number of trees and their searching wooden fingers were enough to obscure the road ahead, which appeared to lead up, up, and around behind a hill, upon which perched the bright, red-brick turrets and black weathervanes of a gigantic gothic mansion, all lit by brilliant afternoon sunshine as if it were on fire, in front of dark, stormy clouds that seemed to have gathered out of nowhere right behind the house.

The sight took her breath away. Not because this was the childhood home of her beloved, or because it was the current home of the incomparable Lady Worthing. Not because it was no doubt also home to every manner of ghost and goblin and horrifying supernatural entity one could imagine. Not even because she knew it would take Eve some time to wind his way through all those hallways and corridors and find what they needed. No. It took Anna's breath away because all at once it was the most beautiful thing she had ever seen. Besides Eve.

Anna drove them up and along the seemingly never-ending driveway until they were finally able to stop the car in a little alcove of paved stone and trimmed hedges. There was still a walk to the house, as the parking area had been set far enough back that any and all guests would be forced to approach the house on foot in order to enjoy the best possible aspect upon arrival.

Anna climbed out of the car, eyes glued to the vicious black spike of a weathervane. "Which wing does Rebecca live in?"

Eve laughed and walked around to her. "This is the last place I can kiss you before she can see us." Fast as lightning, she placed her key on the car, and stood tall on her tiptoes to meet his lips. Then he pulled her in tight to his chest and said, "I could never put into words how much I love you." His voice was soft with a note of melancholy, as though there was any possibility of him losing her now. Still, his tone made her heart ache.

"I feel exactly the same way about you," she said, and stood tall to kiss him again.

He reluctantly let go, placing his hands in his pockets to keep them there, and reminded her to pick up her key. "Are you sure you want to do this?"

"Yes." Then a moment later, a mischievous smile spread across Anna's face. "I bet your bedroom was in the attic and all." He laughed again, just like she had hoped he would.

"To be fair, it was a really big space," he replied, starting up the pathway.

"Wait, are you serious right now?"

He said nothing, smiling quietly at her big-eyed wonder.

"And how many evil governesses did you have?"

"Only a few."

"Really?" She ran after him excitedly on their way to the front door of the sprawling mansion.

The pathway swept underneath what seemed to Anna to be one hundred dense, mossy, ivy-clad, dead-looking trees that lined either side of the path, until all at once, that path broke into stepping stones and turned to the right. The trees cleared and there, front and centre, was Worthing House.

It was long and wide and grand, and indeed, the north wing and south wing swept away into the distance at either side of the lengthy red-brick facade in which Anna counted twelve long, wide windows just in the bottom row. There was another row on top of this, of course, allowing an extra and particularly dramatic stained-glass window in the centre above the forbidding entrance. Then up again, a ramshackle series of towers and turrets and balconies jutting at odd angles here and there, all their rooftops ashen grey tiles and sharply pointed at the top except in the centre, where it went up another level, then up another level, then up and up, high into the dark grey sky, the whole thing culminating in the black railings of the black fence of the spiky, sharp, terrifying widow's walk.

Anna knew Evelyn to be wealthy, but nothing could have prepared her for what she had discovered.

Eve watched her, quietly nervous, and he saw the distance between them grow as her understanding became clear. He wanted to grab her and pull her in close and remind her that none of this made any difference to them at all, but he knew they were under his mother's watchful gaze, and never letting his vindictive mother see his love for Anna was the best protection he felt he could offer her at that time.

Anna sensed Eve's eyes on her, and seeing the concern in his lovely face was enough to bring out the warmth in hers.

It was just Eve.

Whatever separate experiences they had leading up to that point, it was still just Eve, and they would be so perfectly happy together in his little apartment, and none of this needed to matter a few hours from now.

Reassured by her smile, he turned and started up the stairs to the front door. He opened the door with his own key.

Of course he had a key to this huge, grand, glorious mansion, but somehow she had felt as though they would have needed to knock, would have needed permission.

It was his home.

It didn't seem real.

He held the heavy, wooden door, ornate and inlaid with stained glass in dark blues and reds, all twisted around wrought iron, and she stepped onto the plush and no doubt priceless rug that warmed the entryway. A giant, grand staircase, presided over by more stained glass, led up and away to who knew where (Eve knew) and there were doorways off to the right and left.

They were to turn right.

"She'll be in her study," Eve whispered.

The floorboards creaked and their footsteps echoed around the high ceilings as they proceeded through a sitting room, cold and likely rarely used, then through another doorway, French doors thrown open, into a much warmer and more lived-in scene.

Anna, however, only realised the décor and the warmth and the lived-in-ness in hindsight, because walking through that doorway, the room, the house, Eve, absolutely everything disappeared into the vision that was Lady Adeline Worthing.

CHAPTER 13
THE GREAT LADY ADELINE WORTHING

Lady Worthing was tall—tall like Evelyn was—and she had his shimmering, golden hair, too. The eyes were blue, piercing and bright, and the face was delicate and hard at the same time, utterly beautiful with all the right lines and curves at the corners of her cruel-looking lips, lightly twisted into a half-smirk at Anna's deliberately dishevelled appearance.

She wore a black robe, no-less, surely vintage, Anna thought, but who knew? Perhaps it had been especially made for her only recently in the style that was most becoming—a style that followed her lithe form all the way from the tops of her slim shoulders, sweeping over her toes, hiding her feet and making her look utterly other-worldly.

She held in thin, skeletal fingers a cigarette holder, the length of which would have been ridiculous on any other woman, but not on Lady Worthing.

And there she stood, hand on hip, cigarette-holder carelessly aloft, posed in such a way as to intimidate whomever came into that room with her son that day, those blue, blue eyes burning into Anna, ready to completely disarm and tear her apart before she even opened her mouth.

But Anna already hated her with all the fire of Vesuvius, and wanted nothing from her. Nothing more than information and a smattering of revenge. And she didn't care what she had to do to get it.

She remained where she was, there in the doorway by Eve's side, and her fake smile was confident, sweet, as though she didn't wish Lady Worthing any number of catastrophic misfortunes. "Lady Worthing. I'm Anna, Eve's research assistant. I'm so excited to meet you."

Lady Worthing stared another disdainful moment into Anna, then said, "Hello, Evelyn, darling. It's so wonderful of you to drop in like this."

Like Anna, Eve didn't move, but he also didn't smile. "What's that smell?"

"Just a candle, dear." She fixed him with cold eyes. "What are you implying?"

"You knew I was bringing someone here today." Anna felt his disappointment deep inside. She had given up, even as a small child, expecting anything from her own parents. It broke her heart to realise that Evelyn must still have had some kind of expectation of this woman. It broke her heart that the smell, which she recognised, was so fresh in the room. Lady Worthing must have been smoking even as she watched them approach the house.

Anna knew the sickly, sweet smell in the air intimately. She felt the sweat break out on her palms slightly and her heart beat a little harder—a psychosomatic effect. She also knew, from bitter experience, the closest way to a user's heart is to use with them, and recognising her chance, she sniffed the air dramatically, and raised her eyebrows suggestively at Lady Worthing.

Lady Worthing, for her part, was clearly taken aback, and took an instant dislike to Anna, whom she had been planning to despise, anyway.

"Calm down, Evelyn," Lady Worthing hummed. "It's not as though you brought anyone important."

Anna fought hard to hide the fury she felt on Eve's behalf. With little to lose and everything to gain in the coming interview, she launched her attack. "Eve, didn't you say you need to get some books for our research?"

He made no move. "Let's just go."

"It's all right," she replied. "I have so many things I want to say to the illustrious Lady Worthing. You go get your things and I'll wait right here." His worried eyes lightened slightly at the reassurance in hers, and though still hesitant, Eve left to commence his search.

The brief moment of tenderness was not lost on his mother. Anna's calm influence on her son set Lady Worthing's teeth on edge. "Sit down," she said. Anna took a seat on a large leather sofa as directed, and commenced fiddling with her hair anxiously, looking around the room for the drugs, not even attempting to hide the fact she was looking. Lady Worthing came and settled on another large sofa opposite Anna, calm and still. She stayed that way, staring into Anna with those icy eyes, until Eve was well out of earshot.

"Research partner, was it?"

"Yes, that's right."

"At Endymion College?"

"Yes."

The smug smile deepened a little. "And why would a boy like Evelyn need research assistance from someone like *you*?"

Anna met her waiting eyes readily. "I'm actually very clever."

"So you're not after my son?"

She was immediately betrayed by the blush that rose to her cheeks at the direct question. "I'm not after your son."

"Oh good, then you're not going to try to impress me. You'd be amazed at the amount of young women falling all over me to get to him. Far more beautiful than you are." She narrowed her eyes, watching Anna for a sign of jealousy, or of anything she could latch onto. "They're all incredibly boring, too."

"Sounds very difficult to deal with." Anna wondered how long it would take Eve to find the plans. She needed to act fast. "Is that meth?"

Lady Adeline froze. "What did you say?"

"I said, 'is that meth?' I use it to study sometimes and I thought I smelled it in the air."

Lady Adeline eyed her suspiciously. Then Anna saw a tilt of the lips to the right as a half-smile crept over her face. She appeared to have fallen for the trap. "By all means, help yourself." She brought out a small golden tray from under the lounge. On it was a long glass pipe, a packet of very long matches, and the unmistakable pale-blue crystals. It was the most civilised set-up Anna had ever seen, and she had seen many.

"You look like you know what you're doing," Lady Worthing sneered. Anna ignored both her tone and her hypocrisy, loaded the pipe and heated the crystals from beneath. She watched the thin chain of smoke twist and turn into a miniature tornado. She paused and looked at Lady Worthing pleadingly. "You won't tell Eve, will you?"

"Of course not."

So Anna, only a tad reluctantly, did what she had to do.

"There's too much," she said after she blew out the thin wisp of smoke. "You finish it."

Lady Adeline placed the pipe back on the tray and let the crystal burn itself out, watching Anna all the while.

Damn.

Anna had hoped she would have more.

"And you will join me for a drink, won't you?" said Lady Worthing.

"Oh, I would love to!" At least Anna could be honest there.

Lady Adeline poured out two glasses from an already open bottle of champagne. "Drink up, dear."

It was around that time that it occurred to Anna that Lady Adeline was trying to make her as intoxicated as possible—trying to make her look bad in front of Eve. If only she knew Eve as well as Anna did.

Anna drank. Lady Worthing drank.

"Better?" asked Lady Worthing.

"Yes. Thank you. So much better."

"Happy?"

"Yes. Very."

"Good. Now, who the hell are you?"

Shit.

She knew it had been entirely too easy.

"Anna James."

"That's not your name."

"That is my name. Anna James."

"There's only one 'Anna' enrolled at Endymion College, and I personally approved her application. I know her well. That's not you."

Anna remained unruffled. "My scholarship was approved five months ago."

"No, it wasn't."

"Yes, it was."

"Endymion College did not accept scholarship students this year."

"They accepted one." Anna smiled.

"That's not possible."

"Yet here I am."

Lady Worthing leaned forward, savouring her victory. "I don't know how you managed to fool Evelyn, but it stops now. I will be calling security this evening before you make it back to the campus. You won't be allowed on the premises ever again."

"A demon tried to kill your son." The mocking smile fell fast from Lady Worthing's face. Anna enjoyed it more than she should have, but she knew better than to let on lest she lose her moment. "It tried to kill your goddaughter, too. I saved both of them."

Lady Worthing said nothing, her features as still as if they were chiselled from marble, inscrutable.

"It's going to come back." Anna spoke faster now, trying to push Lady Worthing to a sense of urgency that seemed to be completely lacking in her still and perfectly erect frame. "Tell me everything you know. I can't protect them by myself."

Still nothing.

"I don't have time to play games. Eve will be back soon and he has no idea I'm telling you any of this. Tell me what I want to know now or he's going to die."

Finally, Lady Worthing broke her gaze, suitably rattled, perhaps. "Why would he die?"

What to say? "The demon. I did a deal with it."

Lady Adeline stood and walked over to the piano, where she picked a cigarette out of a beautiful silver cigarette box. "You stupid girl," she muttered, shaking her head. "Never do deals with demons."

"Are you speaking from experience?"

Adeline flung herself back down on the sofa, ignoring Anna's impudence, but clearly annoyed. "What is it you want to know?"

"The little boy. Who is he?"

For the first time, Lady Adeline turned pale and averted her eyes. Anna knew she was on the right path.

"What boy?" Adeline mumbled, fidgeting with the cigarette holder and the fresh cigarette.

"The boy in Candide's apartment."

Lady Worthing's eyes snapped over, astonished. "How can you know?"

"Who is he?"

"I won't tell you."

"How did he get there?"

"How should I know?"

Anna raised her voice and stared into Adeline as hard as Adeline had stared into her when she first came in. "I made a promise. To a demon. Now, if I can't get this information, he is coming back, and I'm not making another deal. I will give him your son and Candide, and I'll save myself."

Adeline calmed herself slightly, sitting taller, pushing her shoulders into place. Shaking her hair back, she lit the cigarette with one of the long matches. She breathed out a long plume of smoke. "Which demon?"

Anna searched her mind for a convincing answer. She was unable to find one. "I don't know."

"You don't even know its name? And you made a deal? You stupid, stupid girl!"

"Who's the boy?" Anna raised her voice again, a little too loudly.

Lady Worthing moved swiftly across the room and closed the door. "He's not anyone, 'Anna'. He's just a boy who had an accident a long time ago. How on earth did you find him?"

Anna's stomach tightened. Where could the body be? "That's not important."

"It's important to me. You should never have been able to do that. And... Oh dear God... You didn't let the demon out of him, did you?"

Adeline looked truly terrified now. Anna felt the same. Another demon. A demon where? Where was the body? There was only one place it could be...

"Anna!"

The harsh voice pulled her out of her terrible imaginings. "No. No, we didn't let the demon out."

"Then how—"

"It's not that demon," she gambled.

Lady Worthing stopped still in the middle of the room, aghast. "Two demons? Oh, well, you're really in deep now."

"Cigarette, please?" came Anna's weak voice.

"Help yourself."

Anna stalled for time to think as she walked over to the piano. A boy with a demon in him. A body somewhere with a demon in it? Unless... "Who trapped the demon in him?"

"Ah, that's what it wants to know?"

"Yes," she grasped. "Yes, that's what it wants to know."

"Shit." Lady Worthing crossed the floor to Anna swiftly. "Listen, you're in much deeper than you realise. You need to send it to me."

"The demon? Why?"

"Because I know what I'm doing."

Anna, unprepared for any such response, said simply, "No."

"What do you mean, 'no'?"

"Tell me what you did, and I'll consider it."

"You will consider it?" Lady Worthing laughed in disbelief. "I'm offering to save your life and your soul from a demon and you will '*consider* it'? Anna, you're going to meet a very nasty end if you don't do exactly as I say."

"And so will Eve, if you don't tell me what I want to know."

"Why is this so important to you?"

"I almost died!" Anna snapped. "So many times. I'm going to need several surgeries on my shoulder, let alone the therapy—"

"You want money?"

"No! I want answers. I'll tell that thing whatever you want, but please, for my sake, for Eve's sake, for Candide, tell me everything now, or I'll cut you out of this completely and handle it myself, and I really don't think you want me to do that."

Lady Worthing sat back down on the couch, quiet for a time, her mind working. Anna knew the drugs, the drug-induced camaraderie, were making her more inclined to talk than she normally would be, but she had to act fast before the latest top-up started to taper off. "Start by telling me about paranormal club."

"How do you know about that?" Again Lady Worthing searched Anna's face, looked her over, racked her brain trying to figure out who Anna was, where she had come from, why she appeared to know so very much about whatever this mysterious secret was.

Anna could see from the confusion—confusion mingled with a hint of apprehension—she had her on the hook. "I know a lot more than you think I do. Quickly!"

It wasn't quick at all, but a long silence fell, Lady Worthing's gaze fell, and finally, she gave in. "There was an accident. Many years ago." She concentrated hard on the table in front of her, her still-strong voice wavering ever so slightly here and there as she twisted the expensive-looking rings on her fingers, around and around. "Yes, the accident was to do with paranormal club, but it wasn't our fault. Not really. Perhaps what happened after that was, but we didn't know what to do. Everything went wrong. But—" Her eyes full of horror turned up to Anna. "Now listen, Anna, this is very serious. If the demon ever gets out of that boy, it will be a disaster. You can't ever let that happen. Do you understand?"

"I understand," Anna lied, barely able to get the words out over her thumping heart.

"This other demon, whomever it is you did a deal with, send them to me and I can try to get you out of it. Demons can usually be gotten rid of fairly easily. Not all of them, though. Not the one that remains." She slowed her words, as if to express an undeniable truth, looking deep into Anna's eyes. "He will always remain. He *must* always remain."

Something in the way she delivered those final words. Something in the warning all about her face and person. *Don't touch.* But then why would she? Why would Anna do a thing... Unless she felt compelled to? Unless there was more to the story.

They sat in silence while Anna's mind raced, helped on by the speed at which the drugs pushed it.

The boy's body was possessed by the demon and it was somewhere.

There was only one place it could be.

But his spirit. The ghost. The spirit that remained at Endymion College and tried to protect her from demons. The spirit that controlled her movements, that left the apartment and followed her to a lecture theatre. The spirit that wasn't quite how spirits were supposed to be…

Anna crossed her arms tight across her stomach as a horrifying realisation crept over her.

But no, it was too awful to be true.

She looked into Adeline's face as Adeline watched her, and in that moment she saw the fear—the fear that a long-held and closely guarded secret had finally been discovered. And in that moment, in that expression, Adeline unwittingly confirmed Anna's appalling suspicion.

"Anna." Eve's voice came from the doorway. "I forgot. I have somewhere I need to be. I'll take you back to Endymion and we'll do the research later."

Though her temple was wet with sweat, though her pulse throbbed in her ears, Anna forced out the calm words, "It was very nice to meet you, Lady Worthing. I will come back to see you very soon."

Lady Worthing knew at once that she had been outdone—had given away more than she meant to and was going to get nothing back in return.

"Evelyn." Lady Worthing arose, walked across the room and leaned in close to her son, speaking just loudly enough to make sure Anna heard. "That girl is clearly high. She's been drinking, and she reeks of cigarettes. I don't ever want to see her in your company again."

Evelyn attempted to keep the corners of his handsome mouth down as he looked across at Anna, a proud sparkle in his eye.

He made their excuses and kept a formal distance from her until they were back at the car and out of sight, where (the key being appropriately removed from her pocket) he took her in his arms, kissed her, and insisted on driving them back home under the pretence that Anna should concentrate on their soundtrack. Anna readily acquiesced and did deliver several very-impressive pieces of driving-music while she secretly mulled over her conversation with Lady Worthing.

She couldn't tell Eve any of it yet. His mother had far more to do with everything than he could possibly have imagined. Or could he? She wondered exactly how much he knew of his mother's past association with the haunting, with a demon…

And then there was Percy, the brother whose existence he didn't even want to own up to.

How could she possibly have this conversation with him until he held the key again and was ready to face whatever the truth was?

So she kept it down and waited to see Candide, who clearly still had a lot of time and respect for 'Aunt Addie', not that Candide had any prior knowledge of Percy.

The person she really needed to talk to was Percy… Percy, who knew something of magic, who knew something about that wall or door… Who knew something about that ghost.

Eve, perhaps lost in a haze of not too dissimilar thoughts, finally spoke. "I got the plans."

"Good job. I got champagne!"

He laughed. "How the hell did you do that?"

"Are you impressed?"

"I'm so impressed. You seem totally fine."

"I am. Totally fine. And you told me she was scary." Anna pushed a new cassette into the player and stretched her feet up on the dash happily.

"Everyone except you and Candide, apparently."

"We're kindred spirits."

"I believe that," he smiled. "More now than ever."

"Let's go straight to the apartment and see her. We'll find out if she can do that uncloaking spell." She dropped her feet back down and turned to Eve. "You know, I think we're close to figuring this all out."

"Where the boy's body is?" Evelyn asked grimly.

"Yeah," she said softly. "Maybe. We'll go over those plans tonight, and we'll make our next move tomorrow. We'll probably need tools of some sort if we're going to break that wall open."

"Yeah, I guess we will. And..." Eve tightened his grip on the wheel, changed gears for no very good reason. She knew if he hadn't been driving, his foot would have been tapping anxiously. "Do we need something to put the body in?"

"Oh. I hadn't thought of that. Like... Like a coffin?" There she went again, getting so wrapped up in an adventure that she forgot the brutal heart of the matter. "I wonder who he is. Has he got parents looking for him? Do we tell the police?"

"I think we have to. It's... He's a dead kid." Eve flicked his hair the other way with a tense hand. "Ugh, this is so awful. I mean, we've been talking about a ghost, but it's so real now we're maybe finding... his remains."

They both sat quietly with the horror of it all until Eve said, "I don't think we should even touch that wall. That's not for us to do. We need to tell the police what we know and let them do everything."

No police.

Not yet.

Not if she was right about the clues Lady Worthing had dropped.

"But what do we know?" Anna said quickly. "That our building is haunted? We could be totally wrong about this."

"Do you think we are?"

"I really hope we are."

"But that still doesn't tell us who the boy is. And it's the right thing to do to find out."

He was correct, of course. But she had to stall him. "Can we just take a little more time before we call the police? This has been going on for years. One more night can't hurt, and we'll all make the decision together tomorrow."

"All right. You're right. We'll see Candide tomorrow too and plan everything then. What do you want to do now? Should we get something to eat?"

"I'm not really hungry."

He laughed softly. "No, you wouldn't be."

"And we're not supposed to go out together, anyway. You shouldn't even be driving me around."

"Research partner." He smiled.

She laughed. "I wouldn't believe it either."

"Should we just go home and talk, then?"

"I would love that."

Eve was quiet for a few moments, his lovely smile slowly fading into a troubled brow, until he finally said, "Anna, please don't ever do anything you don't want to do. I don't want you to feel like you have to, um, take hard drugs with my mother. We can always figure things out without you doing that."

"Oh, no, I wanted to take hard drugs."

"Are you sure?"

"Very sure."

He fell quiet again, then, "And… I don't want you to take this the wrong way, because you're your own person and—"

"You don't want me to do that again?"

"Not meth. I know it's not my place to tell you what to do…"

She couldn't help but smile that Eve seemed to think asking her to not take highly addictive and illegal narcotics in order to discover the location of a child's body was overstepping some sort of boundary. "I don't want to do meth again. And I won't. It's not nice. Today was just a means to an end, and I really think if I have to be high for a few hours to help a dead boy, that's a reasonable sacrifice for me. There are worse things. But it won't happen again."

"Okay. Good." And he did look perfectly satisfied until he caught her sly look.

"But now it has happened, I'm going to enjoy it."

He laughed. "That's fair. Will we need more wine?"

"We definitely will."

Eve sat up very late that evening, sipping wine while listening to Anna talk. And talk. And talk. Eventually she took sympathy on him and they went into the bedroom together. She lay down and closed her eyes until she was sure he was sound asleep, then she snuck back into the living room to study the original building plans of her apartment.

The wall with the cold little hole in it should not have been there.

That space, hidden by the oddly-set-back hanging door, should have led the way to a downstairs apartment, which now lay empty, dark, and apparently forgotten by all who did not hold her key.

Anna lasted maybe ten minutes thinking these facts over before her revulsion and sadness became so extreme that she was forced to seek solace back in Evelyn's arms.

CHAPTER 14
SENT PACKING

Eve was careful not to wake Anna as he went out into the college to get on with the day, so as usual, she slept late. Unusually, when she eventually did wake, she climbed out of his bed immediately.

She needed Candide.

She dressed, then slipped silently into the hallway, but as she approached her own apartment, she heard voices coming up the stairs and held back in the dark. Two men dressed in security uniforms approached her door and knocked. Seconds later, Candide answered the door.

They wanted Anna James.

Candide told them they would have to come back another time.

Evelyn appeared on the stairs.

He asked what the problem was.

They informed Professor Worthing a person had been fraudulently posing as a student, living at Endymion College, attending classes. They were to escort one 'Anna James' from the premises immediately.

That was entirely impossible, Evelyn informed them.

They were under strict instruction, they informed him in return.

Shit.

Anna stepped forward. "Sorry, I was just in the bathroom. But I heard everything. I'll go get my acceptance letter to prove I belong here. They gave me a key too! This is a huge misunderstanding. Just look me up at the office. Everything is on file."

The taller of the two men moved his shoulders back, puffing his chest out a little, laying the groundwork of intimidation. "You're Anna James?"

She drifted a little closer to Eve. "I am."

"We've just come from the office," he replied, setting his head on an incredulous tilt. "There is no 'Anna James' in the system. You have twenty minutes to pack your belongings, then you'll have to come with us."

Eve and Anna swapped panicked glances. Her heart beat hard in her chest as she spat out, "No, I won't pack my belongings!"

"I know Anna well," Eve tried, his voice a shade calmer and more professional than Anna's. "She's one of my students. This is a mistake."

"I'm sorry, sir. You'll have to take it up with the police."

"The police!" she yelled.

The door in the hall below slammed.

Everyone fell silent as the stone stairs began to echo with a sound Anna recognised immediately.

Shoes.

Expensive shoes on stone.

Percy!

Now it was panic for an entirely different reason. She held herself back from grabbing him, but pleaded, "Eve, please go inside right now."

He scoffed at the very thought, glaring at the guards. "I'm not going anywhere."

"Please!" She looked imploringly at Candide, who failed to understand the urgency to remove Eve from the situation before he saw his estranged brother, as far as he knew, for the first time in years. But it was too late. Eve's face turned ashen at the appearance of Percy on the landing. The two men took each other in silently for several seconds. Eve didn't move a muscle, nor did he speak, completely in shock as he appeared to be.

Percy was the one to break eye-contact with Eve, turning to the more imposing of the security team with a self-possessed-ness and confidence that made all the guard's posturing instantly ridiculous. "Gentlemen, I work here at Endymion College and I'm afraid there has been a terrible mistake. Ms James is absolutely enrolled, and Lady Worthing has asked me to send you back to the office immediately to sort this out."

As Percy showed the security guards his identification and made explanations, Anna walked around behind Eve and slipped her key into his pocket. He made no more movement than a tensing of hands, a tightening of the jaw, the colour returning to his complexion, and his cold and untrusting eyes never left Percy.

Apologies, led by Percy, were offered to Anna. The security guards made their way back towards the office, assured by Percy that the glitch was now fixed and the necessary information would be found in the system this time.

All four stood at the top of the stairs, waiting for the exterior door to close behind the guards.

They waited. And waited. They heard the soft click.

"Right!" said Percy, turning back to face them. "Time for a little chat."

He strode into the living room and stood patiently in the centre as they came in behind him. Anna saw Percy's confidence slip slightly, if only for a moment, as Evelyn paused to lock the deadbolt on the door, something none of them had ever bothered to do before.

"I can see you're still mad with me, Evelyn," Percy said. "You can thank me later for what I did just there."

Eve said nothing. Anna moved close to him and slipped her index finger into the centre of his clenched fist. She sensed his tension loosen a little as she did so, and she wound her other hand around his lovely, firm biceps. "I can't believe you have an evil brother and he's actually called Percy," she whispered.

A light smirk broke on Evelyn's face and a soft warmth came into his wary eyes.

Candide wasn't so easily placated. "It's the first I'm hearing about it."

"Yes, well, sorry about that," said Percy. "Evelyn hates me, you see, which is fine because I hate him too, but obviously I couldn't tell you who I really was. Even so, I have to say I'm sorry for a few things. I never quite got around to it the other day, Anna, after we were so rudely interrupted."

"Oh!" Candide gasped. "Was that—"

"Not now!" Anna hissed.

Eve's hand tightened slightly on her hand, but that was all. He awaited Percy's explanation.

"This is…" Percy started. He glanced at the window. "Is it past twelve?" He checked his handsome watch. "Yes, yes, it is, so I think we could all use a little drink, don't you?"

"No!" Candide snapped.

He gave a twist of his beautiful lips and half an eye roll in response before assuming an authoritative tone. "Listen, we have a lot of exposition to get through, so let's just find a comfortable place to sit down and relax. I'll try to make it all as easily digestible as possible. Grab a drink. You might need it."

CHAPTER 15
A LOT OF EXPOSITION

"**G**et to the point!" Anna yelled.

"The point is," said Percy, walking into the kitchen and pulling out glasses and a bottle of wine as he spoke, no one noticing Eve's discomfort at Percy's evident prior knowledge of their apartment and belongings, "I didn't mean to get you all almost killed. I didn't mean for anyone to get possessed, so sorry, Candide, about that. But I did, Anna, get you into Endymion College, so you can thank me whenever you're ready."

"How? Why did you do that?" Anna asked, stepping out of his way.

Percy strode back into the living room, put everything down on the table, sat in an armchair, and picked up the wine bottle.

Eve took a seat on the lounge and eyed the bottle carefully as Percy attempted to open it.

Percy caught the look and paused. "You're still sore about that, aren't you?"

Quietly, calmly, Eve replied, "You tried to murder me."

A noncommittal shrug as Percy placed the bottle back on the table. "I said I'm sorry."

"No, you never did."

"Didn't I?" Percy furrowed his brow as though casting his mind back, as though it were the sort of thing one might have forgotten apologising for. "Well… Well, I always meant to. Honestly," he laughed, "I didn't think it would really work."

"It was antifreeze!" Eve seethed. "How would that not really work?"

The innocent smile never left Percy's face. "I just—I didn't think it would be that bad. Or I thought you would just die or something. Not all that…" He waved his hand. "Everything that happened."

"That was Percy?" Candide gasped, sinking into the lounge beside Eve. "But it was months. It took months for him to get better."

"I can't believe you'd do something like that," Anna said. And that was true. She'd had her misgivings about Percy from the start. She knew Eve hated him, but something inside her had genuinely liked him in spite of everything. There had been, she thought, a connection of some sort. But this wasn't at all the same man, in her eyes, as the one she'd talked to all that long night. And her pale face revealed the full extent of how far Percy had fallen in her esteem.

"Things were very different then," he answered softly, lingering a little longer than necessary on Anna's expression.

The brief intimacy was not missed by Eve, though he continued in a calm voice, "It was the one time you were ever nice to me, Percy."

Percy let out a short laugh. "Well, yes, that probably should have made it obvious my intentions weren't good."

"You're five years older than me. I trusted you."

"That was your first mistake."

"I was a kid!"

"I mean, we all were, really. Antifreeze in Pepsi... Stupid kid stuff. Anyway, Evelyn, listen," and he sounded perfectly insincere as he said, "I am sorry I tried to kill you back then."

Eve smiled derisively. "But not this time?"

"What?" whispered Anna.

"It's Percy," said Eve, hate-filled eyes burning into his smug brother's. "Everything has been Percy since that first day. And it's all been because he hates me."

"Anna, key," Candide said. Anna slipped into the seat on the other side of Eve, who still held her key, and she remained very quiet for a few moments as a flood of memories about the ghost came back to her.

"Since before that first day," corrected Percy. "It took me months to find Anna. May I?" He nodded towards the not-yet-open bottle of wine, which Eve took from the coffee table, opened and decanted into three glasses. Percy scowled and filled the fourth.

Eve stretched his arm overhead as he reached back for Anna's cigarette packet.

"You needn't bother. I have some here." Percy threw his golden cigarette case down on the table. Eve rolled his eyes at the gaudy container and pulled out one of Anna's cigarettes. First annoyance, then a malicious smile broke on Percy's face. "Candide, when we had our little party the other night, you much preferred us to smoke in the kitchen. Would you like us to go back in there now? Or is four a crowd?"

The blow landed exactly as desired and Eve's clear and honest face showed the hurt immediately as he realised Candide and Anna had both deceived him, and that they knew Percy far better than either had indicated.

Anna felt a queasy twist of guilt in the pit of her stomach, and she slipped her hand over his arm. "Eve, we agreed we wouldn't talk to you about him. You remember that, don't you?"

Eve looked down at her hand on him, gave it a pat, and nodded. "Yeah, no, I know. I'm just… I'm going to take my smoke over here for a while." He slipped away from her, choosing to sit alone in the armchair opposite Percy, clearly reeling. He didn't look at Anna now as his thoughts raced, and she felt absolutely sick. It was the first time he had ever been upset with her, and even if it wasn't entirely her fault, even if it felt utterly unjust for him to treat her that way, she could feel nothing but his hurt and his distance.

"Eve, could you open the hanging door if you're going to be smoking, please?" asked Candide, pushing open the living room window.

"The door?" Percy's eyes snapped over to Anna, his voice firm. "I told you to never open that door."

"Well, too bad because I opened it lots of times," came Anna's petulant answer. "What does it matter, anyway? Is it demonic or something?"

"Of course it's not demonic. As I told you months ago, the wood is all rotten in there. It's going to fall out any day. It isn't safe."

Anna missed the questioning look on Eve's face, as she was too busy arguing with Percy. "That's it? That's all it was? The door is a bit old. How dramatic of you."

"It's not dramatic—"

"It *is* dramatic."

"It isn't at all dramatic to tell you a door isn't safe. I don't want you to meet your end splattered on the pavement down there. I may have done some terrible things, but I'm not a monster."

Anna rolled her eyes. "That's debatable."

Eve, having kicked the door wide open with a little more energy than strictly necessary, flopped back into his armchair, prompting Candide to ask what they had all been discussing before the door argument.

Eve turned the unlit cigarette over and over in his fingers and eyed Percy warily. "Enchant something for them so they know what's happening."

Percy nodded towards the symbols on the wall behind Eve. "You need to take those ghost sigils down, is the problem. They're hiding your ghost. All recollection of him. And messing with everything else."

"We're not ready," said Eve. "Enchant something."

Candide spoke up. "I can do it."

He looked at her, unsure, but it made more sense to put his faith in her than in Percy, so he agreed.

"Give me your apartment key and mine," she instructed.

Eve passed Candide all the keys, and she moved swiftly to the dining table where the spell book from the library sat waiting. She removed it from the top of a pile, revealing the second book down, the *Necronomicon*, drawing Percy's eye straight to it.

"What the hell is that?" he snapped.

"What the hell is what?" Candide scowled.

"That. There." He pointed at the book, enunciating his words like a school teacher who just discovered his most-hated student's spit-ball launcher. "What is that on the Necronomicon?"

Candide froze. "Just a bit of blood."

"You're not supposed to get blood on the book!"

"I know." She shrugged. "But we had to kill a demon with it."

"It's demon blood?" he yelled. "Do you have any idea what you've done?"

Anna and Eve looked to Candide for an explanation, but the only response she gave was a remarkably tranquil, "I'm trying to concentrate. Please shut up, Percy."

Candide said some words Anna couldn't understand, and a strange glow came into her eyes. Anna recognised it from the night they'd had the argument in the kitchen. A creeping uneasiness swept over her, even though Candide was apparently back to normal within seconds and handing them their keys, now successfully enchanted, now bringing into focus for all of them everything they knew thus far.

Eve had watched Candide cast the spell with something akin to fear in his eyes. Not fear of her, but fear for her. He wouldn't reprimand her now, here, in front of Percy, but Anna knew the next fight would be coming very soon when he asked her to give up her burgeoning practice of dark magic. Something Anna now understood Candide knew far more about than she had told either of them.

Percy, too, realised something had changed. "You did that very quickly."

"It was an easy spell," Candide replied.

He raised an eyebrow. "Only if you know what you're doing."

All eyes on her, Candide's response was a disproportionately sharp, "Cut the crap and get back to the point, Percy!"

CHAPTER 16

BACK TO THE POINT

"Y ou were just getting to the part where you found Anna's application from last year and approved a fake scholarship," said Eve, finally lighting the cigarette he had been playing with.

Anna looked to Eve. "Can he really do that? How come he can do that?"

"His mother has worked here since before I was born. Percy's been hanging around his whole life. He knows the system inside out. He practically grew up in the office."

"Well, my mother could hardly afford childcare on that wage," said Percy.

Candide nodded in agreement.

"I was told," Eve continued, leaning forward, resting his forearms on his thighs, "that he finally slunk off overseas a few years back, but unfortunately, here he is."

"Oh no, I did go overseas. For some time." Percy smiled. "And I got what I went for, too."

"The book," said Eve.

"One and the same," Percy replied. "Of course, owning the Necronomicon is more work than I thought it would be, so, well... I had to get rid of it."

Eve's eyes clashed with Percy's across the table, their mutual hatred permeating the air more noxiously than the streams of smoke emanating from the tips of their cigarettes.

"I don't understand." Anna shifted forward, casting her eyes back and forth between the two. "Where does my scholarship come into this?"

Percy broke Eve's stare, turning to Anna with a jovial air, talking as one might if they were explaining the unnecessarily complicated plot of a book. "Nothing to do with the Necronomicon. I needed someone on the inside. You were supposed to figure out what the ghost is doing here. Then I was supposed to sweep in, free the ghost, and leave the book. Instead, you lost your key, you got that ghost sigil on the wall, and everything went wrong." He glared at Eve. "And you weren't actually supposed to fall in love with him."

"I could have told you that would happen," Candide snorted.

Anna attempted to stifle a laugh. "I mean, look at him."

"God, I'm so sick of him," Candide laughed.

Eve managed a half smile and a blush, and Percy's eyes consequently narrowed. "But then I'm not too sure you did fall in love, did you, Anna?"

Anna's mouth dropped open. "What's that supposed to mean?"

Just as affable as ever, with a slight shrug, "I just wondered, you know, after we spent the night together..." He stifled a grin with his cigarette, tilting his head back lazily to enjoy Evelyn's reaction.

"We did not spend the night together!" Anna snapped, doubly disconcerted by the way Eve's gaze wandered across to her.

"Well, I don't know what time you call that when you finally went back to Evelyn's apartment," Percy drawled. "Two a.m., was it?"

"We did nothing!" she yelled. "Nothing! Candide was here." She turned to Candide for support.

"Yes," Candide said, not quite willing to yell about it. "I was here."

Percy was clearly having a great time and smirked over at Candide, a mischievous but increasingly triumphant warmth all about him. "Not all night, you weren't."

"Anna would never do that," Candide replied simply.

Anna nodded in furious agreement. "How dare you say something like that to me!"

"Anna, calm down." Percy grinned. "I'm not going to tell him what you seem to be worried I might tell him."

Anna did force herself to calm down a little, not because he told her to, but because she hated that she was allowing Percy to rile her up like he was—hated that he was obviously getting so much enjoyment from watching her reactions—but try as she might, she was still hopelessly on the edge of her seat about what he might say next. "I'm not worried," she forced out. "Why would I be worried?"

"No reason at all," Percy said. "It's just that after we spent some time together, at night," he raised an eyebrow towards

Eve, then looked back at Anna, "and we were talking about how Evelyn here has gone off sex with you—"

"What!" she sputtered. "I never said that! Eve, I would never say that!"

"And we were talking about our special connection—"

"Ugh! You shut your mouth right now, Percy!"

Percy remained as relaxed as ever in the face of her fury, laughing, "She accuses me of lying, but you have to wonder, don't you, Evelyn, why Anna wouldn't tell you about me and our months-long history if there wasn't more to the story." The dark hair drifted across his temple as the blue eyes settled with a glint of poison she'd somehow never imagined would be directed at her. "Be honest with him, Anna. You met me before you even laid eyes on Evelyn, didn't you? Yet you never breathed a word."

Anna was shocked into silence. She could hardly believe Percy, who she had thought for a short moment was becoming her friend, would say all these things, these half-truths, lay this trap for her that she had so readily fallen into.

She had kept the details of her relationship with Percy a secret from Eve, just as Percy had suggested she do, even as she went straight from Percy's company to Eve's door, yet would she have done so had she been able to tell Eve everything? She never had the chance to tell him, not really, with the key and the ghost and the spells complicating everything. Yet she knew how much he hated Percy, and somehow she felt she should have told him everything, anyway. She knew it was wrong, that she had done some sort of wrong—broken one of those unspoken social contracts that seemed to plague her life—but the chance to explain had already been ripped away from her.

The heat of her embarrassment and shame brought her cool, shaking hand to her red cheek. Her pulse beat hard in her neck and her breath came harsh and shallow. She felt sick with guilt, worrying how Eve would feel, how much of this he might believe.

Percy cared for none of Anna's suffering. Her silence as she tried to organise her thoughts, her excuses, was a good enough approximation of guilt for him, so he leaned in towards Eve, his voice cold and savage, a venomous glint in his eyes as he prepared to deal the killing blow. "A word of advice, Evelyn—"

"I'm not taking advice from a man in brogues," came Eve's cool and even response.

The hard line of Percy's mouth twisted into a spiteful grimace. "You absolute bastard, Evelyn."

Eve's eyes remained tranquil on Percy's face, though now a light, mocking smile lit them. "There's only one bastard in the room, Percy. And it's not me."

The full import of the comment was lost on Candide and Anna. They could not have known, nor would they have believed Eve capable of the cruelty with which the words were laced, but they hit home exactly as he intended.

Percy's face flushed red and his hands formed into tight fists. "Do you want to step outside?"

"Not unless there's someone more interesting than you to talk to out there." Eve puffed out a long plume of disdainful smoke in Percy's general direction. "Which wouldn't be hard."

"God, I hate you, Evelyn," Percy growled.

"That's good, because I hate you too, Percy," Eve smiled.

Eve looked dashingly handsome to Anna, leaning back in the gigantic armchair, legs crossed languidly, as he carelessly balanced his cigarette in the same beautiful hand as held his wine glass, a little gleam of pleasure in his eye and a slightly cruel lift at the corner of his mouth, having easily unbalanced all Percy's attempted falsity and grandeur with a simple few words.

She could have sworn he was enjoying himself.

As if pulled by invisible strings, she immediately approached and squeezed herself onto the edge of the chair beside him. "Eve?"

He shifted his hips a little further to the side to make space for her, rested his lovely bright eyes on her pensive face, and waited.

"Eve, the way you looked at me that night, months ago, when you were talking about the man in the office and the key... You just looked so unhappy and so angry, and it scared me a little, because I never saw you look like that before. Or since, except when he's involved. And I'm sorry, but I didn't want you to feel whatever you were feeling that night ever again. I know it's bad because this is so selfish, but I didn't want to feel you feeling like that, because when you're unhappy, I'm unhappy. And I know I did the wrong thing and I should have told you every-thing straight away, but I just couldn't be the person to make you feel like that, and so I didn't tell you and I'm sorry and I hope I haven't disappointed you too badly."

And there it was. That look Eve always had for Anna, when nothing else outside of the two of them existed at all. "You could never disappoint me." He threw an arm around her neck, pulled her cheek to his lips, then settled her against his chest, as he slipped a hand around her waist and kissed her hair. "You're perfect."

She flinched inside at those last two words, remembering exactly how imperfect she was.

Percy caught her eye, and she waited for him to say, actually, it wasn't so. She was an awful human who sexually assaulted a possessed priest, and any decent person would throw her away immediately if they had any idea.

But Percy said nothing.

Maybe he didn't know. The look in his eye said he knew. Why an ally in this? Would he use it against her later?

All these ideas were but the work of a second, abruptly pushed aside when Eve continued his thought. "Meanwhile, Percy has been a duplicitous pig since the day he was born."

"Not since the day I was born, Evelyn," Percy replied. "Just since the day your slut of a mother murdered my brother."

CHAPTER 17

SLUT!

"Slut!" Evelyn yelled. "Who even uses that word anymore?"

"Eve," said Candide. "I think you're concentrating on the wrong part of that sentence."

"Sorry. I forget you haven't heard it all before. It's entirely in his head, of course. Percy, when are you going to move on?"

"Never." Percy's index finger slammed down on the coffee table, tapping out every bitterly spoken word. "Not until I find my brother's body and get my revenge for his murder."

"Pathetic," Eve sneered, though all, including Eve, felt the comment was slightly harsh given the circumstances. To his credit, he soon sighed, then more gently, "Percy, I still don't see what any of that has to do with you being here right now."

Percy reacted to Eve's softer tone and softened his own, his eyes almost involuntarily searching the room as he explained, "Because he's here somewhere."

"You've lived here your whole life. Why now? Why would you suddenly think Michael's body is here at Endymion College?"

Percy, pale at the first mention of his brother's name, became quieter still, and his speech took on something of a confiding tenor. "It wasn't until I mastered the dark arts that I discovered the cloaking spell on this building."

That piqued Eve's interest. "And when was that?"

"That was when I came back with the book."

"That was very recent, then?"

"That was when I started living in this apartment."

"Damn it," Eve muttered. "I should have known that was you."

"Yes, you should have. The better part of a year, right under your nose." Percy managed a small, slightly smug smile, but that quickly faded. Anna noted the first hint of vulnerability she had seen in him since the night on the stairs. He looked furtively between them, almost as though he wanted to ask for their trust, but he knew he had no right to expect any such thing. "It was then, when I was trying to find out what was being cloaked in this building, that I saw him. I saw Michael. Right here in this apartment. That was when I realised he had been here all along."

Anna, Eve and Candide understood the implication immediately.

"No," said Anna, not yet willing to accept what was so hideously apparent. "No, that's not right. It can't be. When did he go missing?"

"It was twenty years ago," said Eve.

"Twenty-four," Percy corrected. "It means nothing to Evelyn. He wasn't even born yet, but it should mean something, because it was all his fault."

"Of course it means something to me," said Eve, ignoring the rest of the statement. "What happened was horrible, but my mother, as awful as she is, she couldn't do that."

Anna's heart sank inside her. She could do that. That and a whole lot more. "Percy, are you sure it's him?"

It was a stupid question that Anna regretted as soon as she said it, and Percy reacted with exactly the anger such a stupid question would provoke in anyone. "Do you think I don't know my own brother? Do you think my mother ever took a single one of his pictures down after he went missing? Do you think she doesn't still grieve for him every single day of her life?"

"I'm sorry, Percy," she mumbled.

Candide cut across his response. "I don't believe this for a second. You must know all the same things we do if you had the Necronomicon. More. Why didn't you do a séance and talk to him if that's true? We were able to contact the ghost easily."

"Of course I did séances," Percy replied. "It didn't work. I tried, and I tried, and I could never get more than the most basic things out of him, and then... and then it would change from Michael—before he could ever tell me anything important, it would change to something else. There was a dark presence that always, always interfered. Michael would disappear, it would tell me the foulest things imaginable, and then sometimes I wouldn't see Michael again for weeks, let alone be able to contact him."

Candide and Evelyn exchanged looks, remembering the demon who had interrupted their own séance, who had tried to kill them all, the two of them arriving at the same conclusion at the same time.

Anna, however, had come to a different conclusion entirely, and she stared hard at the floor.

"I know his remains are in here somewhere," said Percy, reverting back to his hard, cold, accusatory tone, "and you, Anna, were supposed to help me find them. I gave you that key to uncloak the building for you. I even showed you the downstairs windows, all bricked up. It's honesty beyond me how you fucked up so completely."

A flush of angry blood rushed to her face, and she pushed herself up off of Evelyn's shirt. "Well, sorry, Percy. I got slightly distracted by almost being killed by a demon."

He shrugged as though he considered it a somewhat valid excuse. "To be fair, that happened a lot faster than I thought it would."

How easy it would have been to throw her wine glass at him. "So you knew that was going to happen?"

"Of course. Not straight away usually, but it's unavoidable in the long run. Where the book goes, bad things follow."

She could have thrown the whole bottle just as easily. "And how did you expect me to juggle the book and 'bad things' *and* find your brother?"

"The ghost mystery was for you, Anna." His eyes and his pointer finger cut across to Candide. "The book was for her."

"Me?" Candide almost spilled her own wine at the surprise allusion to her.

"Candide Lenoir with the Necronomicon." He grinned at his own brilliance. "It was the obvious choice. When I found out you were to be the next tenant of this apartment, I couldn't believe my luck. You're smart, you're capable, and best of all, you would never let your aunt get her filthy hands on it. Everyone else has a price she can meet, but not you. Only you and Evelyn know how dangerous she really is. I know you would never have accepted the book if I simply gave it to you, what with all the difficulties that come along with it, so I simply left it here for you to find. It should have been very easy."

"Unbelievable!" Candide cried. "And why not leave it for Eve? He's just as capable as me. And she's *his* mother."

Once again, Percy's flinty, malevolent eyes glowered over at Eve. "Evelyn was supposed to die."

Another gasp escaped Candide and Anna.

A short, derisive laugh escaped Eve. "That's some plan, Percy."

"Aye, it was a good lay," said Percy.

Anna snorted. "I'll say."

"Not that kind of lay!" Percy spat, and Eve corrected simultaneously.

"Sorry," she said quietly.

"I thought it was funny," Candide whispered.

"Anyway, it mostly worked," Percy sighed. "The book got where it was supposed to go, you got the plans for the building yesterday—"

"How do you know we got the plans?" asked Candide.

"Why do you think I'm here?" This he accompanied with a withering glare before continuing, "Anyway, we're all here now and everything's out in the open. Though I must say, it took a lot longer to explain all that than I thought it would."

Anna snapped him straight out of his cool conclusion with the hot words, "Percy, you can take your stupid book back and get out!"

"I'll do no such thing," he replied. "You owe me, Anna. You wouldn't even be here at Endymion College if not for me."

"Oh, finally the bit about Anna's scholarship," Candide mused. "I've been super curious about this."

CHAPTER 18
THE BIT ABOUT ANNA'S SCHOLARSHIP

Percy narrowed his eyes in Eve's general direction. He uncrossed one beautiful, long leg, dropped his foot to the floor, then brought the other leg across. His strong, masculine fingers, in one smooth movement, pulled the grey wool of his trousers up to reveal a holster, from which he removed an incredibly beautiful, bejewelled dagger.

"I'm sorry to have to do this," he said, then threw the dagger swiftly towards Eve, missing his glorious face by mere centimetres, "but you have spiders."

Eve turned his pale face slightly to the left where Percy's dagger had stuck in the armchair, impaling a gigantic black spider, as big as his hand, now making a horrifying screeching noise and dripping with a yellow, bile-like substance as it wriggled in its disgusting death throes.

"You could have just told me it was there," Eve muttered.

Percy only smiled in response.

Anna looked straight at Candide. "The ash tree!" Their eyes lit up in mutual enthusiasm, but before they could complete their dash to the open window, they were halted in their steps by more of the hideously overgrown arachnids crawling straight from the branches of the tree and into the apartment.

"I hate spiders so much," Eve groaned on his way to the kitchen to obtain tools with which to dispatch them all.

Anna took a step back from the closest of the twelve or so she could see. "Do you think they're very venomous?"

"I don't think we want to find out," said Candide who, with a vague curl of disgust on her beautiful lips, crushed the life out of one of the beasts with her boot.

Percy ripped his dagger from the chair with a flex of muscle against his fitted shirt. "It's because of what you did to the book. You shouldn't get blood on it. Especially demon blood. Things are going to come for it much faster than they ordinarily would." He threw the dagger again. This time, it whizzed past Anna and stabbed through the body of a spider about to crawl from the wall onto her shoulder.

She remained rooted to the floor exactly where she was, and just for a second, on his easy approach to her, he was somehow exactly like the Percy she first thought she knew. The open intimacy was back in his expression, and there was a playful softness about him that belied their current predicament. Nothing like the person sitting in the armchair a few moments ago. Nothing like the person he seemed to be when Eve was close by.

The colour rose to her cheeks as he leaned over to free his dagger, his body pressed gently against hers for a few delicious seconds, that same perfume he wore that very first day bringing her back to the feverish fluster of meeting him. The warmth of his breath ghosted over her ear. "Impressed?"

Eve clattered an armful of kitchen implements noisily down on the couch. "Anna's not the type of person to be impressed by cheap tricks." With that, he launched a kitchen knife across Percy's back, breaking another spider into two repellant halves.

Anna's voice trembled slightly as she said, "That was actually really impressive, Eve."

Eve blushed a little and smiled at her. "To be fair, it took a bit more skill than what he did. My knife is much bigger than his dagger."

Anna giggled like a schoolgirl and she happily accepted his meat tenderiser.

"Puerile little shit," Percy mumbled.

Eve winked at him obnoxiously.

Candide slammed the window closed on the bodies of at least five spiders. "Anyway, Percy, you were saying?"

Percy kicked a spider across the room and into a wall, leaving a sickening yellow trail as its lifeless body slid down. "Do we really need to get into that right now?"

"We certainly do," Anna said, covering herself with spider guts as she smashed a particularly large one. "Why me, Percy? Why, out of all the applicants, did you choose me?"

"The truth?" He dodged the splatter of the remnants Candide created with the back of a wooden spoon. "You weren't even the best. You would have maybe squeezed in this year, as one of the lower-ranking scholarship students, had there been any places. Probably not, though. I spent months searching for someone appropriate, and in the end, I chose you for two reasons. The first…" he paused and sighed. "Do you really want to know? Because you probably won't like me very much after this."

"I already don't like you!" she protested.

"Okay, then… It's that…" Again, that hint of the kinder version of himself, when he looked away from her with a shade of regret. "It's that I knew you wouldn't be missed."

She stared at him, aghast. Then she stomped another spider flat in indignation.

"There was a high…" He also paused to squash a spider. "Yes, I would say there was a high probability the person I chose would die or go missing if anything came for the book. It was better to have someone no one cared about. No one would have come looking for you, Anna."

"Oh shit. Well, don't put too fine a point on it," she said, as Candide rammed a metal skewer through a spider.

"You asked," Percy replied, watching on in disgust.

"And the second reason?"

"Because you did your essay on Keats."

"That was it?" They all paused and looked around the room, covered in the remains of perhaps thirty spiders.

"Yes. It was like… fate. I knew with that essay I could set the ball in motion. I knew if he ever read it, he would instantly jump to your defence, so I simply left it on his desk. You got into Endymion College for those two reasons only."

"Well, shit." Anna threw herself back onto the couch, lit a cigarette, and took up her wine. She acted as nonchalant as she possibly could, tapping her foot a little as she tried to process everything without falling apart completely here and now in front of everyone.

She might have squeezed in.

Might have.

She wasn't nearly as smart or successful as she thought she was, and she *might* have squeezed in.

The others took their places again, except Eve, who watched her expression more intently than she would have liked.

Percy did the same.

"Sorry," Percy said. "There are a lot of very clever people here, and not a lot of places. It was a great essay, though."

Eve settled next to her, winding a reassuring arm around her. "The Passion of Keats. I think I fell for you the day I read it."

Anna forced a smile, which wasn't that hard to force because he really was very sweet. "Well, that's something."

"It is," Eve replied. Then, in an attempt to lighten the mood, he added, "And it turns out I'm a walking cliché."

Percy laughed. "You're just realising this now?"

"Shut up, Percy," Eve replied.

"Snuffed out by an article." Percy smirked.

"And now you quote Byron to me?" Eve spat. "You absolute bastard!"

"Yes, Evelyn, because I hate you!"

"I hate you too, Percy!"

Anna stood and walked to the window, ignoring the foul fluids and twitching legs that now decorated the frame.

It was all Percy.

She owed everything she had in her life to his hatred of Evelyn.

But for that, she would be back with her hateful aunt, miserable, and a failure in life. She never would have met Eve or Candide, she never would have set foot in Endymion College, and she never would have started to become the woman she dreamed of being. She would never, to this day, have felt what it was to be loved.

"Truth hurts, doesn't it?" said Percy, not without sympathy.

Eve walked over to her, trailing a strand of hair behind her ear. "You would have gotten in, Anna. Ignore him." She turned to him, leaning into his gentle index finger that ghosted down her cheek, watching his eyes in the sunshine, which held such faith in her she was just about ready to believe him.

But then Percy kept talking.

"You must realise that's not true, Evelyn." He threw both legs over the side of the armchair and leant back to enjoy his cigarette. "Anna hasn't had a lifetime of tutoring and deportment lessons. There's a reason they do interviews here: to get rid of girls like her. The best grades on earth (which they weren't, by the way, Anna) are simply not enough to get you through that door. She's just not Endymion stuff, Evelyn, so I'm sorry for you too, because she's not the diamond in the rough you want to congratulate yourself for dusting off... She's just your bit of rough."

"Jesus, Percy!" Anna cried. "What the hell is wrong with you?"

Completely unperturbed, he continued, "I don't mean it in a bad way. We're cut from the same cloth, you and I. I hand-picked you and now look at you. If I had known you could fight demons, I would have run away with you before you ever set eyes on him."

Maybe a shoe? She could definitely throw a shoe. "Am I supposed to feel flattered right now?"

"You're not to Evelyn's taste, is all I'm saying. He doesn't know it yet, but it's true." Anna looked uneasily from Eve to Percy. "It's not a nice revelation, is it? Fact is, you could have been any girl. There's nothing special about you. He only likes you because he got to play the hero for a while. Well, that and the Keats. Mostly that though. He'll get bored of you soon enough."

"Wow, Eve," she said. "Your brother really is an asshole."

"Half-brother," Eve muttered.

Candide, quiet until then, made it apparent she was more than ready to wrap the exposition up. "What are we going to do with him?"

"There's nothing you can do," said Percy. "I'm not taking the Necronomicon back. And you can't let that bitch have it."

"Don't call her a bitch," said Eve. "It's sexist."

Percy sighed heavily. "You can't let that evil, murderous, half-demon that birthed you have it."

"He's right." Eve sighed. "We're going to have to keep the book."

"Do you think I can't place a tracking spell on you using the Necronomicon?" said Candide. "I can send all manner of demons after you with the information in here."

"You'd stop, eventually. You don't have the heart."

"I do," said Anna, leading Eve back to the armchair and repositioning herself with her body pressed against his, his arms wrapped around her waist.

"I bet you do," Percy replied quite seriously. "But he doesn't. And he's your weakness." Eve and Anna both, quietly, felt an unsettling wonder at the shrewd words, but before they could process it, Percy moved on. "So here's what's going to happen if you want to keep that scholarship. I'm going to leave now. You're going to take those plans and tear this place apart until you find Michael's bones. When you do, you're going to call me. I'll have the bones investigated and I'll have his mother prosecuted. As for the book, there's really nothing you can do to stop me walking out of here and leaving you all to deal with that mess."

"That's not true," Anna replied. "You have one weakness, and I know what it is."

He looked at her, curious but incredulous. "And what might that be?"

"Your brother."

Percy burst out laughing. "Have you even been listening? I literally tried to get a demon to murder him."

"Not Eve." She swallowed before she went on, steeling herself for his reaction. "I'm talking about Michael."

A vicious cloud fell on Percy's beautiful face and she saw true violence there, deep passion and real hatred. His lip curled in revulsion, his dark eyes flashed, and his voice closed around her like an iron maiden. "It's truly shocking to see such a stupid girl here at Endymion College. In case you hadn't noticed, Anna, my brother has been dead for some time."

"That's the thing," Anna replied. "He's not dead. And I know exactly where to find him."

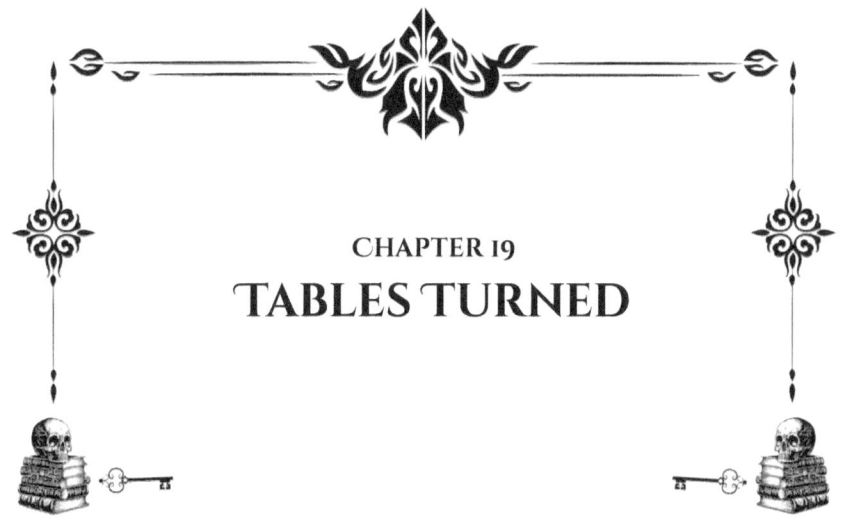

CHAPTER 19
TABLES TURNED

"Y̶ou stupid—"

"Percy, I swear, if you call me a stupid girl one more time, I'm going to punch you in the face!"

"I think you should do it anyway," said Candide.

"Me too," said Eve, and Anna was pleasantly aware of the way his hand, resting on her belly, tightened ever so slightly at the idea.

"Now here's what's actually going to happen," she said. "You're going to take that spell off of Eve first of all, so he doesn't need his key to remember you. Then you're going to take that book and get the hell out of our apartment until I say you can come back."

"No," Candide interrupted quietly. "No, he can't have the book."

Eve's face turned so fast Anna had to duck. "And why not?"

"I mean, we might need it. Anna, we might need it, right?"

Anna detected the plea for support in her tone, but she also decided, regardless of that, Candide was almost certainly correct. "Yes, okay, we keep the book. For now. But Candide, he is going to take it later, okay?"

"Yeah, of course. Of course. It's not like I want to keep—"

"Where is Michael!" Percy yelled so loud all three jumped.

"Percy, you get out right now," Anna said. "Come back this time tomorrow."

"I'm not going anywhere."

"You're doing everything I say from now on."

The intensity of the glare he fixed on her seemed to make Eve, Candide, the room, and everything else disappear until all that was left was Anna and Percy and the ice on his lips. "You do realise I could strangle the life out of you in a heartbeat?"

"But you won't." She met his eyes with the very same glacial cool. Anna had been around genuinely dangerous people since the day she was born. She knew what it was to be prey, and while she sensed that Percy was more than capable of hurting her if he was so inclined, she still instinctively believed he would never touch her. Whatever bond they had developed on the stairs that night held, even now, and the same completely illogical sense of safety in his presence kept her upright in the face of his studied intimidation. She held his gaze until a reluctant blink and an aversion of his eyes showed her that she had won. For good measure, she threw out, "I'll be testing Eve in two hours. If you haven't taken that spell off him, I won't help you."

He knew she had the upper hand—perhaps he even let her take it—but he still passed back one final threat. "You'll lose your scholarship if you cross me."

"You have more to lose than I do," she bluffed.

Percy made his way to the door. He stopped and turned. "Unlock it, Evelyn."

As Eve did so, Percy looked across at Anna, pensive, spent, the strange vulnerability that came and disappeared so readily in him on full display. "Anna, you know I would never do that, don't you? What I just said."

She replied just as softly as he had spoken. "No, I don't know that, Percy. You're twice the size of me, and it was a horrible thing to say."

"It was. I'm sorry I said it. And I am genuinely sorry for everything else I did to you. I hope you know that."

The door slammed shut, and Percy was gone.

After a brief, shell-shocked silence, "Well, shit," said Candide. "Did we even get his number?"

"He's been watching us this whole time," Anna replied. "He'll come when it's time."

"Fucking necromancers," Eve muttered.

"The worst!" Candide agreed, letting her eyes wander about the ceiling before they could ever meet Eve's.

But Eve, fortunately for her, was already focused on Anna. "Why did you tell him Michael's still alive?"

"Because it's true. Your mother told me. Not deliberately, but she let slip. Percy's closer to the truth than he realises, and I'm sorry, Eve, but your mother is behind all of this."

Eve took the news on the chin, like he seemed to do with every miserable thing that happened to him, but it quickly became apparent his mother's lies were well down his list of concerns.

"He's really not dead?" The slightest hint of hope lightened his worried eyes. "How? How can that be possible?"

"He's possessed. I think. That's my best guess. I think his body has been possessed, all this time, by a demon, and from what she said, it sounds like it's keeping him alive."

Eve turned away to process the information, and Candide asked, "Aunt Adeline told you all that? How did you get it out of her?"

On a deep breath, "So, first we got high, then I told her a demon tried to kill you both, and that I saved you, but that I had to do a deal with a demon to do it, and I said the demon was coming back unless she told me the truth about the ghost boy, and I said I would sacrifice you both to save myself unless she told me everything at once."

Eve's shoes scraped to a halt on the floorboards, Candide gaped at him in stunned silence, then, "She's a keeper."

In two steps, Eve was planting a kiss on Anna's cheek. "Right? She's so smart!"

"She is," Candide agreed.

"And so gorgeous," Eve added, with another kiss and an arm moving around her waist.

"She is!"

"Stop it, you two." Anna tried and failed to hide her smile and her blushes. "We're supposed to be very serious right now. Pay attention!" She shoved Eve off and attempted to control herself. "Adeline didn't think anyone would ever find Michael because of the cloaking spell—the one Percy discovered and uncloaked for me with the key. But when she thought I'd discovered it all, she let fly. And one of the most worrying things she said was, no matter what we do, don't release that demon. We're going to have to be really careful this time."

Candide shot an incredulous puff of air through pursed lips. "It wouldn't be the first time we banished a demon. We can take that thing."

Anna shuddered at the thought of what she had done to banish the first demon. "I can't do that to a kid."

Eve brought her hand to his lips with a reassuring squeeze. "Anna, it's all right. It's been twenty-four years since Michael disappeared. We can take our time with this one. We'll figure it out together."

"Even if our parents couldn't?" Candide asked.

Eve's eyes were wary, but he said, confidently enough for Anna to believe him, "We're going to find him, and we're going to fix him. But…" He surveyed the wall beyond the hanging door with a long sigh. "I know what she said, and this all sounds very promising, but you have to remember, she is a liar. And we saw his ghost. I don't understand how he can be alive now. Maybe… Maybe he recently passed or something."

"Astral travel," Candide supplied.

Eve huffed out a laugh. "Just like that? You just know that? How could he do that? And to the extent we thought he was a real ghost?"

"It's the only thing that makes sense. Ghosts or poltergeists are just disembodied souls, right? People have been known to leave their bodies for short periods and return. I know it's a stretch, but he's had decades to work out how to do it. And if anything was going to encourage you to leave your body, it would be having to share it with a demon, don't you think?."

"That does make a lot of sense, actually." Eve furrowed his brow. "You need to stop reading that book."

Cheerfully ignoring him, "Anna, where do we start?"

"Um." She attempted a quick redirection before Eve pressed his argument. "We need tools. We're going to have to take that wall apart. There should be a staircase behind it, and there's another apartment downstairs. You understand downstairs now, don't you, Eve?"

"I do!" Eve grinned. Then frowned again. "That was so weird."

"Wasn't it? But yes, he should be somewhere down there..."

"Just below us. All this time," Eve reflected grimly.

"He can probably hear our footsteps when we're walking around..." Candide trailed off, and they each suffered through their own unsettling images of what must be lurking beneath, waiting for them.

Eve was the first to speak again. "That's horrific."

Anna could see he was on the verge of slipping into a dark reverie that wouldn't serve any of them, so she said, "Don't think about that now." She tugged at his hand. "We're going to have to stay strong and get this job done. We can't think about any of that until later. Will you drive into town with me to get supplies?"

He lightened a little, not least because he understood that she was looking out for him, like she always was. "Yeah. Let's go now."

Candide didn't follow as they quickly turned towards the door. "I was supposed to meet Aubrey. Can you two get everything without me?"

Anna had just about forgotten the spider guts, hairy spider legs, spider eyes, and all the weird yellowish smears that decorated their living room, but Candide's relative availability prompted a whisper of a cheeky smile. "Does that mean you'll clean up here?"

Candide looked around doubtfully. "We probably shouldn't let it dry... I guess... Okay, fine. But I'm not taking that wall down."

"It's a deal." And Anna was quite sure she'd gotten the better half.

"All right." Eve clapped two concluding hands together in a way only a professor can. "We'll meet back here first thing tomorrow and be ready for some serious action."

"Good plan," said Candide. "That was so much talking just then, but I think things are about to get real."

"No more boring dialogue," said Anna.

"Nothing but action from here on out," said Eve.

CHAPTER 20
INTO DARKNESS

Anna and Eve sat on the floor tapping chisels with hammers. They had been at it for several hours now, and they were amassing a nice pile of stones behind them, the hole in the wall growing steadily. The hanging door sat wide open, and though it was winter now, it wasn't especially cold. The sky was a bright and crisp blue, and a soft breeze brought fresh-smelling and invigorating air into the apartment.

Eve looked over at Anna for perhaps the fiftieth time that morning. She was just wearing a sweater she had picked off the bedroom floor, but he didn't think he'd ever seen anyone look so nice in a sweater before. He didn't think anyone's hair ever sat quite so perfectly, or shifted quite so nicely in the breeze. He didn't think anyone ever tapped a chisel quite so well.

"I'm so bored," his beloved sighed over her beautiful lips.

Eve made no reply, trying to judge how inappropriate his thoughts were given the task ahead.

"Eve?"

"Mmm?"

"Do you think that's true, what Percy said?"

A wrinkle of his mouth expressed the switch from enamoured to disgusted. "Which thing that he said?"

"About you and me." She looked across, a little sheepishly, then concentrated on tapping her chisel. "That you were just attracted to me because I was in danger. And it could have been anyone."

"Absolutely not." He laughed, breaking off a big piece of concrete. "When did I ever get to be your hero?"

She threw it in the pile, smiling at his self-deprecatory comment. "So many times."

Eve put down his hammer and chisel and leaned back, stretching his legs out long to engage her completely with his compelling grey-violet eyes. "No. You never needed me. Maybe you thought you did. You didn't. You and Candide would have easily fixed everything. I think I just got in your way, to be honest." Anna remained quiet as she thought over their history, searching for moments like Percy suggested, so Eve took her hand in his and continued, "It was your strength that attracted me, Anna. From the start. And how smart you are. And how funny you are…" His voice took on a longing edge. "And how gorgeous you are."

Anna smiled, stopped looking at his lovely body all stretched out, and met his lovely eyes again. "What if I wasn't any of those things?"

"You are all those things. You can't help it. You're Anna. And I love you." He pulled her in for a kiss, then another kiss, then another. Anna obligingly shuffled across, extending her legs out long beside his, and he took her by the hip, rolling their bodies together. Her hand was at his belt, his teeth on her neck, and the door slammed shut behind them.

They hastily repositioned their tools.

"Any action yet?" called Candide.

"Unfortunately not," Eve mumbled.

"Just tapping and talking," Anna added regretfully.

Candide threw her bag on the couch. "Ugh, I was hoping we could skip over all that."

"Right?" Anna sighed.

"I think we're through!" Eve shoved a brick through the wall with a thump. "It's just about big enough to squeeze through."

Anna peered into the inky black on the other side of the hole. "I wouldn't want to have to leave in a hurry."

"Good point." Eve took his chisel to the next row of mortar.

"No sledge hammer?" asked Candide.

"I told him," Anna grumbled.

"Amateurs."

"It's just a few more bricks," Eve bristled.

Candide clacked her tongue. "Does that mean even more talking?"

Suddenly, the door swung open behind them, crashing into the wall as it did so.

Eve rolled his eyes and tapped his chisel. "Percy."

"You're early," said Anna.

"I thought I could help."

"When there's about two bricks left," said Evelyn. "Typical."

Candide and Anna looked Percy over with cautious eyes. They both noticed he had chosen some rather nice brown boots to wear that day, along with navy trousers, black shirt and grey overcoat, but whether it was simply a costume change in preparation for anticipated action, or if there was more to his choice of shoes, they did not know, nor did they comment.

Percy crossed the room in a few long strides, and knelt down by Anna, his fine shoulder brushing hers as he peered into the dark. "So it was behind the hanging door all the time. No wonder I missed it."

Anna turned her head to reply, her voice coming somewhat weakly as when he also turned his head, their lips millimetres apart. "You never once opened the door to check?"

"What? No. It's going to fall out any day now, I'm telling you." Percy stood, shoved Eve to the side as he made his way between them, and squeezed himself straight through the hole.

"You fuck," Eve muttered.

"This guy," Candide concurred with a shake of her head. "Go with him. I'll get the book."

Percy was already some way along the dark passage when Anna climbed through. "Wait. You have no idea what's down there."

"I have some idea." There was a loud bang as he rammed his shoulder into an old locked door that blocked their path. "Ouch."

"Let me do it," Eve sighed.

Anna started, "Do you think we should wait—"

Eve rammed a shoulder into the door, also failing to move it. "Ouch!"

Percy looked over Eve disparagingly. "Honestly, did you think *you* could move it if I couldn't?"

Eve returned his withering gaze. "Percy, do you think you could go away somewhere quietly and just die?"

"You are such a waste of air, Evelyn," Percy drawled.

"You're such a bag of dicks, you utter—"

"Candide!" Anna called. "Bring the chisel. And a torch."

Percy shook his head at Eve. "How did you not remember to bring a torch into a dark passage?"

"Shut up, Percy!"

"You shut up, Evelyn!"

"Percy—"

"Please, Eve," Anna interrupted. "I kind of need everyone to shut up."

"Sorry."

"Here." Candide passed Anna the chisel and hammer.

She pushed past both ludicrously handsome men and set about loosening the hinges. A levering here, a hammering there, and, "Catch the—"

The door fell the wrong way and made an extended and deafening sound as it plunged, who knew how far, down and down a long and winding staircase. Eventually it hit the bottom with a bang and an echo and all stood stock still, waiting for another sound.

Silence.

Then the smell hit them. A stench nearly unbearable.

Almost involuntarily, they all looked to Percy.

It was the unmistakable smell of death.

A smell Anna knew all too well.

On the verge of a profuse and heartbroken apology, Anna was stayed by Candide's matter-of-fact voice. "If he died twenty-four years ago, it wouldn't still smell like that. Either he's alive, or he died very recently. Prepare yourself, Percy."

"She's right," Anna whispered, in awe of Candide's calm and trying to shake off the guilt of having allowed Percy to be there at all, knowing that what he saw next would probably be terrible for him, whether the boy was dead or alive.

Percy, pale and shaky in a way Anna hadn't thought him capable of until just then, said nothing and held his head high with a becoming dignity.

Evelyn managed an appropriate and genuine sense of concern for his brother, though it was clear his intense dislike of Percy hadn't abated any. "I'll go down first."

"*I'm* going first," Candide rebutted. She aimed her torch through the doorway and illuminated an ageing, broken, undoubtedly incredibly dangerous staircase. It was covered in mounds of dust from its decades-long solitude, and all manner of rat droppings, carcasses of mice, spiders and other small creatures, and hundreds of tiny mounds of shavings of wood, dug out or eaten by numerous insects, were scattered here and there all over the stairs.

"I don't think that's safe, Candide."

"Too late, Eve." She stepped out confidently before he could stop her. The top stair cracked beneath her, but it held.

Each stair after that groaned and creaked under each shoe, but slowly, eventually, they made their way to the base of the stairs where they fanned out to take in the dark space in front of them. There was very little to see. An empty room, other than a hurriedly made brick wall in front of them, which ran about three quarters of the way across the room and did not quite reach the ceiling, as though someone had given up partway through the build.

Led by Candide and her light, they approached the opening. Another sort of passageway appeared in front of them, except the left wall of this one consisted of nothing more than ancient sheets and rags, dusty, hung about with cobwebs, extending to another rudimentary wall.

They paused, all of them knowing what they were looking for must be behind those sheets.

The job fell to Percy, as the person with the highest stakes, to part that forbidding curtain.

Anna moved close by his side. "Do you want me to?"

His head turned slowly, his expression confused at the unexpected kindness. "No, Anna." A sad smile tilted his lips, softening his features. "Thank you. I can do it."

He remained in place for another five seconds, steeling himself, then reached out a shaking hand to grab hold of one of the dusty rags. Candide held the light steady as he pulled it aside and passed through the opening.

"No," he whispered. "No. It can't be."

There, in a cold, rusted, steel chair, sat the child. It was him. It was unmistakably the ghost they had all seen, but here he was, a real child. Chains held him tight to the chair by his wrists, ankles, waist, arms, legs, and neck. He was surrounded on all sides, underneath, on top, by a plethora of warding symbols and seals and sigils and all around were various hex bags, jars and boxes, all manner of small bones and hideous ingredients from the many spells that had been cast to keep him in his place, or to stop anyone finding him, or to do whatever they were supposed to do.

In the centre of all this sat the tiny child, all alone, nothing but the arms of his metal chair within his reach. It was evident he hadn't aged a day since he was first incarcerated in this filthy, pitch-black prison. He was little more than a skeleton draped in pallid flesh. His head hung to the side. His eyes were shut tight. He showed no sign of life.

"Michael!" Percy cried. "Michael!" He held the boy's face in his hands, searching for the smallest reaction. He clasped the tiny fingers, he rubbed the cold, emaciated arms, knew not what to do with himself or with the boy. He was compelled to touch and repulsed in equal measure, desperate to deny the very thing before his eyes, desperate to keep poking and prodding this corpse until it should betray some spark, some confirmation of what he had so desperately hoped for.

Not one breath was perceptible, no pulse, no response to the words—the pleas that soon came.

The boy's younger brother, Percy, now ten times his size, fell at his feet, his whole body heaving with the sobs that escaped him uncontrollably as he gripped at the boney knees, hid his face in the ragged folds of the once-white dress, and wept.

"Percy…" Anna whispered. Her heart was as good as broken for him. Whatever she had imagined down there, in the flesh, it was somehow one thousand times more awful than anything her mind could have conjured. And she, who knew what the destructive obsession with his brother had made Percy do, had brought him face to face with his worst nightmare. "Percy, I'm so sorry."

At her words, Percy snapped back to reality. His eyes flashed anger, desperate hatred, and he launched himself at her with a speed and intent she never could have dodged. But Eve intercepted him before he could touch her. He grabbed Percy, wrenched him close, and pulled his head against his shoulder. Percy, feeling Evelyn's strong arms around him, collapsed instantly into him, and from there the two sank to the floor against a dusty wall, where Evelyn held him, his hand softly stroking Percy's hair as he cried and cried.

Eventually, his face still hidden in Eve's sweater, Percy managed to speak. "You said he was alive."

Anna crouched down and reached out a tentative hand for Percy's shoulder. She spoke softly as she ran her fingers down his arm, hoping with everything she had inside that her instinct was correct. "He is still alive."

At that, a low, deep, evil laugh burst from the child, and his whole tiny frame, the chains and the metal chair, shook with the force of it. It wasn't the laugh of a child, though. It was rasping and guttural and otherworldly. It was demonic.

Percy shoved Eve away, his mouth dropping open in awe. "It can't be…" He made a move towards the child, but Eve tightened a hand around his arm, staring in horror through tearful eyes at the thing in the chair.

Candide, the only member of the party who still seemed to have her full wits about her, spoke up. "Who are you?"

The voice became the child's, hoarse and weak and pleading. "I'm Michael. I'm…" Sludgy eyes fixed on his brother. "Percy? Percy, is it really you? I prayed every day you'd come and save me." On a heart-rending sob, "Please, take me home."

Candide watched on, perfectly unmoved. "Your name isn't Michael. Tell me who you are right now, or I'm going to come back here with a tub of holy water and give you a sponge bath."

Only Anna and the child were in a position to see Candide's face as she spoke. That glow was back in her eyes, as bright as ever. That disturbing greenish glow in the dark. It was unmistakable, and Anna thought the child smiled a little in response to it.

"Candide," Anna whispered.

Candide turned to her, but her eyes, what Anna could see of them by torchlight, were already back to normal. "Anna, you don't have to do a thing this time. I'm going to handle everything."

Percy made another move to stand, and Eve held him back just long enough to say, "Don't do anything stupid."

The two men stood, and Percy approached the boy with cautious steps. He leaned in and looked deep into the creature's foul eyes. "Michael, darling, I know you're in there somewhere. I'm going to get you out, no matter what I have to do. I promise you that. It might take me some time, but know I'm working on it. I won't leave you for long."

Then Percy stood tall again, wiped his tears away, and was apparently back to his usual self as quickly as he refreshed his face. "Incredible," he said. Then a laugh—a short, anxious, slightly insane laugh—broke out of him. "We did it! He's here. He's alive." He shot his dazzling smile right through Anna's heart. "Anna, I knew you could do it!"

Her stomach lurched at the complete change in him. "Percy, he's not—"

"No, he's not, is he, Anna? No…" He stared another moment at the boy, then with a dramatic movement of his arm across his face he yelled, "I can't face this!" And he ran from the room, the stairs then the floorboards above groaning and creaking as he raced back through their apartment, and slammed the apartment door closed behind.

Candide screwed her face up. "Did anyone else find that strange?"

But Eve's only thoughts were for Michael. "What are we going to do?"

Candide moved a little closer, assessing the boy. "We need to nurse him back to health somehow, I guess. Look at him. If we got the demon out now, I don't think he could survive."

"The demon could fix him if it wanted to," said Anna, remembering they murdered the still-living priest at least once. Likely twice. "We just need to give it a reason."

A smile slicked along the blackened teeth of the demon child. "Now you're getting it."

It was Candide he addressed with his yellow, jelly-like eyes, but all three felt their stomach's drop, and Eve's eyes were on Candide immediately. He grabbed her and all but dragged her away from Michael. As soon as they were around the corner and out of the demon's sight, he turned her face up to his and said, "No deals with demons, okay? Can we please agree on that before we do anything else?"

Candide had no time to find the words she needed to express her intentions before Eve went on anxiously. "No deals! We'll do everything we can, but Candide, I am not going to let you do that." Candide's eyes were set and resolute and there was a terror in Evelyn's as he looked back at her, took in her avoidant silence. "No one is to be alone with Michael," he announced. "Not ever. Candide, you never come down here without me."

Finally she pushed back, but with a guilty mumble. "Don't talk to me like that. I'm not an idiot, Eve."

"No, that's exactly right, you're not. I know you and I know exactly what you're thinking. You're not going to compromise yourself in any way to make up for whatever horrible things our parents did. I know it's hard to see him like that, and I know everything Percy and his mum have been through is horrifying, but that's nothing to do with you and me. Do you understand?"

Candide's eyes watered with the vehemence of Eve's words, yet his words came louder still. "Our agreement hasn't changed. Nothing has changed between us. Tell me you understand."

"Of course it's changed." Her eyes flitted across to Anna, only for a brief moment, but the point was made.

Eve shook his head. "No. That never changes. We stick together. You and me. Always. No matter what. Please tell me you know that."

He held her face up to his with a gentle hand belying the violence inside. They searched each other's eyes as though Anna, for the first time in a long time, wasn't there at all. And Eve won his point.

"We'll stick together," Candide whispered.

"Always." Eve brought her head to his shoulder and kissed her hair. "I'm sorry," he said softly. "Candide, you must know Percy would trade you in a second. He will try to talk you into doing a deal. Please don't listen to a word he says. Nothing can happen to you."

"I won't. I won't, Eve."

He ran a thumb over her cheek. "We'll do our best. But it's not our fault."

"I know that. I just can't help but think…" Candide's head tilted down, hiding her face and her words until she changed direction. "It doesn't matter. I would never do anything without you. You can trust me."

"I know I can. I always know that." There was another tight hug, then he released her, and his arm was around Anna again so quickly she felt a twist of guilt at Candide's furtive assessment of her. Eve missed the small, telling detail, saying to them both, "I'm sorry. It's been a shitty few days."

Anna finally spoke, trying to bring them all back to the room, and away from whatever was sitting, thickening, between her and Candide. "I think maybe we should go upstairs. Or to Eve's place. Maybe take some time to think about this situation. We need a really good plan before we do anything else. Nothing spur-of-the-moment, nothing rash, all eventualities considered and thought through to their logical conclusion. We don't need any unnecessary complications."

And that was when they heard footsteps on the stairs.

CHAPTER 21
UNNECESSARY COMPLICATIONS

"Percy, is that you?" called Candide.

"Candide?" It was Aubrey's voice.

"Oh no," Candide whispered, following on with a distraught flurry of, "No, no, no, no…"

Percy emerged from the darkness, refusing to acknowledge any of them, and they heard Aubrey's footsteps close behind him.

"Aubrey! Don't come down here." Candide made a move for the stairs, but Aubrey appeared before them all before she could stop her. "Aubrey, uh, let's go back upstairs. Come on. Please."

The mixture of relief and apprehension on Aubrey's face shifted to confusion. "Percy said you need my help down here."

Candide tugged at her hand. "Come back upstairs."

But it was already too late. Aubrey's now-furious sight was set beyond Candide, locked on to Evelyn and Anna. "What's he doing here? With her?"

Eve let drop the arm he'd forgotten was resting on Anna's shoulders.

Anna took a guilty step away from him, as though it would make any difference.

"Yes!" Candide cried. "Eve and Anna. That's something we all need to discuss. Upstairs. Right now. All of us. Let's go."

Again she pulled at the unwilling hand, only to be interrupted by Percy's loud declaration, "Aubrey, I need you over here."

Aubrey ignored him, turning to Candide with a flash of indignation. "Are you kidding me? Are they together? Did you lie to me?"

"Aubrey!" yelled Percy.

"What!" she snapped.

He flung out an arm of direction. "There's a child here, and he's almost dead. Come do medical things. Quickly."

Aubrey made a move for the opening, and Candide stepped in front of her. "No, please, don't go in there. He's... It's not that. Percy is a liar and a cheat and... You can't believe anything he says."

Aubrey halted, studying the four of them suspiciously. "Why can't I look if there's nothing there?"

"Because you can't. Because..." Candide shot Percy a pleading look. "Tell her you don't need her and this is just a stupid joke. Please, Percy."

Percy kept his attention solely on Aubrey. "He's here. Come see for yourself."

Aubrey pulled herself free of Candide's grip and started forward.

Candide made another desperate grab for her. "If you go in there, your life will never be the same again." Aubrey only dodged away from her, quickening her pace, until Candide moved her body in front of her. "Please stop. What you see in there will ruin everything for you. Please, please, come upstairs with me and just let me explain—"

"He's dying!" Percy yelled. "Come now!"

"He's not dying, Percy!" Candide shouted back. "It's been twenty years! This can wait another day!"

Aubrey's eyes narrowed into a mixture of shock and disgust, all of it levelled at Candide's desperate face. "Are you serious? There's a sick kid in there and you don't want me to help?"

Candide pressed her palms gently against Aubrey's shoulders. "You need to understand... It's not what it looks like—"

In one swift movement, Percy reached out, grabbed Aubrey around the waist, and ignoring her yelp of shock, wrenched her backwards past the partition, dust sparkling in the torch-light as he yanked the curtains down to reveal Michael, still chained to the chair.

The terror with which Aubrey beheld the small child, little more than a corpse, chained up in a dark basement with all the trappings of a satanic cult was only amplified when the boy started to cry, "Please, help me! Please! They keep me here. They torture me. I just want to go home. Please, help me!"

Aubrey staggered back, turning to Candide, the look of abhorrence and reproach in her expression to be forever burned into Candide's memory.

In the space of a breath, Aubrey caught herself, then dashed towards the boy, only to be arrested by Percy's large hand enclosing her slender biceps entirely, his breath hot on her ear, as he growled, "He's possessed by a demon, and he's quite dangerous. Don't touch him."

"What is wrong with you?" Aubrey struggled to push him off, but he held her fast, his grip tightening painfully on her arm.

"It's true," said Candide. "If I could have explained to you—"

"Get off me!" Aubrey cried, shoving an ineffectual elbow in Percy's ribs.

"Percy, let go of her," Eve called, moving forward, only to find himself stalled by Anna's grip on his own arm, not dissimilar to Percy's on Aubrey.

Michael cried out over the top of it all in tones heart-rending enough to make the others almost believe he was telling the truth. "Please, don't go. Please don't leave me. I'm so scared. It's so dark and they never let me out. Please, please, help me."

"I won't leave you," came Aubrey's gentle, terrified voice. "It's okay. I'm going to do something. I'm going to help you. I won't go." She searched the room helplessly, assessing the four other people and the space, wondering if there was any sort of weapon within reach with which to defend both herself and the boy, yet wilting under the towering strength of Percy, hard by her side.

Michael whimpered, "Please, let me hold your hand."

Despite the horrors surrounding her, Aubrey's focus narrowed on the little boy. She reached out for him, and the small, black fingers stretched themselves up for her as far as the tight chains would allow.

Percy yanked her back again. "Don't you understand? You can't touch him!"

"Back off, Percy!" yelled Anna.

Percy spared her a scowl, then turned his full attention back on Aubrey. "Aubrey, listen. I'm going to let go of you. Don't do anything stupid, or, I promise, you will die."

The harsh tone of Percy's voice, combined with the intensity of his eyes, was enough to push Aubrey over the edge.

As he let go of her, she dropped to the floor against a wall, staring at the boy, who continued to cry and plead with her pitifully. Candide came to her side, and Aubrey pushed her away in disgust and fear. Candide turned immediately to Eve, whose arm shot out to her with a movement that was as natural as breathing to him.

"Percy, why must you be such a pathetic excuse for a human being?" Eve said, holding Candide close as she let go a sob on his shoulder.

Aubrey refused to acknowledge anyone in the room other than the crying child, whom she watched in silence with horrified eyes, but neither this nor Eve's reprimand halted Percy's single-minded pursuit. He got down onto the floor next to her and spoke low and intent. "Aubrey, this is my brother, Michael. He's possessed by a demon. I'm sorry you have to find out this way, but demons are real. Michael has been this way some twenty-four years. I have spent that twenty-four years searching for him. Now I've finally found him, and you, Aubrey, are going to make him better. Now, do you want to be a doctor or don't you?"

Aubrey said nothing, made no motion to indicate she had even heard him.

"Tell me what you need," he continued. "Everything you need. I'll get it all. And when he's better—and you *will* make him better—and when he's all better again, just like he was twenty-four years ago, only then can you leave this place."

Aubrey's cry of horror was drowned out by the protestations of the other three.

"No, Aubrey, no, that's not true!" Candide shouted. "You can leave right now. You can leave any time you want."

"What is wrong with you, Percy?" yelled Eve. "Why would you say that to her?"

"Do you want her to go to the police?" said Anna, quite pragmatically.

"I don't care if she goes to the police," Percy spat. "We didn't do anything."

"They can't take Michael like this," Eve protested.

"No, that's true. He would probably kill them all as soon as they tried," Percy agreed. "How powerful do you think it is?"

"Powerful enough to need to be chained up here," Eve replied. "I mean, our parents were experienced at dealing with demons. If this thing had them beat, and it's never given up the body in all that time, it could easily take an inexperienced police officer."

"But how many inexperienced police officers in one go, do you imagine?"

"Exactly how many do you think they would send?"

As Eve and Percy fell into the pointless conversation, Anna sat down quietly, a little distance away from Aubrey. Aubrey didn't react, but Anna could see she was listening to everything that was being said, so Anna waited there without sound or movement.

Eventually, barely loud enough to hear, Aubrey asked, "When did you find him?"

"Not even an hour ago."

"Like this?"

"Yes."

Aubrey reached for her hand, which Anna gladly gave, despite the painfully tight grip of the shaking fingers. Aubrey continued to watch him, study him, until she said, "He shouldn't be crying like that." Anna looked at the boy who, all this time, was pleading with Aubrey, whimpering, begging to be saved. "He shouldn't be able to in that state. He should be dead."

The crying stopped, and a deafening silence smothered the room. A sickening smile spread across the small face as the demon's eyes burned into Aubrey. "Aubrey Agrinya. Your mother, your father, your sisters and brothers, I will take their entrails and shove them down your throat until you choke. I will eat your guts and devour your soul—"

"Don't look at him. Look at me." Anna did her best to hide her terror while Aubrey, now trembling all over, tears streaming down her face, did as she was told. Anna put a hand on her cheek to keep her steady and block the boy's view, even if she couldn't entirely block out the sound of the revolting threats it continued to throw her way. "I know it's scary, but you're safe with us. Demons lie. They're all liars. Never believe a word. We won't let anything happen to you or anyone you love. I'm so sorry you had to find out this way, but you've walked into something very complicated, and so did I. I never wanted any of this and I know exactly how you feel right now, because that's how I felt three months ago when I found out demons are real. But listen. We think we can save this boy, if you help us. He's still in there. A real person. He's trapped in the body with that thing, and all we want is to get rid of it forever and save him."

Aubrey blinked a few times, processing Anna's words, then, "Candide?"

Candide was at her side in an instant, gripping both hands tight at her lips. "Aubrey, I'm so sorry. I never wanted you involved in this." She wrapped Aubrey in her arms, and while Aubrey was as yet unable to begin to think about what she should do, while she was utterly terrified and completely overwhelmed, she lost her face in Candide's hair, in the scent of her, in her warmth, and the nook of her neck, and very slowly, she felt her strength begin to return the longer she stayed that way.

Evelyn and Percy were still discussing how dangerous an emaciated yet possessed ten-year-old could actually be when Anna cut into their conversation. "You're an awful person, Percy, do you know that?"

He readily turned to her with his devilish smile lighting up his handsome face. "Yes, of course I know that. But look, now we have a medic on our team."

Anna, naturally, stared back as though he were an idiot. "She's a student. Just a student. And you didn't need to do it like that."

"You would never have let me bring her on board, so I did have to do that. And what does she matter? She's expendable. All that matters right now is getting the job done."

"Percy!"

"But not you, Anna," came his calm, all-too-personal voice. "You're not expendable. I like you."

She narrowed her eyes at him. "I don't like you."

His smile deepened. "Yes, you do. Just a little bit. I can see it."

Her eyes flared and her stomach flipped. "You're vile."

"Maybe." He leaned a little closer and lowered his voice a little more. "But tell me you wouldn't have done the same thing."

"I wouldn't!" Anna cried.

"Of course you would. And worse." She shrank as his incisive blue eyes seemed to peer straight into her soul. "Don't think I don't know about you." Then he stood tall and snapped back to the same charming man she met in her kitchen three days earlier. "Now let's get this girl some lunch and figure out what supplies she needs."

CHAPTER 22
A SOLID PLAN

Back upstairs in the living room, Anna offered Aubrey a glass of whisky, which she accepted with a shaky hand. Candide sat at her feet, her face resting on the arms she folded across Aubrey's knees, watching her anxiously. Aubrey gently twisted and untwisted a strand of Candide's hair between her fingers as she sipped her drink, then eventually, "So, the demon is keeping his body alive and perpetually young? They can do that?"

"They can," said Candide. "I don't know how long they can do that for. A really long time, apparently."

"They have incredible healing abilities," said Anna. "If it wanted to, it could probably fix him in a few days."

"Okay, but it won't because it's a demon and, therefore, naturally evil. Got it. And you want me to do what? Find a way to give him medical care and do what the demon won't do?"

"Only if you want to," said Candide. "And you can back out any time."

"And you just found him today…" Before anyone could answer, she breathed out an already-defeated-sounding, "I don't understand how this happened. Or why you're involved in any of this Candide. And why is Worthing even here?" She sent an especially foul glare towards Eve, who had deliberately taken a seat at the table, out of Aubrey's line of sight. He chose to say nothing, waiting for Candide to think up some fabulous story to deflect Aubrey from the truth. Anna also looked expectantly at Candide, wondering what she would come up with.

Candide took a deep breath. "Aubrey, my godmother is Lady Adeline Worthing, and as I'm an orphan, I was partially raised by her, and I have always been incredibly close to Eve because our mothers were best friends. We keep all that secret. Our parents had a paranormal club and so Eve and I were also raised around paranormal things. We've spent our lives fighting them off." She glanced at Eve, who dumped his head in his hands and rubbed his eyes, as though that would make it all go away. "We've just discovered that our parents seem to have done something terrible which resulted in the boy downstairs being possessed a long time ago, and now we're going to try to unravel that whole mess. Sadly, this kind of thing isn't new to me, and being with me means accepting all of that."

A white hot fury beat at Anna's temples. "Are you serious right now?" She turned it all on Eve, just as he knew she would. "Just like that! Eve! Do you see how easy Candide made that?"

"I'm sorry!" he cried. "I told you I'm a very anxious person!"

"That's an understatement," Anna seethed.

Though her mouth wrinkled with disapprobation, Aubrey said, "All right. I understand. And why is he here?" Her eyes shifted to Percy, relaxing in the armchair opposite with his own glass of whisky.

"Percy's new to me, too," said Candide. "The kid downstairs is his brother, and he blames Eve's mum for all of this. Eve?"

Evelyn took up the explanation with a twitch at the corner of his eye. "So, a long time ago, my mother made the mistake of falling for Percy's father, and I've been cursed with this idiotic half-brother ever since."

"Oh, that's what you call it, is it?" Percy shot on a breath of cigarette smoke. "Deliberately usurping the Worthing name and fortune from the rightful owner is 'falling for', is it?"

On a weary sigh, "I can't change the decisions our parents made, as much as I wish I could. My mother always made sure you had everything you needed."

"Everything except my true brother, Evelyn," Percy snapped. "Everything except a father. And what do you think that was like for my mother? Taking charity from the woman who stole the father from her children. Thank God she doesn't know the rest."

"Oh, as though your father had no say in the matter."

"Did he?"

"Of course he did. You might want to believe otherwise, but he was every bit as repulsive as you are."

"You take that back immediately, Evelyn!" Percy shouted.

"No, I won't take that back because it's absolutely true," Eve shouted back. "Look at your behaviour today. You're an awful person, inside and out."

Percy fell quiet, took a reflective drag on his cigarette, then let a sly smile cross his face. "Well, not on the outside. Correct, Anna?"

Anna, who had been sitting on the lounge facing Percy and quietly taking in his good looks while listening to them argue, blushed, and swished her head away. "Eve's correct. You're an awful person."

Percy laughed out a puff of swirling air. "Well, you have me at a disadvantage. Things would be quite different between us, I'm sure, if I were the future Lord Worthing."

"How dare you!" It was the first time the idea had even occurred to Anna that Eve, one day, would be Lord Worthing, and once her immediate reaction to Percy's prodding was out, she fell straight back into silence to worry over this latest fact.

Eve, on the other hand, was, as always, prepared to argue with his brother. "You would use the title and all, wouldn't you, Percy? Vulgar to the last."

He got half a disparaging raise of an eyebrow in return. "You're one to talk."

Eve sat up tall and straight, flicked his luscious hair to the side, and smiled an incredibly handsome and, for Percy, incredibly irritating smile. There wasn't the vaguest thing vulgar about his person and both knew it to be true.

"So, all of that. That's all new." Candide waved long fingers in their general direction. "Them and their whole weird thing."

And so Aubrey's gaze returned to Anna, with a sharp nod in Eve's direction. "But not *them*?"

Candide rushed to make their excuses. "I know it seems so wrong at first appearance, but really, it was all very complicated how they got together and it's very appropriate and above board now."

"Anna?" Aubrey awaited her explanation.

"I'm sorry I had to lie to you," Anna explained. "We are together. It's been three months, and he's not like that." She rushed to add, "He's not like... like it seems like he must be... If that makes sense..."

"It makes perfect sense," came the cold reply. "You already both told me what a 'nice guy' he is." Eve flushed at the accusatory tone, and unsure of what to say, bit his finger, wishing the room would swallow him, particularly when she finished her thought. "A very nice teacher who sleeps with his students."

"One!" he cried. "I slept with *one* student!"

"Her first term!" Aubrey threw back.

"It wasn't like that!" he protested.

"No, Aubrey," Anna interrupted. "I pursued him. Relentlessly. Really, I did. And it turns out, I'm very good at getting what I want." Her saucy smile at Evelyn only served to make Aubrey more angry and embarrass Eve further, painfully aware as he was of his intense attraction to his irresistible partner.

Aubrey gave a furious shake of her head. "Candide, I'm doing this for you. And for that little boy. All this," Aubrey swiped her hand across to indicate the rest of the group, "I don't want anything to do with any of them once this is done. Everything inside me is screaming that I need to report Worthing for his predatory behaviour and just look at her." Anna stared back, dumbfounded. "She's so infatuated she doesn't even know how inappropriate this is."

"That's what I said," Eve mumbled.

"Don't even talk to me!" Aubrey snapped, curling her hand into a fist with only her index finger sticking out at him. "Worthing, I don't want you to say one more word to me. You speak to me again and I'm out."

Eve shut his beautiful mouth immediately.

Aubrey sighed and placed her empty glass on the coffee table. "Who's going shopping?"

"Percy," said Anna. "Percy's going shopping."

Percy scowled in response.

"All right." Aubrey linked her fingers together and sat forward to formulate her plan. "I'm just guessing, but I don't think I can get a drip into those veins."

Anna's mind moved swiftly through the options she, too, had been considering. "Are we going to have to force-feed him?"

"Oh, oh no, really?" groaned Eve, despite Aubrey's warning. "I can't. I can't do that to a kid."

"Oh, but that's awful!" Percy uttered, reeling back in distaste. "I couldn't bear it. How could you do that?"

Aubrey rolled her eyes. "Uh, yeah, it's awful, but that may be the only option we have. I can't do it by myself."

"I'm good," said Candide, shuffling her adoring chin a little further up Aubrey's leg.

"Me too," said Anna.

"Great. We have three capable people here." She eyed the half-brothers briefly, but firmly. "It's going to be extremely compli-cated to nurse Michael back to health. I'm talking us, *all* of us, working around the clock. Force-feeding may come later when he's a bit healthier, but if we go straight in with that, his stomach will explode and we'll kill him."

Eve gasped. "No!"

"That's disgusting!" said Percy. "Why would you even say that?"

Aubrey ignored them both. "I need... Oh, I need so much. How are we going to get it all?"

"Eve can pick locks," Anna said proudly. "We can easily get into the med lab."

Aubrey scoffed at her naivety. "Oh, it's much harder than picking a lock now."

"What?" Candide sat up straight. "How come?"

"Someone trashed the med lab a few months back. They stole a bunch of drugs, and there was blood and salt everywhere." Aubrey shook her head. "It was really weird. Some kind of weird, demonic-looking shit, with this chair and bandages and smashed glass."

"Oh..." Candide whispered. "That's unfortunate."

She, Anna, and Eve exchanged none-too-subtle glances.

Which Aubrey caught. "It was you, wasn't it?"

"Uh..." Her chin back on Aubrey's knee, Candide mumbled, "Someone else was possessed. We kind of had to."

Aubrey's eyes drooped to two patient slits. "Right. I'm just going to accept that statement for what it is and move on. Listen, I can't get you into the lab. Only the staff know the code now."

"I can get it," Eve attempted. "There's a database."

Aubrey scowled at him. "Well congratulations. You're not completely useless." And he fell silent again, as she continued, "I'll need scalpels, a drip, maybe a table—"

"Can we do without the table?" asked Percy. "Sounds hard to move."

"Um, if we have to, I guess. I don't know how we would tie him to it anyway, I suppose. I need bandages, needles, tubes. I need food, I need…" Her fingers tapped on her skirt with a pace akin to the mounting obstacles. "I think we might need blood—look, I'll write a list. I'm not going to help get this, by the way. I'll help fix him, but I'm not getting caught stealing this and getting kicked out of Endymion."

Percy pulled a pen from an inner pocket in his coat and threw it down on Anna's notepad on the coffee table. "I'll get it all."

"Ok, good." She commenced scrawling. "The food… He's going to need crystalloid fluids to start, then we'll amp it up to a liquid diet through a nasogastric tube—"

"Down his nose?" Percy shuddered.

"That's terrible," Eve winced.

"That's generally what nasal means, yeah…" She pushed a little harder on the pen. "For the food, you might need to hit a nursing home to get the correct mixture. They won't have anything like that here. He'll also need…" There she paused, twisting the pen in pensive fingers. "God, I wish I could put him to sleep for this. It's so cruel to do all this to a child. How much can he feel, Candide? Do you know?"

Candide shook her head. "I don't know. I'm sorry. Can't we put him to sleep?"

"How am I going to weigh him? If I try to do the anaesthetic and get it wrong... I can't. I... Candide, I could kill him so easily. How am I going to do this?" She ran a shaking hand through her hair and stared out the window. "This is so wrong. Everything inside me says this is so wrong."

"It is," Candide said, taking her hand. "I wish Percy had never got you involved in this. Or any of us. There's no part of this that isn't absolutely horrible."

"But I can't back out either, can I?" Aubrey reflected. "If I don't do this, what's the alternative? Brick him back up for another twenty years? So, no, it's fine. I'm going to do this. We'll push through. I just really hope this little boy isn't the first person I kill." Aubrey wiped a tear away with the mound of her palm, but her firm and determined tone gave little other indication of the intense emotion inside. "We'll do this, and we'll get him ready to... To what? Drive the demon out?"

"Yes. That's exactly right. As soon as he's well enough, we're going to banish the demon and give him his life back." Candide clambered up and perched lightly on the arm of Aubrey's chair, retaining her hand, which she kissed, then held gently. "You're so incredible. A lot of people wouldn't handle this so well."

Aubrey smiled sadly at Candide. "I'm still adjusting. Is it an exorcism you need to do?"

"It is, but we don't know how we're going to do it yet. We did it once before, but, well, it was hard. I think..." The apologetic look she directed at Anna made Anna's stomach jump into her throat. "I think we need a priest."

"No!" Anna's words were instinct and were out before she even registered what was being asked of her. "No, Candide, no. Don't do that."

Eve was by Anna's side in a heartbeat, directing his words at Candide. "We're not going to do anything Anna doesn't want to do."

"But!" Candide leapt up from the chair and took to the other side of Anna. "Whatever happened, Anna, that wasn't Joe. You know that, right?"

"Nothing happened!" Anna protested. "Why won't either of you believe me when I say that?" Their eyes exchanged their silent disbelief right in front of her. "Don't look at each other like that! I'm right here!"

"Anna." Eve knelt on the floor in front of her. "We won't do it. We won't. We can find someone else. Really."

Candide dropped down next to him with a smack into his shoulder. "Anna, Joe knows demons. Better than anyone else we're going to find. You know he's our best shot."

Eve shoved her shoulder back with his. "Candide, don't push her like this."

"She said nothing happened!" Candide snapped. "You should take her word for it."

"She's clearly upset—"

"Ugh! Not again with you being controlling—"

"She said no! I'm being supportive. It's not the same thing. It's the opposite thing!"

"You haven't even given her a second to think about it!"

"Leave her alone!"

"Can you both please leave me alone right now?" Anna withdrew her hands from her two favourite people, who remained on the floor glaring at each other.

She knew Candide was right. She knew Joe Bruno had personal experience and would, this time, hopefully, be prepared to face a demon with them. With the *Necronomicon*. With easy access to all the church could provide—with a safe harbour should they need it. Everything pointed to Joe as being the most obvious person to turn to. She couldn't do another exorcism by herself...

But she also knew what she had done to him. She had kissed him and almost had sex with him when he had no control over his own body. She had beaten him and almost killed him. She had tortured him.

She knew she could never tell Eve all of what she'd done. And, if they went to him for help, she would have to tell Joe, in front of Eve, that she knew what she did, and that she was sorry. Joe, whose body had killed so many people, whose hands had put a stake through her shoulder and almost killed her two closest friends. What kind of trauma would she dredge up for them both when he saw her again?

But overruling all of this, quietly waiting downstairs, sat Michael. Michael, who had tried to help her, tried to warn her about the last demon.

"I don't know if Joe will want to see me," she finally said. "I don't want to make him see me. I think it will upset him."

"It's odd you would be worried about what Joe will think," came Percy's inscrutable voice. "After all, he was the aggressor... Wasn't he?"

On the verge of confessing all under his knowing, watchful eye, waiting for the axe to fall, Anna said only, "I did horrible things to him."

Eve took her hands back gently, shifting to the couch beside her, moving a comforting arm around her shoulder. "Anna, exorcisms are awful for everyone. You saved his life. If anything, he probably wants to thank you. Don't ever feel bad for doing what you had to do to survive."

Evelyn, so earnest in his adoration of Anna, made her sick to her stomach.

Percy spoke again, oh so casually. "Is Joe Bruno as good looking as everyone says?"

Anna gasped loud and clear. "You mean you don't know?"

He smiled his clever smile, playing it off like it was nothing. "No, I haven't ever seen him. Did you think I had?"

The bastard! "You said you were there! You said you knew everything!"

"No, no…" His sexy lower lip pressed out innocently as his fingers traced the pattern of the armchair fabric. "I just heard bits and pieces. I didn't see anything. I don't know everything."

Was it true? Was he lying?

Of course, he couldn't have seen it.

But did he hear it?

He couldn't have, if even Eve and Candide didn't know everything.

But Joe knew.

Yet that little touch of confidence, the hope that she still had her secret, that only Joe knew, was enough to give her the push she needed. "Fine. It's fine. We're going to go see Joe. It's about time I talk to him about all of this, anyway."

Eve didn't move, only held her gaze with his, entirely too sweet, entirely too faithful. "You don't have to do this."

She made a careful study of the floor. "No, I want to. Don't try to make me go over this again. Please. I've made my decision."

"All right." He kissed her hand. "But you can change your mind any time, okay?"

"All right," she whispered, leaning her head on his shoulder, guilty, but so thankful she had him. At least for now.

"All right," said Aubrey. "But who's Joe?"

Candide made her way back over to Aubrey to pull her to her feet. "We'll explain on the way."

"We're doing this now?" asked Aubrey.

"Why not? We've got a solid plan now. Let's do it."

All agreed, they took some time to shove the bricks back into the wall before they closed the hanging door on the whole scene. They took the *Necronomicon*, and walked together down the hill and over the field, winding their way around the picturesque streets of the village and through the church to the adorable cottage where Joe Bruno, blissfully unaware of their approach, was still trying to forget all about them.

CHAPTER 23
A COLD SHOWER

C andide knocked on Joe's red door with the cool bronze ring of a lion's head door knocker.

No response.

She knocked again.

No response.

Just as Anna, Eve and Candide began to wilt under the sickening remembrance that washed over them, Aubrey said, "Is that…" She tilted her head to the side. "Can you hear running water?"

Cautiously, they made their way around the side of the building, and were stopped in their tracks at the unprecedented sight before them.

There, in the dying light of a freezing winter afternoon, was Joe Bruno, steam rising from the heat of his naked body as he washed in the stream of a cold shower.

His thick, hazelnut hair curled even under the weight of the water, which ran in thousands of winding rivers down the curves of his muscular back and chest. His dark nipples were firm and erect with the chill atmosphere. The hard muscles of his chest and abdomen flexed as his breath came in sharp, heavy gasps, his body fighting back against the freezing winter air and icy water. The arms, bulging with muscle—the hands like a sculpture by Michelangelo—the face, eyes closed and lashes long as the day, incomparably beautiful.

Anna, Evelyn, Candide and Percy stopped dead, rooted to the spot, drinking in the splendid sight.

"Why is his shower outside?" said Aubrey.

"It doesn't matter," whispered Percy.

"But that makes no sense—"

"It doesn't matter, Aubrey!" he hissed.

"That's…" said Anna.

"Mmm," Eve agreed.

"Aha," Candide concurred.

Aubrey stomped an affronted foot. "Are you all just going to stand here and watch?"

Candide was the first to snap back to reality. Almost. "No. No! We are not. We're all going to go back to the front door and wait. And not watch…" She gazed back longingly. "This…"

No one moved. Except Percy, who, eyes glued to Joe, shifted a little closer to Anna and whispered, "Does he have scars on his back?"

"Yes!" said Anna, narrowing her eyes for a better view. "Yes, it's scars."

"And he's Catholic, isn't he?" said Percy. "Which means he can't—"

"That's none of your business," Eve snapped under his breath.

Percy, watching in silence for a few more delicious moments, then continued, "Is it wrong of me—"

"You're all perverts!" cried Aubrey. "Go! He's going to see us."

Reluctantly, and with a shove from Aubrey, they all went back to the desolate courtyard with its sleeping grapevines and sat down to wait.

Percy lit a cigarette, looked around, bored. Then his eyes fell on Eve. "Tell me, Evelyn, when you saw that malodorous harpy the other day, did she indicate to you why she felt the need to torture my brother for almost a quarter of a century?"

Eve, a combination of pissed off and resigned, sighed out, "Percy, do you think maybe it's time you stop blaming my mother for the things *your* father chose to do?"

"Well, I would love to do that, but unfortunately, *your* father isn't here to blame."

"And that was his decision."

Percy raised a sharp eyebrow. "Was it?"

"Of course it was. It's no wonder you won't grow up if you're going to spend your life in denial of who *your* father truly was."

Percy moved his gaze down to his boots, which he tapped slowly on the cold stone as he seemed to fall into reflective indecision. When he next spoke, his voice had lost its brittle edge. "Evelyn, what do you remember of your father?"

Eve's entire body visibly tensed at the question. Anna expected him to offer nothing more than a cutting rebuff, so she was surprised when his voice took on a softer, hoarse note. "Not all that much. I was quite young."

"Yes, I suppose you were." Percy hugged his legs in close, his chin on his knee, a faraway look in his eyes. "Old enough to remember some things, though."

"How would you know?"

"I was there more often than you think." Still Percy stared down at the grey stone courtyard ground, toyed with his cigarette, and wouldn't meet Eve's waiting gaze.

Eve shook his head. "No. It was just us. All those years. When Candide was there. Otherwise, I was alone." He added sharply, "You don't know a thing about it."

A sad laugh dropped from Percy. "You're wrong. I was there. On the rare occasion I was invited to my house, I was eventually beaten, then locked in a room at the far end, deep down in the east wing, behind three sets of bolted doors."

Now Percy did look up at Eve, and their eyes met in a brief, miserable, anxious exchange of understanding, then they both looked away again. At anything but each other.

Eve's voice came weak in his throat. "I had no idea. I'm sorry that happened to you."

"No, you wouldn't have had any idea." Then, with only a hint of his recurrent bitterness, "He probably never touched a hair on your head, anyway."

"He did. Only sometimes." Almost subconsciously, Eve stretched his hand open and closed again. "He broke my fingers."

Percy watched the beautiful fingers just as Eve did, suddenly a shade paler, perhaps, a strange look in his eye. Wary yet curious. Distant yet intent. "How many fingers?"

It may have been an odd question to anyone else, but the strange, slight smile on Eve's face showed it was the correct one, and he knew Percy understood. "All of them. Just on the right hand."

"Ah, so you could still write."

"Correct."

"That's just like him." Percy took another puff of his cigarette as he studied Eve. "And how old were you?"

"Percy, I was eight years old. I'm sure you remember my arm in a cast. You used to hit it."

"That's right," he chuckled. The other four scowled at him, and he straightened a little. "I never knew how it happened, or I wouldn't have done that, obviously. I assumed you got it playing polo or something."

"I never played polo," Eve snapped.

"Well now, you are full of surprises." The softness was gone with a flick of his hair and a tap of his ash.

Eve said nothing.

Percy took a final drag and flicked what was left of his cigarette across the courtyard, where it landed on a crisp, dry leaf, fallen from the grapevine. He watched impassively as the thing caught fire, as the edges twisted and curled up, then burnt away slowly into nothingness. "And what did your father say about your broken fingers? The next time you saw him."

Eve kept his own watch on the burning leaf as he spoke. "I never saw him again. He disappeared shortly after that."

"See, now that's interesting, isn't it? Did you ever wonder about that? The timing of his disappearance coinciding with that event?"

"I did. For many years. I assumed he left because he hated me. Or hated being a father. Or some combination of those things."

"And you never thought that bitch had anything to do with it?"

Eve wrinkled a disdainful brow.

Percy clacked his tongue and gave a heavy sigh. "And you never thought that vile, villainous piece of human garbage had anything to do with it?"

"No, I never did. I was told he went away, and I was never to speak of him. Then one day she said he was to be reported missing, and that was all."

"Fascinating." Percy stretched his legs out long, leaning back on his elbows. "If only my mother had access to the resources your mother had."

Through gritted teeth, "I'm sure the money helped."

Also through gritted teeth, "I don't mean the money."

"If she took care of me, by whatever means necessary, then I'm thankful to her," Eve said, hoping to put an end to the conversation. Yet he couldn't help adding, "And I don't really care what happened to him, if I'm honest."

"And you don't care if your mother is a murderer?"

"How many people have you killed now, Percy?"

Percy laughed. "I think it would be rather morbid to keep count, don't you, Evelyn?"

"Not for a cold-hearted bastard like you, Percy."

"And what about you, Evelyn? How many people have you killed?"

Eve must have known it was the obvious retort to his own question, yet Anna felt his muscles tense, and as she looked to his face, she saw that deep, burning hatred levelled at Percy once again. She snuggled further back into him and felt him settle a touch as his arm pressed her close.

Percy's attention shifted to Anna. "You don't even care, do you?"

"Not in the least," she replied with perfect honesty. She had little experience, it was true, but one run-in with a demon was enough for her to imagine and forgive Eve for anything he might have done in order to be alive and right there next to her.

Faced with her calm loyalty, Percy's target became Candide. "And you, Candide? How many?"

Aubrey's face, wan, looked with a shade of distrust towards Candide, whose eyes went straight to Eve, one tear betraying the emotional turmoil within.

"No one," Eve said instantly. "Candide could never do that."

"Eve—" she began.

His words were gentle as he talked over her. "Don't be upset. Don't give him the satisfaction."

It pleased Anna to see that there was no hesitation in the way Aubrey slipped two quiet arms around Candide's waist and rested her head on her shoulder, letting Candide lean into her.

Percy carried on, heedless, with a roll of his eyes. "Aubrey won't have killed anyone. She's far too dull."

"Not everyone's as terrible a person as you, Percy," Eve replied.

"Just you then, Evelyn," he threw back.

"Percy, could you please f—"

"What are you all doing here?"

Five faces snapped over to behold Joe Bruno, standing tall and fresh and gorgeous, if a little apprehensive, awaiting their response.

CHAPTER 24

UNINVITED GUESTS

E ve was up and by Joe's side in an instant, smiling his lovely smile with his infectious, engaging warmth. Apologies were made for the intrusion, and moments later, they were all inside the beautiful old cottage, with its low, exposed beams, doilies and china, and small crackling fire.

Joe refused to look at Anna. She, Aubrey and Candide took their places at a small table against one wall, while Percy wandered around the cottage inspecting Joe's belongings.

Eve disappeared into the kitchen with Joe, under the pretence of helping him make tea, and by the time they returned, perhaps an hour later, Joe was aware of the situation, and looked Anna in the eye with a questioning wariness that was more than Anna could have hoped for. Eve had clearly laid the groundwork for her, saved Joe the misery of revisiting everything in the presence of a sizeable group, and ingratiated himself substantially with their host. All those things being done, he took his place at the table with a kiss on Anna's cheek, and Joe settled opposite him, in an armchair by the window, his face pleasantly flushed, a gentle smile reflecting on the handsome onslaught that was Evelyn Worthing.

Percy threw himself down beside Joe with a disruptive bump. "You look fagged."

Joe's attention, successfully wrenched away from Eve, landed in full on Percy's handsome smirk. "Fagged?"

"You know—worn out, exhausted, tired—*fagged*."

"Oh." Joe's cheeks coloured and Candide scowled at Percy. "Yes, I'm tired. I wasn't expecting all this."

"We're sorry," Anna choked out.

Percy leaned forward on the little table that separated his and Joe's armchairs. "The boy is my brother. Do you think you can help him?"

"Yes, I think I can. We may need to organise a few things, but I think I can do this. And I want to help. If that's all right with everyone?"

Anna felt his gaze on her. "What? Are you… We would love your help…" She made herself look back at him, and the second their eyes met, the heat and the sweat broke out on her palms and on her temples.

He wasn't the demon.

He wasn't at all.

She could see it in his expression, distrustful as it was, and she knew logically that he was warded, just as she was, because she had carved the symbol into his skin herself.

He couldn't be the demon.

But it was the first time they had looked directly at each other since that day, and she felt all the fear of being alone in that room with him crashing in on her in one terrifying heap.

Eve's arm was around her.

Eve pulled her in snug, her cheek against the comforting wool of his sweater, the reassuring press of his muscular arm beneath the fabric, and she was wrapped in the safe scent of him. He didn't say a word, only held her close and rested the open palm of his hand on her chest. At that, an unaccustomed warmth spread straight from his open hand, sinking deep into her skin, deep into her very heart. It was such a strange and deeply soothing sensation that any other day she would have remarked upon it.

But not today.

Today, Joe Bruno sat waiting, and even as she felt her fear slowly dissipate in Eve's protective embrace, it was replaced, as it always was when she remembered the incident, by disgust. Disgust at herself and guilt that made her want to be sick. "I'm so sorry." Her tears began to fall, and she hated them because she had no right to be the upset person in the room. "I'm so sorry for everything I did to you. I don't know what I was doing. I mean, I did, but I didn't, and I can't explain it. And I'm so sorry. And I know you probably hate me, but please know I hate myself. I hate myself every day, and I know that probably makes no difference to you, because it's not about me, or how I feel. I just…" She searched his face. "How do I make it better?"

"You don't apologise. We do an exorcism and then we move on." Joe's voice was calm, but Anna saw the shards of glass hidden in his hard, golden eyes. No one in the room but she and Joe knew what he was really saying: nothing was forgiven and nothing was forgotten. "I've never exorcised a person who's been possessed for such a long time. I don't know anyone who has. I may need your help." He looked away from her, to the fire, but then he added, "You seem to have an intuitive understanding of the nature of demons."

A cold shiver ran down Anna's spine and she felt the urge to slap Eve's hand away as he lovingly tousled her hair, as though Joe had just said she had an intuitive understanding of French Romanticism.

Joe finished, barely audibly, "We'll work together on this, and then maybe we'll try to work through the rest. In time."

"It's more than I deserve," Anna whispered, her heart scrunching into a little ball in her chest.

Candide reached a hand out, wrapping her fingers around Anna's with a kind smile. "Don't be so hard on yourself. It's all right."

Anna smiled back at Candide's sweetness, but pulled her hand away and curled it up, stabbing at her palm with her fingernails.

Percy watched the lot with intelligent eyes—too intelligent—then addressed himself to Joe only. "What do we need? I bet I have everything you need. More than he's got, at any rate." He tossed his head derisively in Eve's direction, which brought a deeper blush to Joe's already flustered cheek.

Joe cleared his throat. "I won't know until I spend some time with the boy. If it's true that it's an extreme case, we may need to find some special items."

"Special items, eh?" Percy nodded his understanding, as though he had done this a thousand times before. "How about a chunk of the true cross? Wart of Saint Fiacre? The Veil of Veronica?"

A very sweet, quietly excited smile lit Joe's face, and he laughed out, "You don't have those things."

"I certainly do," said Percy, his own smile deepening.

"If you had the veil, things would be very different for us."

"I have the veil, Joe. I'm not convinced it works, though. I tried it when I stole it and it failed entirely."

"You can't have stolen it," Joe scoffed. "It was in the Vatican."

"Quite right," Percy grinned. "Twelve hours I spent hiding in Roman sewers to escape with that veil, and it never once stopped the bleeding from the wound those priests gave me. Vicious fighters, they were too. You can't see any of Jesus' blood on there now. It's all obliterated by my own. I was tempted to wash it, actually. I didn't. Just in case. I still don't think it works, though."

Joe raised a questioning eyebrow. "Twelve hours with an open wound in a Roman sewer, yet you didn't die from an infection…"

Percy studied him. "You attribute that to the powers of the veil?"

"I attribute it to fiction."

"You don't believe me?"

"Of course not," Joe laughed. "Next you'll be telling me you have the holy foreskin."

Percy smiled warmly, and his eyes danced as he lowered his voice and leaned in a little closer. "Only in a manner of speaking, Joe."

Evelyn loudly groaned. "Why did we bring him?"

"Anna knows it's true," Percy threw across.

"I do not!" she yelled.

"You wish you knew, though."

"I do not!"

He turned back to Joe. "How about the holy lance?"

With those words, Joe became completely captivated. He took in a little gasp of air, then, "It's not possible."

Percy lifted one beautiful hand theatrically, and pointed to the scar above his eye.

Joe stared hard at Percy, utterly awestruck, clearly taken in by his claims. "So it *was* you! Do you have the heart?"

"Now, that's a secret," said Percy smugly.

"That's incredible! I can't believe it was you!"

"It was me," Percy laughed.

"Let me see the scar." Percy tilted his chin upward, side to side, and Joe's lips parted ever so slightly as he deliberately stilled the hand that wanted to reach out and touch Percy's brow to confirm it was no illusion. "Incredible. It was said he stabbed you right in the eye, and you escaped, only to be eaten by foxes and wildcats, the heart and the lance lost forever."

Percy threw off the grand story as though it were nothing. "A very romantic notion, I'm sure, but as you see, barely more than a flesh wound. Of course, I hear-tell the Church is given to exaggeration."

"You know," Joe spoke more seriously again, "Brother Francis died later from the wounds you gave him."

"I didn't know that. I can't say I'm entirely surprised. And if I'm honest, I can't say I'm sorry either."

"No, nor would I." Joe's lip pulled into a handsome sneer, which Percy narrowed his focus on. "He was a terrible person. You did the right thing to take the lance from him. It holds enormous power. Power that he should never have had."

Percy leaned in closer still, creating a secretive pull between them, and Joe reacted by leaning equally close, the two eye to eye, inches apart, as though there were no one else in the room. "You must know though, the lance, if I had it, is useless without the sheath."

Instantly, Joe announced with complete confidence, "The sheath is in Libya."

Percy's mouth dropped open, just as Joe's had a moment earlier. "It's in Libya? How do you know?"

"Because I also take an interest in such matters." A fire ignited in both their hearts and their eyes as the connection burst into life. "It's kept guarded, locked away at all times, at least three of their fiercest monks always watching, in the reli—"

"The reliquary of Saint Martin!" Percy slammed a hand down on the table. "God, damn it! I knew it!"

Joe shook his head. "It's impossible. No man could ever do it."

"Maybe not one man." Percy looked meaningfully at Joe.

Joe laughed lightly. "I'm not the man for this job. But you…" Joe ran his eyes over Percy, a hot spark all about them. "If anyone could do it, I'm sure it's you."

"You clearly don't put enough trust in yourself." Whatever heat was in Joe's gaze was doubled in Percy's when his voice dropped low and rich and he said, "I think we could do beautiful things together, you and I."

There was the unmistakable chemistry. It was strong and thick in the air, and as Joe and Percy looked pure fire into one another's eyes, and as Joe appeared to be absolutely taken in by Percy's strong, charismatic, superhuman persona, Anna felt another energy behind her. She turned to see Evelyn's eyes locked onto the two of them, his muscles growing tight beneath his sweater in his anger and anxiety.

He relaxed very suddenly, and there was a loud noise as Eve pushed his feet out and scraped his chair backwards on the wooden floor. Joe, his connection to Percy broken that instant, looked over at Evelyn, who pulled his chair up beside Joe and leaned one handsome shoulder into him. Joe flushed, and Anna looked at Candide questioningly. Candide was too busy playing with Aubrey's fingers to have noticed anything until Evelyn spoke.

"Joe, you should know my half-brother is a psychopath, a liar, and a cheat. He would stab you in the back, or poison you, as soon as look at you. And that scar, he got it when a swing came back and hit him in the face when he was twelve years old. For all his studied pretension, he's actually just a clumsy little shit. I strongly suggest you stay far away from him at all costs."

Evelyn stared cooly into Percy's eyes, awaiting his response, which, when it came, was far more measured than any of them had expected.

"A scar can be two things, Evelyn. Do you require more proof?" Percy began to unbutton his shirt.

One, two, three buttons...

"Oh my god…" Anna sighed. The next sound anyone heard was her forehead thunking down on the table.

"Joe, will you come outside for a cigarette with me?" Evelyn linked his arm through Joe's and all but dragged him away from the table. The two were gone in an instant, the door shutting softly behind them.

Anna turned her head, cheek squished against the wood, and watched Eve through the window, beautiful and warm and smiling again. He looked as though there wasn't a thing wrong in the world as he stood there on the freezing ground in the courtyard, telling Joe some kind of entertaining story that got exactly the same smiles and fond engagement Eve was accustomed to getting every time he made the effort to be charming with anyone. Yet behind all the charm, Anna could clearly see that Eve had now found another person, in addition to Candide and herself, that he felt the need to protect from all the horrors of the world. And at the same time her heart swelled in her love for him, it also sank slightly at the knowledge of how much quiet anxiety would be building up inside him as he navigated the latest mess made for him long ago by his parents.

Percy kept the same watch, his bulging chest drawing Anna's eyes when he gave a hefty sigh.

"Do your shirt up, please," she rasped.

"I'm hot," he replied.

"That's not the point!" she snapped, pushing herself back up. "Percy, Joe has been through a lot. He's not here for you to mess with like you do with the rest of us. Leave him out of it."

"I was just making conversation."

"You were not."

Percy and Anna stared out the window at the two men for some time, until Percy said, "He is really beautiful though, isn't he? Even next to Evelyn, who hasn't an altogether displeasing aspect, if you can forget his personality for a while."

"Eve's the most beautiful thing on this planet," Anna responded.

"For goodness' sake," Aubrey sighed.

"Leave her alone," Candide whispered.

Percy turned to Anna. "I'm not sure he's better looking than Joe."

"He's definitely better looking," said Candide.

"He's ethereal," Anna said. "He's like if you took all the greatest and most wonderful things in existence and made them into a person. And then he's more beautiful again."

It was enough to make Aubrey roll her eyes and groan loudly.

"What?" cried Anna. "He is."

"Yes, perhaps." Percy pointed back out the window. "But look at Joe's hair. And scars! Did you see the scars?"

"Oh yes!" said Anna enthusiastically. "All down his back."

"Is it very important?" Aubrey interrupted. "You know, given everything that's going on right now. Maybe we should be talking about possessions or exorcisms or something?"

"Honestly, Aubrey, which one? If you had to," asked Percy.

Eve, having just come back in with Joe, sighed wearily. "Should we go back outside?"

Joe laughed and dropped into his armchair. "It's fine."

"How could I possibly choose?" Aubrey drawled.

Anna, totally missing the sarcasm in her tone, because to her it was an easily answerable but compelling question, asked, "Sorry, is… is everyone here except me bi?"

"Not me," Aubrey said.

"Not me," Joe snapped.

"We never felt the need to label it," Eve murmured.

"Do you know…" Percy started, paused, casting his eye around the room, then continued, "Did you ever think—"

Candide watched his eyes shift back and forth between her and Eve. "No, Percy."

"But look at you two. Did you never want to share?"

"No, Percy!" Eve snapped.

"Are you worried you're related?"

Candide and Eve's ridiculously beautiful faces exchanged knowing glances and Candide said, as much to Aubrey as anyone, "We've always thought there was a distinct possibility."

"It would be quite Roman, though, wouldn't it?" Percy reflected on one of his suggestive smirks.

"Incest?" Eve almost shouted.

"Calm down," Percy chuckled. "No one's going to make you do anything you don't want to do."

Eve sighed heavily, again, then looked as though he were going to throw his cup when Percy continued, "Unless you want to."

Eve narrowed his eyes to furious slits. "With you?"

"No, not with me. That's perverted, Evelyn! There are a lot of people in the room. You and I wouldn't even have to—"

"Oh my god! We're leaving. We're all leaving right now!" Evelyn angrily jumped up from his chair, and all except Percy started going through the motions to depart.

"I thought we could start fresh tomorrow," Percy said, his calm, goading eyes on Eve. "Thought I might stay here and keep Joe company overnight. Prepare him for everything that's... to come..."

"That is never going to happen!" Eve shouted, and Percy burst out laughing at the reaction he had successfully coaxed. Eve glared at him, then softened his tone and said to Joe, "You'll need a scarf. It's a long walk." This he ripped off a nearby coat rack and draped around Joe's neck, pulling a stylish knot below the chin of his blushing face. Then, "Anna, will you be all right?" And he held his coat open for her to shelter in. Her own coat was amply warm enough, but she took the offer without a second thought and wrapped her arms around him as tight as possible in preparation for the dark and spooky walk back to Endymion College.

CHAPTER 25

THE HORROR IN THE FIELD

A chill gale had arisen as they sat, unsuspecting, in Joe's cottage. By the time they alighted, the wind ripped through their coats as though they were nothing, and each quietly dreaded the long walk home across the endless, damp field that lay between the village and the university. The way ahead was black, the only light coming from the occasional flash of the full, yellow moon, as gathering storm clouds occasionally parted, only to regroup soon after, denser and darker than before.

They were about halfway across the boggy green expanse when they saw it.

A vague luminescence.

A glowing ball in the long grass.

They watched it weave around, back and forth, rather aimlessly, until suddenly it stopped dead.

It had seen them.

"What is it?" whispered Anna.

It rose slowly, higher and higher, until it was sitting at the top of the grass-line, fixing the six of them within its sight. Then it came straight forward, moving at an unearthly speed.

"Is that... Is it a ghost?" said Aubrey. "What do we do?"

"That depends what kind of ghost it is," Candide replied, clear eyes assessing the strange apparition.

"It's my first ghost," Aubrey whispered.

Candide snatched up her hand. "Let's hope it's a good one."

It came, and it came, and it got brighter as it came. Then it halted, and they were each struck with the horrifying recognition of the head of a woman crouching down in the grass, staring up at them. Now still, her face was clear as day, as was the desperation in her eyes—a look of crazed despair written all over her. It was a look only seen on the living who have experienced the worst of humanity—who have lived through times of war and violence and extreme starvation. There came into her eyes a note of surprise, quickly followed by a note of pleasure, as though she couldn't quite believe her luck at finding these six people out in a lonely field in the middle of the night. Her slow smile revealed two long rows of sharp, black and yellow teeth glinting in the moonlight. She ascended slowly from the long grass.

"Oh, God," gasped Percy.

"It can't be," said Eve.

"It is," Candide confirmed.

As the thing rose up, beneath the frenzied face came a bare trachea, an oesophagus, the long, bloody, sinewy line reaching down to a stomach, intestines, all human organs attached along the way—heart, lungs, stomach, kidneys, spleen, liver—all hanging off that long, grotesque string. No limbs. No bones. No skin. All head and internal organs.

"Do we run or fight?" asked Joe.

"Percy, stay with me," Eve instructed. "Everyone else, run."

Anna gripped his hand that much tighter. "Eve, no."

Eve gently shifted Anna behind his back, keeping both eyes on the spirit. "You and Candide need to get Aubrey and Joe back safe. We need their help to save Michael. Go."

Percy pulled his lovely dagger forth. "Run along, Evelyn. I can take her."

Eve glanced over at Percy. "I won't."

Percy glanced over at Eve. "You should."

"I won't."

There was but the slightest acknowledgement of the sentiment between the two before Anna pulled her sharp fountain pen from her pocket and stepped back in front of Eve. "You don't even have a weapon, Eve."

By this time, Candide had dragged Aubrey and a protesting Joe halfway up the hill. The creature paid them no attention and weaved back and forth like a red, blue and brown, bulging, bloody snake, ascertaining which of her remaining prey would be the easiest meal. She began to circle. Anna and Percy protectively turned their backs to Eve, readying the two small weapons they had.

"Careful," said Percy. "She's starving, as you can see."

"She'll eat us?" asked Anna.

"If she can."

"How do we kill her?"

"Your guess is as good as mine."

Anna gripped her pen tight. "I'm going to cut her throat."

"Good girl," said Percy.

Hesitantly, Eve started, "I mean, she's..."

"What, Eve?" asked Anna.

"I just... Do we have to kill her?"

"What?"

"I think she's had a hard life," he explained, somewhere between endearing and infuriating. "And a hard death, too."

"She wants to eat you, Evelyn!" Percy snapped.

"I know, it's just—"

The thing lunged at Anna. It narrowly missed her as she stepped aside and slashed the creature's lung with the sharp pen, sending a spatter of blood over the three of them. The monster screeched an ungodly screech, and Percy moved in, slicing straight through her trachea, severing her head completely in one blow. It fell to the ground with a dull thud, accompanied by the sickening squishing sound of the wet mass of organs falling in a heap next to it.

Percy wiped his blade on his dark coat. "Well, that was easier than expected."

"Let's go," said Eve. "We'll come back and bury her when we have more weapons."

"I got weapons!" yelled Candide.

"Candide! We killed it! It was so easy!" called Anna.

"Nice one." She ran down the hill to them. "Was that the Krasue?"

Eve studied the gory heap on the ground. "How is that even possible? She's Indonesian."

"She's Thai," Percy corrected.

"Krasue are all through south-east Asia," Candide said. "My question was, how the hell did she get here?"

Percy stabbed his dagger into the cold ground and began digging a hole for the remains. "It's the book. When you get blood on it, it becomes... It's kind of a... Not quite a portal, but it attracts things, and confuses things. It makes things possible that shouldn't be possi—" A sharp scream escaped his glorious person. "What the fuck!"

As Percy thrashed about in the wet grass, they saw the head of the thing, its teeth digging into his arm, the entrails, now reattached to the head, curling about Percy's legs and neck, squeezing and strangling him.

Candide took one fast and controlled step forward, pressed her boot down on the Krasue's trachea, and stabbed it clean through the heart with a kitchen knife. It relaxed its hold in an instant, falling flaccid to the ground.

"Ow! Fuck! Fuck, that hurt!" Percy yelled.

Eve pulled off his scarf and commenced wrapping it into a tight tourniquet around Percy's arm.

Anna watched on helplessly. "Eve, not your scarf."

"It's fine. Blood won't show on navy."

"I suppose that's true. But you should soak it when we get back, just in case."

Percy only glared at the two of them, unusually for him, refraining from saying whatever he was thinking.

Candide collected her bloody kitchen knife. "Leave the body. Or… All those bits of her. We'll bury her when the sun comes up."

Eve, having finished his first aid, turned away, and Anna asked Percy, "You're not going to turn into a Krasue now, are you?"

"No, that's just zombies," Percy replied through gritted teeth.

"Actually no," Candide interjected. "If the Krasue bites a woman, she could become one."

"Well, shit," Anna replied.

"Sorry. I didn't think to mention it until now." Candide gave a little laugh. "She probably would have just eaten you, anyway."

"That's good to know…" Anna frowned. "I guess…"

They arrived back at the apartment to find it deserted. The hanging door was hanging open, and the bricks had been removed from the wall.

Candide clapped her hands together in delight. "My girlfriend is such a sexy go-getter."

"She is," Percy agreed. "But also, bandages?"

Candide gave a nod at the red liquid seeping between his fingers, that were pressed down hard on the bite. "Don't worry, we have all those things now. Do you want drugs too?"

He gave a half smile. "Not just yet. Maybe later."

Candide took Percy to the kitchen to gather the necessary supplies, while Eve and Anna made their way downstairs.

A surprising scene greeted them, Aubrey leaning close over Michael, surveying him with the cool eye of a scientist, despite his snarling lips and her inexperience. Joe wandering back and forth on the far side of them, one arm crossed, a hand at his chin, apparently thinking hard, but just as fearless and interested as Aubrey now seemed to be.

"How is he?" Eve asked.

Aubrey ignored the question, offering a cold, "Where's Candide?"

Anna heard the soft, tolerant breath Eve let out. "Upstairs." He redirected. "Joe, how is he?"

Anna thought Joe smiled a little more than necessary to see that Eve had returned, and he happily relayed what he had learned. "It's amazing he's alive at all. It makes no sense. Remember when you got me in the back of the head with the Necronomicon?"

Eve grinned, an old tension slipping from him with Joe's good humour. "It was a good shot, wasn't it?"

"It was," Joe laughed. "But it should have killed me. The powers these demons have are incredible. Aubrey, do you want to tell him?"

She didn't even look up, red lips enunciating a firm, "Nope."

Whether Joe knew what was going on between them or not, he happily jumped in to fill the void. "So, Aubrey says she's going to slice the skin open above his vein to get a needle in, because it's too small and dehydrated to put it in the usual way. Is that right?"

Aubrey gave a slight nod. "Mmhmm."

"Then we use a drip for a few days. Then we start with food through the nose."

"Mmm."

"But he might die if the nutrients are too much?"

Joe looked to her for confirmation, and she offered him an encouraging glance. "Yes."

He looked back at Eve, pleased. "So we have to be very careful about our mixtures and how much he absorbs."

"And how long will this take?" asked Anna.

"Weeks," said Joe.

"Weeks!" Anna repeated.

Aubrey took up the explanation as Candide and Percy came downstairs. "For the first forty-eight hours, we'll have to watch him for refeeding syndrome. He might die from the shock of the nutrients entering his system again. If we make it through that, we'll start feeding him through his nose. And I mean, the smallest amount of liquid dripping into his stomach each day. Then we up it, very, *very* slowly, and eventually, hopefully, we'll make it to normal food, blended up. Maybe through a feeding tube in his mouth until we get him exorcised."

"All right." Percy smiled approvingly. "What do you need first?"

"I'll want good light, a few scalpels, needles, tubes, a drip bag and a stand, and…" She looked around the cold, sparse, dusty, dark space, looked over Michael who sat silently all the while, staring, waiting, listening, smiling an evil smile. "I'm going to have to get this myself, aren't I? But there's too much." Sliding her hands into her pockets, she asked, "Who's coming with me? We should leave soon."

"Uh…" Percy's tone was enough to draw everyone's concern, and the way he screwed his face up regretfully was enough to flip their stomachs. "Maybe not just now."

"Why not now?" came Aubrey's sharp words.

He took a deep breath. "Aubrey, I'm sorry to have to tell you this, but you can't leave here."

Aubrey shook her head, slowly and with menace. "Don't you dare try to pull that shit on me again."

"No, it's not that," he replied, calm and collected as ever. "It's something new. Everyone, back upstairs. We have something very important to discuss."

CHAPTER 26
GHOST STORY

"Drinks? Really?"

"Just for nerves, Aubrey, sit down." Percy accepted the glass of whisky that Anna handed to him with a warm wink of thanks that she pretended she hadn't noticed. "Now, that ghost we saw outside. It was the Krasue, which means she came a very long way to be here."

"Is it important how far she's come?" Joe leaned back in the opposite armchair with his own whisky, which Anna had placed near him as unobtrusively as possible before settling back onto the couch between Eve and Candide, Eve and Aubrey having been deliberately placed at opposite ends, out of one another's sight. Happily for the time being, all attention was on Percy.

"It's important because other, closer things should have gotten here first." Percy's finger pointed to the wall over Joe's shoulder. "That ghost sigil there is blocking them."

Aubrey's bright eyes studied the blood-red markings. "But that's good, isn't it?"

"Yes and no," replied Percy. "When you're in this room, you're protected from ghosts of all kinds, and that is good. Unfortunately, that means we've all missed the warning signs of what's coming."

"What is coming?" asked Anna.

"A lot of unpleasantness."

"Unpleasantness?"

"Unpleasantness."

"Percy, I have a sinking feeling right now," said Aubrey. "Please tell me what you're trying to say."

"I'm saying that leaving this room right now could mean certain death for any of us." A general gasp and swilling of drinks occurred before Percy continued, "There should be— there *must* be—dozens of things just outside that door, waiting to have their way with all of us. In fact, we probably shouldn't have the hanging door open right now, because something terrible could come through any second."

"I need to get back," said Joe, ignoring the comment about the door and glaring at Anna. "I can't stay here. For how long?"

"I don't know," Percy replied, letting his gaze wander unguardedly over Joe's well-built chest, the tight grey sweater barely concealing a single contour of muscle. "Perhaps if we stayed in groups… I could accompany you home?"

"No," Eve said sharply. To the various raised eyebrows and frowns he received, he added, "Percy stays where I can see him."

Percy rolled his eyes and returned to the main conversation on a drawn-out breath of boredom. "Has anyone seen anything else we should know about? Anything supernatural we might need to kill before we get on with things here?"

"The thing in the bathroom!" Anna recalled in some excitement. "I'm sure that wasn't there before."

"There's a thing in the bathroom?" Eve asked. "Bathroom ghosts are nasty."

"What did it look like?" asked Percy.

"I didn't get much of a look at it," she explained. "It was human-like, wearing a red robe. But not like a bathrobe. Something nicer than that—a nicer fabric. And its hand was red too."

"Ah, well, you're in trouble now, if it's who I'm thinking of," said Percy. "He should be in Japan."

"Who?" asked Anna.

"Aka Manto," the gorgeous lips announced. "It might be all right if no one talks to him. In fact, don't even acknowledge his presence. Just leave immediately if he's there. I can't guarantee he won't still kill you on the way out, but that's usually how people survive an encounter."

"But that's where the showers are." Candide complained in a way that made her sound exactly like someone who'd had far too many encounters with the supernatural to feel the gravity most people would feel when faced with such circumstances.

Percy nodded his appreciation of the situation. "Showers should be fine. Just don't use the toilet, and whatever you do, don't accept his offer of toilet paper. But look, he's in there and you can still shower and that's fine. More importantly, Anna, did you see his face?"

"No, I didn't. Just his hand and his robe."

"Ah." A little cloud drifted over Percy's face, until he resolved, "Let's not do anything about Aka Manto until I've investigated."

"Why? Is he very dangerous?" Anna, already on the edge of her seat, was very clearly hanging on Percy's every word, and he was very clearly enjoying every second of it.

"Yes, but I want to get a look under his mask. He's said to be very handsome." Percy smiled knowingly at Anna. "*Very* handsome."

"Handsome?" Anna's eyes lit up.

Eve laughed. "Ghosts now, Anna?"

She laughed in return, though she coloured a little with it. "I'm just curious."

A derisive "Ha!" escaped Joe, who, when he caught Eve's confusion and Candide's warning look, coughed loudly and said, "Sorry. It was the wine." Then, looking at Anna, who had shrunk down deeper into the lounge beside Eve, he said, "It was just a little hard to swallow."

"That's not good, Joe," Percy replied tightly, smiling all the while. "You'll have to learn to be more careful in the future. As I was saying… Well…" And his eyes slid straight back to Anna. "Would you like to hear a ghost story?"

"Yes!" Anna cried, speaking enthusiastically enough to represent the entire group.

"All right." Percy waved an authoritative hand, pointing at his audience as he apportioned tasks. "Lights out. Get the candles. More whisky. Let's do this properly."

"But the unpleasantness—" Aubrey started.

"Just close the hanging door," he directed. "It won't take a minute."

They did as instructed, and were soon reassembled around the coffee table, lit only by the light of a candle, and the full moon occasionally shining through the window. A cosy patter of rain fell on the roof, while a harrowing wind tapped the fingers of the ash tree against the glass. Percy lit a cigarette and leaned back in his chair handsomely with his whisky.

"Aka Manto literally translates to—"

"Red cloak," Anna whispered, already utterly enthralled.

"Yes, very good, but don't interrupt." Percy recommenced, "Aka Manto is said to have been an incredibly beautiful young man who often wore a distinctive red cloak, or kimono if you go back far enough, hence the name. And when I say he was beautiful, I mean gloriously beautiful. The kind of beauty that would drive a person insane. In fact," he paused for dramatic effect, "to an extent, that's exactly what happened."

"Literally insane?" Eve asked.

A plume of smoke twisted up into the darkness above Percy's elegant hand. "Have you ever heard of... Stendhal Syndrome?"

"Temporary insanity caused by overwhelming beauty?" Eve replied. "Of course." Then he added, "It happens every time I look at Anna."

She giggled ridiculously and leaned into the arm he happily threw around her.

Percy slightly narrowed his eyes at Eve, but continued in the same low tone, regardless. "Fast-beating heart, dizziness, loss of reality, uncontrollably strong emotions, even hallucinations.

Stendhal experienced it himself while visiting the Basilica of Santa Croce in Florence. It is for this reason that people attack the statue of David every year, driven mad by his aesthetic perfection. Aka Manto was that kind of beautiful."

The tip of Percy's cigarette flashed red as he drew deep, watching his audience to see they were all appropriately captivated before he continued. "Aka Manto became so admired that he could no longer leave his house without being followed. He was accosted everywhere he went. Girls (boys too, I'm sure, but the legend states girls) chased him and hounded him to depression, exhaustion, complete and utter wretchedness. He took to wearing a mask everywhere he went in order to hide his lovely face, but to no avail. They knew. They all wanted him. They pursued him relentlessly, until one day, the young man was so overcome with it all, he went to hide where no one could find him. He hid in the girls' school bathroom, fourth stall, and there he died."

Anna gasped. "How?"

"No one knows. What we do know is that now Aka Manto always haunts the fourth stall in whichever bathroom he inhabits. Even so, I wouldn't be game to try one of the others if I knew he might be in there at all."

"What makes him so dangerous?" Candide stage-whispered.

"I'm glad you asked." Percy smiled. "Aka Manto is an angry, vengeful spirit. He doesn't want to be bothered by anyone now, and if you use his toilet stall, he will make sure you regret it."

Anna grinned over at Candide with excitement. Despite everything, the love of ghost stories that had always drawn them together had never abated, and Candide felt the pull of their warm friendship just as strongly as Anna in that moment.

"If someone knows no better, and they use the fourth stall," Percy went on, "when they have finished doing what they need to do, and they reach for the toilet paper... it will disappear... Then, they hear a shuffling... They hear the sound of Aka Manto's red cape sliding over the floor as he approaches... Then he asks... 'Will you choose the red toilet paper? Or will you choose the blue toilet paper?'"

"Sounds helpful enough," said Candide.

"Yes," Percy replied, "if you want to die horribly. The manner of death changes depending where the legend comes from, but one thing they all have in common is that the colour of paper you choose determines how you meet your end. If you choose the red toilet paper, you will become red. He may simply stab you repeatedly until you're covered in your own blood. He may chop you into little pieces, or, my personal favourite, he may flay you alive and make you wear your own skin as... a red cape."

They all gasped.

"If you choose the blue toilet paper, naturally you become blue. He may strangle you, or you may be exsanguinated, though how he gets all that blood out is beyond my under-standing. It is even said that he may flay you, as in the red method, then strangle you with your own skin."

"How is that even possible?" said Anna.

"There are more things in heaven and Earth, Anna," Percy nodded sagely.

Joe, impressing everyone, but especially Percy, with his game nonchalance, asked, "So, what if I just choose a different colour?"

"I don't know about other colours," Percy replied, "but never choose yellow."

"What happens if I choose yellow?"

"Well… that way leads to being drowned. In the toilet. In your, uh, leavings."

"Awful!" Anna whispered. "I'd just take the red and have done with it."

"I feel like blue would give you more of a fighting chance," Candide suggested.

"Good point," Anna agreed. Then, speaking to Percy again, "What if I tell him I don't want any toilet paper and to go away?"

"Then it gets worse again," said Percy. "He'll drag you straight to Hell."

"Hell!"

"Indeed. Then you're damned, and it's very hard to come back from being damned. Never try to outsmart Aka Manto. The only correct thing to do is to run. If you see him, if you hear him, just run."

"And he's in the bathroom down the hall?" Aubrey asked.

"Apparently so," Percy replied.

"And you want us to just leave him there?"

"Yes."

"Because you want to see his pretty face?"

"Yes."

"And he's very dangerous and might kill anyone who uses the toilet?"

"Yes."

"So maybe… we should kill him?"

Percy let out an amused chuckle. "Aubrey, do you know how to kill Aka Manto?"

"No." She blushed. "Don't you?"

"I don't know if it's even possible to kill Aka Manto."

"So you want to do nothing?"

"Just for now."

"Can we put an 'out of order' sign on the door or something?"

"Yes. Everyone, Aubrey's in charge of organising a sign for the bathroom door." Aubrey scowled at Percy, who carried on unheeding. "When we get through this, we'll see what we can do about helping Aka Manto move on. He's a complicated case, because no one knows who he was before he died. If he's not haunting the area because his bones have been misplaced, then it's a trauma haunting, and that complicates things even more because he's possibly not thinking clearly."

"Hence the evisceration and exsanguination," Candide threw in.

"Precisely," said Percy.

"He sounds so incredibly lonely." Eve's voice was quiet and low, the earnest tenor at complete odds with Percy's compelling ghost-story narration. His hand on his whisky glass shuffled the ice around abstractedly. "Imagine dying all alone in a bathroom like that. As what? A teenager? And even after death, he's so scared he won't let anyone near him."

"Eve, he kills innocent people who are just trying to use the toilet," Candide said. "Please don't try to make friends with him."

"No, I just mean… It's so sad." Eve's brow contracted into the usual worried lines, and he stared hard at the coffee table, reflecting. "People were so obsessed with him that they drove him to his death, but now no one even remembers who he was. It's that… There's something very desolate about that. They killed him because they wanted him so badly, but he was nothing at all to them in the end. What does that say about human nature? It's terrible to think about."

Anna reached out a finger, which she gently ran over Eve's troubled forehead, silently smoothing the lines away, to which he reacted with a beautiful smile, caught her hand and kissed her fingertips.

Percy watched Eve curiously, then said softly, "That's the end of the ghost story. Lights on. Has anyone seen anything else?"

"Just the Krasue and the giant spiders," Candide said.

"Giant ones?" asked Aubrey.

"Yeah," nodded Candide. "I think they qualify as 'giant'."

"Okay. Giant spiders, the Krasue and Aka Manto," Aubrey said. "Oh, and a possessed kid downstairs. Got it. And we all might die if we go outside. No problem." Her whisky was placed on the table with a clank. "Now about our supplies…"

CHAPTER 27

FORCED PROXIMITY

"We'll get the supplies tomorrow," Percy said. "It's easier to fight in daylight. It will still be dangerous and we'll need a group, so we can all go as one or we can split into two. Obviously, it would be the height of stupidity for anyone to go to the med lab alone with something hunting them." Candide and Percy looked at Anna, who flushed and looked at Joe, who looked from her to Eve, and they all looked around the room and said nothing.

Aubrey broke the strained silence. "So until tomorrow, we're all stuck here together." She sent an irrepressible side-eye down to Eve, who was twirling Anna's hair in his fingers, before she turned her head to address Candide quietly. "I'm not really comfortable with… everything. I'm doing my best, but I don't want to spend the night here."

"Aubrey…" Candide let out a long sigh. "It's not that big a deal. I'm sorry, but you're just going to have to get over it."

Eve, realising he was making Aubrey uncomfortable, attempted to remove his fingers from Anna's hair, but he found one was quite trapped, at which point he was forced to wrap his other arm around her to try to disentangle himself, his embarrassment and anxiety growing by the second as Anna complained loudly and poked him in retaliation.

"It's understandable," Percy put in, tilting his head towards Anna. "They are nauseating."

Joe only raised a vague eyebrow in agreement.

"Anyway," Anna attempted to redirect while smoothing her hair back down, "we have class in the morning, so we can't help you get the supplies. Eve, it's your tutorial."

"Oh. Gothic lit." His face quickly changed from happy to not-so-happy. "Oh… That's the four of us all together again." He looked apologetically at Aubrey, who only glared down at the coffee table, her lips in a tight line, her brow contracted, looking like she was trying to decide whether she should say what she was thinking.

"Then that's perfect." Percy switched his crossed legs over and leaned his handsome head against the back of his great armchair to enjoy the view opposite. "Joe and I will get supplies, just the two of us, and we'll all meet back here afterwards to get to work."

None of them had time to react to Percy's grin and Joe's pink cheeks because Aubrey's head snapped across to Eve and she said, "Meanwhile, you can get the code for the med lab first thing. Then you can carry on your secret affair with your first-year student until class."

Candide gasped. "Aubrey!"

Anna felt the heat rise within her, her immediate instinct being to defend Eve, to defend herself, to revert to the least mature and most vicious version of herself, and set Aubrey straight in no uncertain terms. But by chance, before she could do so, she happened to glance at Candide.

Candide, whose hand was already massaging her temple, her eyes closed, bracing. And Anna loved Candide. She loved her truly and deeply and therefore, in a rare show of self-restraint, Anna silently made for the kitchen.

She climbed onto the bench, kicked open the window, sat on the edge of the sink, and lit a cigarette, and she was soon rewarded for such (in her mind) equanimous behaviour when, seconds later, Percy was by her side.

Having already topped up her whisky glass, he snatched the cigarette out of her hand to light his own and whispered, "What a bitch."

"Eve would be so annoyed with you for saying that," she whispered back, trying hard not to laugh at his astute observation.

Percy, as usual, made no attempt to conceal his enjoyment. "Would he, though?"

Aubrey had barely noticed Anna leaving. She certainly hadn't paid any attention to Percy. Aubrey was, very clearly, at the end of her tether, and her business-like tone and her back like a plank made it clear to what remained of the group that she meant to have it all out right then and there. "Candide," she began, "I'm not trying to cause trouble, but I do want you to see this from my perspective."

Candide pushed her hair back, leaned forward a little, took up her whisky, and waited with averted eyes and tense silence for Aubrey to lay it all out.

Aubrey looked between Eve and Candide, and said, "About six hours ago, Percy turned up at my door and told me someone was badly hurt, and that you had told him to get me."

"The bastard!" Candide spat.

Eve nodded in hearty agreement.

"Perhaps," said Aubrey, "but I didn't stop and say, 'Who the fuck is this Percy guy and how does he know where I live?' I came straight away because I thought you needed me."

"Thank you," Candide mumbled.

"I would do it again." Aubrey smiled, briefly, then let her face drop back to serious. "Then I discovered this kid, who's apparently been missing and possessed for twenty-four years. 'Okay,' I said to myself. 'I can do this. He's right there in front of me, clearly possessed. These people need my help. I can do this'."

"Thank you," Candide repeated, thickly.

"Stop saying thank you."

"Okay."

Aubrey shifted a little so by then she was side on, facing Eve, and would have been facing Candide if she wasn't still slumped forward like a child about to be grounded. Aubrey continued, "Then apparently, my girlfriend is some sort of demon hunter. Okay, fine. That explains a lot. It turns out ghosts are real, which is also fine, because I grew up in boarding houses, so I always kind of suspected that, anyway." She paused for dramatic effect, which worked, because both Eve and Candide looked over nervously. "But do you know what's not fine?"

Joe soon arrived in the kitchen. Percy shuffled swiftly back from Anna, passed him a cigarette, and he too hopped up on the bench, and sat pensively smoking and drinking and eavesdropping with the others.

"I think I know what's not fine," Candide murmured, deliberately not looking at Eve, whose knee had begun its recurrent tapping.

Aubrey nodded towards him. "Does he know what happened last year?"

"Yeah," Candide whispered. "He knows everything."

"Ah, okay. So he knows how that professor took advantage of you? Her *first-year student*?"

"Yes," Candide blushed, "but—"

"And does he know what a mess you were after that?"

"He does."

"And does he know I was there to pick up the pieces?"

"Well, not all the details…"

"Does he know how I let you cry on my shoulder for months, made you meals, took you out and got you back in the swing of things?"

"Not really all that…"

"And does he know that even after all that, you still threw me over for Jason fucking Carter?"

Candide's hands, plastered over her red face, muffled her reply. "Yeah, he kind of knows a bit about that…"

"And does he know," Aubrey went on sharply, "that I forgave you for that because I knew how hurt and messed up you were by all the things that professor said and did after she took advantage of you, her *first-year student*?"

"Yes," Candide winced. "Maybe."

"Then please," Aubrey concluded, with some volume behind her voice, "can someone explain to me why, after having watched you go through that—having gone through that *with* you—I should be sitting here, allowing the same thing to happen to Anna? Why you, Candide, think this is okay after the year you just had?"

Candide sat up and took a deep breath. "Yes," she said. "I can do that." She took Eve's hand in hers, unwilling as it was, but she scrunched it remorselessly, and met Aubrey's fiery gaze. "First, Eve is nice. Second, he's in love with Anna. Properly. Really in love. Third, that woman was twenty years older than me, and she was a bitch."

This succinct delivery had the effect of softening the sharp line of Aubrey's mouth. Just a little. "Eve," she said, leaning to the right to see past a now bolt-upright and defensive Candide. "I should tell you that while I didn't want to like you, despite everything, I think you're probably a good person. I do. I think Anna's a nice girl, and I can see how much you like each other. And I know, this is Endymion College, where for some reason the staff and the students are all bizarrely attractive—"

"It's odd, isn't it?" said Candide.

"It's a bit odd," said Aubrey. She shrugged her shoulders. "Anyway, the point is, I can see how this might have happened between you two. But surely you, Eve, of all people, as a member of staff, and as Candide's best friend, surely you can see the possibilities for the fallout here."

Eve, jammed apprehensively into the corner of the lounge until then, turned himself towards Aubrey. "I can, and I do. It's…" He coloured, and made a nervous laugh in the back of his throat. "This is going to sound weird coming from me, but I'm really not okay with teachers dating students."

Aubrey's head dropped a bit further to the side, displaying her full incredulity.

Eve hastened to add, "I know that's not what it looks like, but... Anna's—with us it's—it's an unusual situation."

Aubrey watched him with patient, if doubtful, eyes. "Illuminate me."

"Anna is..." Eve stopped in his tracks. What to say about Anna? The strange way they met, the times they almost died together, their fast and bizarre connection, her having been hand-picked by an evil brother for the express purpose of Eve falling in love with her. The slight sinking feeling that came with acknowledging that Percy somehow knew him well enough to present perhaps the one and only person who could have smashed straight through so many of his barriers to make him utterly devoted to her in a matter of days...

"Well," Candide said thoughtfully to fill the silence, "Anna does have her weird academia fetish thing."

Eve frowned, and in the kitchen Anna shrugged noncommittally to the looks she received.

Aubrey said, "Eve, I'm going to tell you how this appears to me, and I want you to consider it, and tell me why I'm wrong."

"Okay." Eve nodded, happy to have some help to crystallise his thoughts.

"Maybe you don't realise the kind of reputation Anna could end up with over this. Do you know what they still say about Candide?"

Eve nodded again, but slowly and with a regretful glance at Candide.

Aubrey continued, "If you decide to quit, you'll just move on to another job. You're already a professor, but she's just starting out, and you know how vicious academics are. What's Anna going to do when you move on to greener pastures and no one around here will talk to her because she has the reputation of a woman who exchanges sex to get ahead? What happens when no one will take her seriously, and she has years left here of being treated like a slut?"

"Slut!" Eve cried.

"I know it's not a nice word, but that's what people will say. Reputation is everything. Especially for a woman. We all want to think we're living in some golden age where something like this doesn't matter, but that's just not true. One wrong word in the old boy's club that she's the disposable sort, and she's out."

Eve paled slightly.

Candide knew he would be remembering the private boys' school he was sent to, that he hated passionately. That he would be remembering the boys' deportment classes. That he would be thinking of all those masculine clubs and sporting pursuits he was relentlessly pushed into all his life that made him sick to his stomach.

Aubrey, taking in his reaction to her words, pushed on gently. "The point is, Anna has nothing to go back to after this. And if you blow this for her and leave her in the dust, then what?"

Eve's words were firm and immediate. "I'm not going to do that."

"You might truly believe that, but what I see is a rich man in a superior position, with all the power and privilege in that relationship, and a vulnerable girl putting her future on the line."

"Vulnerable?" Eve asked. He looked sharply down at Candide, wondering what she had told Aubrey, but Candide sat perfectly still and refused to make eye contact with either of them.

Aubrey covered the discord smoothly. "Even without those considerations, do you ever think about what you're asking of her, expecting her to sneak around like this? Having to keep your secret? Can you imagine the weight of this on her all the time?"

"First of all," Eve replied, a touch of anger in his voice for the first time since the conversation started, "Anna's not 'vulnerable'. I don't know where you got that idea, but she's probably the least vulnerable person I've ever met in my entire life. Second," he quickly went on before Aubrey could disagree, "I know you're right about everything else. You're absolutely right. I've been living in—in a fantasy this whole time, where I just let this relationship happen, but you're right. It was totally irresponsible. What I did was wrong. And…" He paused for a moment, rubbed his furrowed brow, then sighed heavily. "I shouldn't have let any of this happen, but I did, so… I'm going to have to fix it. And I'll do that. I'll do it tonight, in fact."

"You're going to fix it?" Aubrey's voice came barely audible in disbelief at his quick and firm decision. "Right now?"

"Yeah. I'll go talk to Anna, and I think…" He glanced warily towards the kitchen. "I know she's going to be upset with me when I tell her… Really upset… But it's for the best. She'll see that. Eventually. I hope…"

Anna looked at Percy in alarm while Percy shook his head in disgust.

Joe turned his face away from them both, hiding a smile behind the joyful puff of a cigarette.

The next voice they heard was Candide's. "Eve, no."

"I have to do the right thing," he said, perfectly resolute, though clearly anxious, now playing distractedly with Candide's fingers while his face suggested that every passing second was strengthening his new conviction.

Aubrey sat forward again and took up her whisky with a resigned shrug. "Okay, well, I'm kind of surprised you got there so fast, but if you think that's the right thing to do..." She also sighed, then she paused and looked at Eve sympathetically. "I am sorry. I hate to be the person responsible for breaking you two up—"

Eve's gaze shot over to her, her words having pulled him directly out of his reverie. "What? Oh no, I'm not going to break up with Anna."

"What? Isn't that what..." she blustered. "Didn't you just say all that stuff? Like you understood?"

"No, I do. I understand completely. I know I should never have started this relationship, and if word gets out, all I think about is what that would mean for Anna. Endymion College is every-thing to her and..." Having started his rambling, worried answer, the floodgates opened, and Candide only rested her head on his shoulder as he let go all the thoughts that had been clouding his mind for so long. "Every day I seem to put her in mortal danger just by dating her... Do you have any idea what I would give to be a normal person so I could be with my normal girlfriend and just be happy? And I—I don't know— take her out to dinner or something? But I can't. I exorcise demons with her and we change the dressings on each other's injuries and we run away from ghosts. What the hell kind of boyfriend is that? But I'm so hopelessly in love with her, Aubrey, and I can't leave her, not ever again, and I know that makes me so, so selfish. I almost wish she would leave me sometimes, but I—she's just—" He flicked a hand up in the hope that would bring clarity, but he soon groaned at having no idea what was the right thing to say, so he said, "I love her more than life itself and I can't be without her. I can't. And I'm an awful human and I know that, but I can't and I won't."

Candide, touched, smiled up at him, but Aubrey remained unmoved. "Okay. But it's been how long you've been 'in love' with your student?"

"Three months."

"Three months and you're calling it love?" Aubrey shook her head. "You're as bad as she is."

"Aubrey, believe me, I know… I wish I could explain it to you, how this all happened…" Aubrey watched Eve, waiting, as he studied the strange, Spanish chandelier hanging over them for some time, then he brought his lovely, clear grey eyes down to meet hers, leaned forward and spoke softly, so softly that all those in the kitchen had to strain very hard indeed to hear. "Aubrey, did you ever think you were going to die? Or that someone you love was going to die? And I mean, as in, you watched them being killed right in front of your eyes and you didn't see a way out and you were one-hundred percent sure that person was going to be ripped away from you forever?"

Aubrey turned pale, and a chill went down her spine. Eve thought she looked as though she did indeed understand, but she said, "No. No, I have never experienced that."

"Imagine you had experienced that. Dozens of times. Imagine the person you love most in the world has only just managed to dodge death over and over, and you truly believe you are both cursed. And that one and only person you love—you are convinced one of you will watch the other die any day. Any day. And you hold on to them with both hands, and you never really let anyone else in, because you can't. Because it hurts too much and you can't risk that special person by letting your guard down for a moment. Can you imagine that?"

Aubrey looked at Candide, whose arm had linked through Eve's while he spoke, tears forming in her eyes as she watched his expression carefully. She saw the way he held her hand tight now, much tighter than before. She nodded for him to go on.

"And then imagine someone turns up out of nowhere, like magic, and she takes all that away. An entire lifetime of sadness and loneliness and desperation… She takes all the horrible things you've ever known, and she just destroys them. And for the first time in my entire life, Aubrey, I have found someone I don't have to worry about. I don't have to protect her because she is stronger and smarter than me, and… and she makes me feel safe. And I love her for that. But not just for that. For a thousand reasons. She's brilliant, and she's funny, and she's insightful, and she's possibly slightly unhinged, which is nice, for me. And I know she's completely out of my league, but for some reason, she loves me back. I have nothing worthwhile to offer her, nothing but bullshit, but every day she comes to see me, and she tells me she loves me, and she's just… She's so lovely."

He blinked his hazy eyes, before speaking quieter still. "I know how I must seem to you, but please know, I am aware of everything Anna must be dealing with, and I feel terrible about that. Really, every second we're apart I feel terrible… But I never feel terrible when I'm with her. She makes me feel amazing. And I love her. I think she's the best thing that's ever happened to me. So that's why I'm going to quit Endymion College."

"What!" Aubrey cried.

"You will not!" Candide snapped.

"Get back in the sink," Percy hissed.

"I'm going to quit," Eve said proudly. "I'll get a place in the village and we'll just be a normal couple. We'll read books and... and stuff. Maybe one day she'll come live with me and she can come here and do her thing and I'll just clean her house and write books or something. I don't even know what normal couples do, but it's fine by me. And people will forget I was ever here and... and maybe one day there won't be ghosts and she can just be brilliant all by herself, without me getting in her way."

"Eve, Anna wouldn't want you to do that," Candide said. "I don't want you to do that. Don't ever think about anything like that."

"I think it's the right thing to do," he replied. "I already put her through so much over this stupid job."

"You love your job."

"I love Anna more." He turned his attention back to Aubrey. "Listen, I know this has been a weird and terrible start to... everything, but what I have with Anna doesn't need to interfere with what you have with Candide. I'm sorry you're in this shitty situation. This is so much for a person to handle and you've been amazing. I honestly don't know how you're coping so well. What you're doing for Michael—for all of us... I can never thank you enough for that. And I don't want to make any of this harder for you, so I'm going to stay out of your way from now on. I'm going to quit my job, and I'm going to make sure none of those things you mentioned ever happen to Anna. I know you're just trying to look out for her because you're a good person."

Aubrey sat in stunned silence, about a billion conflicting emotions boiling up inside, before she blurted it all out with a tearful, "I don't want you to quit! And I don't want you to break up with Anna. Don't. Don't do anything. Now I wish I'd never said anything."

Eve's beautiful grin, that very few people found themselves able to resist, broke out in full with earnest thanks. "No, I'm really happy you said all of it. This job—it's making me miserable, it's making Anna miserable—"

"It's not making me miserable!" Anna yelled from the kitchen.

"Stop eavesdropping!" he yelled back.

"Okay!" she called.

"And it's making Candide miserable now, too." Had Aubrey not already been thoroughly won over, the way he looked down at Candide at that moment was enough. Aubrey was mortified. Eve never would have wanted her to feel that way, but in his genuine and open response, she instantly saw in him exactly what Candide, Anna and (it seemed) Joe all saw in him, and she was appalled it had taken her so long.

Candide's response, however, paused the next apology on her lips. "Don't quit, Eve."

It was clear from the peace in his eyes that her words would have little to no effect. "It has to be one of those things, either quitting or leaving Anna. And it would probably take Lucifer himself to tear me away from her at this point." He laughed gently. "And even then, I think she'd be likely to come out on top."

"I agree with Candide," Aubrey said, encouraged and relieved by the smile she got from her girlfriend, who leaned over and refilled their drinks. "And I'm just going to say this, even if I shouldn't, but you know that's very unhealthy behaviour, don't you? Throwing away your career like that?"

"A lot of childhood trauma will do that to a person," Eve half-joked. "Seriously, if I die next year, or next month—or who knows, maybe even this week—I would rather have had that time with Anna. Out in the open. Just like normal people."

Aubrey's voice was soft now, a little shy even, as she leaned back, Candide studying her with an odd smile. "Surely you have dreams and goals of your own, don't you?"

"I want to not die," Eve said. His soft smile remained, but his eyes were suddenly very serious and very sad. "I want to read books and not die and be with the two people I love. That's all my ambition in life, which is a significant step up from what it was before I met Anna."

His honest, dark words brought such a tension over the small group that Candide felt compelled to quell it with a gentle jab to his ribs. "I'll quit if you quit."

She received a scoff. "You won't quit."

"I will, just to spite you. And Anna's more spiteful than me. Do you think she'd let you do that?"

Again, he glanced towards the kitchen, only with a whole lot of longing in his eyes. "I'll talk to Anna."

"She'll talk to you, more like."

Eve laughed. "Maybe I'll see out the term and we'll go from there. But right now I'm going to go smoke cigarettes and drink whisky with my beautiful girlfriend. You want to come?"

"Yes. In a minute." Candide looked over at Aubrey as Eve left for the kitchen.

"I'm so embarrassed I could die," Aubrey said as soon as Eve was out of earshot, she thought. "I was wrong and I'm sorry and…" She closed her eyes and scrunched her face up, as though that would change any of it.

"Come here," Candide said.

Aubrey, resigned to her embarrassment, sunk a little deeper into the space beside Candide. "Sorry."

"Don't be. And don't worry. Everything he said about Anna is true, if slightly exaggerated. She's a force of nature. There's no way she'll let him do that."

Aubrey caught her eye. "I don't just mean that."

"I know." Candide took Aubrey's hand and studied her fingers for a few moments before saying, "I'm sorry I made things so hard for you last year."

Aubrey only watched Candide's fingers, entwined with her own.

"It was a bad time."

"I know."

"And it's over. And you're part of why it's over." Candide pulled her knees up onto the couch and curled towards Aubrey. "Today's been intense."

Aubrey laughed. "Yep. This is probably the strangest day of my entire life."

"Are we still good?" said Candide.

"Yes." Aubrey smiled. "Yes, we are."

"Well, that's good because," Candide kissed Aubrey's lips, "I think I like you more than ever." Candide kissed Aubrey's cheek. "I wouldn't want you to be the kind of person who said nothing in a situation like that." Candide kissed Aubrey's neck. "And I don't want you to change. Not a bit."

Aubrey started to reply, but her speech was thwarted by Candide's kiss on her lips, long and soft and sweet.

When they finally made their way into the kitchen, some time and many affirmations and apologies later, it was just in time to see Anna sit back tall and straight from the firm speech she had given Eve. His only response was to lift her out of the sink and pull her in tight, as though he hadn't seen her in years. "I'm so glad you wrote that essay," he said.

Anna replied lightly, "And that whole time I thought it was true love. It was just Keats."

"It's the same thing," Eve said.

Quite sure it was the most romantic thing any man had ever said, Anna, who was already full to bursting with her love for Eve that night, kissed him with all her heart.

Percy huffed and turned his back on the pair of them, which he'd been intending to do for some time anyway, what with Joe being so nice to look at, and Joe was happy enough to have his attention, what with Anna being all around so nauseating.

Candide evidently agreed, though with a little more humour, moaning at the sight of them, "Oh my god."

"And they've always been this bad?" laughed Aubrey.

"Always. Since the minute they met. It's awful."

"Once the Keats gets in…" said Aubrey.

"It's been months I've been putting up with them and—wait. You know your Keats?"

"I mean…" Aubrey blushed. "Just the basics. Nightingale, Autumn, Grecian Urn, all that."

"Oh, I had no idea. That's really… That's very romantic. You know so many things." Candide fluttered her long lashes and slipped a finger between the buttons of Aubrey's blouse to pull her a little closer. "You're really clever, Aubrey."

"Thanks, Candide. So are you."

As Aubrey looked at Candide's beautiful, happy face, and as she placed a gentle hand under her lovely chin, and as she pulled her in close to kiss her exquisite lips, Aubrey decided she was almost definitely going to be okay with Eve and Anna's romance after all.

CHAPTER 28
ANNA GETS RAILED IN THE KITCHEN

Anna and Eve could both, and not for the first time, have fit comfortably enough in Anna's bed. But after Eve's many sweet words and the little ball of infatuation it produced inside her, she made the quiet suggestion that Aubrey take her bed for the night, because she and Eve would be fine with a few blankets and couch cushions on the kitchen floor. Candide and Aubrey put up a polite, half-hearted argument while Percy and Joe flipped a coin for the armchair or the couch. No one but Joe noticed that Percy never actually showed him the result of the flip, but Percy had flung himself into the armchair with his coat over his face the second Joe brought it up.

Everyone being thus settled, Anna sat on her little mountain of quilts on the kitchen floor, and watched Eve stretch his arm out long to close the window. She watched his shirt lift that little bit, took in that glimpse of his hip, watched his biceps shift, and by the time he turned back around, she was on her tiptoes with her lips pressed against his.

He slid an arm around her waist and wrenched her close against him.

The feeling of his body pressed against hers sent her into overdrive.

She kissed him because he was handsome, because he was sweet, because he was the sexiest man she'd ever seen, but more than all of that, she kissed him, hard, because he loved her. No one had ever spoken about her the way he did that night. No one had ever defended her, and no one, ever, had made it clear they didn't even see a future she wasn't present in. It wasn't thankfulness, or anything vaguely reciprocal. It was simply an outpouring of all her adoration, pent up to an extent she didn't even realise was there until his hand was in her hair and on the small of her back, and her fingers were on his belt.

"We can't," he whispered, with a quick glance at the doorless entrance to the kitchen, but his eyes were soon back on Anna, drinking in her lustful gaze, her pink cheeks, her plump lips, wanting her every bit as badly as she wanted him.

She didn't say a word about it. Just waited for him to halt her. Wondered if he would stop her at all, and when he didn't, she decided to push her luck. She kissed her way down his chest to a rumble of, "Anna," in the back of his beautiful throat.

She lifted his shirt and kissed his abs to a slightly more urgent, "Anna…"

She slipped his zipper down and grasped his big, beautiful, dreamy, hard cock in her hand, dropped to her knees, and took him into her mouth, slowly gliding his length across her flat tongue, then wrapping her lips tight around him, with a rumble of pleasure he felt through every fibre of his being. Eve gripped the bench tight and leaned his head back, and she wanted more than anything to make him moan out loud—to make him completely lose control of himself.

She pulled her lips back to the tip of his cock and looked up at him.

Fuck, she adored that crinkle in his brow. That one, she didn't want to smooth. That one said she was the only problem in his life at that moment, and she was a good problem to have.

She made her way from the base of his dick to the crown, and tilted her head back so he could watch her mouth at work, taking him deep again.

She heard his breath become unsteady, a little louder, and she slowed her movement on the way up, loving that he couldn't tear his eyes away from her. She gripped his balls, and wrapped a finger around the base of his shaft, kissing his perfect dick, savouring that first taste of pre-cum that came with a poorly repressed groan.

Eve slipped his hand into her hair and she made her own soft plea of encouragement in a small sound that broke free all on its own—something akin to a purr. Eve responded by closing his fingers tight, guiding her a little faster, a little deeper, and she ran tight strokes over his shaft as she indulged. His dick hit the back of her throat with a force driven by his need to speak his pleasure—a need he refused to give into. His shoulders caved forward, he brought a second hand into her hair and a whispered, "Fuck, Anna," slipped out, and so she doubled her efforts to make him lose himself.

He let go a ragged sigh, and the sound of her mouth on his cock was so stark in the night she at first marvelled that he didn't stop her, then revelled in the knowledge that he couldn't. He was so completely hers and so in love with her and so thoroughly in her thrall. She squeezed his balls just the way she knew he liked, ran her finger firmly over his perineum and pressed, and was consequently shocked and appalled when he ripped his cock out of her mouth and lifted her to standing.

In a second she was spun around, switching places with Eve, her own back against the bench, and Eve's hand slipped down between her legs. His lips fell on her neck as he pushed his fingers into her slick cunt, and he whispered, "I can't stand the way he looks at you."

Anna, also, did not like the way Joe looked at her, but before she could heartily agree that he was being 'a bit of a dick', Eve said, "Did you see how he winked at you tonight?"

"Percy?" How strange it was the way she said his name on a breath of intense pleasure, all while Eve worked her so deliciously with his perfect fingers, the thrill through her body so all-consuming she could barely speak. She tried her best, and forced out, "No. No, I didn't notice." She had noticed. Of course she'd noticed. And she saw it just then in her mind's eye, and something in the back of her mind noted the way Eve's hand moved a little more firmly. And something in her liked it as much as he evidently did.

"He winked right at you. Because you're gorgeous, and—" One strong arm lifted her onto the bench, two fingers slid inside and Eve pumped them in and out slowly, torturously, speaking low and clear now he had control of himself, all while she slumped against him using everything she had inside to not cry out with the intense pleasure that racked her body. "If I was an asshole—like he is—I'd wink at you, too. But I try not to be an asshole. Unlike him. And he's…" Eve's spare hand took a fist full of hair. Eve's thumb pressed down on her clit. Eve whispered in her ear, "He's really handsome. Really, *really* handsome, and he's *very* charming when he wants to be. And if I was in your position—"

It was such a ridiculous idea that Anna would have laughed out loud. Instead, she let out a pathetic whimper in its place, only to be swiftly shushed by Eve's kiss.

"You're so fucking wet," he whispered, his third finger gliding in and stretching her deliciously.

"For you," she whispered. "Only you."

She felt the approval in his teeth on her neck, that last something she could stand before he squeezed and a wave of ecstasy took her, all the more intense as she tried her best to ride her orgasm out in silence. All the more again, because Eve watched her, adored her, fucked her with his fingers unrelentingly as she came on his hand. Then he said, "Did I ever tell you you have the most perfect cunt?"

"Fuck me," she begged.

Her back was against the fridge faster than she could blink. One arm around her waist, the other beneath her ass, Eve slammed his dick deep into her and she let out a sharp cry of happiness. Eve chuckled at her pitiful attempt to keep quiet, but his humour was short-lived as she braced herself with her thighs on his hips, leaned her head back against the fridge, and raised herself up. She let her hips sink hard and fast, and he groaned loudly.

"Ssh," she goaded.

"Anna!" His stern reprimand served only to make her twice as determined. She reached her arms overhead, took a hold of the top of the fridge door, and arched her back all the way to the tip of his endless dick, then slammed herself back down, forcing another hard gasp of pleasure with an audible moan behind it.

"Quiet, sweetheart," she whispered on another curve of her back. "Don't want everyone to know you're fucking me."

She rammed herself down, but he caught her with two hands on her ass, a wicked sparkle in his eyes. "That's not how this works." Slowly, with control, he pulled back, his grip like iron, while she tried to squirm away from him. Then he pressed in just as mercilessly fast as she had, so profoundly she cried out loud and clear.

"That's better," he whispered.

"Eve," she breathed, his lips on her neck, his fingers in her flesh.

He took charge of her body and sank himself so thoroughly, so perfectly, so repeatedly into her, that she lost all sense of reality, and time, and knowledge of the fact there was no partition between the room where she was being delightfully fucked, and the living room where everyone, hopefully, slept. She didn't hear the way the glasses in the fridge tinkled against each other, didn't notice at all the way its engine had gone into overdrive, or the way its little legs screeched across the floor before it hit the wall. All she noticed was being pounded by Eve in the dying moonlight. She wrapped her arms around him and held on, believing wholeheartedly that the soft moans she let go were so quiet only he could hear. He certainly didn't seem inclined to stop her. If anything, every sound she made seemed to heighten his resolve to eke another out of her, and another, until he finally reacted in kind, letting go one last far-too-loud grunt, which was partially drowned out by her own far-too-loud gasp, as he came hard, as she came harder.

She collapsed into his arms, and he eased her to the floor, onto their pile of quilts, where he kissed her, kissed her, and kissed her, then said, "Do you know how much I love you?"

"I do. All those things you said tonight…"

"I meant every word. You're everything."

"Eve…" She pulled him in and kissed him again, wrapping a blanket over him before his light sweat could turn to a chill in the winter air. He settled his head by her shoulder and sank down into her arms. And she lay there, in a haze of love and sex, floating away on memories of getting so pleasantly railed, until something of a tick or a shift or a murmur drifted in from somewhere else in the apartment.

She lay perfectly still as the haze fell away, eyes wide open, listening intently. No other sounds came, except the beat of her increasing pulse. "Eve?" She nudged him out of the twilight of his sleep.

"Hmm?"

"Do you think I was very noisy?"

He was so quiet for so long that she thought he'd fallen asleep again, until he murmured, "Define 'very'."

"Fuck."

"It's hot."

"No, it isn't!"

"It is, though."

Eve was going to be no use to her at all.

Never had anyone used a toilet so quietly as Anna did that night. Not a light flashed, not a floorboard groaned, and when she returned to Eve's arms, she remained somewhere between utterly satisfied and utterly mortified. Until he pulled her body flush with his, kissed the back of her neck, and she, hopeless little spoon that she was, shuffled her hips back to see if he might be up for a second round.

"Don't flirt with me when I'm trying to correct you."

"Correct me, Eve."

"Stop it, Anna."

"Things I didn't need to hear first thing in the morning," Candide mumbled, staggering into the kitchen.

"Sorry. I didn't know you were there. Also, he's a terrible French teacher, as it goes." Anna cast her eyes over Eve's beautifully built chest and arms and back up to his eyes, in which she could see he was thinking what she was thinking. Again. "A sexy one, though."

Candide visibly shuddered. "Oh, my God. I just wanted some breakfast. And we have a house full of people." Then, with a glare at the pair of them, she offered a pointed, "And I didn't sleep very well."

Reluctantly, guiltily, Anna moved away from Evelyn's warm arms, scrambled up from the kitchen floor where they had spent a perfectly pleasant night, and went about the business of making coffee for six. When Aubrey had emerged from the bedroom, and Percy and Joe sat up from the armchair and the couch, Anna began the discussion of how to go about the day. "It's three hours until our tutorial, so this morning I'm going to drive out and see your mum, Eve."

He paused, toast lingering an inch from his lips. "Seriously?"

"Yes."

"Can I come?"

"If you want."

"Okay…"

She gave his bewildered face a reassuring smile, then continued her instructions. "After that, Eve, Candide, Aubrey and I have a tutorial. That leaves Joe and Percy to get the goods."

Percy rubbed his tired face, muttering, "You all know there's a possessed boy downstairs, don't you?"

"It's just a little longer," said Candide.

"Class is very important," said Anna.

"Fine." Percy's frown changed to a more pleasant expression as he shifted his gaze to Joe. "I'll take care of Joe while you all do that."

Eve shook his head resolutely. "Absolutely not."

Percy sunk a little deeper into his armchair and crossed his fingers over his midline, as if preparing to watch a good show. "What are you worried I'll do to him, Eve? Or, more importantly, what would you like to do to him?"

Eve's mouth dropped open, Percy's grin widened, and Candide moaned loudly, "Why is our house like this?"

"We haven't even had breakfast," Anna agreed, to another glare from Candide.

Aubrey leaned over the arm of the couch towards Joe. "Doesn't this make you terribly uncomfortable?"

Joe surprised everyone, and irritated Anna, by saying with a placid smile, "Strangely, no. It doesn't."

All the while, Eve looked at Percy as though he were last week's dinner. "He's safer with whatever's out there than he would be with you."

Percy gave a chuckle. "And just when I thought we were starting to get along."

"We'll never get along," Eve snapped.

"No, I see that now," Percy spat. "You always were a hateful person, Evelyn."

"Joe," said Eve, changing his tone and expression entirely, as though he hadn't just yelled at his evil, estranged half-brother, "would you like to—"

"He can't come to the tutorial," Candide muttered.

"I know… I wasn't going to suggest that…" Candide raised an accusatory eyebrow at Eve's telling blush. "I was just going to say we have a very nice, very safe library here that Joe might like to look through."

"It's nice of you to think of me." Joe smiled, a little too sweetly for Anna's liking. "But I'm going to go home for a while. Get some things. Take a shower."

Candide and Anna exchanged a secret glance at the comment, but Eve's eyes cut straight to Percy, who said, "I'll definitely keep you company, then. Keep an eye on things for you."

Joe intervened quickly to save Eve the trouble. "I'd like some time alone. But thank you for the offer. I'm quite good at fighting supernatural things, as it goes."

"That's settled then," said Anna, trying to ignore the looks of whatever mutual understanding then passed between Eve and Joe. "Percy, take Aubrey's list and get everything you can from it. We'll meet back here… When?"

"I have a lecture after the tutorial," said Aubrey.

"I have two more classes as well," said Candide.

"I'll just come back here and wait after our tutorial," said Eve.

Anna raised her eyebrows in pleasant surprise. "Does that mean you're free this afternoon?"

"I am." He smiled. "Are you?"

"I am." She smiled back.

"Then it's a date," he said, turning the atmosphere in the room to pure sex with the tone of his voice.

Anna reacted as any young woman might, with a little flex of her hip and fingertips toying with the seam of her shirt. "Good. Because I didn't want to have to shower alone."

"Anna!" Candide snapped.

"What?" Anna remembered the rest of the room. "No-n-no, I didn't mean it like that. It's very scary in that bathroom. There's a ghost in there, you know?"

Candide smooshed her face into her hands to block Anna, and the rest of them, out. "Can we go now, please?"

And finally, they all departed for the hideous day ahead.

CHAPTER 30
HISTORICAL HORROR

Anna and Eve were about three-quarters of the way to Worthing House when Anna slowed the car in the middle of the strangely deserted highway. "Do you see that?"

Eve cast his lovely eyes over the road ahead. "See what?"

"There."

She pointed, and Evelyn traced the line of Anna's finger to the edge of the road where his eyes focused on something—he couldn't say what—lying on the ground. A mass of brown and red that looked jarringly out of place in the shrubbery. "Is it… That's not a person, is it?"

Eve reached for the car door. Anna held him back. Something about the thing, perfectly still but unnaturally so, made her flesh creep. "I'll drive closer."

She set the car slowly in motion, then slammed on the brakes and turned the engine off entirely. "It moved. I saw it."

"They might need help—"

"Wait."

It moved again.

They both saw it this time.

It shifted, sliding towards the road. It slid again, its underside scraping on the rough asphalt. It slid again and again in a horrifying procession neither could look away from until it reached the middle of the highway. There, it paused, until both Eve and Anna were on the verge of investigating, stupid as they both knew that would be. Lucky for them, the unnerving mound suddenly flopped over in one fast, painful-looking movement. A nauseating splatting sound came to their ears as what they discovered to be a head, a gaping wound covering a large portion of it, smashed into the pavement, spilling a disturbing spatter of brains out of the cavity and onto the asphalt. Then they saw the face. What was left of it. It was mostly bone—a bloody, grinning skull on one half where skin should have been; a sagging, misery-ridden expression of death on the other.

Anna started the ignition.

The thing dropped one long, broken-looking arm over its head, and it too hit the pavement with a hard, unsettling slap. It dug its dirty, splintered fingernails into the street and pushed, bending and breaking them with the pressure as it began to rise.

Anna's unrelenting study of the thing, her idling engine and relaxed foot on the brake, began to rattle Eve. "We should go."

She only leaned in closer. "What is it? Is it a zombie?"

He looked back at it, hands absentmindedly searching his pockets for a weapon. "I think it's some sort of ghost."

"Can it hurt us?"

"Almost definitely."

"All right." Anna, eyes intent, set her jaw. "I'm going to take it out."

It continued to push itself up and up until it stood tall on naked, bloody legs with misshapen knees, bending backwards in a way that shouldn't have been able to support the body.

Yet it walked.

One excruciating, backward-kneed lurch at a time. It walked.

Once. Twice. Thrice.

"Anna…"

She floored the accelerator and drove straight into the thing. They felt the impact, the car was splattered in blood, and the head went rolling off in a direction different to its limbs as the wheels bounced over the torso, then screeched to a halt.

"Now behold," Anna announced, tuning her head, "as I back over—" A little touch of white dulled her pink cheeks. "Wait… Where is it? It's gone!"

Eve, dreading what he might find there, also turned his head to look behind them, first out the rear window, then raising himself, into the back seat. "Well, it hasn't materialised in the car, so…"

"Are we okay?"

"I think we're okay," he said cautiously. Then, clocking the barely concealed excitement in Anna's face, he broke his own smile. "Ghost stuff?"

"Ghost stuff," she agreed. "Did I kill it?"

"Probably not." To her sunken face, he added, "But you did good."

Her smile came back twice as bright, and she raised an eyebrow. "Did I impress you?"

He laughed. "You know you did."

"Nice." She put the car in gear. "Weird how it gets easier each time you meet a supernatural thing."

Eve kissed her cheek, Anna flicked on the windscreen wipers to clean off the blood, and she hit the accelerator again, bringing them to Lady Worthing's house within minutes.

This time they traced the path to her front door with Eve's arm luxuriantly slung over Anna's shoulders, and arrived in the great lady's presence in exactly this manner.

"Anna, I'm so happy you've come back to see me!" Lady Worthing came straight forward with a welcoming smile and took Anna's hand, leading her away from Eve and to the same seat she had occupied the last time. She waved him off with a jewel encrusted hand. "I'm sure you have building plans to search for or some such. Please leave us."

Eve waited hesitantly for the surprised but affirming glance from Anna before he left the two alone to go wash the blood off Anna's car.

Lady Worthing spoke casually, as though they were the best of old friends, while she closed the door behind Eve. "You're still enrolled at Endymion College, I hear."

"I'm as surprised as you are," was the curious reply.

"I had a little change of heart."

"I'm very happy to hear it."

She sat down and looked Anna straight in the eye. "Thank you for saving Evelyn and Candide. I failed to say that last time you were here. You took care of the two people I love most in this world, and I am in your debt for that."

Having been prepared for a fight, Anna found herself wholly thrown. In fact, she found herself so overwhelmed, so quickly, she could only mumble a barely coherent, "That's all right."

Lady Worthing glanced towards the window where Eve's beloved form traversed the pathway. "I see you and Evelyn are together, after all."

"We are."

She nodded and kept the same relaxed smile on her face as though it didn't bother her in the least. "And to what do I owe today's visit?"

Anna took a deep breath and steadied herself. It was all very nice and civilised so far, but she knew she couldn't let her sudden and barely acknowledged desire to be liked by Eve's mother get in the way of what she had to do. She pushed it down and said softly, "I found the boy. I found him downstairs. Chained to the chair. He's still there."

Lady Worthing was silent for a short time. She became more serious, the smile falling away, but her tone remained kind and calm. "Does Evelyn know?"

"No."

Lady Worthing studied her to assess whether that might be true, then chanced, "Anna, that's a very good thing. Eve might not be…" Again she glanced to the window, but he was out of sight now. "He might not be as strong as I think you can be. You need to understand: to let that boy out of the chair is to choose incalculable misery for you and everyone you know."

"I remember you implying that last time, but…" Now, finally, she decided to be honest. "I feel awful for that boy. I don't want to leave him like that."

"I feel awful for him, too." Lady Worthing looked clear and earnest into Anna's eyes, and Anna found she believed her. In fact, to Anna, that look felt like the first glimpse she ever had of who Lady Worthing really was. There was a heart in there somewhere, sad and scared like her own. But Lady Worthing soon broke the eye contact. "Believe me when I tell you, I've been over this a thousand times. There is no other way."

"Then you understand why I'm here," Anna said gently. "I need you to explain to me what happened in the past, so I can…" She pushed out the hideous words. "So I can walk away from him and leave him there forever, and still feel okay about this." Lady Worthing nodded her understanding, so Anna moved forward. "He's… The boy is Eve's half-brother, isn't he?"

The mask of Lady Worthing's calm slipped away, to be replaced with the same indignant horror that characterised her last time. "How can you know that?"

"Demon stuff," Anna mumbled.

"God damn it, Anna, you need to stop communing with demons!"

Talk about stating the obvious. "I know!"

"And it's not what it looks like, anyway. It's *very* complicated." Lady Adeline walked to the grand piano, where Anna noticed for the first time that she had laid out champagne with several glasses, her usual cigarette box, ornate lighter and cigarette holder. Today, in addition, was a beautiful silver tray, the bottom of which was a shiny mirror, with several small lines of suspicious, delicious-looking white powder. She had, of course, her own pure silver tube with which to insufflate the drug.

"Are you busy studying again?" Anna joked, looking over the set up. "You're making a very early start."

"I'm up late, not early." Lady Worthing topped up her own glass from the already-open bottle and poured a new one for Anna, as she waffled, "Did you ever wonder exactly how much of Percy Shelley's work was done by Mary Wollstonecraft Shelley?"

"I know she edited and published a great deal of his work after his death. Eve said she's the reason he's so famous. Not the other way around, like most people seem to believe. Or want to believe. He's also working on something to do with that."

"That's exactly correct. And if I don't get my work finished before Evelyn finishes his, I'm screwed."

Anna took in the myriad papers and open books again, this time with a shade of alarm. "You're competing with him?"

"That's academia, dear," she replied coolly, bringing the sparkling glass to Anna. "What do you think you signed up for?"

"I have no idea." Anna sighed, accepted the champagne, and set about wondering if Eve knew. Or if he would want to know.

"It's a fascinating project, but it's exhausting. It's so much to unpick. I need a little help to concentrate, from time to time, as you can imagine." Lady Worthing tilted her head as an invitation for Anna to follow her.

"I understand that much." Anna walked over to the piano, took the silver tube proffered, and did as she was bid. "I can't imagine the champagne helps, though?"

"It has no effect really after the cocaine."

"That's also true."

"It is delicious, though. And evocative, don't you think?"

Anna smiled. "I absolutely do." And then she liked Lady Worthing, if only for that moment. She genuinely liked her. She suddenly seemed like someone Anna would have liked to know well, and it took a Herculean effort on her part not to become distracted, and not to attempt to settle in for the morning with compelling conversation, drugs, books and very good champagne. "I hate to be rude, but have to get back soon, and I need to ask you a lot about everything that's happened."

"I'll start," said Lady Worthing, leaning casually back against the piano next to Anna. "Anna, Evelyn's father wasn't a good man. Unfortunately, when I was a young woman, I thought he was. He was older than me, he was a professor and I was a student, and he was so exciting and handsome, and he thought I was amazing. I was the most beautiful and intelligent woman he had ever met, he told me. And I believed him. Out of all those brilliant, adoring women at Endymion College, I believed I was his chosen one."

Anna lit a cigarette. "But he was already married…"

"Oh, no, he never married Harriet. That was her second mistake. Her first mistake was trusting him. I made that same mistake, but not the second one."

Anna's recent affection for Lady Worthing began to slip. "But surely you knew he had children with her?"

"I did. And as a childless twenty-year-old who had never laid eyes on those boys, they were little more than an abstract idea for me. I didn't really think about them at all, to be honest. Not at first. It seems terrible, and well, I suppose it was. I never thought he would abandon them. I never thought I would become pregnant. I never thought he would try to leave me a single mother with a child, just as he did to Harriet." She didn't look the least bit guilty. She only had a vague air of fond reminiscence as she stared across the room at her glorious silk wallpaper.

"But he did marry you, didn't he?" Anna pushed.

"Ha! He did. And he was every part the brute and the filthy, lying beast Harriet had been putting up with." She turned her eyes, full of bitter humour, back upon Anna. "When the time came, and I was faced with the humiliation and poverty Harriet had been thrown into… Well, let's just say, by that time I had developed *some* skills in the dark arts, and he changed his mind."

Anna gasped. "You put a spell on him!"

Adeline shrugged. "I took nothing less than he owed me."

"But that's terrible!"

"Is it? He was no father to his children. And if I forced him to give me and Evelyn everything he promised to give us, well, what of it? It's not my fault he led Harriet on. It's not my fault she was so easily led. And there was no way I was going to let him do that to me." She took a sip of her champagne and lit a fresh cigarette as though she had barely a care in the world.

Anna watched her, wondering what went on inside her head to allow her to process all of this, to come out the other side, able to speak about it all as if she hadn't been instrumental in destroying several lives. "You don't seem nearly as ashamed as you should be."

"Women like you," Lady Adeline laughed derisively, breathing out a long plume of smoke into the languid sunlight, "you come in here and act like we didn't open the door for you. You act as though no woman ever needed to sell her soul to the devil himself to get you where you are today. Your freedom is built upon the broken and battered bodies of the sisterhood you purport to love so much. Show some respect."

Unbelievable! "Are you suggesting I don't know my feminist theory?"

"Theory? Anna, you don't know it unless you lived it. Things were different then. When I did what I did, I paved the way for Harriet, and for her boys, too. She wasn't strong enough or smart enough to do it, so I did it. She hated me every step of the way, but she knows as well as I do that she has her job and her house and her car and her son's education because of me. I made a hard choice, but I took a stand when I needed to." She turned again to face Anna, who stared back at her, wishing she could say far more than she could if she wanted to get more information from her that morning. But when Lady Worthing spoke again, her words, unexpectedly, went straight to Anna's heart. "You never reproach a woman for doing what she had to do to survive. You don't know how quickly things change unless you've watched it happen. Hang your 'theory'."

Both furious and deeply impressed, Anna said quietly, "Either way, none of this explains how that boy ended up in the chair."

"This is the hard bit…" Lady Worthing leaned over, inhaled a neat white line, took a sip of her champagne, then, when properly fortified, said, "We had our club, as you know, and we… spent more time with certain supernatural things than we perhaps should have. We were young and stupid and didn't know any better. Well, one weekend Harriet's boys were in the house—this house—and they were far away from us, being watched by a nanny, of course, so we did what we usually did. We had our club meeting." There her words slowed and thinned, and with that, Anna sensed real regret, and genuine sadness. "I'll tell it straight." She looked down at the floor as Anna waited, closed her eyes for a moment, then forced out the words. "That night, one of those things, something that came through in our séance, locked onto Mich—the boy—Harriet's eldest son... and he became possessed."

"Why didn't you do an exorcism?" Anna asked softly.

"Anna, we did. We did, over and over. We called priests, we tried to make bargains with other demons. We did everything we could to help him. And then one night..." Now she turned away from Anna, her hands shaking a little, as she walked slowly to the window and stared out. "One night Evelyn's father was alone with the boy, who had been, as far as Harriet knew, missing for some time." She looked across at Anna, guilt written all over her for the first time. "We had, uh, told her that he just went wandering off the grounds, and was never seen again. Poor woman."

"That was it?" Anna stared back in horror. "He was here the whole time and you let her think he'd gone missing? How incredibly heartless."

"What would you have had me tell her?" Lady Worthing snapped. "That her son was possessed? I tried to get him back to her. I did everything I could! But his father..." She turned away again. Anna could no longer see her face, only hear her wavering, cold voice. "That night... his father went too far... and... whatever he did in there, trying to get the demon out..." The silence stretched on in parallel to Lady Worthing's harrowing memories, until her weak voice announced, "There was no heartbeat when we found him. There was no anything. He was battered and bruised, and after all that time, all that work, he was…" Her eyes turned slowly up to meet Anna's. "He killed that boy."

Anna's blood turned to ice in her veins. "No…"

The words came fast and relentless now, a flow that once started couldn't be stopped. "He killed his own son. He said— he *claimed* Michael was already gone, anyway. He said at least the child would find some peace after that. We were already in so deep, and we couldn't let anyone find the body, not the way it was, and after all that time… and so… and so we buried the body."

Anna shuddered, her vision clouding with flashes of Michael's spirit when he came to her. His burial gown, sodden and ripped. His body covered in mud and filth, the sticks in his hair, the broken fingernails…

"We found a place far away from here. A swamp where we thought the body would easily decompose among the bugs and the bacteria, and no one would smell anything out of the ordinary." She stared at Anna, half-mad perhaps, apologetically, but Anna felt only nausea. "Anna, he wasn't dead. He came back. He came back out of that grave and crawled home… and… and a lot of people died."

Anna couldn't find a word to say—nothing at all—so Adeline continued. "He was—is—he *is* very, very dangerous. We did what we had to do, and once we finally found him and trapped him, we put him in the building, in that chair, and we kept him there. The ground floor of my old apartment at Endymion College. The one that I shared with Candide's mother."

Anna's mouth dropped open. "How could you do that? And how cruel of you to put Candide in there!"

"She could never have known anything. And it was safer than..." A fresh worry lit Lady Worthing's eyes. "Candide doesn't know, does she?"

"Oh. No." Anna coloured. "No, I haven't told her anything."

"Good. Because she's completely incapable of keeping anything from Evelyn. Right now, she has nothing but lovely memories of her mother, and we want to keep it that way. Don't ever tell her."

"I won't," Anna whispered.

Lady Worthing went on, more calmly now. "It was really the perfect solution, at the time. No one ever thought anything of us being there all hours because we lived there. That allowed us to work on him every night. Which we did, because we didn't realise at first..." She snuffed out her cigarette and lit another on the spot. "We thought it was just his body that came back possessed. We thought we simply had to get rid of the demon, then bury the body properly. But then when we did our séances, a whim of Lord Worthing's, to assuage the little guilt he was capable of feeling... We couldn't locate the boy's spirit... And it became clear, eventually, that Michael was trapped. Even when his own father had murdered him, even when the body died, that thing would not let the boy's soul escape."

Anna stared up at the ceiling, blinking away the tears that now forced their way to her eyes, trying to control her dismay at hearing what she already knew to be true.

Lady Worthing's relentless words continued to flow. "We doubled our efforts when we realised what had happened, but eventually, we became exhausted. That was long after I had Evelyn. We worked on the boy for years. We did everything we could until one day we just understood… There was nothing else we could do. We simply weren't powerful enough. So… so we sealed him up. We always said if we ever found a way to fix him, we would try again. If Candide's mother had become the powerful witch she always wanted to be, things might have been different… If we'd had access to certain… books or objects, who knows? But she died before any of that could happen, along with her husband. Evelyn's father left years before that, and in the end, it was just me. I couldn't do it alone, so… I left the boy there. Until now."

Adeline came back to Anna's side by the piano and stood silent for some time as Anna sifted through everything she had heard. There they remained, the only two people in the world who knew the extraordinary and terrifying story in full. Adeline waited for Anna to speak, but she did not, unable to figure out how to process the mess.

Eventually, Adeline sighed, walked to the couch and threw herself down. "I want you to understand, Anna, that there were no easy choices. Something awful happened, and it was a stupid, stupid accident, but the repercussions were more than any of us could handle. This is why you need to stay away from whatever demon you've been in contact with. You don't know how quickly things can turn… irreparably bad. When you're dealing with demons, if you set one foot out of place, you may regret it for the rest of your life."

Lady Worthing's eyes filled with tears, but her face remained as hard as Anna had ever seen it. "I still think about him every day, Anna. And about Harriet. And Percy."

"Percy?" Anna, drawn like a moth to a flame, settled opposite Adeline again.

"Percy was the boy's little brother. Harriet's other son. He was there the night Michael turned. He was only five years old." Anna's stomach tightened, sickeningly. It was enough by now. Horror upon horror and more on top. All of it. And yet there was more to come. "He had to watch his brother kill their nanny in the most horrible way imaginable." Lady Worthing closed her eyes, blocking out whatever memories came back to her in that instant, whatever it was that Percy had witnessed that night. "Her screams attracted us before he could hurt Percy, physically, but that boy... No child should ever have to see what he saw. He was..." A little shiver ran over Adeline's shoulders, and she rubbed her arms. "He was permanently damaged from that, I think. And more still from everything that happened afterwards."

Anna swallowed hard. She didn't want to ask, but she couldn't stop herself. "What happened to Percy afterwards?"

"Nothing supernatural that I know of. But he was... changed. As one might expect. He became... a violent child. Had I not known him before, I would have said he was evil incarnate, but I did know him. And he was a sweet little boy, once."

"I'm sure you tried to help him." Anna wasn't sure at all. She knew how much Percy still hated Lady Worthing, but she couldn't stand to think otherwise, her protective heart smarting as the edges folded a little tighter around Percy.

Adeline, eyes on the floor, said, "We told him he dreamed it."

"You didn't."

"We..." She threw her hands up hopelessly. "We didn't know what else to do. He was so little, we hoped he would eventually believe that none of it had ever happened. Not the murder and the possession, at the very least. But he remembered every-thing. He never forgot a single second of it and he told me over and over. And I told him again and again it never happened, and over time, he grew cold inside. Cold and calculating, worse with every year. I tried to be kind, I did. Even after their father disappeared, I let him visit the house, visit Eve, but... He never got better. Despite the money I threw at Harriet for his education, his therapy, whatever else he might have needed, there came a time when he had to be kept away from Evelyn. He was dangerous. A broken, dangerous child, who had to be kept away at all costs."

"But he was the victim!" Anna snapped.

"Yes, he was, for a while," came the strangely distant voice. "Then he became something else entirely. I grew to hate Percy. And Percy grew to hate me."

"But... But poor Percy. All those years. You just told him he didn't see that? How could he possibly process that? He was so little, and sweet, and look what you did to him! No one to talk to about it, no one to understand him. He must have been so alone and so scared. How could you?"

Anna was shocked by her own vehemence, but no more so than Lady Worthing, whose eyes grew wide as her face turned pale. "Please tell me you never met Percy."

"What?" Anna did her best to bluff, but she was sure she was failing, as her heart beat so hard in her chest she was positive Adeline could hear it. "No."

Lady Worthing studied her hard. "Anna, let me be clear. If you ever meet a man called Percy Ashdown, the only smart thing to do is to run. Run fast and far from him, and don't ever let him be near Evelyn."

"I don't know Percy. I've never met anyone called Percy." Anna looked straight into her eyes with as good an approximation of honesty as she could manage, and her voice shook only a little as she couldn't help but ask, "Do you know what happened to him?"

Lady Worthing narrowed her eyes in judgement, but she said, "Not now, no. Last I heard, he was somewhere in the Middle East. I believe he did quite well for himself, all things considered, though I also hear he's every bit as vindictive and brutal as the demon who took his brother. I hope he never comes back." She let out a long breath before continuing, "Percy Ashdown is still the only other person who knows there was more to the story. He blames me entirely. I suppose he might have blamed his father a little, but I was the one who broke up his family, or so he thought. I suppose Harriet probably told him that. And poor Harriet. It was better for her to believe the lie than to see what truly became of her son. Even Percy knew that. Even as a little boy. I don't think he ever said a word to her about what he saw. She had the luxury of grieving, which he never did. If she knew her son was locked in his body with that demon… It's more than any mother could stand to see."

Anna wiped away her tears as Lady Worthing watched, an odd mixture of sympathy and detachment, as though someone else had done all those horrible things. "It's important to me that you understand why I did what I did. Tell me you understand."

"I do." Anna did. The way Lady Worthing had laid it all out for her explained everything. Even if Anna could never approve, she could understand the series of catastrophic events that had led them all down that very dark path.

The frank, calm tone of voice with which Lady Worthing next spoke surprised Anna out of the reverie she was fast sinking into. The atmosphere shifted, and the story, it seemed, was done and dusted and only needed its conclusion. "I've told you everything I know. You can take it all back to whatever demon you've been dealing with and tell them what I've told you. They will probably ask you to trade your soul for the boy, which you may do if you wish. I was never brave enough to do that. Neither was his own father. But now that you do know, I suggest you finish whatever business you have and get rid of it. You may send the demon to me if you have any more trouble, but it probably just wanted to tempt you to make that deal."

Anna had quite forgotten her lies about doing demon deals to get information. "Thank you. And thank you for telling me." She tried to push her many and encroaching thoughts of Percy out of her mind, to concentrate on everything else that had just happened. She wondered how she might have done things differently had she ever let herself get into such a mess with a demon the way Lady Worthing had. Perhaps she would have done everything just the same, and how terrible it would all be now.

"It was good to talk about it. Now I have someone else who knows, it will be a little less lonely." She smiled sadly at Anna, who felt her heart mellow in sympathy. "He needs to be sealed up again. I'm sorry. If you can't bring yourself to do it, I'll do it for you."

"Thank you. You don't need to go back there. I'll take care of everything."

"All right." Then Adeline's tone shifted again, and this time back to the friendly, matter-of-fact woman she had been when Anna walked in. "And now we have that out of the way, there's something else I want to talk to you about." Anna watched Lady Adeline move in a swirl of silk as she walked back to the piano, where she refilled both their glasses and her cigarette holder before walking back to Anna in a cloud of smoke and perfume, placing the two glasses on the table in front of them. "Drink."

Anna did as instructed.

"Anna, I like you." What little was left of Anna's guard instantly fell away. That was all it took. One direct kind word from the lady herself, and Anna was putty. She looked at the lovely face in front of her, the sweet, reassuring smile, and she did feel reassured. "I do like you. Genuinely. I appreciate you, and I appreciate what you've done for my son. You're smart and brave, and you're a woman I can respect."

Anna blushed deeply, and found herself, again, barely able to form words. "Thanks... you."

"Drink."

Anna did so obediently.

"I'm not going to challenge your scholarship. I looked over your application, and you deserve that place. I'm very happy to keep you at Endymion College."

Anna sucked in a breath of air. "Really?"

"Yes, really." Adeline smiled.

Anna couldn't begin to believe what she was hearing. She felt exactly as she had when she first read her acceptance letter. But this was Evelyn's mother. Evelyn's mother approved of Anna? Maybe the first girlfriend she ever approved of! She would be happy for them now, now that Anna had proven herself, and once they sorted through the mountains of trauma and horror, everything would be so much easier for them all. Her heart positively leapt at the thought of how pleased Eve might be that he didn't have to worry about her anymore.

"I'm going to take you under my wing," Lady Worthing continued, her words like a soft hand stroking Anna's hair. "I'm going to see to it that all the right doors open for you exactly when they need to, and I am going to make sure you achieve all the things a brave, smart woman like you deserves. All the things not every brave, smart woman gets the opportunity to pursue."

"Oh," was all Anna could manage, as overwhelmed as she was, her head and her heart reeling from the strange morning.

But Lady Worthing wasn't overwhelmed. She was confident, confiding, and she only smiled wider as she said, "From now on, we'll work together. The two of us. Which means we have to be on the same side, you understand?"

Anna gave a bewildered nod.

"Then let me be frank." Still she kept that smile, still she spoke like the kindest of friends. "Anna, you must know, Evelyn is not for you." It was as though two hands of ice had reached straight into Anna's chest and tore at her heart from either side, breaking it clean in two with the sweetly delivered, vicious words, "You and I both know he can do better."

CHAPTER 31
MODERN HORROR

Anna set her glass down shakily. Her defences had been destroyed only seconds earlier and now the arrow hit its target. Anna blinked back any moisture in her eyes as best she could, determined to keep this woman from seeing her cry. "Evelyn loves me."

"That's irrelevant," came the sugary reply. "Do you love him?"

"Of course I love him!"

As though it were the most logical thing in the world, Adeline replied, "If that were true, then you'd want him to do better than you. Wouldn't you?"

Anna said nothing, trying to decide if she should leave—trying to sort through her frazzled thoughts to figure out if she had all the information she needed. Lady Adeline took the cigarette from her holder and passed it to Anna. Anna smoked it absent-mindedly.

"Anna, you're passionate, exciting, everything a boy like Evelyn wants. But you're a college girlfriend. You're a lot like me, actually. And I don't want Evelyn to be with someone like me. You shouldn't want that either."

"I don't think I'm anything like you," Anna replied.

"That's because you've never been pushed." There was a steely, lifeless smile on her face as she spoke the words. "You would be ruthless, you would make terrible choices, and you would also be a horrible mother."

"I don't want to be a mother!" Anna snapped.

"Don't you think Evelyn would make a wonderful father?"

"Yes." She really did, and all manner of beautiful images of what Eve might one day want to be flashed into her mind, so she sputtered, "But I think that's his decision to make."

"No, not if he wastes his best years with you."

"I think that's very funny coming from you," Anna shot. "He's spent his whole life without your love. Do you have any idea how codependent he and Candide are?"

Lady Worthing rolled her eyes. "That was quite deliberate, I assure you."

Anna ignored the comment, off on her own path. "I won't leave him."

"You will." She delivered the words as though it were a law of physics. "You will because you know everything I've said is true. When you leave here, when you go back to his perfect life and his lovely apartment, every time you look at him, you will know—that wasn't meant for you. You will begin to count every second you spend with him as one more second of his life wasted because it's with you. Because," she pointed a bejewelled finger at Anna for emphasis, "you are not good enough for him."

Anna was too shocked by the audacity, and too scared of the possible truth of the speech, to say anything.

Lady Worthing filled the silence with slow, firm, heart-piercing words. "If you have any depth of character, any compassion, and I know you do, you won't be able to throw his life away so carelessly. Everything he has been through has been for a purpose—a purpose you couldn't possibly understand—and he's almost near the end of that now. There's a life waiting for Evelyn. It's a perfectly curated life that I worked very, very hard to make for him, and I am sorry, Anna, but there is no place in that life for you. Do the right thing and let him have all the love and happiness he deserves."

Then Lady Adeline paused, leaned forward, and looked at Anna with compassion in her eyes, as though she truly did understand. "Sincerely, I'm sorry. You know you're from different worlds. You know that will always, always come between you. You know, as well as I do, as well as Eve does, deep down, that it would never work out in the long run."

Instinctively drawing on her own bitter experience of marrying a wealthy Lord, Lady Worthing had found Anna's weak spot. Anna, she correctly guessed, must have spent hours mulling over the very ideas now put in front of her. Suddenly, with her words, those suspicions had become undeniable fact, and Anna had no choice but to notice that those outside her own insecurities could see the situation as clearly as she did.

And if Lady Adeline knew it, no doubt, soon enough, so would everyone else in their sphere

When their relationship eventually came out at Endymion College, all those rich students would look down on her with disgust, elevating Evelyn even further above her.

What did she do to trick him so, they would ask. She doesn't belong in his world. She's unworthy.

Anna understood, deep inside. How could he be for her? Perfect, ethereal Eve. It was impossible.

It had always been some sort of strange, sad mistake that he should look at her the way he did.

She understood. How ridiculous that she could have thought otherwise…

As the thoughts raced through her mind, Anna's sad, trusting face revealed her defeat to Lady Adeline.

And that might have been it, had Anna not caught the slight but vicious smile lifting the very corners of Lady Adeline's mouth, hidden almost as soon as it was revealed.

A new and sickening realisation spread over Anna as she was then hit with the depth of the manipulation.

Lady Worthing knew all about her now. Of course she did. She said herself she'd read her application, accessed her school records. She knew the poverty, she knew the sense of alienation and disparity Anna must feel on a daily basis in a place like Endymion College.

But worse than that, she knew Anna was an orphan, and she had deliberately, ever so briefly, given her the experience of what it was to have a warm, confiding, caring older woman in her life. Someone who valued her opinion. Someone she had a bond with. Someone who would look out for her, who would set her on the best path using their own wise, thoughtful experience.

She had very deliberately given Anna the brief experience of mothering that she had never had. That she had never realised she so badly craved.

And Anna had fallen for it so easily.

In one short interview, Lady Worthing had managed to gain Anna's sympathy and loyalty to such an extent she almost managed to have her hideous past covered up again without one careless whisper and with a thanks on top.

And from there, she would have had Anna destroy her relationship with Eve, then walked away from their two broken hearts, appearing totally innocent in it all.

Eve had warned Anna how deeply manipulative his mother was. She hadn't begun to imagine the extent of it until that exact moment.

Anna felt all the old feelings that carried her through her childhood and her teenage years returning in a flood. Anger, resentment, pride, disdain. She became cold and focused, like she had been before Lady Worthing had managed to get under her skin.

Anna stood tall, drawing herself up to her full height, which, to be honest, wasn't particularly tall, but she felt quite lofty at the time. She took her champagne glass and walked calmly to the piano, snuffed out her cigarette, and helped herself to another. As Lady Adeline watched on, Anna desperately willed her hand to remain steady as she refilled her glass. She didn't spill a drop. But her face showed no sign of the relief and self-satisfaction she felt in that moment.

She took a sip of champagne and placed the glass carefully back down on the piano. "I'm sorry too, Lady Worthing," she said. She took a long drag on her cigarette, puffed out a plume of smoke, then said, "but your wallpaper is hideous." It was a bald-faced lie. The wallpaper was fabulous, and they both knew it. "When you shuffle off this mortal coil, and when I inherit this place, through my relationship with your son, I'm going to have the whole place repapered."

"I'd have you killed before I'd ever let you lay a finger on my wallpaper."

Anna tried her best to play off the unexpected response. "You'd already be dead."

"Do you think that would stop me?" It should have been a joke, but Anna had the unsettling feeling there was a grain of truth in what she said.

Lady Adeline walked over to stand on the opposite side of the piano and held out her glass. Anna refilled it for her and passed her the cigarette, which Lady Adeline smoked sans holder, assessing Anna all the while.

"Damn it," she eventually said. "I would have loved you for a daughter-in-law."

Anna was ready this time. "It's a shame I'm not the marrying type," she replied, lighting another cigarette. "But I'm in love with your son. And I'm not going anywhere."

Neither said anything, and it was in that instant of silence that both became aware of Eve's presence in the doorway. The look of delight on his face was like a knife in each woman's heart, in her own unique way. The mother's overwhelmingly selfish and protective love, willing to break her own child's heart to know he would be safe and successful when she was no longer there to pick up the pieces. The selfish and protective care of a lover, the only other person in this world who could see him at his happiest, who would destroy worlds before she would let that happiness be touched, who knew she was the cornerstone of everything and would not, could not, give an inch.

Both women recognised the other as an opponent, but a worthy opponent. Both would have preferred things to be different, but they were far too similar to back down.

Lady Adeline's mouth curved into a victorious smile, as though the battle were already won. She launched the next attack. "Won't you two stay for breakfast?"

Eve's response was quicker than the knot tightening in Anna's stomach. "Sorry, we can't. Anna and I have somewhere else to be."

Anna looked at him and she saw it was true: he was, every inch of him, just the hero she had always needed.

When they were well away in Anna's car on the road home, Eve finally broached the subject. "It sounds like you held your own. Again."

How untrue that was, Anna thought to herself. "How much did you hear?"

"Just that she wants me to marry you." A little sheepishly, "And that you won't marry me."

She would almost have considered it just to spite his mother, but Anna said, "Is that going to be a problem?"

He shook his head with a smile and a squeeze of her knee. "Nothing's a problem so long as we're together."

Lovely Eve. Eve, who believed in nothing more than he believed in Anna. Eve, who was so radiant and true in the morning sunshine. Eve, whose father was a murderer, whose father beat Percy, whose father broke every finger on his son's right hand one by one. Eve, whose mother allowed it all to go on and on right under her nose until the three brothers were torn apart, two of them left to grow up lonely and distant, and the third to never grow up at all. And Anna, who knew in her soul she would stop at nothing to protect Eve from whatever evils the world would throw at them next.

CHAPTER 32
A HAUNTING TUTORIAL

"The Picture of Dorian Gray," Evelyn began. "Who here wishes Basil Hallward would paint their portrait in just such a way?"

There was some light joking around the room about sins each student may or may not have had, skeletons in closets, and so on.

Anna's hand was slow to rise, not only because she didn't want to appear overly keen and responsive to her alluring teacher, but also because she couldn't help but feel she perhaps had a different insight into certain aspects of the story compared to others in the tutorial. "Dorian is amoral, wouldn't you say? Right from the start."

"You don't think he was corrupted?" asked Eve.

"Only a little. I think he was trouble all by himself, and he let it happen very easily. And it was a very pleasant form of corruption, wasn't it? I know this is the story of a beautiful man of a certain class, but I can't help but wonder…"

She looked around the room at the clear, rich, happy, hopeful faces turned towards her, and imagined they probably didn't even know the sins their fathers and grandfathers chose to commit to gain the wealth that gave them access to that exclusive room on that glorious winter's day.

They had probably been raised since birth with enough distance from the various meat-grinding businesses that brought them their daily money, that perhaps they no longer even had the capacity to feel as deeply as they should about it.

"I can't help but wonder what the portrait would show if Dorian wasn't born into that world," Anna ventured. "What if he only did terrible things, not because he wanted to, but because he just didn't know any better? Or because he didn't have a choice? Because the very world he was born into was so evil, in and of itself, that, well, he became more a victim of no one stepping in and preventing his corruption, than of being a corrupting influence himself."

"But," Aubrey piped up, "doesn't he have a personal responsibility, just as a human, to try to do the right thing?"

"Maybe," said Anna, "but how do you know what the right thing is when you're already lost from the start? What if Dorian lost his moral compass early in life, not because he was gently led astray, but because it became a matter of survival?"

On a chuckle, Candide threw out, "What survival is that, exactly? Sex and drinking?"

"Yes, possibly." Anna laughed. "It was expected of him, though, wasn't it? But what I want to know is, say he was once young and innocent, like the youth we meet right at the start of the book, is it fair that the portrait reflects only his actions, rather than, possibly, who he really is. Or was. The portrait reflects what he did, but not the struggle within as he made those choices, and it was that insidious image that served to make him worse. It was that cruel and incomplete reflection of himself that made him sink deeper into amorality."

"Wilde's whole premise was that art does not corrupt. You're clearly wrong."

The words 'shut up, Mark' were close on Anna's lips, but she quickly rearranged them and instead replied to the smug face opposite her, "Was it?"

"Yes. Dorian acted, and the portrait served only as a reflection of his sins."

"But it was the very existence of the portrait that spurred him on to become evil. Had there been no portrait, he might have become a Lord Henry type, but he went above and beyond because of the constant reminder of his failure—the complete inability to ever make it better even if he tried. Whenever he tried to do good, if he checked the portrait, it only ever reflected the bad."

"So you're actually disagreeing with Oscar Wilde?" Mark scoffed. "You're saying art *does* corrupt?"

"I'm not disagreeing with him at all. I think you've misunderstood the book." She knew she shouldn't, but she quickly added the words, "As usual." He opened his mouth to argue, but she spoke over the top of him. "Anything has the ability to corrupt, if used the right way. And I believe that's what Wilde was saying. It isn't the art in and of itself, it's the way we engage with it. One temperament might remain completely unmoved by the aesthetic perfection in Hallward's painting, but another might be driven mad. You can't blame the art or the artist, innocently made as it was. But what shapes the way we engage with art is a combination of the individual's soul *and* the society they're a part of."

Candide coughed loudly to draw attention away from the adoring sigh that escaped Eve's lips, though Anna hadn't heard, involved as she was with her own thoughts.

"Of course, this situation is supernatural, which only complicates things further. How twisted, how cruel that each of his desperate acts should have become imprinted on his permanent record, for all the world to see and judge, without any understanding of the sadness and desperation behind that. What will that do to a sensitive soul? I just think, P-uh-Dorian," she blushed, but maintained her speech, "might never have become that terrible person if not for a series of events that were set in motion, outside of his control. And then when it happened, and he reacted badly, no one was there to catch him. He needed help, and it was denied because he was surrounded by bad people and bad things, and then all he was left with was this hideous reflection of himself, always haunting him, with no hope of a reprieve. What must that do to a person?"

"Are we still talking about the book?" A young man Anna had never seen before ripped her straight out of her train of thought. A young man, with a particularly odd and cruel sparkle in his eye.

"Yes." She twisted her fountain pen in her fingers uneasily. "We're still talking about the book."

"Just making sure." He stared hard into her, even if his words were delivered casually. "It seemed like you were going somewhere else with that. Somewhere personal."

"No. I'm just reflecting—"

"It seems as though you don't see Dorian's portrait as a window to his soul."

"I'm not sure it is because——"

"It is," the lips seethed starkly. And on a rising and vehement cacophony of words, "You may not have realised this yet, Anna James, but all your sins are writ large, all over your face, for all to see. No one cares what your excuses are for doing what you did. All that matters is that you did wrong. And you can never erase the terrible things you did just because you wish you hadn't done them. It's too late. And when the time comes, you will be judged. And you *will* pay."

The blood drained from at least four faces in the room. An evil smile spread across the face of the student as he finished his speech, then, just as if he had said nothing, he blinked and looked back at Eve with a blank expression.

"What the fuck, Greg?" Candide yelled.

He looked across at her, befuddled. "What?"

"Why did you just attack her like that? Why would you say that?"

"Huh? I don't even..." He gazed around the room, everyone staring back at him, and turned red. "I don't know. Sorry." He glanced at Anna, then the table, then Anna. "I'm sorry. I don't even know what that was about..."

He was clearly embarrassed and confused, so Candide and Anna kept tensely silent, while Eve addressed a distracting question to the group, getting everyone back in hand quickly, except Mark, who sent Anna a particularly foul smirk.

Anna was too busy studying Greg to notice Mark.

Greg sat there, furrowed brow, playing with his pencil and obviously not listening to the discussion any more than she was. He seemed like a normal person again... But he hadn't been.

He'd been… Before she could admit the horrifying truth to herself, her gaze was drawn past him, slowly, and to the doorway beyond.

She had caught a glimpse of a movement through the open door.

She searched the space.

Nothing.

She kept her watch, then, just at the base of the door, another movement.

A black finger.

The finger pulled back and out of sight.

Anna's blood turned cold for perhaps the fiftieth time that morning. A thousand thoughts ran through her mind, at the forefront of which was that the ghost-child, Michael, had more than once managed somehow to hold her physically in place in the past. He had held her in place and no one else could see him when he did. Even here in this room with all these people, she wasn't safe if his intentions were bad. But why would they be? He had never hurt her once. When he so easily could have. Then why had he come?

Suddenly, Anna was hit with the hard conviction that, for whatever reason, Michael needed her.

Her heart beating violently in her chest, she slid her papers into her bag. Eve, eyes on Anna, kept talking with the class until he said, "It's cold. Should we close the door?"

Pale, with shaking hands collecting her coat, she said, "I will." She moved quickly before Eve could say anything else, and slipped out of the room, closing the door behind her. It was the work of a second, and she cursed her stupidity only moments later, as she found herself alone at the end of a long, dark hallway.

And there he was.

How he had crawled such a distance in that time she didn't know, but he was there at the end of the hall, peeking around the side of the doorway, watching for her.

He disappeared out of sight as he descended the central staircase.

Anna hesitated by the tutorial door.

In there, all the students, Eve and Candide, possible safety.

Out here, a ghost.

But there must be a reason he wanted her.

She walked straight forward.

As she approached the corner, she slowed and looked over the bannister. She was on the second floor and she could see straight down the middle to the hard granite below. There was no sign of the boy.

She jumped as she heard a door slam on the third floor. Footsteps on the stairs above.

Something inside screamed at her to run.

She flew down the stairs after the boy, driven by she knew not what sort of madness. She came out into the beautiful central atrium and heard the pursuing footsteps sound louder as they increased their speed. She ran across the granite floor, past the coloured light of the stained-glass windows, through the solid oak doors, and saw the boy across the courtyard. He disappeared into the black mouth of her apartment building.

She heard shoes hit the stone floor behind her and she sprinted as fast as she could after the boy, too scared to look back, across the courtyard and up the staircase and into her own apartment. She slammed the door shut and locked it, and she heard the steps in her own building. On the stairs. Outside her door. She waited, her breath harsh and fast, her blood pulsing in her ears. Then, finally, she heard the sound of someone walking back down the stairs.

She ran to her bedroom window and looked down into the courtyard. There was no one.

She ran back to her door and listened hard. Not a sound.

She looked around for the boy, but she knew he couldn't enter the warded space.

Anna took her key from her pocket and opened the hanging door, quite safe at that great height from whoever had chased her, she hoped. She pulled at the loose stones, piled up in the hole in the wall. She was only just able to get enough purchase on either side of the huge top stone with her fingertips. It pained her frozen fingers to pull it loose, but out it came, slowly, scraping over the rocks underneath. Her hands closed around the base of it to lift it down, and as she revealed the space, the child's deathly face appeared, inches away from her own. She reeled back in fright, she stumbled, and the huge rock fell hard on her stomach, knocking the breath out of her.

Gasping for air, retching, she rolled and almost plunged straight to her death out the side of the building, catching the rotting door frame just in time.

She pulled herself in, climbed onto all fours and heaved in spurts of cold air, grasping her stomach where a large bruise was already forming. In short instalments, her breath slowly came back, and she looked again at the boy.

He stood there, still, terrified, his mouth moving, but no sound came out.

"I know you didn't mean to do that," she whispered.

His face cleared a little.

"I guess you want me to stay out of there for some reason, huh?"

Anna looked around the room. They had long since disposed of their ouija board, and as quickly as the thought occurred to her, she realised how utterly ridiculous the idea was and moved on.

She could try automatic writing. But she would have to let the boy channel her somehow. Invite him in to use her body… She thought of Candide's possession and let her mind move along.

Electronic voice phenomena? There was no recording device she knew of nearby.

She looked at the boy apologetically and did the only thing she knew to do.

Half an hour later, Eve burst into the apartment in no small panic to find an unexpected scene.

Anna sat with a neat pile of rocks against the wall, her back to the open hanging door, wrapped in a thick, soft, shaggy throw, every candle they owned lit and placed inside, outside and all around the opening in the wall, reading aloud.

He listened as she finished the paragraph. "Jane Eyre?"

"Yeah, it's…" She blushed and cast her eyes down at her book. "I thought she was a nice role model for… I don't know. Is that awful? I didn't have anything more appropriate for a child."

Anna looked up at him hopefully, and received one of the most adoring smiles she'd ever seen in her life. "I think that's a beautiful choice."

Eve made them both warm drinks and he and the boy, now unseen by either of them on the other side of the wall, sat and listened to Anna read for the next two hours.

CHAPTER 33
MEDICAL HORROR

Aubrey, the first to arrive, took the portion of blanket offered by Anna, the coffee offered by Evelyn, and waited, nervous about the task ahead of her, but buoyed somewhat by the reassurance of her new friends, and the confidence and proper decorum they had finally started to show as the task grew near.

Candide, the next to arrive, was first thrilled by the intimacy that greeted her, then set about easing Aubrey's anxiety by letting her unburden herself of the process she had in mind in all its gory detail.

Percy and Joe arrived. Together. Eve said nothing, cautious to not create any undue tension, but the first person Joe addressed was Eve, making apologies for the situation. Eve responded that it was really none of his business and Joe responded that there was really nothing to talk about, anyway. Eve refused to look at Percy, and to Percy's credit, he neither looked at nor spoke to Eve. He went about unpacking and unloading with barely a word until he eventually moved close to Anna when the others were deep in conversation, leaned in, and whispered, "What is it?"

It was only then she realised she had been watching him intently all the while.

The myriad thoughts that had clouded her mind for hours hit her head on. How frightened that little boy must have been. What it must have been like keeping the hideous secret to himself all those years. Being told it never happened at all, by the only people he ever could have turned to.

Anna wanted more than anything to reach for Percy's hand and tell him she knew everything—that there was at least one person in the world who knew and who believed him. One person he could unburden himself to completely and expect nothing but friendship in return. But unable to unscramble and articulate the mess of dark and distressing thoughts, she only said, "I'm sorry this happened to you."

Percy clearly hadn't been expecting the comment, or the look of genuine care that came with it. She saw a flash of panic in his eyes, his mouth drawn to the side in a light grimace, his fast assessment of her as he took a few slightly quicker, slightly deeper breaths, then he forced it all down and smiled his lovely smile as though it were nothing. "It will all be over soon enough."

She allowed him to brush it off, knowing too well the feeling of being trapped to try to push him. "Did you get everything we need?"

He understood the exit she had given him and seemed for a moment as though he wasn't going to take it. His lips parted, then whatever he was about to say disappeared as he searched her face. For what, she didn't know. He gave a soft, shy, sweet smile, like the one she had received only once before from

Percy, out on the stairs that first night, and he backed out of the conversation completely. "I think we did. Come see."

There was clearly some truth in the claim that Percy had needed Joe's help to obtain what was required, as they had brought with them several cumbersome bags full of medical supplies.

Aubrey watched the display of stolen goods with a calm and resigned eye. "You did well." She washed and dressed appropriately, then they all went downstairs to set up the necessary items for the first medical procedure the boy's body had needed to endure for over two decades.

"Light?" Aubrey asked.

Joe and Percy looked at one another uncomfortably.

"We brought torches," Percy said.

"Are you kidding?" Aubrey glared at the pair of them. "We haven't even started this, and you already messed up with the light?"

While she gave them a firm dressing down, for which Percy had many opposing arguments, Anna collected the candles from upstairs and began setting them upon every surface she could find in the dusty little bunker. The act possibly annoyed Aubrey even more than Percy and Joe's failure, but she said nothing and let Anna feel useful. Anna's usual bravado had long since evaporated as her attachment to the boy grew stronger during the time she spent in his presence that day, and they all sensed a certain something lacking in their midst. But Aubrey was the only one to address it openly. "Anna, are you going to be able to watch this?"

Slightly caught off guard, Anna nodded. "I am."

"Good." Aubrey adjusted her gaze. "Joe, how about you?"

"I'm fine," Joe said.

"Okay. I know you're good, Candide. Percy and Eve, do you need to go upstairs?"

Eve looked warily at Percy. "No."

Percy looked warily at Eve. "No."

Aubrey's mouth scrunched. "I don't want to hear a word from either of you, okay?"

They each gave a sullen nod.

The boy, or more, the demon, sat quietly, waiting. His big, scared eyes fell on Aubrey, and his black and broken fingernails gripped the edges of the rusted chair as best they could.

Percy came around, leaned down in front of him, and put his hands softly on Michael's arms. He looked him straight in his devilish eyes. "Michael, we're going to start to fix you now. If you haven't already, this would be a very good time to take leave of that body for a while, if that's something you can do. Otherwise, know this will hurt a bit, but it will heal in time, and we'll have you all better soon. Then I'm going to take you home with me. And I'll never let anything bad touch you ever again." Percy visibly fought off the urge to move any closer to the boy, though his caring tone and gentle touch had several people in the room forgive several ills that afternoon. Not least of all, Anna.

Once all the necessary items were laid out nearby, the drip set on its stand behind and out of reach of the demon, Aubrey took a deep breath and instructed, "Anna, hold the torch. Candide, I need the antiseptic."

Aubrey reached out and touched the boy's arm with her gloved hand. She was thankful for the glove. His skin was ice-cold, mottled, and foul.

As Candide unwrapped a scalpel, Percy began slowly pacing, silently, his arms crossed over his stomach. Aubrey's movements showed no sign of her noticing him, but she said, "We're going to need some heating in here. Percy, can you take care of that, please?"

He came to a stop, both unwilling and unconvinced. "Right now?"

"Please. He needs to be warm if we're going to get his blood flowing again. And it will make him more comfortable."

"There's one in my apartment." Eve held his keys out to Percy, who hesitated only briefly, then gave a slight nod before accepting the offer, and left without another word.

Aubrey pushed her fingers against the boy's eggshell skin. "His veins are so tiny from all this time with no liquid, no blood flowing, no anything… This is going to be bad."

She first washed the little arm, then spread the antiseptic along the length of his wrist. "Scalpel please, Candide."

The boy turned his head, and his eyes didn't close to blink once as his gaze bore into her.

She brought the scalpel down to his skin, and just as she was about to make the first cut, he screamed. It was a deafening scream, and after his complete and total silence up until that point, it shocked Aubrey so that she stabbed him slightly with the scalpel. The blood came to the surface faster and in more volume than she or anyone in the room would have thought possible.

"All right," she said calmly. "Please clean that."

As Candide brought the cloth down, the boy screamed again.

"Can…" Aubrey looked up at the others. "Can someone do something about that?"

Without any hesitation, Joe picked up a length of bandages and began winding them around and around the boy's jaw until his mouth was completely covered. "Do you want me to do the eyes too?"

"No." Aubrey shook her head slowly. "No, that feels even worse somehow."

Candide gave Aubrey's arm a little squeeze. "Try to remember, it's not him. He knows you're here to help."

Aubrey stiffened a little, pushing away any vulnerability Candide's words called up as best she could. "Just the mouth is fine. Let's do it." And she brought the scalpel back down to the boy's skin. On first contact, he yanked his arm back and flailed his hand around as much as his restrictions allowed. "Eve, hand."

"Oh… Yep. I'll get it." Eve, far-too-gently, pushed the skeletal hand down. The demon gave a small laugh behind the gag, then snapped its fingers shut on him. Eve held a little tighter, and grit his teeth as the demon curled its hand, its broken fingernails piercing Eve's skin, drawing blood within seconds.

"All right, Eve?" said Aubrey.

"Mmhmm."

"Hold on tight."

Aubrey, once again, brought the scalpel down, and this time was able to make a long, neat incision above the vein. She sliced lengthways down his arm a small way in order to pull the skin back. She lifted the vein out of the skin to get better purchase, allowing her to push the needle into the shrunken and desiccated blood vessel.

Candide absolutely beamed as Aubrey stitched the skin back together and applied the bandages to keep the drip in place. "You're amazing. Do you know that?"

With the task complete, Aubrey's entire demeanour changed. She finally relaxed her shoulders and let herself smile a little. "I wish I did. We'll just have to see how he copes over the next few days. Now, I'm going to change and wash and have a stiff drink. Who's taking the first shift?"

"I will," said Joe.

"I can stay," said Eve.

Aubrey pulled off her gloves and dumped them in a bin. "You can both stay for a while. When Percy gets back, I need to talk to you all about something, so I'll call you upstairs then. You can take that gag off now. Anything out of the ordinary—whatever that is—you call me straight away, all right?"

Eve turned immediately to Anna. "Will you stay, too?"

She looked doubtfully at Joe, who let out a quiet sigh and stared absently at the floor. "No. No, I think I'll go get us all something to eat." She hated to leave the two of them alone, not only because of the growing jealousy she was trying constantly to keep under wraps, but it was obvious Joe still despised her. Why wouldn't he? But what might he say to Eve?

Regardless of her misgivings, she accepted Eve's kiss on her cheek, hoped it wouldn't be the last, and followed Aubrey and Candide upstairs.

They two disappeared into the bedroom, and, left alone, she felt the size and the cold of the apartment more than ever. She did her best to make the place as bright and cheery as she knew how, switching on every light, tidying a little, turning up the heat. Then she went to the kitchen by herself to mull over the long and difficult day. Which was the last thing she wanted to do. She chopped some things, arranged some others, and just as she felt her bravery about to collapse entirely, she smelled the heady comfort of Percy's perfume, and was able to discreetly take in his well-formed physique as he heaved his glorious-looking body up onto the kitchen bench beside her.

CHAPTER 34

PERCY AND ANNA, ALONE AT LAST

Percy's alluring warmth was just as engaging for Anna as it had been several days earlier, the last time they were alone together, when he had inserted himself so recklessly into their lives. But now things had changed. She knew the awful things he had done—some of them. She knew the hideous things he had seen. She knew the lonely, heart-breaking life he must have lived. And no matter how much she disliked herself for it, she was even more drawn to him.

"How are you holding up?" she asked.

"I don't know," he replied. "On the one hand, I'm probably the happiest I've ever been. Finding Michael has been the purpose of my existence for pretty much my entire life. But that's done now. Wine?"

"Please."

"I think I'm slightly terrified of what happens next. I don't think I'm going to know who I am anymore. But I'm happy to be here. For now. With you." He smiled his breezy smile, handed her a glass of wine, and hopped back up onto the bench, kicking the window open and lighting a cigarette. "How are you holding up, Anna? I don't know why you're still talking to me after everything I said to you, and everything I did, but I'm glad you are."

Percy, able to talk so frankly about such a tragic life as though it barely touched him, keeping everything under his studied, well-presented facade, until it escaped in vile bursts of anger and violence.

Anna glanced over at him, a little hesitantly. "Percy?"

He must have known it was coming. He spoke gently. "What is it?"

"You didn't really mean to kill him, did you?"

"Which time?" he joked.

"Percy!" she snapped.

He pulled his legs up and rested his chin on his knee as he leaned against the window frame. He made rather a beautiful, if melancholy picture as he sat there, smoke escaping into the moonlight, reflective. "I honestly don't know. I think maybe I did that first time. I can't explain how terrible things were back then... I wish now I hadn't done it. But then, last time... I still don't know." He sighed, drank his wine, and sat thinking for a time. "I don't think I ever really knew Evelyn at all. And I don't think I do even now. He would never let me know him, you know? With good reason, I suppose. But he's not who I thought he was."

Anna, pleased to hear what seemed like sweet words about Eve, said, "He has a very forgiving nature."

"I can only hope so." Then Percy turned his head slightly to glance at her, a soft smile on his handsome face. "Not least because I'm more than a little in love with you."

She almost dropped her spoon. "Percy! You can't say that!"

He watched her perturbation without the slightest ripple of alarm. "Why not?"

As usual, his relaxed nature annoyed Anna even more, so she adjusted her heat and her pots, pointlessly grabbed a new spoon from the drawer, and set about furiously stirring. "Just when I thought there might be a good person in there somewhere."

"I thought you and I could be frank?"

"How do you think Eve would feel if he knew you were up here saying that to me?"

"He must know." He continued to watch her calmly. "I've hardly made a secret of it."

"No, maybe not," she sputtered, knowing that was perfectly true, "but that's different. That's just—"

"And he's very tolerant of your wandering eye."

"That's not—it's just—it's my eye! Not me!"

"Funny, I thought I heard you say my name last night." He leaned his head languidly against the window frame. "Late last night…"

She wished very much that she could die. Or at the very least that she could hide her deep blush somehow, but the kitchen lights were harsh and true, so she let her hair fall around her face as she gave dinner far more attention than was necessary. "You're not allowed to come in here and tell me you love me."

She could hear in Percy's voice that he was having a marvellous time at her expense, as usual, and she knew if she looked up just then, she would probably be caught by his mischievous grin.

He let her off the hook about the night before, much to her surprise and relief, following her lead chivalrously. "It sounds so much nicer to say 'love' than 'lust', though, don't you think? Imagine if I walked in and said, 'Anna, I want you right now'." Then she did look up and he curled his lip in just the way she liked, before continuing in a low tone, "'I'm lusting after you.'"

Her body responded in a way quite the opposite of her mind, which made her blush even more deeply than his declaration had. She rasped out, "Did you think this conversation might make me slightly uncomfortable?"

He raised that sexy eyebrow of his. "Not in a bad way."

"Stop that!" But despite everything, a smile finally broke though, and she realised she had given him exactly the reaction he'd hoped for. He laughed in response, happy to see her smile for the first time that afternoon, try as she might to repress it.

"Anyway," she said, with a roll of her eyes, "I thought you may have developed interests elsewhere."

"Oh, I have." He gave a heavy sigh. "But he's also hopelessly devoted to you know who. He'll barely even look at me now, especially after everything Evelyn told him about me. And you should have seen the two of them down there."

"Seen what?" She stirred her pot as casually as possible, listening more intently than ever.

Percy leaned in a little, lowering his voice like the dreadful gossip he was. "Evelyn acts like he has no idea about this little crush of Joe's, but he's pushed himself right up against Joe, and they're whispering together like… like a pair of old lovers!"

Anna burst out laughing. "Don't be ridiculous."

"Then what's he doing sitting with him like that? He sits there, making his little jokes, all warm and sweet with his nice sweaters, and Joe takes it all, hook, line and sinker. Evelyn needs to stop leading him on."

"I think Eve has been very clear about how he feels about me and our relationship."

"Even so."

"'Even so,' what?" She felt herself getting properly annoyed now, but not with Percy. "You're allowed to be jealous of them, but don't accuse Eve of something he isn't doing. Eve can't help it if Joe has feelings."

Percy scoffed. "I think you're kidding yourself slightly there."

"Oh, please." She slammed down her spoon with a splatter all over the bench, turning to Percy. "If Joe's going to throw himself shamelessly at a taken man—"

"Shamelessly?"

"Shamelessly! Always with the big eyes, looking at him like a lost kitten. How can Eve help but be nice to him if he's going to act so pathetic?"

"Nice?" Percy repeated with clear disbelief at her naivety. "There's 'nice' and there's making eyes back at those kitten eyes. Does he really have to help him get his scarf on? He's a grown man! And I'm telling you, I've seen him playing with his hair."

"He was not!"

"He was too!"

Anna had seen it. Eve had been playing with his hair. She turned away again, mumbling, "Maybe just moving it a little. Once ever. I mean, his hair gets all in his eyes."

"Yes. It does." Percy relaxed against the wall again. "It's beautiful hair."

"It is," she conceded.

"They would make a beautiful couple."

"They're not going to be a couple!"

For a few seconds he was quiet, perhaps considering his next words, and in that few seconds the atmosphere shifted. Before he even spoke, Anna felt the knot inside, but then he did speak, softly, seriously. "But what if they did end up together? I think we could make a pretty good go of it. Don't you?"

She neither blushed nor smiled this time. "No, Percy."

"It would have been you and me, though, wouldn't it? If that demon had never come, you would never have been pushed together with Evelyn, and he would have refused you every step of the way. You would never have gone to the church, and neither you, nor I, nor Evelyn for that matter, would ever have met Joe. Evelyn would be a distant memory by now… but you and I…"

She glanced at him just long enough to confirm that he was quite genuine, then concentrated hard on the spice rack. "You're very sure of yourself."

"Why pretend you don't feel it?"

"Because I'm in love with your brother."

"Half-brother. Is that the only reason?"

"There doesn't need to be another reason."

"No. Not unless he wasn't here."

A stark, cold shiver came over her and she glared back at him. "Why would you say that?"

"Don't be like that." He spoke with such an air of distaste, disgust even, that he made her feel guilty for ever having had the dark thought. "I didn't mean it like that. One can't help but reflect sometimes, is all. There are so many things in this life that should have been mine." He puffed bitterly on his cigarette as she fixed him with her steely gaze.

"We would have lasted about four seconds if you were going to refer to me as 'yours'."

"That's not what I meant."

"Of course that's what you meant. You're only flirting with me because I'm with Eve. You see me as an extension of him. Another thing that belongs to him. That's why you said all those horrible things to me the other day. You didn't even care how much you might have hurt me. You just wanted to get to him."

He threw back, angrily, "It would be easier for you to believe that, wouldn't it? Much less complicated than considering whatever feelings we each may have. But you're wrong." Percy cast his eyes almost involuntarily over her, and she felt the warmth in him and she felt more self-conscious than she ever had in his presence.

He seemed to sense it and he looked back out the window, controlling his tone, yet speaking with an edge of ardour to his voice that was all new to her, and more frighteningly compelling than ever before. "I love your hands. I love the way you hold that spoon with your beautiful fingers that were the first thing I ever noticed about you. Back when I handed you that stupid key."

Those fingers shook a little now as her heart beat hard and she forced her eyes down. He stole another glance at her.

"I love your wrists and your arms. I love your mouth. I love your hips, Anna. I love the way you move about a room—"

"Percy, stop."

He spoke faster, louder. "I love the way you think and the way you dress and the way your eyes flare when you're annoyed with me. I love the way you look at me like you do. Like no one else does. I love the way you try to hide it all from him, right there in front of him, the way you try to protect him when you know as well as I do—"

"Stop it right now," she yelled.

He raised his voice over the top of her. "And I *hate* that you would never have to keep things from me the way you do with him because I'm like you and you're like me and it isn't fair." Anna was too shocked to say anything, so he continued, "I know I went about things the wrong way, and yes, I would have loved to have torn you away from Evelyn—"

"Shut up!"

"It wasn't just the essay, Anna, or anything else I said the other day. You're smart. You're resilient. So many things fell into place when I found your application, but at the bottom of it all… I liked you. I liked you before I even met you. Before Evelyn met you. And then I met you and I really like you now.

And I know it's too late for any of that because I did the stupid, desperate things I did. And now you've chosen the golden boy—"

"Okay, I've had enough." She threw down her spoons, switched the stove off entirely, and walked across the small room to Percy. "You're going to stop talking to me like that right now. What do you think gives you the right to come in here and say that to me?"

He met her eyes easily, defiantly. "It's all true."

"I don't care if it is. Would you go and put this all on Joe? Or any other man? Or do you feel like you can force these ideas onto me just because I'm a woman? If you're going to make these claims that you care about me at all, then you owe me the basic respect of friendship, and that means not deliberately upsetting me and dumping your feelings on me. I'm with Eve. I'm staying with Eve. I don't care what you do or what you say —everything else stops right now or I will kick you out. Eve's a beautiful person—"

"Ha!"

"Inside and out. And that's not even the point at all. Stop making this all about him. I know you had a shitty childhood—"

"You don't know anything about my childhood."

"No, I suppose I don't," she stumbled, "other than the obvious fact that we're trying to exorcise your older brother who you lost as a kid because you have an evil step-mother."

Percy shrugged his agreement, so she carried on. "I'm not going to pretend with you, of all people. I know you saw my application and all the school reports. I know you know where I came from. That means you know, in theory at least, that I grew up with people who are worse than anyone you ever spent time with, for all your murderous monks. People far worse than Lady Adeline Worthing, worse than any demon we're likely to come across here at Endymion College, and far, far worse than you, Percy, whatever you believe yourself to be. You were a kid when you did those horrible things. And you're still horrible sometimes, really you are, but I'm horrible sometimes too and I can understand that. But you and I are friends, and I want you to drink wine with me and tell me all your stories and I really enjoy your company, but you need to never say anything like that to me ever again. I don't want to hear it. And it's not fair to Eve. He's so sweet, and he's so kind, and all he does is take care of other people, and I don't think you even realise that includes you."

Percy broke the intimate moment to tap a disgusted touch of cigarette smoke out the window. "Evelyn hates me."

Anna leaned forward, her elbows on the counter next to him. "Do you think anyone else would put up with you being here after what you did? He lets you stay, he lets you watch Michael heal, he lets you help. He puts aside his feelings every second you're here to do what's best for you and for Michael. He could demand you were out at any time, and he knows Candide and I would back him up."

Percy scoffed again, but with far less heart than before. "You would not."

"Of course I would. I bet you thought it was me letting you stay this whole time, but it's not at all. I'd throw you out in a heartbeat if Eve said to. I'm sorry, but that's the truth. You don't understand him at all. He's such a good person. He deserves so much better than he gets from you. And so do I."

Percy chose silence, so she took the moment to drive her point home. "If you don't want to be the villain of this piece, then just stop being the villain. It really is that easy."

Percy furrowed his brow and sat for a time. Anna wandered about the kitchen, cleaning up the mess she'd made throwing spoons around, and she set everything back on heat. He stole the occasional glance at her as she went about her tasks, but it wasn't like before. There was less intensity, less tension, but more intimacy somehow. And after a long silence, he said, "I'm sorry I upset you. I hadn't thought about it that way. I won't say anything like that to you again."

"Thank you." She flinched only slightly as she said it, because although his previous words had been entirely inappropriate, although she hated to have to openly acknowledge and manage his feelings, he was beautiful and he had her heart in a vice, and deep down, she had loved every delicious word he spoke. In another life, things would have been very, very different, and they both knew it. But this was the life she had chosen.

He said, "I do want to be your friend. I don't want to throw that away over... this. Whatever this is. Or was. Or what I mistakenly thought it might be. I'm sorry."

The logical part of Anna suggested that his relatively fast switch was entirely too good to be true. But Anna had already discovered she had an almost innate tendency to trust Percy, therefore the much larger part of her judgement, driven by her heart, won the day. "It's all right." She smiled. "We are friends. We'll forget all about it and just be friends from now on."

He opened his mouth as if to say something more, but he apparently thought better of it, which pleased Anna. He sent her a half-smile instead, and looking, she thought, rather ashamed of himself, they turned away from each other.

Anna cooked and sipped her wine, Percy smoked and sipped his wine, and he stared silently out at the full moon. They stayed that way for so long, each lost in their own thoughts, that she quite forgot about him, beyond the sense of comfortable silence in the company of another.

The last thing she expected to feel at that time was her entire body thrilling with delight as two strong, warm arms came from behind and wrapped themselves tight around her waist, pulling her gently back until she was pressed against his beautiful body. She moved her head to one side to allow her neck to be kissed, and a delicious shiver ran from her neck to her toes. She turned to kiss his beautiful lips. "Eve," she whispered.

He stood tall again, with a glance towards Percy. "Sorry. I didn't realise he was here, or I would have come up sooner."

"Don't be sorry." She kissed him again. "We had a good talk."

"I guess even murderers have their charms."

"Evelyn." Percy's voice held none of its usual venom, and he remained as confiding and melancholy as he had when he was alone with Anna. "Do you think it would be possible, someday, that you would forgive me for what I've done?"

"Never," Eve said. "Not as long as I live." He kept his tone light and calm, and the dreamlike smile never left his lovely face, as he spoke the brutal words. "Until Michael's better, you can pretend you have some sort of relationship with the people here. But you and I both know this is all part of the deal. As soon as he's well, you take him and the Necronomicon and you leave. You sure-up Anna's scholarship, and you never set eyes on any of us ever again. Then we'll both be happy, because we'll both have everything we want, right, Percy?"

Percy sighed, flicked his lit cigarette out the window, and hopped down from the bench. He paused just long enough to look his brother in the eye, and say, "You're absolutely correct, Evelyn. You're a hateful little shit, and I dearly hope I never have to see your smug face again, for as long as I live."

CHAPTER 35
A SERIOUS CONVERSATION

Spread into small clusters throughout the apartment, they ate their food disparately before being called together for what Aubrey had labelled 'a serious conversation'. Eve and Anna remained at the table where they ate, Percy and Joe at opposite ends of the couch, while Aubrey and Candide took an armchair each.

"All right," said Aubrey, looking cautiously over the group. "There's no easy way to say this, so I'm just going to come out with it…" She glanced at Candide for reassurance, and on her nod, Aubrey announced, "I don't know if what we're doing is ethical."

"Ethical?" Percy spat, still furious after his last interaction with Eve. "Since when did demon possession become a matter of ethics?"

Aubrey leaned towards him, looking every part the doctor delivering the worst sort of diagnosis. "Michael's recovery, his physical recovery, is going to be long and hard and painful. No human body that we know of has ever been through something like this. On top of that, we haven't been able to ask him if this is what he wants us to do to him."

"Don't you worry about that," Percy replied. "I have plenty of time and money, and I'll nurse him myself. With his mother, of course."

"And there's that." Aubrey blew out a long, reluctant breath. "I don't know how old your mother is, or what kind of health she's in, but… I worry how she's going to react to this. And, well, whether she would…" Aubrey, again, looked to Candide for assistance.

Candide took up the argument. "Percy, your mother didn't sign up to raise a chronically ill, high-needs, mentally unstable ten-year-old at her age. She's grieved for him. She let him go. And she's moved on."

Percy lay his molten gaze on Candide. "Are you suggesting she doesn't want her own son back?"

"No." A nervous hand pushed a strange of hair back, and she forced herself to meet his glare. "You need to understand. Even if we can get that thing out of him, even if we can make him healthy again, what kind of person can he be now? He's been locked in there for twenty years. In the same room for over two decades, with no one, nothing but a demon to talk to." She took a beat to decide if she would carry on with what she had to get out, then said, "He's not your brother anymore. Whoever's in there… they'll probably be damaged beyond repair."

Percy slung his foot over his knee and began to tap it anxiously. "No. No, that's not true. He got out. Anna, you saw him, didn't you? He came to you. He tried to talk to you—to warn you. He understands everything."

"Percy's right," Anna said, and not only because of her increasing if unspoken defensiveness wherever Percy was concerned. "I think Michael knows exactly what's going on."

"And if he doesn't?" Candide asked.

Percy shook his head resolutely. "I won't hear it. You're going to fix him—we—we are going to fix him, and I'm going to take him home to his mother. And I will take care of him. For the rest of his life, if I have to."

Aubrey recommenced, "That's very noble, it really is, but I don't know if you have any idea of what that would be like for Michael. He'll probably have no moral compass. Just think— he's learned every life lesson he has from a demon. Consider what it must have said to him, told him, all those years he's spent with it."

Joe, who had for some time remained quiet near Percy, watching his averted face with worried eyes, spoke as gently as he could. "She's right. I was only possessed for a few days, but… The demon lets you see what it sees. You see the world in a very different way when the demon controls you. Your belief system, I think, may begin to change when you understand what motivates demons. It can become the same thing that motivates you…"

Percy shouted back at him furiously, "Then what's the alternative?"

"We euthanize him." Candide was quick and calm with the words, but they lost none of their punch.

Percy dropped his foot to the floor and leaned forward, his speech slow and cold and full of loathing. "You want to murder my brother? Right after I got him back?"

"It's not murder," Candide replied. "It's just something that…" She trailed off, passing the hot potato back to Aubrey.

"It would let him rest," said Aubrey. "Before he does anything that—that might not let him rest…"

A vicious chuckle crept up Percy's throat, his face and voice hiding none of his revulsion. "I'm sorry, but to be clear, are you on a mission to save his mortal soul?"

Joe started, "Aubrey makes a good point—"

"That's quite enough out of you, Captain Cross!" Percy snapped.

Anna choked back the inappropriate laugh rising inside her own throat, and instead forced out the calm words, "We're not bringing religion into this."

"If he goes out there and kills someone, then what?" said Aubrey. "You don't know what he might do."

"And there's the very root of the problem with this whole stupid belief system," Anna replied. "If he's not of sound mind and he's been forced onto this path, he's somehow supposed to go straight to Hell? As though he's responsible for this awful life he's been forced to live? Some God you both have there."

"Anna, maybe not right now," Candide sighed.

Anna rolled her eyes at Candide, knowing she felt exactly the same, but wouldn't admit as much in front of Aubrey. "I'm just saying it's not okay to make a huge decision like this based on some stupid superstition. No one's making religion a part of this conversation."

"Anna's right," said Percy.

Candide continued, "Even if we forget the religious side of things for a moment, that doesn't mean he won't be dangerous when we release him."

"You can't execute him for something he hasn't even done yet," Percy yelled.

"Execute?" Candide yelled back. "Don't you think maybe he would just like to move on now? Almost his entire life has been misery. Maybe he would like to rest."

"You don't know that. You don't know a thing about any of it." Percy turned to look behind him, where Eve had sat silent and still during the entire discussion. "Evelyn? Eve, are you going to let them do this?"

Eve's face and knuckles were white as he broke his silence. "No, Percy. No, I'm not. We're just talking."

"No, Evelyn. Not like that."

"Percy—"

"He's your brother too, Evelyn."

Eve stared down at the table. "I know he is. We just need to think about what's best. For Michael and for Harriet. And Percy, for you, too. We're not going to make a decision about this right now—"

"Evelyn." The strong, sad, bitter, heart-wrenching tone of Percy's voice cut through the room. "I know you hate me, and I know you want me out of your life, and I am sorry for that. I know now how very wrong I've been—my entire life—my whole, entire life without him… and without you."

Percy's voice finally broke, and tears filled his eyes. Eve, still staring hard at the table, wiped his own tears away.

"You cannot know what it is to be the only remaining child of a single mother who believes her son was abducted and murdered. You cannot imagine the pain every time she looks at you, to know you're not the one she wants. That no matter what you do, or how much you love her, you can never make her whole again." He swallowed, trying to keep firm his wavering voice. "It drives you insane. It was always, always just us and this missing child. And I loved him and I wanted him, and I never could say a word, or her heart would break even more. And I needed what was left of it, with every fibre of my being. And all I could do was push it down and dream of bringing him back to her. Dream of making her whole again. And then finally, maybe, I could have a piece of that love that I needed all those years, that I deserved, as much as any child." He pointed a furious hand at Eve's avoidant frame. "That you, Evelyn, that you had every day with your adoring mother, who would move worlds for you. And she took it all away from me!" The hand scrunched into a fist, hard and white, and he dropped it to his side, lowering his tone. "And I am sorry, Evelyn, but oh, how I hated you. I think sometimes the only thing that kept me going all those years was my hatred of you and the revenge I would have on your mother when I did to her what she did to my mother. But I'm sorry now. I'm so, so sorry." He said softly, "You are my brother." Eve, finally, raised his eyes to meet Percy's. "You are my brother and I needed you all those years more than I could ever have imagined."

Eve was up like a shot, around the couch, where Percy was standing, waiting, and in an instant their arms were around each other, pulling one another in close, and they held on and they both cried in messy, racking sobs. "I needed you too," said Evelyn, between heaving breaths and more tears. "Every day. More than you could imagine. It was so hard. Percy, it was so hard." Two sets of wide and handsome shoulders shook with the violence of the emotion as they clung tight, covering each other's necks and shirts and glorious hair in tears. "But you're here now. And we're not going to do this alone. Not ever again."

"No, Evelyn, not ever." Percy placed his hands on either side of Eve's face, looking deep into his eyes. "Please forgive me. Please. For everything."

"I do," Eve nodded. "Of course I do. I'm so sorry I said all those things."

Percy threw his arms around Eve and pulled him in tight again. "No, you were right to say that. All of it. I deserved everything. I'm so sorry."

Candide's shocked eyes found Anna's, and she silently mouthed, "What the fuck?"

Anna's equally shocked if somewhat tear-stained face shook slowly back and forth in response.

Eve looked up at his brother, a hand on his cheek. A confident smile broke out, and he gave a small nod. "All right," he said. "That's settled."

"Is it?" Anna and Candide cried in unison.

"It is." He swept the tears from his still miraculously beautiful face. "Aubrey, can we go check how Michael's doing?"

Receiving a blank face from Candide, Aubrey offered a bewildered, "Uh, yes. Yes, we can do that."

"Great." Eve turned back to Percy and held out his hand. "Percy?"

"All right, Eve. Let's go." Percy linked his arm through Eve's and grasped his hand tight. "Let's go together."

Evelyn and Percy didn't break physical contact once as they made their way downstairs, leaving the rest of the group in astonished silence. Eventually, Aubrey managed to pull herself together enough to go after them, followed shortly by the remaining three.

CHAPTER 36

NASOGASTRIC INTUBATION

"That's strange," said Aubrey.

"What is?" asked Anna.

Aubrey leaned forward, touching Michael's arm gently, studying his face. "He's... He's hardly had any fluid at all, but... look at him. He looks so much better. He's warm, the colour's coming back..." She turned to the group. "Is this supernatural? Is this what they do?"

"It's what they do." This, Joe accompanied with half a shrug.

Percy started forward to examine Michael up close. "This is fantastic."

Anna, meanwhile, watched his excitement warily. "But why would it do that?"

"Does it matter?" he called back, his fingers sweeping lovingly across Michael's little arm.

"Very much," said Candide. "Why would it help us?"

Percy ignored her and looked up at Aubrey instead. "What's the next step?"

"I'll have to examine him, but if that goes well, I guess we can intubate him."

Percy screwed his handsome face up in disgust. "Oh, that's the nose thing?"

"Yes, Percy," she sighed.

He climbed to his feet. "And you can... can... Do you need me? While you're doing that?"

"No." She smiled. "Not a bit."

"Perfect." He clapped his hands together, rubbing them for warmth. "All right, do I need to break in anywhere to steal anything?" He looked over at Eve, who watched him and all proceedings with a sweet, softly excited smile. "Eve, will you come steal things with me?"

Eve grinned wide and true. "You know I will."

Percy made his way back to Eve's side with an equally large smile. "This is going to be so much fun."

"Ah, no, that's fine," Aubrey interrupted. "You got everything before. We're good for break-ins."

Two handsome faces fell.

So Aubrey suggested, "Maybe you can just go sit for a while? Upstairs. And make sure nothing supernatural kills us?"

Their faces lit up again.

"Imagine that, Eve," said Percy. "Two estranged brothers, side by side, fighting supernatural things. What an odd concept."

"Ridiculous," Eve laughed.

Anna and Candide squinted incredulously at them both.

Percy had already started to drag a more-than-willing Eve upstairs, but Eve called back over his shoulder, "Anna, do you want to come?"

"No." She frowned. "I'm going to stay here and help Aubrey. I imagine this will be quite stressful for her."

"Oh!" His feet screeched to a halt. "Should I stay? Aubrey, should I stay?"

A doubtful shake of the head from Anna and a firm 'No' from Aubrey, and Percy said, "Let's go, little brother."

"Let's go, big brother," said Eve, and they disappeared out of the room together, still arm in arm.

"I think they're probably more nauseating than Eve and I," said Anna, watching them disappear into the dark.

"Could it be a spell?" Candide asked.

"I didn't see him cast one. How could it be possible?"

"Maybe they're just… happy?" suggested Joe.

"Maybe," said Anna.

"I don't like it," said Candide.

"I don't know how to feel," said Anna.

"I'm going to examine him now," said Aubrey.

A little time later, Candide and Anna were sent upstairs to gather supplies for the next procedure. There they found the floor slick with blood from whatever supernatural things had already crept through the open hanging door, and Percy and Evelyn sat on the couch, faces close together, eye to eye, hanging on one another's every word, as Eve wiped more blood from what had become his favourite kitchen knife.

"So, we're just going to stick a tube up his nose now," Candide called.

Percy gave a wave of his hand. "Let us know when you're done. We'll be down."

"You're still watching this door, right?" Anna said. "I don't want to die if something comes in…"

Eve tilted his head on the side and held up his knife. "I'm on it." He offered a gorgeous smile, and he and Percy quickly returned to their intimate tête-à-tête.

"Right. We'll just go then," Candide called, to no response whatsoever, prompting her to stomp on the stairs so hard on the way back down that she cracked several more.

Anna caught up to her with far lighter steps. "Are you okay?"

"Of course I'm okay. Why wouldn't I be okay?"

Anna dodged the sharp flick of blonde hair. "No reason."

"Good. Let's get to work."

Upon their return, Aubrey, in full medical kit and holding a thin transparent tube, announced rather grimly, "I've never done this before and if I don't get it right, I'll fill his lung up with food and he'll die. So, I'm a bit nervous. And this should be an interesting experiment." She breathed out a short, sharp breath. "Joe, Anna, I want you to push his head back and hold him very, very steady."

Anna paused in her place and her eyes met Joe's. It was the closest they'd have been since she kissed him. Her stomach did a particularly grotesque flip, sliding a burst of bile up her throat, but Joe quickly attempted to break the tension, stepping forward and saying, "You take the top half."

Anna walked around behind Michael, beside Joe, who was still tall and beautiful, but now wholly terrifying, and she placed two hands on the boy's forehead. She pulled his head back gently, and it moved easily, Michael rolling his sickening eyes back to look at her. Then he spoke. "If your boyfriend hadn't come in, you would have raped this priest."

Anna let go a yelp of horror and jumped back from the thing. "Joe..." She stared up at his horrified face, aghast, her breath coming hot and fast, then promptly turned and threw up on the floor, at which point she fell on the floor and burst into tears.

"Anna!" Candide was by her side in the space of a second.

Anna wiped away her tears and the strings of vomit clinging to her lips. "I'm so sorry. I'll clean that up." Then she threw up some more, heaving out every bit of dinner with stabbing pangs of guilt and disgust, until it was nothing but dry retches and more tears.

Candide ran her hand over Anna's back. "What was that? Are you okay?"

"Yes. Yep." She swept the sleeve of her shirt over her mouth. "Can we please intubate him right now?"

Anna stood shakily and grabbed hold of the boy's head again, pulling it back just as gently as she had the first time, only a thousand times more reluctantly. The head came back, and the eyes rolled back, and the black tongue and the black mouth spoke again. "He hasn't forgotten about you."

To Anna's great surprise and slight relief, Joe's hand swept across and forced the mouth shut. "Does he need this to breathe while we intubate him?"

"He, uh, he still has one good nostril, I guess," said Aubrey.

"And the other's going to be full of tube and food. Right." Candide took a deep breath, watching the boy struggle to release his jaw from Joe's grip.

"And we're going in." Aubrey moved the tube to Michael's nose, and his thrashing, twisting and grunting became more extreme. "Hold him tighter!" Anna pushed her chest against the head to try to get a better grip. Joe attempted to move his hands to the boy's cheeks to hold him still, and feeling the shift, the boy's teeth parted and ripped a long chunk of flesh from the side of Joe's hand.

"Fuck! Fuck!"

"Oh shit!" yelled Candide. She grabbed a bottle of disinfectant, pulled Joe's hand towards her, fumbled, and dropped the entire bottle, spilling brownish-yellow liquid all over herself and Joe and Michael and the floor. "It's okay! We have another!"

"Yeah, he'll want lots of that," said Aubrey, looking over the torn flesh on Joe's hand. "And a course of antibiotics. I can't imagine the bacteria on those teeth."

"That's really helpful right now, thank you, Aubrey," Joe gritted out, holding his hand still for Candide's second attempted dousing.

All the while Anna waited as inconspicuously as possible, looking forward to the moment she could disappear from sight. The creature, free of Joe's restraint, had dropped its head back again, glowering at her as she tried to maintain control of herself. Then loudly, clearly, it said, "He's already here."

Anna jumped and let out a cry, this time shocked at the violence with which Joe sharply reached up with his wounded hand and snapped the mouth shut, cracking at least one tooth and covering the boy's chin, neck and chest in the blood still streaming from his open wound.

"What the hell was that, Joe? He's still a kid in there!" Candide yelled.

"Sorry. Sorry, he's upsetting Anna." Anna didn't believe for a second the violent gesture had been for her benefit. She said nothing, staring at Joe in horror. The sudden, aggressive move, at the mention of the demon, had pushed her straight back again to the med lab and that night. But Joe didn't look back at her. He averted his gaze and for the first time, instead of the anger, the avoidance, the defensiveness, she thought she saw fear. The same fear she felt. His gaze, had he looked up, she was sure would be a mirror to her own.

Candide was too upset about the act to notice, all-but-shouting at Joe, "Don't do it again, or you can go straight upstairs with the others."

He nodded and apologised again under his breath as he struggled to hold the mouth shut.

Aubrey's eyes went from Anna and Joe, then to Candide. "Gag him. And we'll get a vice to hold his head still if we have to."

Candide wrapped the bandages around and around the bottom half of Michael's struggling face. She wrapped Joe's hand next, and these two things being done, Joe moved his strong arms right around the boy's head. When his hand brushed Anna's, she shuddered and pulled back from him. His head leaned in close against her face, his soft hair on her cheek, the scent of him—the disturbing and pungent scent of church incense. Anna fought back a fresh retch and pulled away as much as she could while still trying to grip the top half of the boy's head. Michael continued to writhe as much as the chains would allow him to, but this time Aubrey got the tube in.

Deeper and deeper she pushed it, and for all of them, it felt like the slow procession of plastic would never end. But finally, she said, "Now I put the saline fluid in, and we watch for bubbles."

They waited patiently as Aubrey added the solution.

The boy writhed even more and made some sort of hideous screeching sound, and then they saw what Aubrey had predicted.

"Yay! Bubbles!" Candide clapped.

"Yeah, no, that's a lung." Aubrey pulled the tube loose. "Let's go again."

"Right... Languages are really my thing," Candide waffled with a flush. "And art. And chemistry. And maths. But not medicine."

"You just haven't learned yet," said Aubrey, and Candide bent over and kissed her cheek, both of them thankful for a short moment of levity amongst the medical horror. But then Aubrey said, "Wait... is that... is that smoke coming out of his nose?"

"Oh. Oh, um. Will there be much more saline solution?" Candide asked.

Aubrey narrowed her eyes. "I don't know. Why?"

"Uh. Demons don't like salt."

"Don't 'like' it?"

Candide shook her head. "Not a bit."

"Am I hurting him?"

"Maybe. A little."

"All right. Okay. I wish I didn't know that." Aubrey glanced up. "Have you two got him?"

Anna and Joe grunted their assurance, and Aubrey tried the tube again, which curled up inside the boy's nasal cavity three more times, and had to be removed and reinserted each time, until eventually, it went through. She tried the solution again. There were more screams, but this time, at least, there were no bubbles.

Candide watched on nervously. "Did you do it? Is that it?"

"Yes," Aubrey confirmed. "Unless I broke a bone and the tube went into his brain, in which case he'll die as soon as we exorcise him." She deliberately brightened. "But it looks good for now."

Candide threw an arm around her and kissed her. "You're incredible."

"We'll see." She laughed.

Anna, desperate to have it all over with, asked, "Is there anything else we need to do?"

Aubrey gently pulled Candide's arms down from her neck. "I'll get the food going in now. Only a few teaspoons each day to start. We'll watch him carefully for refeeding syndrome, especially given this whole salt situation no one told me about, and then if that goes well, we'll step it up over the next few weeks."

"Sounds good." Anna swept her hair back with a shaking hand. "I'll take the first shift, then."

Aubrey looked her over bluntly, and said, even more bluntly, "You don't look well. I'll watch him. You go upstairs and get some rest."

"I'm fine," she lied. As Aubrey's incredulous face was the only response Anna received, she continued, "I mean, I'm not great. But I want to be alone for a while. And this is a good place to do it. There's a lot going on up there. With all of us. I'm definitely better here. For a while."

Anna held herself as still and confident as she could manage for the next few seconds while Aubrey assessed her.

Finally, Aubrey relented. "You'll need to take the gag off."

"I can do that," said Anna.

Candide's arm pressed against hers. "Can I stay with you?"

"No, please, I'm really embarrassed about throwing up, and I really wish everyone would go. Just give me a few minutes, okay?" Anna walked to the bench and started tidying to hide her tears.

She felt Candide watching her, as she asked, "Are you sure?"

"I'm sure."

But then Joe, his voice stark in the cold and claustrophobic room, said, "I'm going to stay, too. If that's okay."

Anna froze, back to the group, then whispered, "Okay."

She felt Candide's reassuring hand sweep across her shoulder, but Candide quietly ushered Aubrey out as requested, leaving Anna alone with Joe for the first time since the day she had exorcised him.

CHAPTER 37
JOE AND ANNA, ALONE AGAIN

When the room was quiet, Anna remained with her face to the wall. She heard Joe's shoes creak as he shifted his weight, waiting for her.

She made herself turn to look at him.

He stood tall and handsome, his face neutral but his eyes wary. Her breath caught in her throat. "I don't think I can be alone with you."

He remained where he was, arms folded across his chest. "I'm not him, Anna."

"I know." Her fingers gripped the metal bench behind her. "But I'm still very scared of you."

He gave a small shrug. "I'm not particularly comfortable around you, either."

Another silence stretched on, in which her voice seemed to evaporate into the dusty air, until she found, "I don't know what else to say to you. I already said I'm sorry. If he comes back—"

His tone was remarkably brutal as he said, "Are you worried about what you might do?"

"No," she whispered, stomach churning anew. "No, I would never do that again."

"Do what?" His golden eyes under long, dark lashes were hard and unsympathetic, and it was a direct challenge—a new kind of torture. He was going to make her say it. Out loud.

She looked straight into those cold eyes and she wondered, was it really him? How could she know he was really Joe?

Anna saw no choice but to speak or run, so she, staring hard at the black and filthy floor, laid it all out—every vile thought she'd been thinking for the last three months—every word she'd said to herself a thousand times over. "I'm sorry I kissed you. I'm sorry I touched you. I'm sorry I let your body do that to mine. I'm sorry for anything else I would have done, because I like to think I would have stopped, but I honestly don't know if I could have. Or would have. I can't blame the demon because… because even if he said that was what you wanted, I didn't want to believe that wasn't true… when I did it. So I did it, anyway. I know that's horrible." She looked up at him. "Is that what you wanted to hear? You didn't want me and I assaulted you, and I'm sorry."

Now it was Joe's breath that came deep and fast, and his beautifully sculpted face turned away from her. "I didn't expect you to say any of that." He paced back and forth, then placed a trembling hand over his eyes until he was ready to face her again. "Now, at least, I know you understand what you did. But… I think I need to tell you something you don't know. About what happened." He dropped his hands to his hips, and looked back at her, just the way she'd looked at him when she made her confession. "Anna… You think you did that against my will, but the truth is..." How those beautiful dark eyes smouldered under the curls of his chestnut hair. "I wanted you to do it."

"No." Anna, pale and shaking, felt sure she was going to throw up again.

"No?"

"No. I can't hear that. Don't say that." She backed away from him, stumbling over the bench and almost falling to the floor. "You're not..." The tears came hot on her cheeks. "Are you him? Why would you say that to me?"

"Anna, no." Joe took a step towards her. "I'm not him."

"Joe wouldn't say that to me." She cast her eyes around for a weapon, grasping a bag of saline solution and a scalpel.

"Stop. Anna, stop. You want to put the salt on me to check?"

"Yes!" At that, she stabbed the scalpel into the bag and let the whole thing burst over him.

Seconds later, as he stood there soaking wet, admirably patient, she dropped the scalpel and the bag to the floor. "I'm so sorry. I'm sorry."

"No, that's totally all right." She watched him flick the water off his hands and wring out his sleeves a little.

"It's not really."

"No, I'm glad you know, now. And..." He quickly gave up any hope of getting more water off himself, crossing his arms against the cold. "Can we talk now? Do you want to sit?"

"Yes." She dropped to the freezing, wet, concrete floor where she was, and he did the same.

He spoke gently as he watched her, while she avoided making eye contact. "I can see you're not coping too well with this."

"I'm doing very well, I think. Under the circumstances." She wiped away her tears. "You seem better than I thought you would be."

Joe pulled his knees up, and wrapped his arms around himself. "Anna, I'm still… really angry with you, but what I said just then is true. I wanted you to do what you did. That day. I needed to tell you that, because I can see it's really weighing on you, and it wouldn't be fair of me to let you think I didn't want you to… to do what you did. Some of that…"

She brightened. "Are you saying I didn't assault you?"

"No, you totally assaulted me."

"Oh." Her face dropped back to miserable. "But you said… I'm confused."

"You assaulted me, because you weren't sure, and I couldn't tell you yes or no, and you knew that, and you went ahead anyway, and it was totally your intention to keep going."

"That's true." She nodded. "Yes, that's definitely assault."

"I don't know if you realise…" All at once, Joe seemed to grow more reserved, yet more trusting. He looked at her like he wasn't sure he wanted to go ahead, but he said, "I had never wanted a woman like that before. And now you, Anna, are the first and only woman I've ever kissed."

"Oh shit." She wished absently that someone would come and punch her in the stomach and leave her to retch on the floor until all the disgust was gone. "I'm so sorry."

"And not just the first woman, but…" He sighed, and with words barely audible, revealed, "That was my first kiss. Ever."

Anna's insides felt like they were glued together, from her clenching stomach to her un-breathing lungs, to her throat, clamped shut. "I'm sorry," she choked.

He swallowed hard, but still he pushed on. "If I wasn't possessed by a demon for days, seeing things through his eyes, hearing his thoughts, feeling his emotions, then I never would have wanted that. He changed me, and he changed what I wanted, and he made me someone else. So, when he told you I wanted you, he wasn't lying to you. But it wasn't really me either. But it was. All at the same time."

"Okay," Anna mumbled. "I don't know how to feel about that."

"You're still a terrible person," he helpfully clarified.

"I know," she agreed.

"Good." Then he took a deep breath, calmed himself, and continued, "It's been really hard for me because… because I spent so much of my life wishing I could be attracted to women. It was… It was never easy where I grew up. My parents disowned me. They would have been so happy if I could have felt that way, and it was so simple for that minute and it was… strange. And then it was over. But those feelings, just for those few minutes, were so intense, and my memory of you and what happened between us…" He brushed his hair back, and it did fall into his eyes again, so he tilted his head to the side and said a little reluctantly, "I don't know how to feel about that now when I'm with you."

She waited for the axe to fall. That night's conversation with Percy was fresh in her mind, and she stared at Joe apprehensively. She knew it was really Joe. It was really Joe, and these were really his feelings, so she waited with bated breath for what he would say next. Another declaration of love was the last thing Anna needed that evening, despite how attractive her many paramours may have been.

"Do…" She hesitated. She pushed forward. "Do you have feelings now? For me?"

"No!" he cried in alarm. "I'm a very gay man!"

"No, I didn't think so!" Anna yelled and blushed, drawing distracting lines on the concrete with the saline solution. "Just asking. To be clear."

"I'm not saying this because of," he blustered, "that sort of thing. It's that… There's no one I can talk to about this. You're the only person who knows what really happened, or who might understand, and I haven't been able to talk to you. I've been working through everything else that happened with the Church. They provide a counsellor and that helps a lot—"

"I wondered if they would do that." She smiled across hopefully.

"Oh yeah, they do." He smiled back. "It's a great program, actually. And I practically live on valium."

"Really?"

"Oh yeah."

She raised an eyebrow. "You don't seem that relaxed."

"I killed a lot of people."

"That's true. Therapy seems like the least the Church can do for you, considering."

"It's really good therapy, but they don't cover things like, 'that time a gay priest who took a vow of chastity got possessed and developed some kind of demonic sexual feelings for an insane person which resulted in his first ever sexual encounter with a woman'."

Anna's jaw almost hit the floor. "You took a vow of chastity?"

Joe's response was not dissimilar. "That's the part of that whole sentence you pause on?"

"It's a big thing," she gasped out.

"Yeah." On an anxious laugh, he admitted, "I sometimes wish I hadn't done that."

Anna's head moved up and down with extreme understanding. "Can you take it back?"

"That's not really how vows work."

"You should definitely take it back."

"What? Why should I?"

"I just…" She looked around the empty room as though it might give her the answers she sought. "It's a big thing. A *big* thing. It's a big part of life, and of being a person, and—"

"I couldn't be a priest if I took it back."

"But why would you want to, if they're going to make you deny such a basic part of who you are?"

Joe's cheeks coloured, a little in frustration, a little in embarrassment at the unexpected turn of conversation. "There are other reasons to be a priest, you know. Demons are real. Isn't that proof enough for you that God's real, too?"

"Not at all." She blinked away the thousand or so hideous memories that assailed her at that moment, that reminded her exactly how absent any sort of higher being must always have been from her life, unless said being specifically had it in for her from day one. "All that says to me is there are bad things in the world, and no one's coming to help me. So if I want to survive, I have to put my faith in me. But if you believe that— that God exists, and that he doesn't hate you—why do you think he would want you to be miserable?"

He screwed his face up at her. "Who said I'm miserable?"

She tilted hers to the side. "Joe, you just said, 'vow of chastity'."

"It's not the same thing."

Anna rolled her eyes. "Please."

He yelled, "Some of us can control ourselves!"

She yelled back, "I said I'm sorry!"

"I don't even mean what you did to me." He gesticulated wildly into the air in his exasperation. "Anna, you cheated on Eve! How could you do that? He's so nice. Do you have any idea how much he loves you?"

It was both shock and realisation that crossed her face. "I didn't! I would never do that! What? Is that what you think of me?"

He shouted, "I was right there!"

She shouted, "We weren't together then!"

"I saw you! Even before that night. Even before I got possessed. Remember at his apartment? You two were arguing, and I liked him straight away, and it was so obvious there was something going on between you two."

"No." Anna laughed at the memory, somewhat bitterly. How badly she had wished she was with Eve that day. "No, he dumped me right before I assaulted you."

Joe's anger simmered down a little on hearing her words. "Really? Right before?"

Anna nodded. "I mean, more or less right before. He wouldn't go out with me at all in the first place, but he kept holding my hand and all that, making it like he liked me, and then he said we could never be together—after he kissed me three times, I'll add—and he completely crushed me—"

"Eve did that?" Joe whispered conspiratorially, clearly enjoying the drama.

Anna was more than happy to unload. "He did! And!" she stage-whispered, "that's right after he told me he was falling in love with me."

Joe gasped. "I don't believe it!"

"Right before!" she reiterated.

"No!" His eyes widened.

"It's true! I'd only known him for three days and he was like, 'Anna, I think I'm falling in love with you. Oh, also, you're dumped forever and we can never be together'. No explanation. All while we're being hunted by this demon. I mean, how was that supposed to make me feel?"

Joe shook his head. "That's terrible."

Anna nodded again, fiercely. "Right? And everyone thinks I'm the crazy one."

"Well, to be fair—"

"Anyway, when you turned up, I was a free agent, and I'm sorry, but I didn't know I had a thing for demons, and I already had a big crush on you from before you even got possessed, and then it was you, and you were him, and he had whatever supernatural powers, and all those promises he made to keep Eve and Candide safe, and with everything else going on it was… overwhelming."

Joe considered for a time, then, shyly, with a blush, "You had a crush on me?"

"I did." Her blush and shyness matched his, but she added distracted fingers playing in the puddle again. "But I don't know, probably mostly because Eve was… I thought he was with Candide…"

Joe laughed, which sounded so good in amongst the tension. "Seriously?"

A darker shade of pink that Anna threw off with, "It was complicated. Anyway, he was messing me around, and I just thought you were good looking, and… I'm a mess, basically."

"Ah. Ah, well, that changes things. A bit. To know all of that."

"It does?"

"It helps me understand you better. It all makes you slightly less awful than I thought you were."

"That's something." She laughed softly, then mumbled, "I can't believe you thought I would cheat on Eve."

He raised a withering eyebrow. "I've seen you do worse."

"Yeah, but still… It's Eve."

Joe, well settled into the conversation by now, stretched his legs out long and leaned back on his palms. "That's what made it even more galling. You know, when he took me home after the exorcism, he stayed with me for a long time. All day. He really took care of me. He wanted to come back another day, but I said no."

She listened in wonder, but not too much wonder. It was, after all, typical of Eve to be so kind. And then to not even mention what he'd done in case Joe's name upset her. To carry his own burden of care that whole time to protect her from any thought of it. "He never told me that," she admitted. "Why did you tell him not to come back?"

He smiled sadly, confidingly. "Why do you think?"

Anna hardly needed Joe to tell her to figure it out, but it was sweet how open he was about his crush. Something she could completely relate to. "My plan was just to never see him again if we couldn't be together."

"He's a really lovely person." His words drifted off into a meditative silence, and Anna began to wonder if they had reached the end of the interview, when Joe quietly added, "I was very jealous of you."

No surprise again, perhaps, but miserable all the same. That same old feeling rose up inside. Why her? Why not Joe in her place? What had she ever done to deserve Eve?

She looked at Joe and thought he was a thousand times more beautiful than she would ever be. And the same again for kindness. "Why haven't you told him what I did?"

"Because it would crush him." He didn't need to think twice to figure out the answer. "I didn't want to do that to him. He doesn't deserve that." He chuckled, and continued, "I thought he would eventually figure out how awful you were and end it himself, so I let it go. But then when I heard him say all those things last night…" He trailed off, looking at her, really studying her, as though it would allow him to see whatever Eve saw. "He loves you so much. And I thought to myself, how could such a smart, sweet person be so wrong about that? It made me think about you differently." Anna chose to say nothing, so Joe continued in a gentler tone, "He talks about you like you're some sort of brave warrior. Not a woman who throws up over a few harsh words from a demon."

Anna groaned at the reminder of the pile of vomit sitting in the corner, and she said hoarsely, "I wasn't expecting it was all."

"There will be more of that, you know? Not vomit, hopefully, but the things he said."

"I know." She felt the urge to curl into a ball and die, but Joe pulled her straight out of it.

"I'll tell them all he's lying."

Her heart sank inside her at his kindness after everything she had done to him. "I can't ask you to do that. I know what I did."

"I don't think you do. You realise you were coerced too, don't you?"

"Maybe a little, but that's the thing that scares me." She refused to look up from the wet floor as she whispered the words. "I wanted to do it. I wanted to… submit to him."

Joe kept his gaze steady upon her. "But the important question is, would you have wanted to, if he didn't have you at a disadvantage?"

"I knew he would kill Candide, then Eve, if I didn't do what he wanted. I thought he'd kill me too, and you, and take the book, and I don't know what else he might have done after that. Those were all very good reasons, plus all the promises he made. It seemed like a reasonable sacrifice, my soul for all that. But those considerations aside…" She hated to admit it, because right there with Joe was the first time she had truly admitted it, even to herself. "Deep down, I know I wanted to. All on my own. I wanted to do what he asked of me, and I wanted all the things he told me I could have, and I wanted… I wanted to be with him. It felt safe."

When she finally lifted her eyes, she saw that Joe remained patient and caring, and he didn't seem at all surprised or perturbed by her confession. "It doesn't mean anything. You didn't get to make that decision on your own terms."

"Candide didn't submit when he asked her," she softly protested.

"That's different. You had more to lose and more to gain than Candide. Imagine if you were her, and your friends were there with you, and you had always been loved and taken care of like she has. You would have had so much to risk by accepting him. Maybe you wouldn't have done it either if you were her. But I don't believe the demon would have asked you if he didn't see something in you that he thought he could take advantage of."

Joe's words were so perceptive, they cut to the core of her, and she wondered if he, like the demon, had been able to see straight into her soul, when he was trapped with it. "How much do you know about me?"

"Just what the demon said to you," Joe replied. "I know the demon said you had always been alone, and seen awful things, and in my experience, lonely people will try to grab love in bad places—in any places. I've seen it so many times. You think you have a darkness in you, but desperation isn't the same as darkness. It's survival. He took advantage of you, and he made you think it was your choice. That's what demons do, every time. They make you believe you have the power of autonomy, but they set the parameters first, so you don't even realise you're already trapped."

Anna was dumbstruck. For months she had wrestled with the guilt, not only of what she had done, but the fear, the abhorrence of who she might really be. With a few words, Joe had changed everything. He was so completely correct. It had, all of it, been a perfect trap that she fell straight into. And while she still felt awful, while the sadness and shame might always linger, she also felt indignation. The good sort of anger that came with knowing it wasn't entirely on her. And that, she felt right then and there, was the first small step to, maybe, one day, healing. "Damn. You're a really good priest, Joe."

He laughed. "Thank you."

They heard floorboards creak overhead as the others wandered around the warm apartment. Anna said, "I wonder every day what would have happened if Eve hadn't come in when he did."

Joe looked up at the dusty ceiling as he reflected. "Things would probably be much the same as they are now. Until the demon called in the debt. And he would have, eventually."

"What are we going to do when he comes back?"

"You think he's coming back?"

"I do."

"Me too," he admitted. "He wanted you and he wanted Candide. I don't know why. There's an anger in both of you, and a power, and that's all I know about it. He wants the book, but he wants you both with it. Even so, he'll still kill either of you if you cross him. And he's very powerful. I don't know when, or how hard it is for him to come back after you banished him, but I believe he will try."

She narrowed her eyes at him. "And you're just telling me all this now?"

Joe shrugged, with his handsome lower lip pushed out. "I didn't want to talk to you before." Anna rolled her eyes. He went on, "But also, I didn't think we needed to talk just yet. Not until Michael said the demon was coming back."

"Thank you for telling me now, then," she muttered. Then more genuinely, "And thank you for talking to me. About everything. I feel much better about fighting demons with you now."

"Me too." He gave her a bolstering smile. "And I do forgive you."

"Thank you. It means a lot to hear you say that. I'll never stop feeling terrible about it—"

"That's a good thing. You should feel terrible."

"I do."

"Good." Joe dragged his legs back in close with a shiver. "Also, I'm cold. Can I get changed now?"

"Oh. Oh yes, sorry." Anna jiggled the pins and needles out of her own legs in preparation to stand. "Eve will have a change of clothes for you. He has lots of nice stuff."

"I noticed that." Before Anna could be annoyed at the deliberately provoking comment, Joe turned his attention to Michel. "Should we take this gag off first?"

"Oh shit, I totally forgot. I hope we haven't killed him."

They jumped up, then halted simultaneously as their eyes fell on the boy.

"His fingers..." It was with a combination of horror and amazement that Joe and Anna beheld those tiny little hands, long, and pink, and clean, and not a nail broken or chipped in the slightest. Their study traced up his arms, which were plump and healthy and full of life. His eyes, those once disgusting eyes, were now a bright and clear blue, and so lovely, just like those of his younger brother.

Joe reached for the bandages that wrapped Michael's face. Around and around and around he unwound them to reveal smooth, luminous skin dotted with pale brown freckles and a rosy glow about the cheeks. Beautiful bright pink lips and two rows of glorious white teeth smiled back at them. The voice came in the sweet, happy tones of a healthy little boy. "Will you take me back to my mommy now, please?"

Anna turned to Joe. "Give me five minutes to clean up this vomit and we'll get the others."

CHAPTER 38
AN EXORCISM

"All right, let's do it," said Candide.

Just like that, they, all six, launched into the Latin verse that was known to drive demons from the bodies of humans.

And just like that, nothing happened.

"Anna, what do we do?"

Touched by the faith Eve put in her, Anna coloured a little. "Last time, I thought it best to make the body inhospitable. That's why I gave Joe the mark. That's why I put all that salt into you, Joe."

"I was so thirsty for days," Joe laughed.

"I'm honestly amazed you didn't die," Anna laughed.

"Anyway…" said Percy.

"Anyway," Anna continued, "I can't—I won't—carve that symbol into Michael. And I won't fill his body up with salt. And I won't torture him. Does anyone else want to do that?"

All being in agreement with Anna that torturing small children was strictly off-limits, Percy was the first to put forth some other ideas. "All those things I said before, about those special objects I own, that was all true."

Earnestly, Eve said, "I'm sorry I ever doubted you, Percy."

"That's quite all right, Eve." Percy smiled lovingly over at him. "You had every reason to doubt me. But you have my word I'm going to be a better brother from now on."

"I don't doubt that at all," Eve replied, his eyes sparkling faithfully.

"Oh my god, can we not?" Candide sighed.

"As I was trying to say," Percy scowled at Candide, "Joe, you know as much as I do about these objects. Let's all go to my place and take what we need so we can get this over and done with."

"Great!" Anna clapped her hands together. "I've been wanting to see Room 238."

"Oh, Anna." It was probably the first time she ever saw Percy look remotely embarrassed, but she soon realised the embarrassment was on her behalf. "Do you still believe I live there?"

"What? Yes—I—" She blustered and blushed. "—I believed you—you may have…"

He watched on. "*Still?*"

"I mean. Yes?" She turned to Joe to explain, rather pettishly, "Percy said he's our neighbour."

"Percy says a lot of things," said Joe disapprovingly.

Now Percy scowled at Anna, even more severely than he had at Candide. "The point is, I have a lot of very useful things at home, so we need to go there at once, and get what we need. It's just slightly further away than Room 238 is all."

Joe's lips wrinkled, and he asked, "Does someone need to stay with the boy?"

"I think that would be a very bad idea," Candide replied.

"I think it'd be fine," Eve said. "He's still chained up."

Candide cast her eyes over Michael, who, all this time, sat smiling sweetly at them. "He's healed himself completely in preparation for us messing up. He knows his abilities better than any of us do. We can't be stupid enough to leave one person alone with him while he's in this state."

"Candide's right," said Anna.

Which elicited immediate agreement from Eve. "So what do we do instead?"

"We take him," said Candide.

"What?" everyone else exclaimed.

"We take him. We get what we need, and we exorcise him somewhere safe."

A general cry of disapproval came from four of the six present, until Anna said, "I think Candide's right again. It's not safe to do it here, anyway. Not if it's going to be a long, drawn-out process. And we have a sanctuary we can use at the church, right, Joe?"

"I don't know." Joe stretched a reluctant arm back behind his neck, drawing Percy's full attention and causing a sharp intake of breath to sweep over his parted lips.

"Why not?" Aubrey asked loudly.

"I've never tried to force a possessed person into a church before. I don't know what might happen. What if he just bursts into flames or something?"

"You clearly watch too much television," Candide scoffed.

"Oh, says the woman who stole her exorcism from a tv show," Joe threw back.

"I did my research first. And it totally worked."

"So why wouldn't that also be true?"

"You're not burning my brother," Percy said flatly.

"And I'm not anaesthetising him first, either," Aubrey added.

"Really, Aubrey?" Percy's ever-present scowl was now hard on her. "Did you have to make the point quite so graphically?"

Aubrey only shrugged in response.

"Explain to me again why we can't just do it here?" As the words left Eve's handsome mouth, the stairs creaked. "Ah, shit," he said. "Percy?" And the two drew their knives, returning shortly after, all but covered in blood. "Candide makes a good point. We should leave soon."

"What was it?" Anna asked, sliding her hand around Eve's biceps.

"It was like a dog thing. No hair. You can take a look on the way out if you want."

"I will." Anna reached up to wipe a drop of blood from Eve's cheek as he smiled down at her.

Percy coughed as obtrusively as possible. "My place is definitely safer than here. If we could just close that godforsaken door…"

"That's settled then," said Eve, dropping a languid arm over Anna's shoulders. "We're going to need a van if we want to keep him in the chair. Or something with a big boot."

"There are lots of very big cars in the carpark," suggested Candide.

"As a student, I have to say that feels very wrong," said Anna.

"They can afford it," Eve muttered. "So long as we can find something I can start."

Percy looked over at Eve with proud surprise in his eyes. "Can you hot-wire a car?"

Eve's ready smile grew a little wider. "I can."

"My little brother," said Percy, positively glowing. "Isn't he wonderful?"

"Oh, shut up!" snapped Candide. Then, "How are we going to smuggle this kid out if he's chained up in a metal chair?"

"Which is bolted to the floor, by the way," Aubrey added.

"We can handle that," said Eve. "We found a wrench upstairs. It's a bit bloody now, but it should do the job."

Anna's eyes sparkled. "Did you have to kill lots more things up there?"

"Lots," he replied, which led to mutual appreciative blushes on both their cheeks, and Anna's hand finding its way to his chest.

"Okay…" Aubrey glanced at them, shook her head, and got back on topic. "So we get a van from the carpark, swing by here somehow, get Michael in it somehow, and drive to Percy's house where we use his special objects to exorcise the kid?"

"Yes." Candide gave a firm nod of approval. "And failing that, we take our chances with the church."

"We'll all go together." Anna commenced a fast circle around the room, blowing out candles as she went. "Upstairs is warded, so even if Michael escapes the chair somehow while we're gone, he can't get out of this room."

"If upstairs is warded, how do we get him out the door?" asked Aubrey.

"We'll have to break the seal." Candide looked to Anna, who looked immediately to Joe, with whom she shared the same frightened understanding.

"I'll bring some fluid to fix the seals when we're done," he said. "We won't leave it long."

Anna gave him a thankful smile, then asked Percy. "Your house isn't warded?"

"One room isn't," he replied with a suggestive wink.

Eve's pretty mouth dropped open, and he shoved Percy's shoulder playfully. "Do you have an exorcism room you didn't tell us about?"

Coyly, Percy replied, "Of sorts."

Eve remained leaning against Percy's shoulder. "You're brilliant, Percy."

Percy leaned just as fondly back against him. "Thanks, Eve. You're brilliant too."

"Well, you might have told us that in the first place," Candide huffed, with a lofty roll of her eyes. "Everyone, get a weapon. We're leaving right now. I feel like stabbing something."

CHAPTER 39
BLOODY BURGLARY

Anna opted for the bloody wrench, refusing Eve's offer to wash it first, stating that the dried blood gave it better grip. Of course she still had her fabulously sharp fountain pen, too.

Candide made sure Aubrey and Joe had kitchen knives slightly larger than the one Eve gave her, which until that time had been his weapon of choice.

They took the extra scalpels Percy and Joe had stolen, still in their protective wrappings.

As all were aware by that time, Percy had his own dagger, which he proudly showed off to Eve and Anna, leaning back against the kitchen bench, turning it here and there to shine in the light. He said it came from Spain, was almost four-hundred years old, and had belonged to the painter Velazquez himself.

Anna, admiring the beautiful weapon, wondered aloud how many times the unblemished blade must have been replaced, or the golden clasps that held the jewels in place, or the jewels themselves, as it really was a very sturdy weapon for something so old and ornate.

Percy advised her sharply that they should all be preparing to leave rather than staring at his lovely blade.

Evelyn found a hammer in a drawer and declared it quite satisfactory, but at Candide's insistence, he also secreted a small steak-knife about his person, making sure Anna did the same.

He checked the time. "It's eight. And I have a lecture at nine tomorrow morning."

With her chin on his shoulder, Anna moaned up at him, "Why would you schedule a lecture for nine?"

"It's not up to me at all."

"I just think the whole system needs to change. They're setting sleepy people up for failure."

"We'll start the petition as soon as we're done exorcising Michael," said Candide. "Let's go."

They all laced their boots, pulled on their overcoats, and made their way, with surprisingly little trouble, down the staircase, through the central courtyard, under the grand Ancaster stone entranceway, around and down, down under the ground and into the carpark, hidden under perfectly manicured green grass.

They wandered through the dark, damp garage, which was undoubtedly the most rundown part of the entire campus. They passed one oversized car after another until Anna paused and kicked the wheel of a particularly large black jeep. "This one."

Eve passed his flashlight over the license plate. MARKY1. "You're still holding that grudge?"

"He's such a jerk. Wouldn't have a clue about Frankenstein."

"That's true." Eve grimaced. "You should have seen his essay."

Anna's lips pulled into a sly grin. "Can I?"

"Absolutely not!"

She huffed a disappointed, "Well, it has to be someone's car. Why not his? It's poetic justice."

Eve, as agreeable as he always was for Anna, said, "I guess it's the least we can do." He pulled two black gloves from his navy-blue overcoat—gloves that Anna recognised from a few nights earlier—and her eyes lit, and he caught her look, and he blushed, and she all but pounced on him. "Anna, we need to steal a car!" he mumbled through her kisses.

"Yes, okay," she relented breathlessly. "But we're going to burn it anyway, right?"

"Yes, we'll definitely burn it."

Raising an eyebrow, "So the gloves *were* just for me, then?"

"Anna!" He remonstrated with all the energy he could summon for the task, but he was, as usual, loving every second.

"Sorry. Sorry, I'll let you steal it now." She took a few steps back and ignored Candide's shaking head and the averted eyes of Joe and Aubrey, noticing only Percy's inquisitive gaze on her. "Haven't you got anything better to do?"

"I'm just trying to figure something out about how one might—"

They heard Eve's hammer smash a side window, then the creak and the rip as he pulled the dash off.

"My boyfriend is so awesome!" Anna jumped into the car and unlocked all the doors for the others. She released the boot and came around the back to open it. "Everyone in."

Percy and Joe climbed into the boot, and Aubrey into the back seat. Candide had just placed her foot on the step of the car to clamber in next to Aubrey, when she noticed the sudden and complete absence of Anna's somewhat-irritating exuberance.

She slammed the door shut behind Aubrey, pulled her knife out, and closed the boot.

The engine sprang to life as she moved around the other side and shut the remaining doors.

Seconds later Anna took a huge breath in and let out a cough and a half-scream as she felt her left side become drenched in warm blood from the giant slit Candide had carved in the creature that had pulled Anna beneath the car, and that had been, until that time, suffocating the life out of her with her friends only inches away.

"Anna, out!" Candide yelled.

Anna, grappling to retain her wits, rolled to her right and out from under the jeep, still gasping for air. She heard the bang as Candide was thrown against a neighbouring car. The engine was cut as Eve realised what was happening. Anna pulled the wrench from her pocket, and rounding the corner, smashed it down on what was most likely the thing's head. The yellow-grey mass had so many lumps and bulges amongst the festering mess of pustules that she couldn't quite be sure it was the head until the blow had the desired effect of knocking the thing to the ground to reveal something akin to teeth.

"Is it dead?" Eve called.

"I don't think so," said Anna. Then, "Start the car."

Naturally, his immediate response was, "No!"

"Get back in and start it!" Candide yelled, as a pleasantly grotesque understanding passed between her and Anna.

Eve watched Candide's blade thrust back into the thing as it reached for her, and seeing she was fine and in control, he smiled and relented. The engine roared once again, and with another swing of Anna's wrench, the creature's head smashed back down on the carpark pavement. Anna and Candide pushed the repulsive mass across the floor, and each kept a boot on it as Anna motioned for Eve to reverse.

To say the head popped like a watermelon would be to know what it is to back a car over a watermelon. None of the group were party to that information that day, but Candide and Anna did express some surprise at the amount of brain-matter and blood that covered each of them and also MARKY1.

"I'm so glad you talked me into buying the black coat," Anna said to Candide as she climbed into the front seat next to Eve.

"Argh, it's brains." He picked a lump out of her hair, tossing it on the floor.

"It looks so good on you," said Candide, clicking her seatbelt into place and snuggling up against Aubrey, who, happily, much like Eve, was more impressed than repulsed by the state of them.

Eve turned the car and drove through the ever-increasing puddle of blood, leaving a long, red trail through the dark carpark. He took the long way around the campus, through the long grass of their neighbouring field, where they may or may not have run over the remains of the Krasue they had completely forgotten to bury, then he pulled the car up at the bottom of the hill just down from their apartment. "I think this is as close as we'll be able to get."

"Beautiful," said Anna. "Now, how are we going to lower him from the hanging door to the pavement?"

CHAPTER 40
A STUPID PLAN

Once they were all back in the apartment, Candide roundly declared it to be a stupid plan, even if it was the only one they had.

"He couldn't get out of those binds last time," Anna protested. "We'll just use the exact same combination. That's right, isn't it, Joe?"

Joe, a little reluctantly, said, "I'm not sure the demon was really trying to escape last time."

"What? Why wouldn't he try?"

Joe flushed, fumbling for the words in the face of Anna's surprising ignorance while all eyes were on him. "He, uh... I think he was hoping you would untie him yourself."

"Well, that was pretty dumb then." And she laughed a little too loudly as she wondered if the demon might have thought they had actually made some kind of deal that night. Joe also laughed with her, just as loudly, which she was thankful for, so she carried on with the plan. "So, Eve and I will hit the med lab and get those really strong ties."

"And some electrical cables," said Eve.

"You all do the bandages while we're gone. Tie him up good. We'll be back in no time with the rest of the stuff." With that, Anna grabbed Eve's arm and pulled him towards the door.

"Wait," Aubrey called after them. "I thought we weren't supposed to go out at night, which we already did tonight."

"No, that was last night, Aubrey," said Percy. "That was different. We have a plan now."

"But—"

"And I've got this nine am lecture," Eve explained. "I can't be late for that."

"Yes, but—"

"And there's a stolen car waiting," said Anna.

"But do you think splitting up right now at night is a good idea?" said Aubrey.

"Of course! We'll be fine. Wrap him up well, okay?" And Anna and Eve disappeared into the darkness of the hallway.

CHAPTER 41
AN UNEXPECTED TURN OF EVENTS

To everyone's great surprise, Anna and Eve returned almost immediately with everything required of them. Upon arrival, they found the boy partially tied and gagged again.

"Is that necessary?" asked Anna.

"I don't want him upsetting you," Candide said in an off-hand sort of way, dropping medical supplies into a bag.

Anna's heart sank. As much as she didn't want to ask, she still did. "Did he say something to you while I was gone?"

"No." Candide flashed a bright smile. "And he won't say anything now, either."

"Candide…" Anna whispered, and she got a quick, loving look in return before Candide ordered everyone to get back to work. If the boy had said anything, not a single person in the room alluded to it, and all was casual business as usual.

They tied the boy even more thoroughly, and once they were all satisfied with the bandages, cable ties and electrical cables that held the boy to the metal chair, Anna got down on her knees and used her wrench to loosen the screws that held the chair in place. They took some work, having been screwed as tightly as Lady Worthing's own strong hands could manage, but after a time, Anna threw the last screw to the floor, then stood tall. "It's the moment of truth."

Eve easily opened the ancient padlock that had been holding the chains in place for twenty-four years, then he and Candide unwound the mass of heavy metal from the boy.

Where days ago the chains had left deep, black indentures in his thin, sickly skin, now the flesh bounced back fresh and plump upon their removal.

They waited and watched anxiously, but the placid boy made no break for freedom.

"It looks like you had a good plan after all," Candide said to Anna. "Let's get him upstairs."

This was achieved quickly and easily, with Michael weighing very little, even in his healthier state. They soon had him precariously balanced on the edge of the precipice outside the hanging door.

There was a brief discussion, and it was decided, much at Percy's insistence, that he and Joe should remain at the top and from there, using the chains, they could lower the boy down to the rest of the group waiting below.

Another brilliant plan.

Minutes later, the boy was successfully on the ground, and with a great deal of excitement at their success, particularly from Anna, they made their way along the path towards their stolen car, all seven of them.

None of them could have said precisely what it was, or pinpointed in the moment how or why the chair suddenly slipped from their grasp and hit the pavement. It hit with very little force, yet it was somehow enough to break the old, rusted chair apart.

In the blink of an eye, the boy slipped his binds from the metal of the chair and disappeared into the forest.

CHAPTER 42
FUCK!

"Fuck!" Candide did a faster assessment of the situation than anyone else. "Eve, Anna, I'm taking Aubrey and Joe back to the apartment. I'll be back very soon. Joe, you'll find a way to fix the demon warding and keep her safe, okay?"

Candide had already begun a purposeful stride away from the group, but Eve caught her arm. "We're not splitting up."

"First rule of horror," Anna agreed.

"This isn't fiction!" Candid hissed back at her.

Aubrey was around the front of Candide by this time. "Exactly how useless do you think I am? I'm not leaving you."

"I didn't mean it like that. I just don't want you to die tonight," said Candide.

"Great, then I'm staying," Aubrey replied.

"Okay, then don't die, all right?"

"All right. I'll try not to die."

The brief standoff was concluded with a kiss, then another, and Candide's arm around Aubrey.

"Then I'm staying too," said Joe, before adding, "And try to remember, everything Michael sees now, it will be fresh in his mind. Try not to let him see too much horror. And try to be kind."

"Funny coming from the guy who almost broke his jaw," Candide muttered under her breath.

"What was that?" Percy, his handsome face darkening dangerously in the half-light, fixed on Joe for the first time, angry, disdainful eyes. There followed a particularly uncomfortable moment in which all present except Joe and Percy themselves saw the change in Joe—the realisation that he had gone down significantly in Percy's estimation in that split second—and with that, the clear realisation that it bothered him, written all over his face.

"He bit him," Anna said quickly. "Have you seen his hand? He needs a whole course of antibiotics for it. Right, Aubrey?"

"Mmmm, that much is true, Anna," Aubrey mumbled.

"He ripped half his arm off," Anna continued. "Just about. Blood everywhere. It was brutal."

Percy surveyed the bandage on Joe's hand, which had bled through quite convincingly. Even if the resentment hung about him in the night air, he managed a softer, "Are you okay now?"

"It's fine," Joe mumbled, turning pink. "I didn't mean to… It was an accident."

"Six is easier," Eve interrupted. "Let's split into pairs and look for him. Stay close, Candide."

With a nod, she led Aubrey a small distance away to the left. Joe picked the heavy chains off the ground and threw them over his shoulder as he and Percy moved off to the right. Anna clasped Eve's gentle hand, and they walked straight forward together into the damp, mossy forest.

The trees had mostly lost their leaves and their naked, silvery branches let through ample light from the full moon that shone overhead as they took their first tentative steps into the forest. Within seconds, of course, the small gap of cloud around the moon closed up and all became pitch black except for the light from their torches.

"All right, Candide?" Eve called.

"Fine, Eve," Candide called back. "It's been about thirty seconds."

"Good," he said. Then to Anna, "Where would you go if you were a demon set free for the first time in twenty years?"

"After what we did to him the last few days?" She glanced around the forbidding forest. "I would wait right here in the dark and kill us all, one by one."

"That's not comforting," he said.

"You like my honesty," she replied.

Before he could concur, Eve dropped to the ground with a piercing cry of pure agony. Anna was on the dirt with him in a second, and once his screaming and flailing had abated a little, they made the grisly discovery of a sharp stick, expertly pushed straight through the skin at the top of his knee, and forced down behind his kneecap, her flashlight revealing the unsettling extent of the bloody stick poking out the top of his leg.

"Little shit!" she exclaimed, scanning the trees for the boy, her arms a strong support for Eve, who was trying to sit up.

Within seconds, Candide and Aubrey appeared from one side of the forest, Joe and Percy from the other. "Protect him," Anna said. They formed a circle around Eve and Anna. She put her boot on Eve's stomach to hold him still, and she yanked the huge stick free from his leg with a spatter of blood and a scream of horror from both of them.

Aubrey spun around in shock, yelling, "What the fuck did you just do? You leave things in! You always leave them in!"

"I didn't know!" Anna cried.

"No, no, it's actually much better," said Eve through tears and gritted teeth, accepting both the oxycodone and whisky that were handed to him one after the other by Candide and Percy. "It's all right, little buddy," Eve called into the wilderness, swallowing everything down. "I know you didn't mean to do that. We'll get you all fixed up soon."

Percy helped Eve to his functioning leg and supported him as they moved deeper into the forest. They had only taken about six slow and painful steps when they heard the sound of a branch snapping. To be specific, it was not the sound of a dry twig or stick on the ground that one might step on with their boot. It was the sound of a branch of a decent size being snapped from the side of a tree with great force, and it came from somewhere very close by.

Joe's jaw was dislocated entirely, cracking at least one tooth, as the branch in question smashed into the side of his face. The branch swung back around and crashed into Percy's stomach, knocking the air out of him and felling both him and Eve in an instant. Anna held her wrench ready, and she and Candide turned back to back, safeguarding the pile of beautiful but sorely injured men sitting on the forest floor. Aubrey sank into the middle of them. "Hold still," she said to Joe, who couldn't speak to protest, but was so surprised by the onslaught he did only as instructed, and Aubrey was therefore able to manoeuvre his jaw back into place within seconds. "Hey, that really works," she said, admiring her work on the bruised but still handsome face. She handed Joe some of Candide's painkillers, which he took with Percy's whisky, without a second thought.

Anna, until that time watching for another attack, only noticed what was happening as Joe swallowed the lot. "Wait. Is that okay with Valium?"

"Valium?" Aubrey's eyes grew wide as they snapped back to Joe. "You're on Valium?"

"Just a bit." He rubbed his aching jaw. "But it's probably wearing off by now. Why? Is that bad?"

Aubrey shook her head slowly, her brow more deeply wrinkled than Anna had ever seen it. "I don't know."

"It's fine," Candide called over her shoulder. "It might make him fall asleep, is all."

Aubrey tilted her head to the side. "And how do you know that, Candide?"

Anna and Candide exchanged inscrutable looks. "Chemistry... I'm good at chemistry."

Anna stifled a laugh. Aubrey ignored her with the flash of an eye roll and moved on to the more pressing concern. "What are we going to do with this lot if he falls asleep? We can't carry them all back."

"I'm good." In an attempt to prove his point, Eve jumped up, the drugs and alcohol already taking their miraculous effect on him. He bolstered himself with a tree, and reached a hand down to pull Joe to his feet, then shifted his weight against Joe, who was still running a hand around his face, feeling over the fast-forming lumps and bumps. Percy, meanwhile, remained coughing and convulsing at their feet.

Anna sidled over to Candide. "How many pills did you give Eve?"

"Six."

"Aha." She watched him take another sip of the whisky Joe handed over. "And drinks. On an empty stomach. This should be fun."

"Really, I'm good," Eve insisted with a worrying grin.

"Michael," Anna called into the night. "I want to thank you for everything you tried to do for me. I'm not going to hold you to blame for anything that happens tonight, so I hope you won't blame me for doing what I have to do, either. I think you've been stuck inside a demon long enough to know what that means."

Percy made some kind of gagging sound in protest, but she spoke over him.

"Demon! You should know I'm not the mothering type. If you lay one more hand on any of my friends, I'm going to have to kill your host. I won't hesitate just because he's small."

Silence reigned for perhaps half a minute, which felt like aeons to the group, before a large rock came hurtling through the darkness, smashing into Anna's shoulder and knocking her to the ground next to Percy. "Bastard! That's my bad shoulder! I bet he knew that!"

"We all need to leave. Now," said Candide.

"We can't just let him escape!" Anna protested.

"We don't have a choice. We'd be better off going back to the campus and watching over things there."

"And what if he goes to the village?"

"We can't let him get to the village," said Joe, shuddering at his own horrid memories of what his possessed body had done once it got to the village.

"We have to do something," said Anna, getting to her feet with the aid of Eve's unsteady hand. "Candide, can't you *do* something?"

An even more deafening silence than before fell over the group.

Throwing a very pointed look at Anna, Candide said, "No, Anna, I can't *do* anything."

Anna slipped away from Eve and lowered her voice. "Don't think I don't know what you can do."

Candide lowered her voice to equal Anna's. "What is it you think you know?"

Anna thrust her arms out in exasperation. "You sleep with the book! You know all about that book. Don't tell me you don't know how to do things from the book. I've seen you do things."

Candide threw her hands up in denial. "I didn't do anything. That doesn't mean a thing that I sleep—"

"I know what that means." Anna waggled the finger of her sore arm right in Candide's face. "And don't you dare suggest that I don't know what that means."

A slightly panicked, though mostly annoyed, look from Candide bore into Anna, but she wasn't about to back down.

"Do something!" Anna shouted.

Both pairs of eyes snapped over to Eve, whose head rested on Joe's shoulder, his eyes glazed, a soft smile on his handsome face as he watched the interaction. "Do it, Candi."

Candide melted on contact. "Eve... I don't know if I can do it in this situ—"

"Hurry up!" yelled Aubrey.

"Okay, I'll try." Candide looked down at her hands, closed them tight into fists, then closed her eyes. They all sensed an eerie calm spread over her body, and somehow, into the surrounding air, too. When she opened her eyes again, they glowed green, just as Anna had seen before.

Anna looked at Eve, who, even in his artificially congenial state, held a wariness in his eyes. He said nothing. He did nothing more than to send a half smile to Anna to reassure her, but she could see how frightened he was.

"There," said Candide, pointing to a small cluster of trees nearby. She wrenched the gigantic knife out of her pocket, making fast strides forward. They heard the rustle of leaves on the other side of the trees as the boy retreated. Candide broke into a run.

"Oh no, you don't." Percy lunged forward and tripped Candide up, quickly overtaking the group and disappearing into the forest after Michael.

"What the fuck was that?" Anna yelled.

"I knew we couldn't trust him!" Candide shouted.

"What, Percy?" Eve hopped forward to pull Candide to her feet. "Nah, we can trust Percy."

"Eve, seriously?" said Candide, furiously brushing dried leaves and dirt from her coat.

"I'm sure he didn't mean…" Eve looked off into the woods. "He's just trying to take care of Michael. Are you all right?"

"Of course I'm all right. Except now I have two people to stab."

"We're not stabbing Michael," said Anna.

"Nowhere lethal," said Candide, sneaking a half a glance in Aubrey's direction.

"What?" Aubrey's eyebrows just about shot over her hairline. "I'm not telling you where to stab a kid to not kill him."

"I think we all might die soon if we don't get moving," came Joe's tired voice.

Joe's tired voice attracted Eve's attention, lingering with a little bloom of pink in his cheeks, and calling up a very earnest, "Those chains look so good on you."

Until that time slumped against the tree, Joe stood a little taller, and Anna saw that Eve was correct. The way the chains fell across Joe's chest only made his pecs appear even bigger than usual, and something about the softness of the grey sweater in juxtaposition with the hard, rusty, cold of the chains gave him a rugged, but not too rugged look. The loop of them swept down past Joe's hips, accentuating the whole area, and Joe's hurt jaw looked twice as handsome with the fresh smile Eve's comment brought to his lips. "You want to try them?"

"Yeah, I do!" Eve lunged forward, and Anna's and Joe's eyes both lit up as she went about helping Joe unburden himself of the heavy load.

"Oh God, Candide, can you find him again before this all happens?" Aubrey pleaded, watching them with a strain of utter hopelessness in her voice. "What's her excuse? She's not even high."

Candide's eyes glowed as she scanned the forest. "You three! He's this way."

With a resigned shrug and eye roll from Eve, accompanied by a disappointed jangling of Joe's chains, they dashed off through the trees again. Over fallen and rotting logs, through thick branches hung with dubious webs, across mossy rocks and damp earth, they ran as fast as they could over a short distance, whence they came upon a clearing.

There Michael stood, at the other end, waiting for them. His smile was wide, self-assured and expectant.

Anna felt Eve's protective arm curl around her as Candide pulled up on her other side.

"I wasn't expecting that," Anna whispered.

"I'm going in with my knife," Candide whispered back.

"I'll back you up."

"Anna," Eve whispered, but she had already slipped from his grasp.

She and Candide flanked the boy, right and left, but as they did so, he began a slow procession forward, allowing himself to be completely encircled by the five of them.

Eve began, "He seems very confid—"

Candide darted forward, in a move perhaps intended to drive her knife into Michael's foot to hold him in place. He stepped his foot back a second before the blade would have connected and drove his knee up to meet Candide's cheek with a nauseating crunch, throwing her onto the ground.

In an instant, Joe's chain swung forward. The boy caught it in his small hand, and with appalling ease, he pulled Joe over onto his stomach. He kicked Joe onto his back with the smack of his bare foot into his stomach, and dropped a length of chain down, wrapping it around his neck. He yanked it back, cutting off Joe's air, and effortlessly resisting Joe kicking back into him, his body writhing desperately for a breath.

Eve dropped his hammer, opting to use his arms to tackle the child, but the boy swung Joe's entire body into Eve with enough force to bring them both crashing down, inflicting not an inconsiderable amount of pain and suffering on them both.

Anna was able to connect her wrench with the child's side but to very little effect before it reached around and pulled the wrench clean out of her hands. Only Aubrey's ability to pull one leg from beneath the boy and unbalance his aim was enough to save Anna's brains painting the forest clearing that evening. As it was, the wrench caught her wrist, which fractured on impact, sending her to the ground with a scream of pain.

The child turned, and with the back of his hand, he smacked Aubrey's face so hard he sent her tumbling over Eve and Joe and onto the hard, frozen floor of the forest.

By this time, Candide had retrieved her knife, and taking Anna's less-sympathetic view of the situation, she aimed it right at the boy's chest. She brought the weapon down, fast, but he caught the blade in his own bare hand. The blood, as the demon allowed it to slice into the little boy's fingers, was more than Candide could bear to see, and she eased her pressure on the knife. Her horror, as the demon looked her in the eyes and continued to close the tiny fingers deeper into the blade, was such that her eyes glowed and instinct took over. She punched Michael right in the face as hard as she could with as firm a fist as humanly possible. The boy fell to the floor, and Candide and Anna were on top of him. Aubrey pushed his head to the ground as Eve grabbed his feet and pulled the chains from Joe.

As they wound the chains around and around the boy's legs, he reached one preternaturally strong arm up, grabbed Aubrey by the hair, and slammed her into Anna, the impact making them both lose their sense temporarily. With his other arm, he returned the punch Candide had given him, but in her stomach, sending her to the ground gasping for air and vomiting in turn. Michael kicked one foot free of the chains, which he then connected with Joe's jaw, knocking it out of alignment again, and sending Joe's head spiralling into the trunk of a nearby tree. Then the demon was on top of Eve.

Michael's cut and bleeding fingers held tight around Eve's neck, and Eve struggled beneath him, smoke rising from his naked skin as the demon's murderous hand made contact with his warded flesh.

The child smiled.

Eve saw the knife glint in the moonlight.

Michael moved it slowly to the centre of Eve's forehead, and as Eve struggled beneath the superhuman strength of the hideous creature, he felt the warmth of his own blood as the creature indulged in the slow torture of slicing into him. Eve closed his eyes in horror of what was to come.

But the next thing Eve felt was the full weight of Michael's body falling back onto his legs.

All five sat up in astonishment to see Percy's bejewelled dagger sticking out of the boy's chest. "Chain him, quickly, before you pull that knife out," Percy directed.

Joe struggled to his feet, grabbed the chain, and they got to work binding the boy to a tree as Percy threw himself to the ground next to Eve and pulled him against his chest.

"I'm fine," Eve mumbled, his face smooshed against the thick brown wool of Percy's overcoat.

Percy turned Eve's face up, clasping his cheek tight with loving fingers. "If I'd been a second later—"

"You weren't." Eve smiled up at his big brother.

Percy dropped a kiss on Eve's cheek, another on his hair, wiped the blood from his brow, then stood tall again, pulling Eve to his feet beside him, saying to the others, "That knife's poisoned, by the way. Don't touch the blade if you have an open wound. And make sure he can't get free this time. It won't be long till he reanimates."

With an arm around and supporting Eve, Percy turned his attention to Candide, who still stood doubled over, holding her stomach and catching her breath, bracing herself against a tree, and he said, "Now, Candide, this is important. Exactly how long have you been sleeping with that book?"

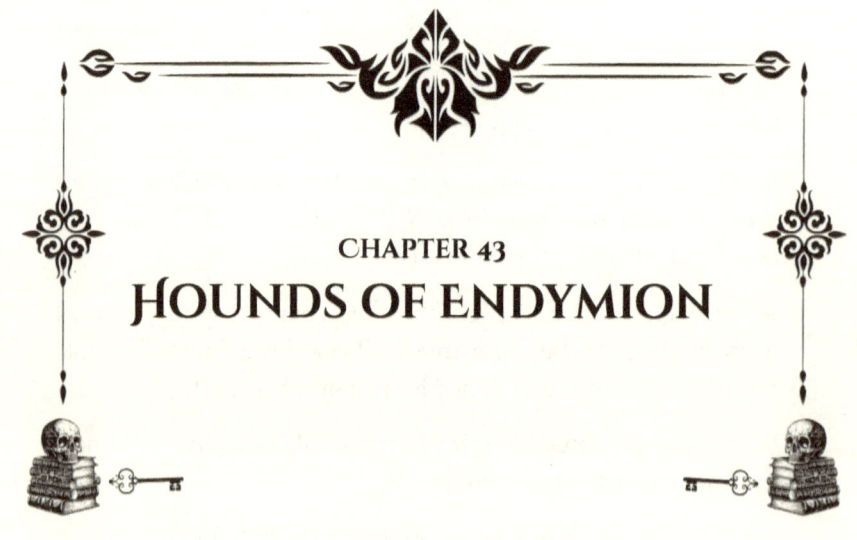

CHAPTER 43
HOUNDS OF ENDYMION

Candide said nothing. Anna said nothing. Percy's eyes darted back and forth between the pair of them, and his tone became sharp. "Candide, if you have more magic than we thought, we can do this. We can do the exorcism right here, right now. How long?"

She looked at Eve as though she'd been caught skipping class, excuses the first words pouring out of her mouth. "I'm not that magical. I just practised a little. I'm not—"

"Practice is just for control," Percy cut her off. "Has it been the whole three months?"

"It's been…" She blushed in the dark. "Yes, pretty much the whole three months."

Percy gave a harsh laugh, half relief, half disgust at her stupidity. "You're lucky you're not completely insane by now."

Eve snapped the padlock shut on the chains. "How could we tell the difference?"

Candide stayed stock still, mouth gaping. "What did you say?"

"You know…" He clambered back up onto his one good leg. "How could we tell the difference from what you're usually like?"

"Yes, we get the terrible joke, Eve! But—but I thought you'd be mad at me."

"Of course I'm not mad at you."

Anna guffawed out loud at the comment which Candide chose to address head on, stating, "Oh, yes, you are!"

"Okay, yes, a bit," he admitted, "when I'm not on drugs. You shouldn't be absorbing magical, probably evil powers from the Book of the Dead while you sleep."

"See, I knew—"

"But it's done now. And that was your decision. You knew what would happen." He commenced a slow hobble over to her.

"Then why didn't you say anything until now?"

"I'm trying very hard to stay out of your way."

"Is that it? I thought you were just… busy… with everything else going on…" She glanced at Anna. "And everyone else…" She glanced at Percy.

"No." He smiled, shaking his head. "I wanted to argue with you so many times, but I just didn't. I'm being supportive of your life choices."

"Oh Eve, that's so sweet!" Candide leaned her head against his shoulder as he wrapped an arm around her, but she looked up at him and said, "Don't do that. Too much. It's weird. I miss you arguing with me."

He pulled his head back a bit to focus, as though he wasn't sure he understood her correctly. "Sorry. I thought you wanted me to stop."

"No. I don't, really. Not completely anyway."

Taking her shy rebuff to heart in the blink of an eye, Eve redirected with, "Okay, well, just so you know, I don't want you to become a necromancer."

"It's a bit too late for that," Percy muttered.

Candide's eyes, still quite green, flashed at him. "I'm not a necromancer."

"You most certainly are," he replied.

Eve pulled her glare away from Percy and back to himself, where it lightened at his words. "You do what you want. If that's what you want—to be a necromancer—then I'll just have to deal with it. I think you should be an art historian, though."

"I could do both—"

Anna stood up, interrupting with, "So I carved the demon-warding symbol into Michael's chest while you were all talking. Can I take the knife out now?"

"What the hell did you just do?" yelled Percy.

"Anna, you're the best!" shouted Eve.

She looked guiltily at her bloody fingers. "I mean, he was totally unconscious. And it should make the exorcism easier, shouldn't it?" She glanced back at Michel. "The knife?"

"Yes, yes, take the knife out," Percy blustered, starting forward to claim back his glorious dagger.

Aubrey winced as the blade was yanked free. "Do we need to wait for Michael to wake up to get started?"

Anna nodded wisely, as one who has been around the demon block a few times. "I could tell the exorcisms had worked with Joe and Candide by the look in their eyes."

Percy stopped dead, staring at her, astonished. "That was it, Anna? Really?"

"Yeah. Joe and Candide looked absolutely horrified. Then they spewed *everywhere*."

He narrowed his eyes at her with what seemed to her extreme prejudice. "It's a wonder you're not all dead already. You must realise how easy it would be for a demon to fake that?"

She coloured. "Oh… I… guess…"

"Salt, Anna." He slapped his hands together, the sound ringing out harshly in the night air. "You always use salt!"

"Calm down, Percy," Anna mumbled. "So I learned one more thing about exorcising demons today. Can we do this now?"

"Wake up, Joe!" Percy snapped. "This is serious!"

Aubrey quickly bent down and slid Joe's jaw back into place as he slept.

"Wake up!" Percy yelled.

Joe, vaguely roused, was hauled to his feet by Eve, who vastly overestimated his own strength, and fell back to the ground with Joe on top of him.

"Pathetic," said Percy.

"He's very heavy," Eve protested.

"I don't mean you, Eve, darling. You're doing your best with a bad lot and I'm very stressed right now." Percy took one of Joe's arms, Eve the other, and they brought him back up to a standing position where he wavered drowsily from his heels and his toes, trying to get his bearings.

"Joe?" Eve slapped his cheek gently. "Can you help us do this exorcism?"

Joe forced his eyelids wide. "Yep. Let's do an exorcism."

Aubrey, the only one present who still needed notes, pulled them from her pocket, and they all began to recite the words, this time with Candide incorporating as much dark magic as she knew how. And when they reached the end of those lines, said with as much belief and feeling as each could muster, nothing happened at all.

"Fuck!" Percy yelled. While all agreed internally with the sentiment, the growling that suddenly came from the surrounding trees silenced them.

Six sets of eyes searched the darkness all around. It was a swish of leaves here—a crack of twigs there—a wet, hungry, guttural snarl everywhere.

Aubrey was the first to fall. She gave a shrill scream as one great beast pounced on her from behind. Its claws easily ripped through her overcoat, slicing wide red gashes into her skin.

Candide's blade instantly slid between the ribs of the creature, Percy's boot coming down to hold it in place as Candide continued her bloody assault.

Before she could help, another wolf-like creature tackled Anna to the cold ground, its stinking breath hot on her face and disgusting enough to instil a lifelong revulsion of everything canine. It opened its filthy, gaping jaws to tear her neck to pieces, and at that precise moment, Eve stabbed his knife into the creature's throat and sliced it wide open. Simultaneously, Anna stuck hers deep into the guts of the creature and ripped it apart from beneath. Thus she was doused not only with the entrails, the guts and the last meal of the thing, but also with a scarlet shower of hot blood gushing from the jugular. Eve pushed the beast off of her and helped her to her feet. He noticed neither the blood nor the guts nor the warmth of the dead thing's interior that soaked him through as he pulled Anna close and kissed her, then refused to let go of her, despite her half-hearted protests.

With Aubrey now wrapped in Candide's coat, Candide portioning out painkillers for her, Eve and Anna quite unaware of anyone else's presence, Percy finally said, "Where's Joe?"

Stomachs sinking to their knees, they desperately searched the forest until Anna caught the faint paleness of his fingers, just for a split second, as he was dragged, perfectly unconscious, into darkness. "There!"

They heard Joe's scream. They heard a yelp and a terminal cry, and then the gigantic beast was flung straight across the clearing, where it smashed into a tree, splitting its head from its legs, falling in a furry, bloody, revolting mess at the base of the tree.

Percy made his was swiftly to Joe's side, hauling him back to the group single-handedly while the others searched the dark for an explanation.

"Eve!" Candide whispered. His head snapped across to her at the urgent tone of her voice. She held his gaze and took a sniff of the air, as though it meant something. Anna did the same, noting nothing more than a vague smell of cigarette smoke, but Eve's eyes showed he understood whatever Candide meant.

"Exorcism now!" he yelled, and he commenced his recitation, loud and clear. With some confusion, the others followed his lead, even Joe, leaning hard into Percy's strong, supportive arms, barely holding onto consciousness, bleeding out through an enormous gash the beast had given him down the side of his leg, which Percy had made a makeshift bandage for with his scarf.

Anna, who said the words in time with the others, sensed the difference in Eve. His gaze was fixed on the boy, as though he refused to look at anything else that might be in the forest that night.

Then she sensed the other presence.

She looked around cautiously, but she didn't see what Eve and Candide obviously realised was there, so she put all her attention into the words, into her belief in them, into her sadness for the life Michael had lived, her thankfulness for his care of her, the desolation that Percy and Harriet had suffered all those years, and the catastrophic effect their pain had on Percy and Eve their entire lives.

Then she realised who that other person must be.

And she knew how powerful she must be, and why Eve and Candide made no move whatsoever to let Percy know she was there, lest he break his own very necessary concentration.

Michael roused from his slumber. His body shook, he convulsed, and a demonic moan ripped out of his small frame. He spoke in a furious stream of angry Latin, but Anna didn't understand a thing he said. She only saw that Percy frowned a little deeper, and Candide and Eve exchanged worried glances before they redoubled their concentration on the task at hand.

The boy's body trembled violently, his legs went stiff, and his head smacked back against the tree. He convulsed, and he retched, and finally, he vomited. What it was he threw up, no one could have said because no food or drink had passed those lips for twenty-four long years. Yet there came a swirling, stinking gush of putrid, sticky black, racking the little body with screams and grunts, for so long not one of them thought they could take any more. Then the boy, his beautiful, pale face, sick and wan, the familiar expression of horror, disgust and shock written all over it, spat one last time on the ground, let his head roll back, and settled his eyes on Percy.

Eve caught Joe as Percy started forward, only to be arrested by Anna's grip on his arm as Candide yelled, "Banishing spell!"

They quickly switched to the next spell, and as the last words were uttered, Percy fell to his brother's side. "Michael? Michael, is it you?"

"Percy," the voice rasped, weak and exhausted.

Percy pulled a hessian bag from his overcoat pocket. He sprinkled the salt onto the bare skin of Michael's hand, and there it sat, innocuous, sparkling in the moonlight.

The smile that crossed Percy's face was utterly dazzling. Tears in his eyes, hand on the boy's cheek, he said firmly, adoringly, with so much heart it just about broke Anna's, "Michael, you're back. I've got you now. Forever."

Eve had already unlocked the padlock and together they pulled the heavy chains from Michael, who was scooped up and kissed and held tight by Percy. Without another word he turned and carried the boy out of the forest, while the others trailed their various injuries slowly behind, Candide helping Aubrey, Anna supporting Eve who, barely able to walk himself, was almost carrying Joe.

Percy had already loaded Michael into the car when they caught up. He made his way straight to Eve, placing a hand on his shoulder with a squeeze. "I have to go right now. You understand?"

Eve, clearly a little shaken at the abrupt end of things, said, "Of course. Go."

Percy pulled him in and hugged him tight. "I'll come when I can." He dropped a kiss on his cheek, and moved for the jeep.

Anna called after him, "Please, can you burn the car too?"

Percy smiled back. "I knew I was right to choose you. Don't worry. I'll take care of Marky."

The car rumbled into movement, and Anna slid back under Eve's waiting arm as they watched Percy drive away across the field with Michael.

"I need a shower," Anna eventually sighed. "Hey, should we all go shower together?"

"Anna," Aubrey said. "I'm going to the hospital. Now."

"Yeah, I'm coming to the hospital too," said Joe.

"I'll drive you both," said Candide. "Bear attack."

"Oh." Anna turned her suggestive eyes up to Eve. "That just leaves you and me, then."

Eve pushed her hair back from her face and kissed her before delivering the blow.

He was also going to the hospital.

And he was quite insistent that she come along.

CHAPTER 44

ALL'S WELL THAT ENDS WELL

For three days, no one mentioned Percy's name to Evelyn. There was no call, no visit, and Candide had all but concluded that he'd used and discarded them once he got what he wanted.

There was a wistfulness in Eve's eyes at times when he would stare off into space and sigh, then make the sudden physical transformation into his sweet, confident, professional self, swallowing down whatever thoughts he had in order to process them at some distant date.

But that Sunday night, as Anna, Eve, Candide and Aubrey sat down to their wine and conversation, discussing how much longer Joe was likely to be kept in the hospital, there was an unexpected knock at the door.

Anna answered.

At first, he only stood there, hidden from the sight of all but Anna, his piercing blue eyes burning into hers. The intensity as he ran those eyes over her body, then, slowly, back up to meet hers, took her breath away. Every time he had talked to her, flirted with her, even when he tried to kiss her—he had never looked at her like that. He was sex, but with none of the warmth. He was beautiful, and he was powerful, and for the first time ever, she shrank from him.

He took a step towards her and she took a step aside, her back pressing against the frame of the door.

A shameful heat spread from her head to her toes as he brushed his body against hers, sending an intimate, sly, seductive smile down at her as he moved past, and she turned her gaze to the floor and shrank a little deeper into herself.

He entered the room and turned to the group.

"Percy!" Eve was up from the lounge at once.

"Evelyn," Percy drawled. "How good to see you again." His tone was cold and bored and the brilliant smile disappeared from Eve's face, to be replaced by hurt, anxious confusion.

Percy side-stepped him and took a seat on the lounge. It was clear his manner with Eve ruffled Candide as she pushed herself back against the arm of the chair and looked across at him accusingly. "We didn't expect you."

He ignored her entirely, gaze on Anna as she curled back into her armchair.

Eve sat down by Percy. "How's Michael?"

Percy's eyes never left Anna as he spoke, that same lascivious glint of pleasure in them, even as she attempted to avoid looking up. "He's doing very well."

"And Harriet?"

"She's doing very well, too."

"That's really good to hear," said Eve.

"And how about you, Evelyn? How are you doing?" The words spoke to Eve, but Percy didn't. Not really.

Eve followed his eyes, still locked onto Anna, who remained looking at the floor, and his leg shook as he started to tap his foot. "I'm fine. I was hoping you'd come by."

"Were you now, Evelyn?" A hint of that same old malice was back in his voice, but somehow darker than before.

"I was," Eve said softly. "I wanted to thank you. You saved my life."

Percy gave a short laugh. "That's funny, isn't it? I keep mulling that over, actually. I keep thinking, had that blade landed anywhere else on Michael's body, it might have killed him instantly. Had the poison been just a little more, that would have killed him, too. In that second, I had to make a choice between you and the brother I spent my entire life searching for. How strange that I should choose to save you and possibly murder Michael in your place. It would take a lot of love to do something like that."

"Percy—"

"So much love." Finally, he turned his head and regarded Eve with a lightly mocking smile, watching his expression intently. "Can you imagine how it would feel for me to watch you die? Given that I love you so very much."

"Percy, it's over." Eve shifted his knees towards his brother, looking as though he wanted to touch him, but didn't dare to. "We're all okay. Michael's fine and we're fine. It's done."

"Evelyn," Percy's eyes narrowed, and his smile deepened, "did you really believe I loved you that much?"

Eve was quiet, the realisation settling over him. His eyes dimmed. The defeat, the sadness, were written all over his face, in the resigned sigh he gave, in the reluctant smile and the gentle words, "I did. I did believe you."

Percy leaned a little closer, his smile more cruel than any of them had ever imagined it could ever be. "So tell me, Evelyn, would it break your heart if I told you she was right all along?" Percy motioned in Candide's direction. "Would it break your heart if I told you none of those nice things I said to you were true at all?"

Eve held his gaze. "Yes. I think it would."

Percy moved his face closer still and spoke with pure venom. "Then what if I told you that when I hit Michael with the knife… I was really aiming for you?"

Eve visibly winced at the words, but he forced himself to rally and replied, "All right, Percy. I guess you've said what you came to say. I honestly didn't think even you were capable—"

Percy cut him off with one lone word said carefully, obtrusively, as though there were no one else in the room with them. "Anna."

Her frightened eyes looked up at him. The cruel smile disappeared from his face and he sneered, "Did you really think it would be that easy?"

With a fast flick of Percy's arm, Eve's head was smashed, face down, into the coffee table. Candide reached for Percy, and he snapped her wrist back with a loud crack, breaking it in one swift movement accompanied by her loud scream. He stood, kicked his foot straight across Aubrey's face, knocking her to the floor, then picked up her struggling body and threw her into the wall, her head smashing hard against the window frame.

As Anna stepped forward, she felt the sharp sting of the back of Percy's hand, swung with immeasurable force to hit her so hard it smashed her sense of hearing into no more than a ringing peal of terror.

Percy had already picked Candide up by her collar, curled his great hand into a fist, and punched her face, breaking her cheekbone with a crunch, before flinging her down onto an unconscious Aubrey.

Eve, already brutally injured, pushed himself to standing, and Percy knocked him back to his knees, then simultaneously slammed his shoe down on Evelyn's back and ripped his right arm upward with such violence the arm was pulled completely out of the socket, a hideous cry ripping out of Eve's wrecked body. But Percy wasn't done. He twisted Eve around and slammed him down on the coffee table with such force it smashed to pieces beneath him, piercing him through with shards of broken glass.

All was the matter of a mere seconds, and before she had vaguely registered everything that had happened, Anna was kicked in the stomach and thrown against the wall.

Percy dragged her up to standing with a fist in her hair, and the other, he folded into an iron knot and smashed it into her stomach.

He tightened his grip on her hair when her body tried to double over, smacked her head back against the wall as she gasped for air, and fixed one impossibly strong hand around her neck. "Now we can finally be together."

A furious pain shot from Anna's neck and all throughout her body. An acrid smoke rose from the place his bare hand held her flesh.

Percy's hand on Anna's skin burned on contact.

He leaned in close and his breath came hot against her face as he growled the fatal word in her ear: "Submit."

A cry of hopelessness escaped her, and she tried to turn her face away, but he held her tight. She cast her eyes desperately around the room, at Eve and Candide struggling to their feet behind him. She saw the gold glint of the tip of her fountain pen as it rested on the table beside her, and without a second thought, she grabbed it and plunged it deep into Percy's neck. Deep enough to kill him.

And he didn't even flinch.

He did nothing more than smile his evil smile.

Slowly, he reached up, and with an enormous streak of blood, he ripped the pen free. She watched in horror as the skin, before her very eyes, began to heal. He twirled the pen around and pushed it under her chin, the sharp point drawing a drop of blood. "You'll pay for that."

Eve reached out for him. The demon swung around, and Percy's hand pushed Anna's sharp fountain pen straight through Eve's eye and deep into his skull.

Evelyn Worthing dropped dead then and there on the floor of the apartment in front of the people who loved him most in the world.

Finally, the demon let go, and Anna fell to the floor beside Eve's lifeless body.

There were screams and tears and protestations, begging, wailing, cursing, and the demon stood and watched it all, drinking in every second of their grief.

Candide crawled to his body and thought no more of the demon, of nothing but Eve, and as she cried and screamed and pleaded for her reality to be different, she didn't even notice when, some time later, Anna fell silent. She didn't notice the cold—the glacial cold nothingness—that took Anna then and there. The emptiness that took that once warm and loving woman, and turned her inside out, until the centre was steel and all about her was flayed and red and raw and untouchable.

Anna pushed herself away from the once-beautiful body of the man she loved. The body she had clung to and bathed in her tears only seconds earlier.

She clawed her way to Percy's feet, and looked up at him, her knees pressing hard into the cold wooden floor, and she whispered, "I submit."

His smile widened, but only a little.

"Fix him," she begged. "Fix him now, and I submit. I'll do anything you want. Anything. Please, take me, take my soul, take everything. Please. Please, just fix him."

Anna stared up at the demon, and his eyes shifted, coming to rest on Candide. He flicked them back down to Anna, and Anna understood. And she moved slowly, her head bowed to him, her tears falling silently, but she did move.

"Stay down," she whispered as she staggered to her feet.

Candide paid no attention to Anna's words as Anna walked past the broken coffee table and back again to Candide's side.

"I love you, Candide," Anna whimpered.

Candide was unconscious on the floor from the blow, her blood already pooling in her beautiful hair, before the words could have registered.

Anna dropped the wine bottle to the floor with a shaking hand, then turned wild, desperate eyes on Percy. She fell back at his feet. "Do you see? I'll do anything you want. Anything, anyone. Anyone! Just not Eve. Please, now, go to him, fix him, give him back to me, and I am your slave."

The demon's lips kept their silence, but he gave a slight tilt of his chin. He moved a hand into his overcoat and pulled out Percy's own lovely dagger, which he held out for Anna.

Shakily, she climbed to her feet and accepted the knife. "I don't underst—" She looked down at Eve. "Oh. Oh. Okay."

And that was when Anna fell apart. Her body shook all over and she could barely see a thing through the tears and the panic as she made her way back to Eve's body. She gently pushed Candide off him, then she unbuttoned his once lovely, fresh, crisp linen shirt.

She cried, and she cursed every aspect of her life, every single thing, every single moment that had occurred to lead her to this existence which she hated with every fibre of her being, as her gentle hand came to rest on the mark she had carved so lovingly, to protectively, into his flesh.

Then, with a sob, she forced her shaking hand to take the sharp blade to Evelyn's skin, and she sliced into it. Her tears turned his red blood pink as she moved the blade back and forth, back and forth, until she had removed the demon warding symbol from his body. She threw the bloody lump of skin to the floor, then, utterly defeated, a shell of the person she once was, she turned her eyes up to Percy.

"*Please.*"

Percy's body fell limp to the floor.

She looked expectantly at Eve.

Nothing.

No sign of life at all.

She took in the scene around her. Candide's blood was trickling under her shoes. Aubrey lay still and silent against the wall. Percy was an unmoving heap on the floor. And her beautiful, darling Eve lay there, in the centre of the room, covered from head to toe in blood, still not breathing, still just as dead as the second he hit the floor.

"No," she cried. "Please—please don't do this to me!" She collapsed onto Eve's chest and cried hopelessly, scrunching his shirt in her fists, soaking his blood-drenched clothes with her tears, wailing piteously, pointlessly... until the thought finally occurred to her to take Percy's dagger and slit her own throat. For it was all there was left to do in this horrible, bereft life.

She rolled off her one and only love.

She reached for the dagger.

She pressed it to her neck.

She took one last look at what was left of Evelyn.

And a sudden movement stayed her hand.

There, out of the corner of her eye, she caught Percy, awake now, staring back at her in disbelief. "What have you done?"

"It isn't working," she wept. "It isn't working!" She screamed in her frustration.

"It will work, Anna," he said quietly. "I don't think you know what you've done."

She dropped the dagger to the floor with a sharp clatter and pounced towards him. "It will work? How can you know?"

Percy shook his head in shock at the exhilaration, the complete change in her demeanour given the one small crumb of hope. "This is a terrible thing that you've done. Don't you understand?"

"Percy..." Trembling, desperate fingers gripped his shirt, and her mad eyes stared into his pleadingly. "Percy, do you know what it will do? Please, will he fix Eve?"

Percy's head turned to look over Anna's shoulder. His face fell ashen and sickly. His eyes, cast upward, were the very soul of terror.

Even in her overwrought state, she understood. She followed Percy's line of sight in breathless excitement, and a look of pure, radiant happiness spread over her face.

Eve stood before her once again, tall, strong, breathing. Blood stained his clothes, blood covered his face, blood dripped from his fingertips, one arm hung loose where it had been dislocated, his face was expressionless, his remaining eye, glazed and unseeing.

Anna approached him, reaching out a shaking hand in awe. The fountain pen, deep in his brain, still protruded from his eye. She put her hand to his cheek, cut, swollen and bruised, his face barely recognisable from the beating he had taken. He said nothing, made no movement or sound to indicate life, other than to stand before her taking those incredible, miraculous breaths.

"Eve," she sighed as she looked him over, stroking his cheek reverently. The tears fell fast and hot from her eyes, and she begged, "My one and only love, please, please forgive me for everything I am about to do."

Her tears mingled with the blood and cerebral fluid pouring from his wounded eye as she stood on her tiptoes and put her lips up to meet his. She felt his heartbeat in her own chest and a wild madness of ecstasy overtook her as she felt, ever so softly, Eve's own precious lips return her kiss.

The End

CHAPTER ONE - AN EDUCATION IN EVIL

"Welcome to Russian Literature. You can call me Professor Worthing." He printed his name slowly on the blackboard in large ugly letters. He turned back to face the packed lecture theatre and fixed Anna with his cold, cruel eye. "Death, misery, regret, agony. This is what you have chosen."

Anna lowered her eyes to the page in front of her and watched as a few tears dropped into the ink before her, obliterating the tiny modicum of progress she had made.

"We'll start, of course, with Fyodor Dostoyevsky's masterpiece, Crime and Punishment. If you never wanted to drink a pint of vodka before, this may be the moment that pushes you over the edge…"

Continued in…

AN EDUCATION IN EVIL

THANK YOU FOR READING!

If you enjoyed *A Study in Survival*, please leave a review. This is a great way to support authors and to help the series thrive.

Sign up for the newsletter at www.whlockwood.com for special content, new release news, ARC opportunities, and to keep up to date.

ALSO BY W. H. LOCKWOOD

Find the first Endymion College trilogy here:

Endymion College 1: A Lesson in Love and Death

Endymion College 2: A Study in Survival

Endymion College 3: An Education in Evil

But wait… What's that I hear? Someone typing out a brand new Endymion College novel? A whole new Endymion College adventure kicks off with *Endymion College 4: A Vicious Vacation* in 2024.

Meanwhile…

There's something a little unsettling happening in Manchester… In the year 1844. A brand new historical gothic romance with lashings of monster horror is also coming your way in 2024.

Visit www.whlockwood.com for more information.

LOOK AWAY NOW IF YOU DON'T LIKE SPOILERS. SERIOUSLY. I'LL WAIT.

Yes, there's an Endymion College spinoff, and you can find the action-packed novella series below.

Degenerate Art

The Reliquary of Saint Martin

Kidnap the Girl

A Sicilian Romance

The Beast of Barmiston Hall

The Horrendous Haunted Heist of Horror

Coming Soon:

Low Down in London

ACKNOWLEDGMENTS

A huge thank you to everyone who supported me, offered advice and helped me shape this novel into what it is today.

Specifically, a huge thank you to Letizia Lorini for the monumental amount of work you put into this, and for forgiving me when I made you cry. You have forgiven me, right? If not, I have a bottle of wine with your name on it. Kisses.

No one out there can comprehend exactly what this woman does for the world of literature, but there are hundreds authors whose books might never see the light of day without this gorgeous woman in their corner. I cannot say enough about her and I am honoured to have her as my friend. She's too talented, too clever, just too kind to even describe. Please go read her wonderful books.

Lety, I love you!!

Ally Blythe, you have been a rock. Thank you for the many hours of hilarious discussions and for sharing your writing with me. Thanks for being on call for every one of my author breakdowns about how many orgasms Anna may or may not have, etc, and for all your help with all my books. I love you.

Shelby, thank you so much for helping me whip this into shape. You are an absolute delight and I'm so happy we met. Thank you.

TJ Rose, same goes for you. Thank you for the hours you spent on this, but also for writing one of my favourite books.

Krystel, Joe (the other one) and Daphanie. Thanks so much for all the back and forth and listening to me. You three know how much I love you.

Emma, Mycroft and Hannah for being the best book club in town who put up with me talking about my own books for months, and especially to Emma for all the time you put into my books, even if you are the fastest reader I ever met. Thank you!!

Thank you to Atalienart (Anna and Eve, front and back) and Jenn Dove (interior portraits) for the beautiful artwork. Go check them out. Their work is amazing.

Tiffany, Alyssa, Natalie, Annie, Katie, Kim and Bethany. Thank you for the time you spent on these books. I will always appreciate all your help and advice.

Last but not least, Matthew. This could never have happened without you. To the most romantic romantic lead in all romances: thank you. To you, to Alex, Ada and Mary, too, I love you all so much!

ABOUT THE AUTHOR

Author of the Endymion College series, W. H. Lockwood writes gothic romance, MM action-romance, historical fiction, dark academia and cosy horror.

Raised on a diet of teen horror books and Pepsi, only willing to leave her den to attend chess club at public school, W.H. Lockwood started writing at a young age and has kept this passion throughout her life.

Always a voracious reader, she obtained an undergraduate degree in literary studies from a gorgeous sandstone university, following that with a masters in publishing and editing, then a masters in astronomy, thus uniting her two great loves of the arts and science, leaving her utterly unqualified to cope with the real world.

These days, W.H. Lockwood can often be found aimlessly wandering the coffee shops and bookstores of the beautiful city she calls home.

She's known to be a scatty writer, but updates Instagram most frequently, so follow her there for news and random pictures of skulls, coffees, and books.

Thank you so much for taking the time to read the series.

 instagram.com/w.h.lockwood.books